CORNWALL COUNTY COUNCIL
LIBRARIES AND ARTS DEPARTMENT

DISTANT
RELATIONS

DISTANT RELATIONS

Kathleen Conlon

GRAFTON BOOKS

A Division of the Collins Publishing Group

LONDON GLASGOW
TORONTO SYDNEY AUCKLAND

Grafton Books
A Division of the Collins Publishing Group
8 Grafton Street, London W1X 3LA

Published by Grafton Books 1989

Copyright © Kathleen Conlon 1989

A CIP catalogue record for this book is available
from the British Library

ISBN 0-246-13365-1

Printed in Great Britain by
William Collins Sons & Co. Ltd, Glasgow

DISTANT
RELATIONS

PART ONE

Leaving Max

1

Calendars start in January, but for many people the year turns, like the leaves on the trees, in the autumn: the death of an old season, the beginning of a new term, a new class. For Christina Conway, crossing the road between John Lewis's, where she had just bought a coffee pot, and Habitat, where she intended to buy a table lamp, Monday, October 7th 1985 signified the beginning of a new life.

As yet, Monday, October 7th was three days away and Christina Conway, heavily-laden with new life purchases, was still only en route to becoming part of a statistical trend: that concerning the failure rate of marriages (one in every three, to be precise) rather than an actual statistic. As yet she still wore the wedding ring that Max, her husband, had placed on her finger twenty years before. She kept it on because a ringless wedding finger indicates availability and she had no wish to give the wrong impression, and also because, despite successive applications of soap, butter and Vaseline, it wouldn't budge (it had been on the tight side in the first place; now it was embedded and she'd need to visit the jeweller's to have it cut off when Livingstone, her lover, was finally free to replace it with a new one).

In Habitat, Christina, a woman now in her fortieth year, who had spent a fair proportion of the most recent of them wondering whether (a) she'd ever have the guts, impetus or wherewithal to walk out of a marriage that had become increasingly joyless and (b) if she'd survive were she to do so, chose a ceramic table lamp of severely minimalist design and as unlike anything that furnished the matrimonial home as could possibly be, then betook herself round the corner to George Henry Lee's where she added a pair of silk sheets to her purchases: blush-pink, they were, and sporting a price tag of the sort that can send the blood pressure soaring. They matched the lingerie she'd already bought: Janet Reger, crêpe de Chine and clotted with lace. (During her first honeymoon, the real one, she'd worn an Aertex vest and knickers, being not long out of school and having no money and no mother to advise; 'Baby,' Max had said, taking them off and covering each portion of the flesh thus exposed with kisses.)

Then, at nineteen, she had been young – and young-looking – for her age, unformed, unaware of her own style. Cousin Gwen, contemporaneous and clued up about everything that mattered, had said, with such dispassion as she was capable of, 'You *could* look all right, you just don't make the best of yourself.' Perhaps that was a skill she'd never completely mastered, but there had certainly been improvement. On the escalator, going up to the third floor, a man, youngish, good-looking, smiled at her and, as befits a woman confident of her attractiveness and the attention it attracts, she smiled back.

The world was smiling. And the weather. Compensating in fine style for a dismal summer. She took it – as she took everything these days – for an omen, a cosmic indication that, despite the feeling she had that with every step she took a yawning chasm might open up in front of her, she was doing the right thing, that, after all the seemingly purposeless treadmill years, at last her life seemed to have direction.

In the audio department she bought a tape: 'Verdi: *La Traviata*: Dramatic Highlights', though, as yet, there was nothing to play it on. It was 'Verdi: *La Traviata*: Dramatic Highlights', or similar, on tape, that had provided the background music for her first, proper, acknowledgedly-clandestine, meeting with Livingstone: he'd taken her to an Italian restaurant. She'd looked across at him and met his glance and felt as though there were a flower inside her – dormant for years – that was beginning to burst into bloom.

She would have continued to buy: a new life demands new possessions; her spending was curtailed only because she couldn't carry anything more. As it was, she had to take a taxi back to the flat. All the way there she was excusing her prodigality to herself. Once this initial euphoric nest-feathering was achieved she wouldn't want to spend much. Compulsive shopping is symptomatic of the unhappy marriage, the unfulfilled female destiny; once she had Livingstone she would need little else. In the weeks and months and years to come he would not be irritated by her extravagance but rather impressed by her frugality.

Indoors, the first thing she did was to take off her clothes and, in front of the wardrobe mirror, try on the honeymoon lingerie. The satisfaction thus derived went some way to justifying the expense. Though she knew that the translation from housewife-and-mother-hurtling-towards-middle-age into desirable female had been achieved without Janet Reger's assistance, had begun as soon as she realised that she had become an object of desire.

She changed back into her wifely clothes, carefully folded the mistress garments and placed them on the silk sheets. 'Oh really?' Livingstone would say when he saw them and they'd both laugh at this faintly ludicrous attempt at stereotypical love-nest build-ing, but he'd know why she'd attempted it, why, after a year of back-seat love-making, or snatched matinées in the flat of an obliging colleague, it had been necessary, before they embarked upon real life, for her to indulge in a bit of romantic play-acting.

She filled the new pot with Blue Mountain coffee and checked the kitchen cupboards. Soup: the lobster bisque that he liked so much, Dover sole in the fridge, smoked salmon (in restaurants he eschewed the meat menu entirely in favour of fish. Unsurpris-ingly, he was Pisces – she read his horoscope in the paper before reading her own. Pisces was unstable as its natural element, but – given the right encouragement – tender and true.)

There was a bottle of champagne and a half bottle of brandy and a pineapple gâteau and a triangle of Brie. There was butter in the butter dish and Tiptree jam and Frank Cooper's Oxford marmalade. The croissants she would buy in fresh, early each day, from the bakery around the corner, and the milkman had already been alerted to begin his deliveries on Monday morning.

Everything was organised. The deed was done. And there could be no backing out. Having found a flat and ordered the milk, she felt therefore obliged to live in it. Doing things arse-upwards, some might have said, but there was a buried logic, the same that had prevailed when, years ago, squeamish at the thought of having her ears pierced, she'd first bought some earrings, consequently making it difficult for her to chicken out of undergoing the slight discomfort involved in enabling her to wear them.

Now, as then, she had gathered her meagre courage, stiffened her faltering resolve, overcome her constitutional trepidation and, arse-upwardly, dared to dare. Though now there was rather more than slight discomfort involved. This morning she had awoken terrified; this evening, as she faced up to the task of formally announcing her intention to leave home, she would shake and gulp and tremble, but right now she felt calm and curiously fatalistic as though she were at the far side of all the unpleasantness that must intervene before the dust of her departure finally settled and she could embark upon life as she thought it ought to be.

Friends, discontented wives, met for coffee, bemoaned their lot, but said, 'How *can* we change it? What about money, the kids, the upheaval?' They wanted a man to come and do it all for them as their grown-out-of, fed-up-with husbands had once done.

But it could be done. If you wanted it enough. If hearing him say 'together' made you aware that the alternative was misery; when listening to him tell you that he couldn't even *ask* it of you brought you to the realisation that you had nothing – apart from your children's affection (and why should that alter?) – of value to lose.

And she'd almost done it. She was nearly there. She'd plotted and planned and manoeuvred and now she sat in the midst of her carefully-prepared set, waiting for Act One to begin.

Merely looking around gave her immense pleasure. It was a rented flat, furnished to someone else's taste, but someone else's taste was far more to her own than that which prevailed in the matrimonial home. An inheritance: they'd moved in when Max's father moved out to a retirement home in the country; it was a large Edwardian-built villa, all passages and cubby-holes and redundant servants' bells and great high cobweb-harbouring ceilings. And along with the house they had inherited the furniture: big solid carved pieces in oak and mahogany and rosewood, tallboys and chiffoniers, wardrobes and chests of drawers so massive that to contemplate moving them was to risk rupture or prolapse. Max often ran a proprietorial hand over the bow fronts and the ball and claw feet and remarked complacently on the price they'd fetch from a dealer. That was when he wasn't running a finger across their horizontal surfaces, pretending to leave a clearer trail in the dust than was actually the case and saying, 'What in hell's name do you do all day?'

At least he used to say that. When she was nothing more than housewife-and-mother and had absolutely no excuse for falling down on the job, dust-wise. After she'd registered at the University to resume the degree course that she'd had to abandon twenty years before, he knew perfectly well what she did all day and was less than enthusiastic about it.

Well – some of it, he'd known, not all. He hadn't known, for example, that she'd met a man there, a lecturer who, when introducing her to the mysterious workings of the computer, had casually placed an arm across her shoulders and she'd suddenly realised that she could feel the pulse you have there, but otherwise never notice, beating away in her neck.

It was the pulse they tested to check whether you were dead or alive. And the reason she hadn't noticed it before was because, until he touched her, she *had* been dead, in terms of her womanly responses, at least.

She'd fallen in love in a moment, between the hand gently coming to rest upon her shoulder and then moving away, between stumblingly typing in her identification number on the computer keyboard and seeing the information being recorded. She didn't ask herself why. She only asked, 'Why him?' And, naturally, it took quite a while before any satisfactory answer was vouchsafed. She had to get to know him: to drink endless cups of foul coffee in the canteen across a table from him, to bump into him accidentally-on-purpose in the library, or the pub, to exchange carefully-rehearsed and deliberately-expurgated mini-biographies with him, before she recognised the reason: it was because he had identified her to herself, presented her with exactly the sort of favourable representation that she required: Christina Conway. Not Christina Conway, wife of Max, or Christina Conway, mother of David and Adam, and nothing much else besides, but the *only* Christina Conway who, alone, could smile at him across the table in the canteen or brush his sleeve as they passed on the stairs and change his perception of everything.

She had been waiting for that identification, waiting to be found and named. She thought it highly significant that *his* name was Livingstone. It was a name that, after she'd fallen in love with him, jumped out at her from newspapers, magazines and the list of credits at the end of television programmes – she wouldn't have thought it nearly common enough for this occurrence to be so frequent. Once, it wasn't just his name, it was he himself, in person. In his role as convenient local telly pundit. Being fairly eminent in his field – which was Urban Studies – they tended to call upon him every time they ran a studio discussion searching for the causes of riots or vandalism or glue-sniffing, whatever the current fashionable media preoccupation happened to be.

She'd sat, frozen with shock, not taking in a word of what he was saying, looking at his Jonathan Miller gesticulations, his Gary Cooper smile, the evidence of knowledge that ought to have been beyond her ken all over her face. Who could fail to interpret that reaction? Who could ignore the signs that said, 'That man is my lover'? Max could. Max did. He crossed the room and, as usual, without consultation, changed channels. 'Mouth, mouth, mouth,' he said. 'Is this what we pay fifty-eight pounds a year for?'

He never did know. Not until she told him. And even that had been in response to one of his derogatory remarks: 'Who, in his right mind, would take you on?' 'Someone has done, someone will,' she'd replied, quite unaware, at the time, of the contradictory order of her tenses. 'Well God help him, whoever he is,' Max had said. 'Unless, of course, he likes the idea of living in a pig-sty. Will you *look* at this place?'

She remembered looking but couldn't remember what had sparked off that particular row: a button missing from his suit, a spillage on the kitchen floor, a library book moved so that his place was lost?

He'd always been a neat, fastidious man but, during the early years of their marriage, easy-going. This passion for order and symmetry had festered furtively, grown gradually, until he was complaining because the curtains were pulled back unevenly. And the more he carped and quibbled and criticised, the more nervous and ham-fisted she became: plates and cups leapt from her fingers and smashed into smithereens, the bottoms of pans burned through when left unattended for the merest moment, inches of dust accumulated the instant after she'd wiped a surface clean.

Perhaps, she'd thought, it was some sort of male menopausal thing – he was thirteen years older than she. Perhaps, if she could keep her head down and sit it out . . . Surely, somewhere beneath the accretions of age and disillusion and disappointment, there must remain traces of the Max and Christina who had been sufficiently attracted to each other to accept the idea of setting up home together, to acknowledge that, in pursuance of this aim, they must undertake to tolerate each other's faults?

But she suspected that the real Max and Christina, the one finicking, precise, hypercritical, the other disorganised and over-anxious, had been there all along, unacknowledged, while their false selves went ahead with attracting each other, making a nest, producing a family. And once that was done with . . .

Though it wasn't quite done with. Not quite.

She brought the brandy from the kitchen and poured herself a glass and realised that now, at the end of all the indecision and procrastination, now it was stand-up-and-be-counted time minus a couple of hours, her courage unaided might not be enough.

Not because of Max. She could rely upon Max's nastiness. And the nastier he became, the easier it would be for her to leave. Anyway, it could scarcely come as a complete surprise to him: each having acknowledged their growing dissatisfaction since long before Livingstone came on the scene.

Though it was only since Livingstone that she'd moved into the spare bedroom. She'd started staying up later and later, postponing bed, pleading the excuse of essays to finish, until it seemed only logical to sleep elsewhere so as not to disturb Max. And he'd let her go. Only once, in six months, when slightly intoxicated, had he made it plain that he intended to join her. She'd been unprepared, resistant, and as dry as the desert, she remembered, and he'd hurt her, relentlessly driving himself into her as if, at a certain depth of penetration, some long-dead affection could be re-kindled between them.

She could have struggled and fought and cried rape, but she complied for fear of a row that might wake Adam.

Adam.

The brandy made her blink and gasp, but its effect was rapid enough. She refilled her glass and drank and it became easier to believe that a new home could be made for Adam too. 'I always wanted sons,' Livingstone had once said, rather wistfully. He and his wife were childless. Nobody's fault, he'd said, though apparently Louise had womb problems and was forever going for smears. Whereas most women have them every five years and those at risk are advised to repeat them annually, it seemed to Christina, listening to Livingstone, that Louise had them on an hourly basis.

'I always wanted sons.'

Well, there was still time for that . . .

Meanwhile, there were those she had . . .

Not that it would matter a great deal to David who, apart from being nearly twenty years old and away at university, was of a philosophical turn of mind; she foresaw that telling David (the cowardly way, by letter; it couldn't be face to face anyway since he was staying with friends before going straight back to college) would only involve a certain amount of embarrassment; the totality of guilt would be reserved for her younger child. He was fifteen but she found herself, more and more frequently these days, remembering him as a little boy. She remembered a school-made Christmas card sticky with glue and drenched in glitter and its deeply-scored, tongue-between-the-teeth, unevenly-printed inscription: 'From your loving son, Adam'; she remembered the red-faced, unable-to-be-concealed swelling pride when he'd announced to her news of his first unaided trip down the garden on a bicycle/gold star for handiwork/success-fully-tied shoe lace – even though remembering these things only served to increase the guilt-in-advance that she was experiencing.

But the brandy enabled her to rehearse again, with a measure of confidence, the explanation she had prepared for him, the solemn undertaking: 'It will be better from now on, Adam. I promise.'

Different from now on. And it didn't have to be along the lines of the pessimistic litany delivered by those trapped married women friends: broken home, emotional deprivation, lifelong insecurity, terminal guilt. It didn't *have* to be tragic.

The buzz of the entryphone startled her and she spilled brandy on the carpet. Her first instinct was to run for a cloth and mop it up before Max could pounce upon the stain as yet another example of her slovenly housekeeping, and then she remembered where she was and that never again would she need to react in that panic-stricken fashion.

'Well I'm here,' Livingstone said, when she picked up the phone, 'as directed. On the dot. And fairly agog with curiosity.'

She'd had to leave a cryptic note for him at the Porter's Lodge in the Social Science Department – which they'd used as a *poste restante* during the summer vacation: 'I shall be at Flat 2,

Swinburne Court, Queen's Road, between three and four o'clock on Friday afternoon. Can you meet me there?'

'Come on up. First floor. I haven't had the chance to get a card yet.'

'Mysteriouser and mysteriouser,' Livingstone said.

She pressed the door release and awaited his appearance. Perspiration from her palm misted the surface of the brandy glass, and she was aware of pulses beating not just in her neck but all over her body. She hadn't been as nervous as this the first time in that borrowed bedroom when, for a moment, all desire had deserted her and she felt like someone emerging from one of those dreams that are sufficiently lucid to convince you they're real, yet disconcertingly deficient in logic.

Then, it had only been for a moment. He'd looked at her with an expression that combined lust and reverence in exactly the correct ratio and desire had reasserted itself and all the things that could have gone wrong had gone right.

Now it was necessary to hum the tune of the love-duet from *La Traviata* in an attempt to resurrect the appropriate emotion, to remind herself of her reason for being here.

She had left the living-room door ajar. He pushed it open and stood still for a moment, framed within the aperture, his glance taking in the unfamiliar surroundings, his nose twitching slightly as he smelled the odours of newness: recently-planed wood, sanded floors, fresh paint. She looked at him. She could have looked at him until her eyes gave out for, apart from anything else, he was so good to look at. His handsomeness had impinged long before he put his arm around her shoulder and everything changed: he was tall, broad-shouldered, long-legged, slim-thighed; black hair grew in a widow's peak and then fell across a broad forehead. And, oh, what else? A long upper lip, a heart-shaped smile, dark eyes, tarn-deep . . . all the girls in her year had pronounced him luscious. And they *were* girls: nubile, pretty, available. She'd been astonished that he'd chosen her in preference to any one of them, having been quite resigned to her falling in love being a strictly uni-directional activity.

Now he smiled, displaying teeth dazzlingly white against the tan acquired during his holiday in the Swiss Alps, smiled and then kissed her and put a finger against her lips. 'Don't tell me,' he said, 'you've become the mistress of a man rich enough to set you up in luxury and complaisant enough to allow you to entertain your boyfriends in the afternoon. Like that Françoise Sagan story . . .'

She'd read them too, in the days of her youth, those particular Françoise Sagan stories. She had a suspicion that the secret of a contented middle life might lie in having had the great good fortune to avoid reading the wrong sort of books at an impressionable age.

He had read those same books at approximately the same time. They had grown up contemporaneously. Whereas Max's childhood reminiscences: ITMA and Empire Day, shrapnel collections and coupons, lay outside her experience, *their* memories were mutual: *Sunny Stories* and Uncle Mac, watching the Coronation on specially-acquired black and white television sets afflicted with flicker, defying parental orders to queue all night for tickets for a Dylan concert, sitting down on the same day – she in the North, he in the South, to tackle their scholarship papers: they could even recite to each other the passage of Virgil they'd been required to translate. For them, the activity of 'Do you remember?' could never pall. It had been their favourite pastime in that cruelly-curtailed recovery period after love. 'Do you remember?' and 'How would it be?' How would it be if: I were to presume to ask you to leave your husband and children for me?; you were to make that ultimate decision, take that irrevocable step?

He walked to the window. 'So quiet!' he said, raising the sash, leaning out and looking down towards the garden: lawns, a shrubbery, a fountain in the form of two dolphins disporting themselves – it reminded her of a stylised version of his horoscope sign; there were omens everywhere, if you cared to look.

The act of leaning caused his jeans to tighten across his buttocks; spontaneous desire coupled with slight inebriation made her want to move to him, to stroke him and fondle him, but she restrained herself. There was a lifetime ahead of them for succumbing to their sexual chemistry. She kept her distance. Now they must not kiss and caress and melt and swoon, now they must talk: organise, arrange, make provision.

'It's still so *hot*. We could have gone to the coast. Nookie behind a sand dune. How does that sound?'

He drew back his head and shoulders, let the curtain fall, turned to face her, silhouetted by the sun.

'So what *is* it all about? You drinking brandy at three o'clock of an afternoon in an empty flat in Queen's Road? Are we *entitled* to be here? Christina?'

'We couldn't be more entitled.'

She moved slightly; the light behind him dazzled her. 'It's ours.'

'What?'

'There's a month's rent paid. It's ours. I did it. I think you thought I never would.'

Occasionally she'd wondered if he suspected her of brinkmanship, had felt that she'd never quite convinced him that games-playing was not in her nature, least of all the game of see-how-far-I-can-go. And least of all with Max.

'When?'

'When what?'

'When did you actually – make up your mind?'

Her mind had been made up long ago. What he meant was: when had she decided to implement the decision.

'I think it was when we were on holiday.'

Had David accompanied them it might not have been so bad: David had a way of cheering her, diverting Max's gloom and bullying Adam out of his sulks. But David had been back-packing around Europe and the unceasing Breton rain had bounced off the shingle and the shutters had creaked in the wind and Adam's lower lip had jutted and Max had mixed Neutra-donna in the vain hope that it might appease the gnawings of his ulcer.

The rain had beat a tattoo on the roof of the beach hut: 'No, no, no,' it had repeated; 'Not any longer,' the wind had wailed.

'It seemed to me,' she said, 'that all the changes might as well be made at once: my job, us . . .'

They'd discussed it endlessly, their being together, from the time it had been merely a wish, through its development into a possibility, right up until the moment when it matured into a real alternative, so why then the sense that she'd shocked him into immobility, rendered him speechless?

He didn't move, but eventually he did moisten his lips and words found utterance. He said, 'A month's rent? However did you afford a month's rent?'

She told him: by means of the credit card, the Family Allowance, and in anticipation of her first salary cheque. 'It's expensive,' she said, 'but between us . . . Look, do move over here. I hate talking to someone I can't see.'

He moved then. To the sofa. And sat down stiffly on the very edge of the cushion. She couldn't tell from his face whether he was delighted at the news or appalled: he still looked dazed.

'I should have forewarned you, I know, but you were away so long . . .' (A couple of postcards from Switzerland, enclosed in envelopes, sent to the University: 'Darling love, every night I dream of you, every minute I long for you. The days cannot pass fast enough.' Before meeting him, she'd have considered the expression of such sentiments between people of their age somehow not quite seemly – imagine David reading them, or Adam!)

'In Brittany, I knew if I didn't do it soon I never would. And I just couldn't face the thought of any more.'

The deceit and the difficulties, she meant, and all those dreary Sunday afternoons re-reading newspaper articles about child abuse and AIDS and gazing at ads for sofa-beds, and watching Max's snores waking him up, the interminable separations, her increasing inability to make do, put up with, endure.

'Have you told him – them?'

She nodded her head, though she hadn't – yet.

'I know you'll need some time to sort everything out . . .'

Though, as in her case, it was really only a matter of the final step. Louise had known for years, just as Max had known for years, that her marriage was a sham.

And he had no children to complicate the issue.

'Put your arms around me.'

He did as she asked. Tension was evident in his every muscle. It was only to be expected. Men were faint-hearted. The prospect of confrontation scared even the best of them. She was terrified to her soul at the idea of facing Max, and she was a woman. And women, as everybody knew, were far braver.

∽ 2 ∽

She walked from the station. She walked slowly, limping slightly. She had on new shoes which rubbed her heels, and her shopping – the mundane matrimonial sort this time (fish fingers, Scotch broth, mousetrap cheese) – weighed her down. But the slowing of her pace was not entirely due to sore feet and heavy shopping. Winchester Road was long and straight and sloping and she could see her house as soon as she turned the corner; the distance between it and herself seemed to decrease with startling rapidity, no matter how slow her progress. She stopped and put down her bags as if in need of a breather and, once more, rehearsed the opening lines of her farewell speech.

In fact she rehearsed alternative opening lines. There was the crisp, cold-blooded approach: 'Max, on Monday morning I intend to move out of this house and take up residence in Flat 2, Swinburne Court, Queen's Road. Adam will be accompanying me, though I don't want you to think for a minute that I have any intention of seducing his affections away from you. I will, of course, require you to maintain him, but *I* shan't ask you for anything – even supposing, as a woman ensconced with her lover, I would be entitled to make any such claim. Besides, I start my job the week after next.'

Or, there was a more subtle way of going about it: 'Max, we've got to face facts: we can't keep on pretending that this misery stroke antagonism stroke soul-destroying stasis which forms the fabric of our marriage can continue much longer without driving you, me or Adam, or all three of us, to distraction. You can't honestly claim that you'd be *more* unhappy if I wasn't here?'

And so on and so forth.

The house was empty. She went through the rooms, calling

for her husband, her son, becoming more and more annoyed. It is highly frustrating to nerve yourself for confrontation, to scramble out of the trench, bayonet fixed, fuelled with Dutch courage, only to find that the enemy lines have been disbanded, the engagement postponed. By the time they returned, anxiety had entirely swamped the justified anger that she'd relied upon to carry her through. Even the effects of the alcohol had begun to wear off.

She sat in the bay window, watching them as they got out of the car. She saw Max's mouth moving, knew that he was saying, '*Don't* slam the door,' knew from the wince that followed directly upon the issuing of this caution that Adam had done just that.

She didn't get up. She waited and watched as Max fumbled for his key, looking at him with a stranger's eye, trying to remember a time before the mere sight of him was an irritation. A stranger would have seen a man whom age was treating kindly: he had kept his figure; his hair was turning silver in exactly the correct, aesthetically-satisfying sequence; he was closely-shaved, neatly-barbered, pleasing of countenance. And a stranger, glancing at his *curriculum vitae*, would have been obliged to concede that it told of an upright citizen, a conscientious provider, a responsible parent. A stranger, unaware of his ill humour, of the tension generated by the merest of glances, the slightest of gestures, might well have proclaimed that some people didn't know when they were well off.

She watched him jabbing his key into the lock. Not all his fault, of course. Self-deceiving to pretend that it was. No wonder that he was ill-humoured when she could not prevent herself from making it plain that she found his company tedious, his conversation uninteresting and his amorous attentions entirely unwelcome.

But which had come first?

There had been words between them that morning to do with her failure to collect his dinner jacket from the cleaner's the previous day. She remembered now that she'd forgotten again. She knew that he was unlikely to let it rest. He didn't. He walked into the sitting-room and looked at her and he said, without preamble, 'Did you get it? No? You forgot. I knew you would. Last thing that was said before I left the house: "*I'll* pick him up from the rugby match, *you* collect my dinner jacket." I knew you'd forget.'

I forget, she thought, because you expect me to forget. 'What's the panic?' she said. 'You don't need it till tomorrow night. I'll pick it up in the morning.'

Perhaps her last housewifely commission. Tomorrow night he had one of those ghastly lodge dinners. Women were not invited, but if they had been she wouldn't have gone.

'You needn't bother. God forbid I should put you to any trouble. I'll get it myself.'

'Good,' she said. It *was* good, that he should launch straight into attack via fault-finding. Briefly, while she awaited their return, she had found that she *could* remember happier times: Max's face behind a vast bunch of purple gladioli on the day of David's birth (she loathed gladioli, most particularly purple ones): an expression of mingled bewilderment and awe; Max gravely choosing a little red and white pair of baby shoes and hanging them on the Christmas tree for the six-month-old Adam; Max relieving the monotony of traffic-jam-bedevilled journeys by singing silly songs, excruciatingly off-key, before putting his foot down and discovering a detour.

Rarely did the needle touch sixty-five now when he was driving (David said he'd seen hearses travelling faster), and he'd stopped singing years ago.

He sat down, balancing the evening paper on his knee. All the time he was reading it he was pushing back his cuticles. He was a printer and once, when he'd still been actively involved in the practice of his trade, his hands had always been stained with ink. He'd been happier then, she'd thought. Often he'd brought home examples of his work, in order to show her this new technique or that, had, briefly (and to the immense chagrin of his father, who owned the firm), joined with a couple of artists in the production of illustrated texts, had spoken of founding a press which would publish the work of local poets. But, some-how, the dream had died: the artists were unreliable, the losses too large to sustain and, as his father grew older, Max had been obliged to move full time into administration.

Now he made decisions and conferred with accountants. Now the firm produced only that which was commercially viable. Now his manicure was impeccable and his hands were always clean.

She began to take deep breaths, preparatory to speaking. He

sniffed and said, without looking up from his paper, 'What's burning?'

She'd put a fish pie in the oven. She got up to attend to it. 'Where's Adam?' she said.

'Gone up to his room.'

'It's his guitar lesson this evening, isn't it?'

'No. It's been changed to next Wednesday.'

'Drat! That's why I put the pie in – I thought he'd need to eat early.'

'He said he doesn't want anything to eat. He's going round to – whatshisname's – Parkinson's.'

Adam's cronies were a fairly unsavoury bunch and Parkinson the least attractive of them: an elderly-looking, surly, scruffy, glowering youth, a bad example, she was certain. Max maintained that he needed his arse kicking, but then Max said that about most of them, whether childish or mature, clean or dirty, impudent or respectful.

In the event, Adam came down and ate a portion of the despised fish pie after all, and then sat on at the table, absently crumbling bread around his plate. Max read *The Mayor of Casterbridge*. Rarely did he appear at table without a book (usually Hardy; when he reached the end of *Jude the Obscure* he'd start again with *Desperate Remedies*); it got them through many a mealtime.

'Oughtn't you to be moving if you're going out?' she suggested to Adam.

He shrugged. 'Doesn't start till eight.'

'What doesn't?'

'Disco.'

'I thought,' she said, 'that you were going to Parkinson's.'

'Am. Disco after.'

Did he have to talk in monosyllables? 'Where is this disco?' she asked sharply, and Adam made a gesture with his knife that encompassed approximately half of the south side of the city.

'*Where?*' she persisted. You *couldn't* just let them run loose. Not these days, not with tins of Evostick and little carefully-folded newspaper squares that contained smack and perverts parked round every corner. Max sighed heavily, without raising his eyes from his book. She knew how fervently he must wish that you could still sell wives on the open market. Except that, no doubt, *he'd* consider himself lucky if he could *give* her away.

'Well, Adam, where?'

'St Mary's.'

'Then why not say so in the first place? Why do I have to drag information out of you, as though everything's top secret?'

His reaction was to stare long and hard at her, his face totally devoid of expression. Doubtless a Parkinson trick. And extremely disconcerting, in that it never failed to make her feel that her criticism was entirely unwarranted, a product of her own personality problems rather than a reaction to his behaviour.

The meal came to an end. She cleared the table and washed and dried the pots. She washed and dried them very conscientiously: scrubbing away at every last stubborn stain on the pie dish, applying scouring powder to the insides of the cups. All the time, the pre-rehearsed explanation was running through her head like a loop of tape jammed on fast-forward: sentences jostled each other for prominence, were gone before she had time to register anything but their general inadequacy. When she passed the kitchen door and looked across the hall she could see Max. He'd taken some papers from his briefcase and was checking through them. He usually managed to appear occupied; it was insurance against unwelcome approach.

'Do you *want* something?' he said. And she became aware that she'd been standing in the doorway looking at him, twisting a tea towel between her hands, for quite some time.

She opened her mouth and tried to force the words through it and thus into the domain of public knowledge.

'Well?' Max said, and pushed his spectacles more firmly on to the bridge of his nose: a gesture that she found only slightly less irritating than the way he had of crossing his legs and describing a circle in the air with his foot, or his throat-clearing in the morning. This was possibly retaliatory irritation for his objecting to the way that she chewed on her lower lip when absorbed, cracked her knuckle joints, twitched. Often the time they spent in each other's company seemed to be wholly devoted to a battle of wills in the matter of who could first succeed, by means of judiciously-orchestrated fidgeting, in driving the other to screaming pitch.

'Well?' Max repeated. 'What do you want?'

I want . . . you to be the way you were when we met, when you called me 'Baby' and pulled my Aertex vest ever so gently over my head, when you held my hand at the graveside on the day of my mother's funeral, exerting a faint but constant pressure that kept me from total disintegration, that promised strength and support for ever and ever, world without end.

They'd met in hospital (their mothers were being terminally ill in adjacent beds). He had guided her: a young girl, fatherless, clueless, around a kind of Monopoly board of registrar's offices and undertakers and death certificates and chapels of rest. None of her contemporaries could have offered her the same degree of assistance. Max, being older, was neither frightened nor embarrassed by grief. 'I'll look after you,' Max had said, enfolding her in his embrace, gently parting her thighs, inserting an intelligent finger into her interior and massaging her clitoris until she was drowned in sensation; it was the only method of stemming her tears. 'Little love,' Max had whispered, taking advantage of her swoon to ease himself into her. It was unlikely that any of her undergraduate friends knew what a clitoris was, let alone where it might be located, and as for comfort: most of them blushed when they met her or crossed the road to avoid meeting her.

Getting pregnant had seemed somehow logical, fitting, in that it meant delivering herself over to him entirely. Her tutors at university were regretful, talking of wasted potential; she sacrificed the possibility of that sort of future quite philosophically, believing herself to be unequipped for tackling life head-on, alone.

'Baby.'

But she wasn't, any longer. She had started to grow up, to strike out on her own account, to question his opinions and argue with conclusions that hitherto had been taken as read. And she suspected that most of their troubles stemmed from her growing up, her demanding a life free of his control and guidance. This being so, it was hardly rational to ask him to revert to being the Max who had fallen in love with a child, and to whom she had responded as such.

'I've got to talk to you.'

But explanation number one was a non-starter. And explanation number two fared no better. 'Max,' she said, and could get no further. She was aware of a solitary bird singing in the garden, of music issuing from Adam's room, though she could scarcely hear them above the noise of her heart. And then that organ, instead of hammering against her ribs, seemed to suspend its activity altogether and she was aware of the enormous and hostile silence enclosing them, and she was also aware – as though she'd suddenly been granted a completely different and unfamiliar perspective on the situation – of the enormity of the step she was taking. I'm mad, she thought, I can't *do* this. And then he said, 'Would you mind moving out of my light please?' and the time-suspended, frozen moment was past and all the rehearsed sentences deserted her and she could only splutter incoherently: 'I'm leaving. I have to go. On Monday. I've taken a flat. It was no good trying to talk to you first and then . . . Anyway, you *won't* talk. Every time I've tried you take some papers out of your briefcase, or switch on the television, or open your bloody *book*. If we *could* . . . If you'd just, occasionally, act like I existed . . . Max, listen to me.'

Tick, tick, tick, went the pen, so steadily-held, against the row of figures upon the paper from which he never raised his eyes. During previous rows this tactic had so incensed her that she'd been known to fly at him, her hands clawed, her nails ready to plough furrows down the sides of his face. But he was a big, strong, muscular man and he had no trouble in fending her off.

Very deliberately, he replaced the cap on his pen, screwed it up tight, gathered his papers together and got to his feet. 'I don't have to listen to this nonsense,' he said.

'No you don't. I can't make you. But it doesn't alter the fact that I'm leaving. On Monday. I've taken a flat in Queen's Road. I'm moving out. And refusing to listen won't make it not so.'

It was said not in the hysterical fashion that he'd obviously expected, but with a calm certainty that surprised her and brought him to a standstill. He stood tapping the papers against his thigh, turning the pen over and over in his other hand. He said, 'What are you talking about?'

'You know what I'm talking about.'

And she could see that he knew, now, that although she had screamed 'I'm leaving you' dozens of times before, this time he was listening to a statement of intent rather than an empty threat.

'Why?'

Why? Where to start? What could she tell him that he didn't already know?

'Because there isn't anything left between us.'

No empathy, no tenderness, no passion. Or if there is, your

27

rigidity, your inability to change with the changes, has warped it out of all recognition.

'You murdered it,' he said. 'You allowed it to die.'

He was breathing very heavily, through his nose. He was also very pale.

'No. It's me that's being murdered. Stifled. You're *killing* me. Trying to keep me in some sort of time-warp. Trying to keep me as I used to be: looking up to you as though you were God. Did you really believe that it could stay that way? As though I was a piece of this bloody awful furniture in this bloody awful Rip-Van-Winkle house? I *had* to try to change and you wouldn't *let* me . . . Max, you know as well as I do that this isn't just some whim, some spur of the moment thing . . . I've *got* to go.'

'You've got to go? You've got to go only because there's someone to go to.'

'What makes you so sure of that?'

How distant Livingstone suddenly seemed, how remote from all this.

'Because you haven't the gumption to do it off your own bat.'

'Is it surprising? You won't let me *be*. You didn't want me to get my degree, to look for a job . . . Max, you cannot . . . keep . . . me . . . as . . . your . . . property . . .'

His arm rose, as though in response to some hypnotic command, as though whatever action he performed would only be at the instigation of an irresistible external force. She thought he might be going to hit her (he never had, but then she'd never left him before) and, irrationally, under the circumstances, moved towards him rather than away. Maybe she deserved to be hit. Maybe he needed to externalise his rage. In the past she had often wanted to say: 'Match me, shout for shout, yell for yell. Express your pain. Whatever it is that you keep suppressed surely can't be so terrible that you daren't risk allowing it its freedom?' But his way of responding to aggression had always been to walk out of the room, if not the house.

His arm fell to his side. His face was working furiously. It took a moment to grasp that he was attempting to prevent himself from crying and then she was overcome with such embarrassment that she couldn't look at him. She hadn't seen him cry since his mother died. It was inconceivable. She'd *rather* he'd hit her.

'We can – do something about it – change. You can't just – '

28

She stared at the wall. She knew how much it was costing him in terms of pride to plead with her. She knew however he tried, whatever promises he made, he was incapable of changing, of coming anywhere close to meeting the requirements necessary for harmonious living. She knew that her transferred affections would sabotage whatever attempts he might make. She wished, more than anything, that he, whose refusal to respond had so often driven her to gibbering fury, would regain control over himself.

'Please . . . Christina . . .'

'Please, please, don't.'

The phone rang. And continued to ring, without either of them making any move to respond to it. Eventually, another sound was added to its strident summons: that of Adam's feet thudding down the stairs. He put his head around the door. 'Isn't anybody going to answer that?' he said.

'Well?'

'Leave it,' they both said simultaneously, and Adam said, 'For heaven's *sake*,' and crossed the hall and picked up the receiver but, by then, whoever it was had rung off.

'Right then. I'll get going.'

She followed him to the door. He had on all his disco finery: 501s, Lacoste pullover, Puma training shoes. A dandy. David, who acquired his clothing from second-hand stalls, mocked this unhealthy preoccupation with style, or actually – what was worse – cost. 'Little snobs, posing in the playground,' he called those of Adam's persuasion, criticised him for allowing himself to be seduced by the prevailing climate of materialism.

Her thoughts meandered, swung out of control, no matter how determinedly she tried to keep them addressed to the matter in hand. Adam lingered, waiting no doubt for the ritual farewell warnings: variations on the theme that had persisted since childhood; after all, strange men were strange men, it was only the nature of their blandishments that changed.

Instead, she merely touched him on the shoulder and said, 'Enjoy yourself,' and saw him blink with surprise.

'Right then . . .'

'Adam!' called Max from the sitting-room. 'Can you come in here for a minute?'

'What *is* it? I'm going to be *late*.'

In passing her on the threshold, a lock of his carefully-arranged hair had been displaced. He took a comb from his pocket and attended to it, was combing when Max turned to face them and said, 'I gather that your mother has something to say to you,' was still combing with the utmost concentration when Max said, 'Well come on, tell him what you've told me, about this new arrangement you've decided upon,' and she said, 'Not now, Max,' and Max went right ahead and repeated, 'Adam, your mother has something to say to you.'

She hadn't planned for this. She had envisaged a heart-to-heart over the weekend, a walk in the park, a calm and sensible discussion, an acknowledgement of his maturity: 'I know I can rely on you, Adam, to understand . . .'

Max had mastered his tears. You'd never have known. Except for the muscle jumping at the side of his mouth, you'd never have suspected that anything was amiss. But she knew she had to speak before he did. He had abased himself, she had spurned him, and therefore nothing that he said, however brutal, could surprise her. 'Adam,' she said, 'you know how things have been. Your father and I just haven't been getting along lately. We think it's best if we part . . . See how things go . . . I didn't want to tell you like this, obviously . . .'

The comb was suspended in mid-air. The bird in the garden sang full-throatedly, like an off-stage effect that had wandered by mistake into the wrong theatre.

'We?' Max said.

'I've taken a place in Queen's Road,' she continued. 'It's a lovely flat. Masses of room. I think it'll suit us very well. For one thing it'll be more convenient for school – you've always said what a trek it is . . .'

'Us?' Max said. 'That would be "us" as in you and your boyfriend, I take it?'

The comb was slowly returned to Adam's pocket. A tuft of his hair was still sticking up at the back.

'Because I hope you're not under the misapprehension that "us" might possibly include your son,' said Max.

His hands were loosely clasped, his stance hadn't altered, but the tic beat frantically.

'Well, naturally . . .'

'Well you can think again,' Max said. 'Adam isn't going anywhere.'

She looked at her son, remembered the glitter-drenched

Christmas card, the egg-shell fragility of his baby skull before the bones knitted together, his hand in hers as they walked to school for the very first time, the way he'd clung to her at the threshold and couldn't be detached.

His hands now were pushed deep into the pockets of his jacket. Even so, she could see that they were trembling. So was his upper lip. His eyes darted all over the place, directed everywhere except at her or his father. When he spoke, the words emerged perhaps an octave higher in pitch than he had intended. 'Dead right I'm not,' he said.

3

'Dead right I'm not.'

And, very soon afterwards, he'd left.

'He went to the disco. Just as if it had been any ordinary Friday night. And on Saturday he went to the football match and then back to that awful Parkinson's.'

Livingstone handed her another tissue, taking receipt of the one she'd already drenched rather too fastidiously between finger and thumb.

'Max went straight out after breakfast on Saturday too.'

He'd got up from the table and addressed a point in the air above her left shoulder: 'Whenever it is that you're going, will you make sure you leave your credit card before you do? I'll call into the bank on Monday about the account.'

'Max,' she'd said, and put out a hand. He'd side-stepped so that he didn't have to come within a yard of her as he walked out of the room.

'Sunday,' she told Livingstone, 'I spent chasing them through the house, knocking on locked doors. All Adam would say was, "Lay off, will you? It's nothing to do with me. It's between you and him." Do you think he reacted like that because of the horribly crude way that Max described it to him? Do you think he felt he'd be in the *way* here or something?'

She'd taken it for granted; she'd just assumed . . . There'd been so much friction of late, with herself acting as arbiter, conciliator, pig-in-the-middle: 'Adam, turn off that television set, you know your father can't stand noise first thing in the morning.' 'Adam, clear up this mess, your father'll have a fit if he sees it.' 'Of course he doesn't know the value of money, Max. Did you, at his age?'

She'd just assumed because making an assumption was easier than facing up to the problem of explaining the situation.

'I should have done it gradually, shouldn't I? Introduced the idea to him gently. But how *could* I? The time between telling him and actually leaving would have been unbearable. These last two days have been bad enough.'

Having exhausted the tissues, she wiped her nose on her sleeve. Her nose was twice its normal size, her eyes almost closed with crying. On first seeing her, Livingstone had said, with a very obvious tremor of unease, 'Oh my God! Did he *hit* you?'

'It isn't as if it meant such an *enormous* change for him,' she continued. 'I mean, it isn't as if I was dragging him off to another *town*. A couple of miles away, for heaven's sake! Oh *why* do you think he wants to stay with Max?'

'I don't know,' Livingstone said, moving his cuff slightly so that he could see the face of his watch. Though he did it very surreptitiously, and her eyes were half-closed and clouded with tears, she noticed.

'I don't know anything about children,' Livingstone said.

'You can have an opinion, can't you?'

'If he says he wants to stay with his father, then presumably that's where he feels happiest. I think you have to accept that – however much it hurts. After all, he's not an infant. Presumably you'll have every opportunity to see him.'

Presumably.

'I tried to put my arms round him. He shook me off as though I had something contagious.'

'Well, he's at that age, isn't he?'

'I thought you didn't know about children,' she said.

'I know that fifteen-year-old boys don't usually welcome displays of affection. I remember my mother once kissing me in Peter Jones, in the china department. I almost hit her. Oh look, please, use this!'

He handed her his own clean handkerchief. Apparently he found use of the sleeve very off-putting. Once, after love, he'd told her that he couldn't imagine anything that she might do that could repel him.

'Are you worried that he won't look after himself, or be looked after?'

'Well of course.'

Although Max was not a neglectful parent. He would make sure that Adam was properly fed and clothed. He would make certain that he was clean! There was a programme currently on the television: a comedy series, purportedly told from the point of view of an adolescent boy, which dealt with a very similar situation: mother run off with lover, leaving father and son to cope as best they might. Being a comedy, everything – not surprisingly – was made out to be comical; all the domestic disasters that were supposed to result from the withdrawal of a woman's touch: washing-machine floodings and gas supply disconnections and burnt offerings masquerading as square meals.

In emotional terms, the boy in the television series seemed to cope admirably. She wondered not why life couldn't be more like the movies (it seemed to be proceeding in exactly that direction in terms of cruelty and violence), but why it couldn't, just now and again, resemble those sort of increasingly prevalent situation comedies.

She blew her nose into his handkerchief. It was very clean and carefully ironed (by Louise or the laundry? At any rate, it gave her great pleasure to despoil it). She said, 'I *was* going to do us a meal, but . . .'

It had all been prepared in advance: lace tablecloth, candle, Swedish glass water jug, Blue Mountain coffee. Tonight was to have been the first of the meals acknowledging the creation of a new family circle – though she had been quite prepared for there to be just herself and Adam, supposed that Livingstone's leaving might well involve several long evenings devoted to the sort of discussion and planning that must take place if a husband and wife are to part in anything like a civilised fashion.

There were amicable partings, where each partner, having recognised the failure of the marriage, also recognised the necessity to bite their tongues and swallow their pride and address themselves to sorting out the compromise most advantageous to both.

And there were partings where one person ducked to avoid whatever the other threw at him, partings characterised, if not by physical violence, then certainly by verbal abuse, where children huddled wide-eyed on the bottom step of the stairs and overdoses were swallowed and the services of highly-persuasive divorce lawyers engaged.

Was Louise an hysterical woman? As a womb-sufferer, male

tradition would suggest that she was. Christina had only ever seen her once, and then only briefly. She'd been lunching with a woman friend when a group of people had passed their table and one or two of them had acknowledged her. When they were out of earshot the friend had said, 'They're buyers. You remember when I worked for Kayser-Bondor? I got to know them then. It'll be the spring collections. You see that blonde woman? That's Louise Livingstone. You know: the one who designs those knitted things. *Gorgeous*. But *horrendously* expensive. What's wrong, Christina? Isn't your mousse very nice?'

Smallish, ash-blonde. Cool and composed. He'd met her, when they were both very young, at an art school dance. She was a student of fashion design. He said that only her reticence: an inability to push herself forward in a highly-competitive field, had prevented her from really going places.

She'd looked, to Christina, even in that brief glimpse, like someone who was perfectly capable of reaching the place that suited her best and, having reached it, of defending her territory.

'It's all right,' Livingstone said now, zipping his jacket. He hadn't even taken it off. 'I don't want anything to eat. I can't stay anyway.'

'But it's only half-past eight.'

'You knew that this week was going to be chaotic.'

She did know. He'd told her. It was not only the week marked down for departure from his home; it was also the first week of term and he – having been granted a year's sabbatical – had to show his replacement the ropes. It was leave of absence to allow him to write a book, a sociological study dealing with racial tensions in deprived inner-city areas.

Her job, his sabbatical; they'd discussed it often: the un-strained days there'd be when he, having serenely finished his latest chapter, would prepare a simple meal for her, returning weary but replete with job satisfaction from her day's work. They would eat at a table set in a recess, facing a window. In their fantasy, the window was curtained in white muslin billow-ing gently in the breeze which rippled the surface of the lake below.

She couldn't manage a lake, but the sight of muslin curtains had been a definite plus when she'd first inspected the flat.

'You knew I'd hardly have a minute to myself. And now . . .' he said, gently extricating his arm from behind her shoulders.

Well yes of course she'd known, but then she'd banked on having Adam with her.

'It looks like you've plenty to occupy yourself with anyway,' he said, indicating the cases that waited to be unpacked. She'd deliberately used her own, pre-marriage luggage: ancient stuff, it was, heavy – and her trunk, labelled still with her maiden name and her college address. She'd had to give the taxi-driver a huge tip in advance to induce him to drag it down the stairs: 'What do you think I am, missis, Pickfords?'

'Can't you stay just a little longer? Please?'

He rubbed his nose, tugged at an earlobe, shuffled his feet on the carpet. He was normally very composed, but these were not normal times. 'Well all right,' he said, 'just a little longer. Her sister's over for the evening and I promised to drive her back.'

She didn't say anything. She thought: I have made my own way here, laden with luggage, pulled each of my cases and then my trunk, up the stairs. There's a pain in my side and blisters on my hands, and you've promised to drive Louise's sister home.

She couldn't get Adam's face out of her head. She'd made him promise to visit her on Wednesday after school. They finished early on Wednesdays. She'd hugged him to her, but it had felt as though she were embracing an inanimate object. After he'd gone, she'd written letters to both of her sons. Adam's, she'd propped up against the photograph on the sideboard that depicted herself and Max on holiday at Lake Como. Having no close relatives upon whom they could dump the children (Max, like herself, was an only child), they'd never managed a holiday by themselves, but that day the hotel had arranged children's entertainment – even timid Adam whose eternal cry, as a small child, had been: 'Mummy, don't leave me!' had allowed himself to be bribed with the prospect of circus clowns and Charlie Chaplin films. They'd slipped off for the afternoon, strolled by the lake, held hands. Disembarking from the steamer, she'd turned her ankle. How solicitous he'd been: lifting and carrying her across to a taxi, kissing it better.

Perhaps it had been perverse, objecting to being his baby when she considered how well he'd looked after her.

She and Livingstone would look after each other. Dependence would not enter into it. She mopped her eyes. Things would improve, she was certain: the guilt that clung to her skin like some terrible contagion would evaporate, David would write back saying, 'Don't worry, Mum, I'm sure you're doing the right thing,' Adam would turn up on Wednesday, smile, and allow himself to be embraced, Louise would gracefully acknowledge that what is dead cannot – as a general rule – be resurrected.

She embraced Livingstone. 'You get off,' she said. 'Do your duty.'

'Sure you'll be all right?'

'Of course. As long as – just – '

He paused with his hand on the doorknob. 'Just what?'

'Nothing.'

She bit back the query she'd been going to make as to his exact intentions. Innocent queries could so easily be construed as demands. He would do what had to be done in his own good time; she must leave him to it.

It only occurred to her after he'd gone that this was the first night she'd spent alone in her entire life. At college she'd shared a room; when her mother was in hospital she'd stayed at her cousin Gwen's, and after that, after her mother never came out of hospital, Gwen's father, her guardian, having given his permission, she'd married Max.

When Max was away there'd been the children, and the only time she'd been away from home without either Max or the children was to spend a night in a hotel with Livingstone.

It was the quietness that was so uncanny. Even the gloomiest of households, if it contains children, will rarely be quiet. There will be television sets and record players and cassette decks and Sony Walkmans, there will be recorder practice and electric guitars and the chatter of home computers. Friends will call, thundering up and down the stairs. The garden will double as go-kart track, cricket pitch, tennis court. Motor cycles will roar away from the front gates and, later, cars. Even in a household presided over by someone as intolerant of noise and disorder as Max, if it contains growing children, periods of uninterrupted quiet will be few and far between.

Whereas here: it was a residential area, filled with huge Victorian houses, most of which had been converted into flats, and flat-dwellers tend to be a childless population. Below Christina, there resided, from April until the end of September, an elderly lady who spent the rest of the year on the Costa del Sol. The flat above was reserved for some sort of company letting and was, at present, vacant.

No buses passed along Queen's Road and, as it didn't lie between any major thoroughfares, no cars used it as a short cut. If there was to be noise, then she must make it herself. She switched on the radio and, for ten minutes or so, unpacked her cases to a background of Mantovani, Swedish interference and crackle. And then there was just crackle. And then there was nothing at all except for some barely-audible muttering sounds, and she remembered all the times she'd said to her sons, 'When you replace batteries, throw the old ones away, *don't* just shove them into a drawer where people will assume they're new and use them again', 'people' being Max who always seemed to be at the receiving end of this practice: taking a torch to investigate sinister noises in the garden at night and having it fail on him and nearly breaking his neck as some dustbin-marauding tom cat fled across his path.

It had taken her far longer to pack her suitcases than it did to unpack them. It took no time at all to prepare a bit of bread and cheese for supper and eat it. As she ate it, she pulled back the curtain and looked down to the street. All she could see was the dark clump of shrubbery, a sodium lamp and the branches of some trees; there wasn't a living soul abroad. Some sort of bird suddenly emitted a scream. Perhaps there were owls about. She had always been afraid of owls, of the look of them as much as their predatory habits and the bloodcurdling noises they made.

She had nothing else to do but go to bed. She lay very still on what she already thought of as her side of it, waiting to be overtaken by sleep.

Strange beds. It took a night, at least, to get used to a strange bed. Even if you weren't emotionally shattered, remorseful, apprehensive. Ridiculous, really, to have expected to sleep.

At half-past twelve she did drop off for ten minutes or so, then she awoke with a start, heart beating twenty to the dozen, hands tingling with cramp. Slowly she unclenched them. In her dream, they had been at Max's throat and she had been prevented from squeezing the life out of him only by that timely awakening. 'We were all right,' he had said, in the dream, before she flew at him. 'We were all right until you spoiled it.'

She thought it was the dream that had wakened her, but it wasn't, it was a scream: shrill, piercing. It happened again. She shot bolt upright, pulse racing, mouth dry, and then she remembered the owls. But the intermittent tapping that became audible as soon as she began to calm down could not be attributed to the owls. She couldn't locate it, nor find any reassuring explanation for it. Was it coming from the flat above or the one below? Was it coming from outside in the corridor or inside in the hall? Had she dropped the latch on the door? Which was worse: to lie where she was, wondering, or to risk getting up and encountering – whatever might be responsible for that noise? It took ages, and a long intermission in the tapping, before she plucked up enough courage to swing her legs out of bed and run full-pelt into the hall and fumble frantically for the light switch.

There was nothing there and the door was locked and the tapping had ceased. It didn't recur until three forty-five, but by then she'd switched on every light in the place and propped a chair under the door handle. When she woke the second time, she said, 'Max' and then she remembered and said, 'Livingstone' and then she remembered properly and the realisation of the futility of saying anything at all came as quite a shock.

◡ 4 ◡

The next afternoon when Livingstone arrived the sun was shining and the night and its attendant frights seemed so remote as to be figments of her imagination. That night, a repeat performance of creakings and tappings was sufficient to project her, full-tilt into his arms when he arrived the following day. 'Hey,' he said. 'Hey!' But was dismissive when she explained the reason for her distress. The noises she'd heard could be easily accounted for: these flats were recently converted, were they not? New wood has a habit of expanding and contracting; floorboards creak; plumbing takes time to settle down; radiators have been known to produce a positive symphony of sound.

'Why only at night?'

'It isn't only at night. It's just that you notice it more when it's quiet.'

'And the tapping?' she said. 'Floorboards can't tap, radiators can't tap.'

'Oh yes, they can. But actually – have you noticed, there are blinds at the windows of the top flat? We used to have blinds. The slightest draught and those wooden thingamajigs at the bottom of the cords can tap like fury at the glass. We got rid of them in the end.'

'Oh did you?'

'Oh come on, Christina. You're quite safe. There's a lock on that front door that could withstand a horde of crazed vandals, and this one is perfectly secure. *And* you've got a bolt.'

'I just feel so isolated here, so vulnerable . . .'

She could feel his hand in her hair, stroking, smoothing away the tension. 'You've worked yourself up into a state,' he said. 'Come on, come and sit down and have a drink and relax.'

'I was hoping you'd get here earlier. Adam came. I wanted you to meet him.'

Adam had stayed in the flat for exactly nineteen and a half minutes, for only seven of which he had been persuaded to sit down. And as soon as she'd said, 'There's someone I'd like you to meet,' he'd leapt to his feet and made for the door, reciting a list of excuses too comprehensive to be convincing. She'd been left contemplating an untouched plate of *mille-feuilles* (his favourites, bought specially); 'No thanks,' he'd said. 'I'm not hungry.'

Interrogation would not be welcomed; she saw that from his face as soon as she let him in, saw him begin to wriggle beneath her scrutiny: his collar was clean, his shoes were polished, moss had not yet started to grow on his teeth – she forced herself to leave it at that. She offered him a guided tour. 'Yeah,' he said, 'very nice,' every time she opened a door.

'And this is what I thought of as being your room . . .'

Then, he'd produced a deep blush.

'You haven't changed your mind?'

A vigorous shaking of the head, a jutting of the lower lip.

'But you'll come to stay? Very soon?'

She had sunk down on to the bed with its severely masculine duvet cover – chosen especially for him. 'Adam,' she said, 'I didn't leave just on a whim. I left because – for a very long time – life has been impossible.'

He gave every sign of not having heard her and then he said suddenly, 'How could it have been impossible? You've lived it.'

'But I don't think I could have continued to live it.'

Quaking every morning as she came down to make the breakfast: what sort of mood will he be in today? What sort of mood am *I* in? Is combustion inevitable?

'Adam,' she'd said. 'There's someone I'd like you to meet . . .'

And it was then that he'd picked up his schoolcase and rushed for the door, talking of guitar lessons and Parkinson and homework.

'You missed him by only a matter of minutes,' she told Livingstone. She saw no reason – from his point of view anyway – for their meeting to be strained; she had told him so much about her sons, during the months of their love affair, and he had seemed to display an eagerness to listen. It could only be paranoia on her part that made it appear as though an expression of relief passed fleetingly across his face.

Generalised paranoia: the imputing to people of feelings that didn't exist, the translation of perfectly innocent noises into a horror-film soundtrack. 'I'm being an idiot, aren't I?' she said. She said, 'Ignore me and come and eat. I hope your appetite's good. I did enough for Adam as well.'

His appetite wasn't good, that much soon became apparent. She recalled reading stories about errant husbands who found themselves gaining stones of excess weight simply because they were obliged to avert suspicion by eating the meals their wives provided for them and then, in order not to offend their mistresses, having to start all over again.

But it was too early for him to have eaten already. She watched him struggling. She said, 'You don't have to *force* it down.'

'It isn't a question of that . . .' But he put down his fork.

She put hers down too. It didn't matter. There would be weeks, months, years, for them to enjoy home-cooked meals *à deux*.

'I do know what you're going through,' she said. 'I can only say that the doing of it is slightly less dreadful than the contemplation of it.'

He produced a faint approximation to a smile, and then began to rearrange the unused cutlery (and there was a lot of it: he hadn't eaten any bread, the pineapple gâteau was untouched, and the cheese) into battle stations on the tablecloth.

'It's saying the first sentence that's the worst. After that, it's easier. All you're doing, really, anyway, is confirming what's already known. You always said that she must have realised what was happening. Just as Max did – '

He demolished his careful knife and fork and spoon arrangement and sent them bouncing across the cloth. 'Why do you assume,' he said, 'that what's true for you and Max is bound to be true for everyone else?'

Never before had she heard that querulous note in his voice. She'd always thought of him as possessing the most equable of temperaments, couldn't – however hard she tried – imagine what might possibly ruffle him, never had reason to believe that his charm was anything but a reflection of himself.

Of course, neither had he any cause to suppose that she'd turn into a whimpering neurotic, having the vapours because the floorboards creaked.

'I'm sorry.'

They both spoke at the same time. They were used to being polite to each other, even in their passion.

'I'm sorry,' and into each other's arms. Where everything could be made right. Even if the silk sheets did strike a somewhat inappropriate note: this was not unbridled passion, but rather comfort-sex – the first time they'd felt the need for it. And, she hoped, at the end of all her futile attempts to bring him to the requisite pitch of arousal, the last.

'It doesn't matter,' she said. 'It doesn't matter in the least.' (Weeks, months, years ahead of them for gourmet meals and good sex.) 'I just wanted you to hold me, that's all.'

She hadn't. She'd wanted him to bring her to orgasm, the most thrilling climax of her life. As a statement. As a symbolic christening of the new bed. Because, among all the abnormality, his response to her was one way of reassuring herself that there were still constants.

Plus which, it might have helped her to sleep.

She tried to jolly him up: 'Don't men usually say, on these occasions, "This has never happened to me before"?'

'Men are liars. Don't you know that by now?'

The weather was pretending to be summer, but it was actually autumn. Getting chilly. She pulled the coverlet over them, drew his head on to her shoulder, but despite the coverlet and her cradling of him, his skin beneath hers felt cold and clammy. It was fear that caused it, fear that prevented him from getting an erection. She had always thought of him as being far stronger than herself, looked to him for guidance. After all, it was he who had showed her how things worked: computers and flow-charts and the coffee machine in the foyer of the Department, he who had encouraged her when her enthusiasm began to flag and graduation seemed impossibly remote, he who had directed her towards careers' officers and relevant publications and asserted, in defiance of her protest that no one would give her a job, that she wouldn't know until she tried.

Well, strength and courage waxed and waned, were known to be situation-specific: she was afraid of the dark, he was scared of confrontation; both these fears could, and must, be overcome.

'Let's go and finish the wine,' she said. Courage must be derived how and where it could be found. Was that why they called it bottle?

43

Wine, candlelight, and a background of some sort of palm-court orchestra (she'd bought new batteries for the radio first thing on Tuesday morning. It was surprising how much the flat was *not* furnished with, how much twenty settled years of accumulation allowed you to take for granted. Kitchen tools, she'd had to buy, and a clock for the lounge, another lamp for the bedside, and a plug, and a screwdriver and wire-strippers in order that she could assemble it. She'd begun to wish that she'd been rather less high-minded in the matter of bringing nothing with her from home except her personal belongings).

She said, very casually, 'You haven't brought any of your stuff yet then, have you?' He might say that he had a car full downstairs, but she doubted it.

'I can hardly do that until there's been some sort of decision as to dividing up – '

He couldn't bring himself to say 'the spoils', and nor could she say it for him. It surprised her that such division should be considered necessary. During their discussions, both had spoken of marriages that were held together first by children, and then by possessions. Women friends of hers, male acquaintances of his, said, 'I'm not leaving him, I'd end up with nothing,' or 'Why should she get the benefit of everything I've sweated my balls off to provide?' This attitude, they had found incomprehensible. Neither of them, they had said, placed much value upon possessions, *things*.

And now, it seemed, there was to be some sort of share-out between himself and Louise. Two separate piles, she imagined, with the pair of them perusing a sort of wedding-present list in reverse, holding up books, ornaments, tin-openers, enquiring politely, 'Yours? Mine?'

He drank steadily, holding her hand so tightly that she got pins and needles. And he was quiet for so long that she'd had time to rehearse a good few indirect versions of the question: '*When* are you going to move in here?' when he suddenly said, 'Louise has the chance of a contract with an American company, to supply several top stores over there.'

'*Really?*'

'Mm-hm. It's happened before, tentatively, but this looks like a firm offer.'

'That's marvellous,' she said. 'Isn't it?'

She was thinking: sometimes, amazingly, you get your timing right. Your children grow up, you go out into the world, you fall in love, you get a job and you're able to contemplate at last pleasing yourself. (Well – almost right; perhaps another couple of years with Adam safely away at college too might have been preferable.) And then, lo and behold, your lover's wife has a stroke of the sort of good luck that must mean that he'll be able to leave her secure in the knowledge that life is smiling on her, that, compared with that kind of opportunity, the mere defection of an already-estranged husband can only be incidental.

'She must be delighted.'

She remembered how, after her glimpse of his wife in that restaurant, she'd gone into one of those exclusive little shops that drape just one or two unpriced garments in their windows and tried on an intricately-embroidered jersey that said 'Louise Livingstone' in gold on the label, blushing, ridiculously, all the while as the saleswoman told her how popular they were, and then she took it home and put it in a drawer under some other jerseys and never put it on again.

'Will she have to go over there?'

Louise, the retiring violet, conquering America! Had she become more forceful? One did. One had to.

'Yes, of course.'

'When?'

'The week after next. That's why things are so hectic at the moment. She's working like stink to get everything ready . . .'

. . . so it was perfectly understandable that, until everything *was* ready: the final sequined rose appliquéd to the front of an evening jumper, the last bugle bead sewn on to a hem, he would find himself unable to broach the subject of their separation.

But once she'd left!

It was simply a matter of stealing oneself to cope with the loneliness and those inexplicable nocturnal noises until that moment arrived.

'Yoo-hoo! Christina! Yoo-hoo!'

She looked across the road and saw a figure standing outside the Army and Navy stores, semaphoring wildly. It was her next-door-but-one neighbour, her ex-next-door-but-one neighbour, Alison Harrington, who now, having succeeded in attracting

Christina's attention, began a dangerous weaving progress through the Pelican-halted traffic.

It was too late to pretend not to have seen her. Still, people would have to know, sooner or later, and telling Alison Harrington, who had a mouth like the Mersey Tunnel, would be tantamount to putting it in the paper.

Anyway, she was a career-woman (an occupational therapist, her speciality being sex for the disabled; once, in Christina's sitting-room, she'd started talking about her work: the accommodations necessary, the ingenious prostheses involved, blithely unaware that fastidious Max, within earshot, was embarrassed beyond measure) and, as a career-woman, had always stressed the need for female autonomy. Alison Harrington, as well as acting as carrier-pigeon, ought to be the first to offer her congratulation.

She was out of breath. Panting punctuated her combined greeting and request for information: 'Hello, Christina,' she said. 'Where on earth were you going the other day with all those suitcases?'

The great thing about people like Alison Harrington was that, if you let them talk, sooner or later they answered their own questions.

'Have you left home? You *have*? Good God. I said to Derek, "She can't be taking all that just for a couple of nights away" – Derek thought you might be going to see David. I said, "It looks like she's doing a bunk" – Derek said don't be so daft. And then yesterday, when I called, Max opened the door to me and I said, "Is Christina in?" and he said, "No she is not," and practically shut the door in my face. Good God!' said Alison Harrington. 'Where are you living? Who are you living with?'

'Queen's Road. I'm not living with anybody.'

And even if she had been, she couldn't have said so. Not yet. Unseemly somehow to admit to it. Yet.

'Look,' said Alison Harrington, 'I've got half an hour free. Come and have a coffee and a chat. You know,' she said, steering Christina towards a nearby café, 'Derek said he'd seen Adam leaving for school yesterday morning and the morning before. I said, "Either you're puddled or you need your glasses changing." I said, "If Christina's left, she'll have taken Adam with her. It stands to reason."'

'I have to go. I've an appointment and I'm late already.'

The green man came to her aid, started to flash; she dashed across the road, leaving Alison Harrington gaping on the pavement.

It started to rain as she was walking up to the Polytechnic but instead of opening her umbrella she raised her face to it in the hope that it would cool her burning forehead, her flushed cheek. Alison Harrington was blunt and outspoken, but she was only articulating what would, when the news was bruited abroad, be a tacit consensus. And where, last week, she had walked the city streets, filled with anticipatory delight, seeing nothing but goodwill in the faces of passers-by, now they appeared to look at her and condemn her as an unnatural woman.

By the time she reached the top of the hill and the Social Sciences Department of the Poly, she was panting almost as heavily as Alison Harrington had done – and without the excuse of excess weight. Out of condition. She envisaged a totally new recreational regime when Livingstone moved in. He actively kept himself fit: swimming, tennis, squash. Louise, sickly, had been obliged to sit on the sidelines: *she* would join in.

Everything would change. It had to. She'd realised that when she first contemplated the terrifying notion of leaving home. Half measures wouldn't do: it would be too easy to abandon them, to find oneself slipping back into the old ways. And if one was to be terrified, then one might as well be terrified on all counts at once: new home, new man, new job, and get it over with.

Though she had to admit that getting a job hadn't demanded quite the same sort of pioneering spirit that was entailed in finding a place to live and actually leaving to live in it. Livingstone had steered her in its direction: a year's research assistantship on a project dealing with aspects of interpersonal relations: and though she had a good degree, the fact that it turned out to be Hilary Roberts whom she was required to assist had undoubtedly enhanced her chances.

'Hilary Roberts?' Livingstone had said. He knew her vaguely; they'd met at conferences.

'Yes,' she'd said, 'I didn't realise that it was *that* Hilary Roberts. We were at college together.'

For a brief time they had shared a room in hall. This had not been a convenient arrangement for either of them: Hilary

47

Roberts being prone to sleeping with men and therefore requiring at least a modicum of privacy. Sleeping with men was only allowed to take place before eight pm (in fact, it wasn't allowed to take place at all, but men had to be out of female rooms by that hour), so many of Christina's late afternoons and early evenings had been spent sitting in the communal kitchen trying to concentrate on Kierkegaard while, around her, girls heated tins of soup and wondered if their hair would go another day before washing and remarked that Hilary Roberts was fast achieving college-wide notoriety as a slut.

At nineteen, she had not been particularly good-looking. Her enviable success with men was due to her sexual generosity rather than her physical charms. The style of the day: severely geometric haircuts, skirts so short that they barely skimmed one's knicker elastic, demanded, for best effect, a kind of chicken-boned fragility, and Hilary Roberts had been rather a hefty young woman. But there comes a time for every physical type, and 1985, with its fashion emphasis on wide shoulders, big teeth and large amounts of unruly hair, had allowed her to come into her own.

Today, she had on a bright cerise parachute suit, the sort of footwear that – in Christina's kindergarten days – had been known as pumps, and a great quantity of the sort of jewellery that looks as though it has been fashioned from the fossilised bones of prehistoric creatures. Compared with this, the appearance of the punk girl in the outer office: a vermilion Mohican sprouting from a baby-pink shaved dome, black lips, a spiked collar and a single handcuff enclosing her wrist, seemed slightly less outlandish.

'Christina!'

'Hilary.'

On guard. Not a great deal of love lost between them during the room-sharing days, when Christina had been considered (and they had both been aware of this) far and away the brighter of the two. But times change and beggars can't be choosers and bullets must be bitten, and now that Hilary Roberts finds herself in a superior position, who can blame her if she is inclined to condescend?

'Right. Now. To put you in the picture – '

And then her phone rang. She picked up the receiver and spoke into it. Then she settled herself more comfortably into her chair, motioned Christina to take the one opposite and lit a small cigar. It was obviously going to be a long conversation.

And, judging by what one could hear, a very boring one: all to do with resources and allocations and the apportioning of available grants. Christina's glance travelled around the room and came to rest upon a kind of Scrabble-letters arrangement in a holder that proclaimed to the world that it was in the presence of Dr H E Roberts – or would have done, had not the gremlins who always got at those arrangements, changed the O to a U and substituted a B for a T.

'Dr H E Rubbers.'

They'd called them 'You *know*' during the days of the shared room in hall. But then, they hadn't been readily available or perhaps, in the heat of the moment, the necessity to take precautions hadn't always been observed. Christina remembered having her moral support solicited while Hilary Roberts sat in the bath and swallowed great quantities of Beecham's Pills soaked in vinegar. Nothing had happened. Not to Hilary Roberts. The temperature in the bathroom had soared and the steam had condensed and run down the walls in rivulets and Hilary Roberts had been obliged to get out of the bath in order to resuscitate Christina, who had fainted – the reason for this being, as they were soon to discover, that it was Christina who was pregnant; Hilary Roberts had merely been suffering from a hormonal hiccough.

'Oh come on, Ron,' she was saying now. 'Don't give me that kind of supercrap. It's me you're talking to. Remember?'

While she talked on the telephone she fiddled with her nameplate, turned it round, realised what it said and, tutting with irritation, rescrambled the letters.

They had the same method of identification at the University. Christina remembered walking along a corridor towards her first tutorial, looking at each door as she passed it: 'Dr G. Evans', 'Dr L. Fraser'. On Livingstone's door it just said 'Livingstone'. 'Yes, just Livingstone,' he'd said, after she'd knocked and entered and introduced herself and then stood at a loss, unsure of how to address him. 'After you've heard it for the ten-thousandth time the joke wears a bit thin. Just Livingstone will do.'

The others eventually got to call him Alan, but she never did. It was their joke, their secret.

'OK, Ron,' Hilary Roberts was saying. 'We'll leave it at that. You don't bullshit me, I won't bullshit you.'

She put down the phone. She said again, 'Christina!' and offered her cigar packet. Then her face changed and she became very much the employer, the head of the team, the recognised authority, put on her glasses and started to shuffle papers.

'Recap on job profile – the details being still somewhat sparse, I remember, when you came for the interview. That's because we knew *what* the focus of our research was to be, but we still weren't sure where it was to be concentrated. Anyway, as everything's now finalised, I can gen you up properly. You've heard of The System?'

She continued without pause as though only those who'd been excavating the earth's core within recent memory could have failed to have heard of it. Christina, actually, hadn't, but held her peace.

'It's a resource scheme whereby people exchange skills and services with each other: for example, *I'll* dig your garden if *you'll* sort out my tax problems; you can have my old washing-machine in return for your lawn-mower . . . In other words, a self-help system functioning outside the strict confines of a cash economy – and these sort of arrangements are going to have to be implemented more and more frequently as jobs become scarcer . . .'

It was hard to tell from her expression whether she approved of these alternative economic arrangements, or welcomed them reluctantly as a way of salvaging some kind of adequate livelihood from the social deprivation wrought by opportunistic capitalism that prevailed all around them. Of course, she'd hardly be Poly and Social Sciences if her politics were school-of-Max: employees largely categorised as work-shy, bone-idle or bolshie ('You can't sack the buggers these days, that's the problem'), but you never knew.

'The scheme is administered jointly by the Manpower Services Commission and the Standish Trust,' Hilary Roberts continued. 'The Polytechnic has undertaken to monitor its progress as part of our Interpersonal Relations Project, which we hope to complete by 1987. Of course, if we can get funding beyond eighty-seven this will give us the opportunity to expand our focus . . .' She had a far-away look in her eye that suggested absorption with ambitious future plans. 'And my function?' Christina prompted.

'Observing and recording,' Hilary Roberts said. 'We need a research assistant who can collect the basic data and liaise between the group and ourselves. You are, of course, familiar with the sort of participant observation and interviewing techniques that I have in mind?'

The manner in which this query was put was enough to drive out every scrap of knowledge concerning observational methods and interviewing techniques from the head of the world's foremost authority on the subject; Christina could only nod and hope that she would not be required to furnish immediate proof of this familiarity.

But Hilary Roberts had moved on, was busily recapping. What they were after, primarily, she said, was information as to whether and in what way people's perceptions of one another changed when the conventional profit-motive was absent from their transactions. To this end, Christina's initial observing and interviewing of a representative sample of The System's membership would be used as a basis for the formulation of a questionnaire, which would then be administered to the whole of its population.

They talked a little longer and then Hilary Roberts gathered together a great armful of bumf: off-prints, mostly, smudgily photocopied, and handed them over. 'These might give you some hints as to the best sort of organisational methods. If you can read them before next week . . .'

No problem. Doubtless there would be plenty of empty hours to fill before next week.

Hilary Roberts extended a hand. 'See you then, then.' But having taken Christina's and shaken it, she held on. 'How's the domestic situation?' she said, the tone of her voice altering from brisk to sombre-yet-supportive.

Christina had been obliged to mention the possibility of a change in her circumstances during the first interview. Her mouth had been stiff with embarrassment. As it was now.

'There isn't one any more. Well – only me. I'm living on my own now.'

Alison Harrington had looked at her with an expression of deepest sympathy, as though she'd just announced news of a terminal illness; Hilary Roberts' reaction: a sort of nod-nod, wink-wink, join-the-club, we're all girls together and aren't men an utter waste of space, was no easier to tolerate. She didn't want pity and she didn't want praise. Her case was an individual case, unique to herself, and could not be fitted into some convenient pre-existing system of classification.

Not that that was going to stop anybody from trying.

Hilary Roberts ground the life out of her cigar stub. 'It's something, I suspect, that more and more of us are going to have to go through.'

She'd mentioned, during their previous meeting, an early, brief, marriage, the dissolution of which hadn't caused much grief to either participant.

'Like measles,' she was saying. 'Or chicken-pox. The best you can hope for is a legacy of immunity from the next attack.'

From the studiedly-casual look on her face this was a phrase she'd used often, for effect, a phrase establishing her in the guise she'd chosen: sophisticated Hilary Roberts with the wry sense of humour, who refused to have truck with any of that sentimental, two-hearts-beating-as-one nonsense, who maintained a healthily sardonic attitude to the smeary film of romance that – due to a history of patriarchal attitudes and phallocentric hierarchies – has attached itself to the basic functional honesty of the mating game.

It was the declaration of a philosophy that might impress most people – as long as they didn't remember her from years ago, remember the steam in that college bathroom and her tears dripping into the water and a different sort of statement being made: something to the effect that throughout all the promiscuity, she, Hilary Roberts, had simply been searching for someone to love her. Just like everyone else.

She visited the DHSS and the Income Tax Office and the bank in order to register her new identity: 'Conway, Christina Mary, Ms,' separated woman, no longer entitled to plunder any joint account or to pledge a husband-sponsored Access card against the more impulsive of her purchases. From now on, as a separated woman, living in rented accommodation and possessed of no acceptable form of collateral, she would have to earn her financial privileges.

The rain became heavier as she made her way back to the flat. She opened her umbrella, but it was a very old and ragged umbrella (selflessly, she'd left behind the two that worked properly), and did not afford much protection. She ran up the drive, head down, splashing through the puddles, fumbling in her pocket for her keys. She didn't see the figure lurking behind the shrubbery until it had stepped out and was almost on top of her. She screamed.

'Christina! For God's sake!'

'Oh! You gave me such a fright. I couldn't see you properly, just out of the corner of my eye . . .'

'I'm sorry. I didn't mean to startle you.'

The lurking, looming figure was Livingstone. He had been sheltering under the eaves. All the same, he was drenched. So were the flowers that he held out to her: freesias; the rain on them enhanced their scent to an almost overpowering sweetness.

Hothouse blooms. They had to be, at this time of year. She let her umbrella fall to the ground and, holding the flowers out of harm's way, embraced him. The rain poured down, soaking their hair, seeping into their collars, dripping off their chins as they kissed. A camera crew should have arrived and filmed them for a television commercial.

'I thought you'd be back before now,' he said. 'Hey, this rain's getting beyond a joke. Let's go inside.'

'I thought *you* were going to be desperately busy all this week.'

'I am. I'm skiving. Anyway, this new chap can cope perfectly well on his own. I just thought: "Which would I rather do: hang around pestering this guy who probably only wants to be left alone to get on with it, or visit Christina?" I've even brought my lunch. Look!'

Producing goodies from the pocket of his trenchcoat like rabbits from a hat: cheese, bread, and a couple of splits of champagne. 'I know it should be a jeroboam or something, but Sainsbury's was right out of jeroboams.'

Something had happened, some resolution had been reached, that had led to the clearing of his brow, the disappearance of that trapped look from his face. They climbed the stairs, entwined, and entered the flat where they took off their clothes and hung them up to dry and spread out their feast on the coffee table and he, the bath-towel wrapped, toga-like, around him, she, having donned the lace-trimmed underwear, knelt to eat it. They fed each other morsels of food, sipped from each other's glasses, were irresistibly drawn to touching each other between every sip, every bite: caressing the curve of her thigh, planting a kiss upon his collar-bone, nibbling an earlobe. There was no doubt that they had regained their appetites and one was more insistent in its demands for assuagement than the rest. There was still cheese left and bread and champagne when they decided that the bed might be more comfortable than the floor.

No question this time of a fiasco. Everything was in perfect working order and, in terms of ardour, it was probably their most memorable making of love since that very first time when they'd both hesitated, wide-eyed, not knowing whether what they were about to do would turn out to be among the best or the worst things they'd ever done.

He exclaimed and subsided. He sighed. 'Stay inside me,' she pleaded. It was an involuntary request, always made but rarely before satisfied. There hadn't been time in the back of the car, or the borrowed bed, for that sort of indulgence, just a moment or two, hearts thudding in unison, sweat beginning to cool on their skin, and then they'd had to leap up, buttoning and zipping, combing and smoothing, clearing away the evidence from the scene of the crime. Now, he could comply with her request for as long as nature allowed. Now, if either of them had smoked, they could have lit a couple of cigarettes.

And when he was no longer capable of inhabiting her body and they had to acknowledge their separateness, he could put his arm around her shoulders and kiss her cheek and echo what she'd said earlier, to herself: 'This is how it should be.'

Lovers. Lying in each other's arms in the afternoon, listening to the raindrops pattering on to the leaves of the shrubbery, draining a champagne bottle. How they had longed, throughout the hole and corner months, to be able to do this. 'If we could only have a room of our own,' they had sighed, like a couple of latter-day Virginia Woolfs. 'If we could only have a bed that didn't belong to somebody who wasn't all that particular concerning the laundering of the sheets, and some uninterrupted hours to ourselves.'

These simple requirements being satisfied, then their cups would have no reason not to run over. Perhaps it was only she who had looked beyond that to a more mundane sort of companionship: pushing a trolley with him through a supermarket, choosing Christmas presents together, planting roses in a garden and watching them sprout. And, of course, with Adam, enacting all those scenes that you glimpsed through other people's lighted windows and took to be authentically representative of domestic bliss.

He squeezed her hand. Because their fingers were laced together and she was still wearing Max's wedding ring, this was somewhat painful, but she knew that there could be no pleasure without pain.

'I don't want it ever to be spoiled.'

The rain had ceased very suddenly. It gave her the feeling that the whole world was holding its breath. In the quietness his words emerged very clear and distinct.

'Why should it be spoiled?'

'I don't know. Things get spoiled, don't they?'

'Not if they're right, *good*, in the first place, surely? Changed, perhaps, but not spoiled.'

(Max, in the dream, saying: 'We were all right until you spoiled it.' But they hadn't been all right. Something, from the very beginning, must have been wrong: a weak spot, a bit of unhealthy tissue – only a matter of time before the disease took hold and rampaged through the entire body of the relationship.)

'Wasn't it like this for you and Max? Once upon a time?'

He had used the question as a way of conveying information: this is how it used to be between me and Louise. And she was conscious of starting to feel slightly irritated by his insistence upon dwelling on how it was: a rosy past, lost and gone for ever; or else some impossibly remote future, wistfully contemplated: 'How would it be if . . . ?'

'I can't remember,' she said. 'All I know is that it's not like that now.'

The thing was, surely, to concentrate on the now, but a now that stretched some little way beyond an oasis of love, a sneaked afternoon.

'I thought perhaps,' she said, 'that this evening we might try to make some kind of a financial plan. It'll be tedious, I know, but I'd rather we started off with everything sorted out. Otherwise . . . well, you know how it can be? There's nothing worse than wrangling about money.'

Actually, there was. And perhaps he *didn't* know how it could be: Louise, after all, had an income. No question of *her* having had twenty years' total dependence.

'I thought if we sort of listed household expenses, and

disposable income and so forth . . . Basically, it's about pooling our resources. And I'm unused to the procedure, never having had any resources to pool before . . .'

She burbled on, endeavouring to ignore the fact that he was unwinding his fingers, one by one, from her own. Eventually he interrupted her. 'Love,' he said. 'I can't possibly make it tonight. There's a departmental meeting. Didn't I tell you?'

'No, you didn't.'

'I'm sure I *did*.'

She thought of the fridge stuffed full of food (some of which wouldn't last much longer), thought of the long evening ahead. Why was the prospect of solitude so uninviting? There had been so many interminable afternoons and endless evenings: kids out, trapped with Max in a state of frozen non-communication, when she had longed, firstly, to be with Livingstone and, failing that, to be on her own.

'Well, anyway, I think we should get those sort of details sorted out as soon as possible.'

'We will, we will. I'll bring a ledger with me next time. Double-entry book-keeping. Income and outgoings. Every item recorded.'

Said jokingly. But she sensed an edge of irritation, as though he resented being organised in this way. Was he, she wondered, one of those men who were secretive about their earnings, who thought of it as somehow unmanly to confess the exact extent of their material worth? Surely not? But she didn't know.

He started to kiss her. 'This is how it ought to be,' he said again. She assumed that when he said 'ought to be' he meant 'can be' or 'is'.

5

That evening she tried to concentrate, to fix her attention upon the page, the smudgily-printed page: 'Descriptive and Analytic Survey Designs', 'Attitude-Scaling Methods', 'A Nomograph for the Testing of Statistical Significance of Percentage Differentials', but found herself reading the same sentences over and over again until they were transformed into a string of meaningless monophones.

Her problems in making sense of Hilary Roberts' bumf had nothing to do with an inability to grasp the fundamentals of research methodology, but everything to do with want of enthusiasm. The brief autumn afternoon came to a close. The daylight died. But she postponed drawing the curtains, closing out the world. She laid aside all the incomprehensible extracts from learned journals and boiled herself an egg. And when she'd eaten it and washed her plate and her cup, 'A Nomograph for the Testing of Statistical Significance of Percentage Differentials' seemed even less inviting than before.

She glanced to where the telephone, smugly silent, rested upon a shelf. There was no likelihood of it ringing. Only Livingstone and Max and Adam had her number.

And David, of course. David could have rung. Why hadn't he? Or written? Although she knew the answers to those questions before she asked them: he was, always had been, less than diligent in the matter of communication. Other mothers had received postcards from Scout camps, foreign exchange visits, school skiing trips. Not she. When challenged, he'd clap his hand to his forehead and say, 'Didn't I post it? I could have sworn I posted it.' He'd say that every time.

But she could ring him. There was a coin-box in the hall of the house in which he lived and, occasionally, a resident or passer-by willing to answer the telephone. Sometimes, if you were extraordinarily lucky, he answered it himself.

Not today. Today the phone was answered by a person whose understanding and command of English was limited in the extreme.

'Davi' Co'way? Seco' floor? No. No' in.'

A most peculiar accent: oriental? David said that the place was swarming with Vietnamese mathematicians and Mongolian astro-physicists.

'No' in.'

'Could you take a message for me?' she said, but the total incomprehension conveyed by his repetition of the word 'message' decided her against venturing further.

'It doesn't matter. Thank you. I'll ring again.'

She walked to the window, gazed down upon the shrubbery, the dolphins, the deserted street. Soon the clocks would go back and the darkness would have descended before she'd finished her boiled egg (although, by then, it wouldn't be a solitary tea-time boiled egg; it would be salmon mousse or grilled sole or sardines on toast – depending upon their finances). Now there was still enough daylight to make her feel claustrophobic at the thought of being obliged to stay indoors. But where to go?

There was only one place that readily suggested itself. And she realised that her visit would serve a dual purpose: not only providing her with a destination, but giving her the impetus to do what she must, sooner rather than later, which was to put her cousin Gwen in the picture. They didn't get on, she and Gwen, and they had nothing in common except kinship, but the consciousness of that kinship had, somehow, throughout the years, kept them in tenuous contact.

It was situated in the city centre, Gwen's wine bar: Klosters, named after a memorable skiing holiday, which she ran with the assistance of Corky, her business partner and resident cook. 'Closets', most of its regular clientele referred to it as, egged on by the young barmen who rolled their eyes a great deal and exchanged endless meaningful glances. 'Pansies,' Corky called them, mistakenly, being of a generation unused to witnessing thorough-going male narcissism and therefore unable to distinguish it from homosexuality.

A very up-market establishment. Christina stood for a moment admiring the frontage which was decorated in Harrods' green and gold: blinds and brass fitments and gilt lettering and windows with such tiny panes that the passer-by was denied the merest glimpse of the interior – she was reminded of those sort of clothes shops that exhibited their Louise Livingstone jerseys without price tags, suspected that the same principle applied: that if you needed to see, or ask, then you couldn't afford to go in.

The unseen interior was even more resplendent: dark green velvet banquettes, crystal chandeliers, menus covered in gold fabric and a bar festooned with glittering gilt and silver-sprayed foliage, the lighting dimmed to a green-tinted sub-aqueous gloom. Perhaps this was deliberate, in order to obscure the prices which were as spectacular as the décor.

Although, presumably, affordable by Gwen's yuppie clientele: rising young executives all: Dunhill lighters and Cartier watches, reeking of Gucci, and their girlfriends: brittle young women who gave one the impression that whatever employment they undertook – secretary, PA, design-assistant – it would always come second to their real-life's mission, which was a total and undeviating dedication to self-presentation.

They would be in there now, sipping and nibbling and posing. Christina took the alternative route: down a passage to the backyard where the rotted door of a defunct outside lavatory hung askew from its one remaining hinge, and dustbins overflowed.

The evening rush was just starting. The young men in their bottle-green trousers and gold lamé waistcoats tripped in and out of the kitchen, their trays piled high, the washers-up were elbow-deep in suds. A young chef decorated a peach flan with whipped cream.

'How about that then, Corky?'

He had produced quite an accurate representation of male genitalia atop the orange glaze. Corky, who was sitting at the kitchen table, rolling a cigarette, calm amid the uproar, turned round in order to survey this confectionary masterpiece.

'And that's about as much use as most of them are,' she declared. 'Decoration.' And then she noticed Christina and said, 'Well hello stranger,' and made the brief teeth-baring movement that was her version of a welcoming smile.

'So what brings you round here?'

She folded the *Echo* that she'd been reading and laid it down on the table, drank from her George VI Coronation mug: Miss

Something McCorquodale, late of the Catering Corps, a tall, muscular woman, age indeterminate but probably (going on the evidence of the Coronation mug) somewhere on the downhill side of fifty, her pepper and salt hair cropped with regard for utility rather than style, a favourer of tracksuits, both for exercise and daily wear, Miss Something McCorquodale with big plimsoll-shod feet and big red hands that could, nonetheless, produce the wafer-thin crêpes and melting pastries that helped to make Klosters such a success.

'Hello.'

In all the time she'd known her – five years or so, since Gwen had taken her on, agreed to a partnership and, soon afterwards, decided to share her house – Christina had never been able to bring herself to use that ridiculous cartoon title. She couldn't call her Miss McCorquodale, so she was obliged to call her nothing. One day she would remember to ask Gwen what Corky's Christian name actually was. There must *be* one.

'Is it Her Ladyship you're after? She's in the office, fiddling the VAT, or painting on a new phizzog. One of the two.'

But her tone betrayed no real hostility. It was as though, due to continual repetition, the words had been stripped of their meaning, were mere tokens of an animosity too time-wearied and taken for granted to be capable of any practical application. She and Gwen squabbled; they shared a squabbling relationship, as valid in its way, perhaps, as one characterised by passion or accord.

Was it also characterised by a physical attachment? The cruder among their acquaintances had been known to refer to them as a couple of dykes, but somehow . . . For her part, Christina had never, when close to Corky, experienced that bristling of the neck hairs that told of lesbian proximity, and Gwen, she was sure, would have been appalled at the idea that anyone might even consider . . . would cite her late husband at length, hint at cohorts of male admirers.

Which, to be fair, she'd had, had still.

'I'll go in then.'

But before she could suit action to words she was waylaid by Albert-the-dwarf, chief washer-up, most venerable of Gwen's employees. (Misfits and cripples seemed to figure largely among her behind-the-scenes staff; perhaps it was a philanthropic gesture, or perhaps she could get away with paying them less than the going rate.)

He barred her path, sticking his large head within a couple of inches of her midriff and enquiring of her the name of the capital city of Venezuela.

She shook her head.

'Caracas. What was the orchestra founded by Sir Thomas Beecham?'

'The Hallé?'

'London Philharmonic. Date of Caruso's death?'

'1930 – something?'

'1921. Former name of Nijni Novgorod?'

She shook her head again. He smacked his malformed hands together gleefully. 'Got you there,' he said. 'Got you there all right. Not so clever as you thought you were, are you?'

'Albert!' Corky said warningly, and he waddled off back to his sink which had an orange box set before it so that he could reach to wash the crockery.

'Take on all-comers and beat 'em,' he announced. Above the sink, only his head and his hands were visible. He was, as Corky had told her, the star of the quiz team at his local pub, a mine of that sort of obscure information that forms the basis for tests of general knowledge. Whenever his team scored a victory, he was prone to marathon bouts of drunkenness. 'Gets completely kalied,' was how Corky described it. If she and Gwen were in the midst of a falling-out, and most particularly if Gwen was entertaining someone she wished to impress, she'd deliberately and provocatively vary her description to: 'utterly arseholed'.

Gwen set great store by appearance, insisted on doing the proper thing properly, thus providing Corky with innumerable opportunities for the puncturing of pomposity. As Christina knocked at the office door, she could hear Corky calling from the kitchen, 'Mind how you approach her. We're a bit nowty these days. Got the old trouble back, I think.'

The old trouble was haemorrhoids – 'Farmer Giles' was Corky's name for them. Gwen was a chronic sufferer.

But it was impossible to tell, apart from the odd wince (and that could equally well be due to annoyance at being interrupted – particularly being interrupted by Christina), whether Gwen was actually currently afflicted.

'My word! To what do we owe this honour?'

61

It was fair comment. Christmas, Easter and, in earlier years, the children's birthdays, those were the traditional times for meeting. She'd drag the boys along ('Do we *have* to go?' They didn't care for Gwen, but it was mutual: Gwen didn't care for children), persuading a reluctant Max ('Do we *have* to go?' In this case she wasn't sure whether a mutuality of aversion existed; Gwen took no nonsense from him, but she'd never been the sort to take any nonsense from any man, even the ones she'd had her sights set on).

She'd never needed to. In that department, she'd been a roaring success from the word go: she'd attracted little boys, bigger boys, youths and, eventually, men, without any need to employ the desperate strategies adopted by the less favoured of her peers.

One of whom had been Christina. A late developer. Unconfident. Taking refuge in the controllable world of books and exams and scholarships. 'My cousin,' Gwen had introduced her as, during their teenage years. 'She's an intellectual.' The words 'cripple' or 'imbecile' could have been substituted without there having been any need for an alteration in her tone.

Gwen had been a pretty child, a beautiful girl; even now, heading towards middle age, she was still quite an eyeful. And for a moment the two distantly related cousins eyed each other: Daddy's girl Gwendoline, tall, hour-glass figure still on the safe side of plumpness, thick tawny-coloured hair professionally highlighted, china blue eyes set wide, mouth gently and generously curved, possessed of that opaque, creamy-coloured skin that ages well, and the kind of sheen that money can buy – the adjectives that sprang to mind were vivid, abundant, luxurious – and, comparatively, Christina, who was built from an altogether less extravagant blueprint, had always felt somehow blurred.

Well, comparisons were odious. And beauty was in the eye of the beholder. And a dozen other appropriate clichés that ought not to be necessary. (She might be smaller in stature, less generously endowed, her colouring not so striking, but she had also been admired, desired – never mind had been, *was*, was admired and desired.) It was a measure of the legacy of all those years of uneven development that they were.

'A drink?' Gwen said.

'That would be nice. I'll have a glass of wine, if I may.'

Interesting to see which bottle Gwen opted for. Usually, you could judge both your status and her current opinion of you by what was uncorked. But this evening there appeared to be only one bottle on the go: a mid-range, thoroughly inoffensive white Bordeaux. However, the fact that she got up still clutching her calculator in one hand gave some indication that you weren't considered important enough to warrant more than a brief hiatus in the calculation of her VAT returns.

Soon change that, Christina thought, but was content to postpone the moment, sipping her wine, admiring Gwen's tremendously desirable grey suit that was made from a suede so soft that even whilst lusting after it, you couldn't help but be reminded of the very young things that must have been slaughtered to provide it.

There probably wasn't an item in Gwen's wardrobe that wouldn't evoke lust and envy. She'd had money for long enough to have developed good taste: only daughter of a rich and doting daddy, only wife of an equally rich and doting husband; the wine bar was really no more than a hobby, acquired to renew her interest in life after her husband's death. She could have forfeited what she earned from it without noticing.

Could have done but didn't. She was her father's daughter and could conceive of no situation which, somehow or other, could not be manipulated to yield profit. Christina remembered reluctantly-shared childhood holidays in Bournemouth and Herne Bay, enlivened (or, more accurately, rendered terrifying due to the threat of discovery and retribution) by Gwen's stealing of chewing gum or sherbet fountains from the edge of the counter in Woolworth's. She remembered their kindergarten days when Gwen had appropriated the report card that said 'Christina Carroll' and prized off the gold stars in order to stick them on to her own.

Nice to remind her of those days. Particularly when she directed one of her less-than-the-dust looks at you. But what would be the point? She'd deny it so vehemently that you'd wind up thinking you'd invented it simply to discredit her.

'How's the family?'

A perfunctory enquiry. She had started to depress the keys of the calculator, was glancing at her accounts book. There was a computer on the desk which the manager used for all calculations and projections to do with the business, but there were certain things that Gwen preferred to check for herself, in the traditional way. Managers could rob you blind and probably, with the aid of electronic intelligence, even blinder.

Christina drained her glass and pushed it forward again, not quite so subtly that Gwen was able to ignore it. Eventually she offered a refill.

'They were all right when I saw them last. Which was on Monday.'

Gwen's head, which had been bent over her figures, jerked upwards, the finely plucked arcs of her eyebrows rose almost into her hairline, her jaw dropped to the extent that a fair amount of expensive bridge-work could be seen within it.

'I've left home.'

'You've what?'

Her face could be read more easily than the accounts book. Neither approval nor disapproval was displayed there, only utter and absolute astonishment: Christina Carroll, who never had any gumption, who used to jump at her own shadow, who couldn't even be induced to keep a look-out while sherbet and chewing gum were misappropriated from Woolworth's counters, who became Christina Conway because of lack of gumption and never developed any afterwards (Daddy used to say that it was because she was a Caesarean child – she never learned to push), gumption-less Christina Conway, Carroll-that-was, the last person in the world whom you would think of in connection with that sort of declaration.

'Where are you living?' she said, when she'd got her breath back.

Christina told her.

'On your own?'

'For the time being, yes.'

'What do you mean: for the time being?'

Briefly, Christina related the facts of the case: how she'd met Livingstone, fallen in love with him, known – as he too had known – that they must be together or go mad from deprivation, that now she simply awaited his coming, calmly crossing the days off her own personal advent calendar.

Gwen listened, open-mouthed still, and then she cleared her throat and tapped her pen slowly and rhythmically on the edge of the desk and said, without looking at Christina, 'Well, I'm afraid that I should want a little more assurance than that.'

'Than what?'

Gwen laid aside her pen and her book and her calculator, took a compact out of her handbag and began a critical reappraisal of her make-up. 'Than some vague airy-fairy promises. I should want the money to be put where the mouth is before I stuck my neck out.'

Well, she would, wouldn't she? She'd want to know the statistical significance of percentage differentials, she'd want sworn affidavits, she'd want to know the ins and outs of a duck's arsehole, as Corky so crudely put it, before she'd put her trust in anything that couldn't be counted.

'Well I hope you know what you're doing. I, personally, think you're off your head.'

'You do?'

But then she always had done.

'I think,' Gwen said, 'that I'd need to be pretty certain to give up everything: my home, my children . . .'

'They're not children. Well, hardly. And that place never felt like home. It felt like a bloody mausoleum most of the time . . .'

It hadn't been so bad in the early years: a small modern house, babies, never a minute to spare for thinking, assessing, regretting; it was when they moved back to the family home that the rot set in. Her heart used to sink as soon as she opened the front gate.

'It was like being in the army. Or prison.'

(That truly terrible unfaltering routine: breakfast at eight, on the dot, dinner at seven-thirty. A round of golf on Saturday morning, sex on Saturday night and – every second week – on Wednesday too. Lodge meetings every month, ditto a haircut. Clothes to the cleaners quarterly, a change of car every year. Three weeks in August in Brittany. Cutting his toe-nails on Friday. Always shaving his face in the same order: right side, then left. His chair having to be replaced after vacuuming in exactly the same position as before. Suggest even the slightest deviation: a different type of breakfast cereal, painting a ceiling blush-white instead of magnolia, plotting a new route to the supermarket, and he'd react as though you were trying to engineer a change so radical as to rock the very foundations of his carefully-ordered existence.)

'And it'll be different with this man, will it?'

Gwen's attention appeared to be focused upon her reflection to the exclusion of everything else, but she was taking it in all right. Every word. And wasn't there just a hint of chagrin, just a suggestion that Christina Conway, that well-known lacker of gumption, ought not to be allowed to get away with acting out of character?

'Yes, I think it will.'

Corky stuck her head round the door and addressed Gwen: 'Your panorama's arrived. Baldy. *I'm* not entertaining him. I've put him in the bar.'

Did she mean paramour? Inamorata?

Apparently Gwen knew what she meant. She directed one final searching glance at her reflection. 'Right,' she said. 'I'm coming. I'm sorry,' she said to Christina, 'I've got to go. I've someone waiting.'

Gwen's escorts, these days, tended to be inexorably-middle-aged, enormously-solid citizens: bank managers, accountants, solicitors, who would favour *intime* dinners *à deux* in echoing hotel dining-rooms with lots of heavy silver and discreetly familiar headwaiters and vast leathery sides of beef. Probably they would fail to figure out Gwen's reason for accepting the invitations, which was as much to do with picking their professional brains as responding to their personal advances.

Though tonight's gentleman caller seemed, at first, to be an exception to this rule: 'That vet chap with the Adam's apple,' Corky said, as Christina accompanied her back to the kitchen, but then went on to explain that Gwen's cat had been suffering from what had been diagnosed as post-castration hormonal alopecia.

'Bleedin' thing's got mange, if you ask me,' she said, pulling a tray of patties from the oven. One got the impression that the cat evoked as much jealousy as the vet.

'Could you go a pancake, or a couple of these?' she enquired.

The aroma was enticing. So was the prospect of company, even if it was only Corky's, whose conversation – apart from derogatory comments about Gwen's admirers – consisted mainly of derogatory comments about any and all of the public figures who might have featured in that day's news: Reagan or Gorbachev, Macgregor or Scargill, Kinnock or Thatcher, union leaders who pretended not to be Commies, Commie Yids who masqueraded as Conservatives For Their Own Ends, bloated plutocrats who'd bottle the sweat from their workers' brows and flog it if it'd bring in a few bob, lazy bastards who basked in

66

public sector sinecures, loony Lefties and Fascist swine who were hell-bent on dismantling the Welfare State, privatising everything upon which they could lay their greedy paws, turning the country into a bleedin' Persian market.

There might be some coherent thread linking these apparently contradictory prejudices, but it had always eluded Christina who was therefore cautious of making anything but the least controversial of conversational contributions in case she might be putting her foot in it.

'No,' she said. 'I'd better be making tracks.' Perhaps Livingstone might have abandoned his meeting and be, even now, waiting for her behind the shrubbery. She picked up a stray piece of pastry from the tray and started to nibble at it. She said, 'No doubt Gwen will tell you, but as I'm here now, I might as well . . .'

How embarrassing it was. Much more embarrassing than telling Gwen. At least, with *her*, there'd been an element of stick-that-in-your-pipe-and-smoke-it to carry her through.

'I've left my husband.'

What reaction had she expected? She pondered this as she waited at the bus-stop. What had she supposed that husbandless, childless Corky might say?

She had been engaged in transferring the patties from their baking trays to plates and Christina's news was not sufficiently startling to give her pause. 'That Max?' she said, as though there existed a multiplicity of husbands eligible to be deserted.

'Yes.'

'And have you got a fancy man?'

How did a fancy man differ from a panorama that Gwen's friend should deserve the latter title whereas Livingstone only qualified for the first? Or was there no difference? What could she do but nod?

'Well then, let's hope you've picked a good 'un.'

You could die waiting for the bus. And there were so many unsavoury-looking characters wandering around. Christina thought of hailing a taxi then thought that she ought to be saving money and then a bus arrived (not the one she wanted) and all the rest of the queue boarded it except for herself and a man who had been talking to himself all the while, so she thought again and made for the cab-rank.

Riding through the streets of the city, trying to slow down the inexorable progress of the meter by an effort of will, she wondered whether she had picked herself a good 'un. Of course, it rather depended upon your definition. Max undoubtedly satisfied the conventional criteria: law-abiding, conscientious, dependable. She didn't seriously believe that she was prepared to trade all those virtues just for the promise of having a fantasy made real – traditionally it was always the bad 'uns that made your head spin and your pulse race – but surely you could have all those qualities *and* something more? She saw the expression on her face, pale in the dark window, so anxious to be convinced.

Dark. Very. The taxi dropped her at the end of the drive and she let it go, remembering too late that she could have asked the driver to accompany her to the door.

She took deep breaths and set off with measured tread, hearing only the sound of her steel-shod heels on the tarmac. Why, in the name of God, hadn't she thought to leave on the hall light at the very least? Why? Because it had never occurred to her: a woman protected, cosseted, made soft by twenty years of handing over personal responsibility to somebody else, that such stratagems might be necessary.

The drive's length seemed to increase in exact proportion to that part of the distance already covered. She negotiated the gate-posts' shadow, she made it around the side of the disporting dolphins; it was the rustling in the shrubbery that made her realise that, rather than walking steadily, she had begun to trot, to canter, and then to gallop towards the front door, key held shaft forwards, scrabbling for the lock.

And then she was inside, her breath escaping in a great sigh of relief, not yet admitting to herself that she was almost as frightened inside the house as she was outside it.

⌒ 6 ⌒

She didn't *want* to admit it to herself, she didn't want to admit it to him, to present herself in such a feeble light, but fear being stronger than embarrassment, she told him. In bed. He had surprised her with another afternoon visit. This time he brought figs and apricots and peaches. She was delighted to see him. She got out the smoked salmon from the fridge (its eat-by date was getting ominously closer) and opened a bottle of Graves. 'A book of verse?' she said, but he could only offer her a copy of *Social Trends, 1985*.

'Most of my books are still at Winchester Road,' she said. 'I had a fair bit of poetry.'

Acquired mainly during adolescence: Donne, Yeats, Tennyson. 'Mooning again, Christina?' Gwen's father, 'Daddy', or 'Jumbo', as he was known to his country-club cronies, would remark. He understood only real teenagers like Gwen who had squads of real young men hot on one another's heels at the front door, couldn't fathom a girl who preferred to stick her head into a book all day long.

'I used to recite out loud,' she said, pouring wine. '"Mariana in the Moated Grange", "The Lady of Shalott", "Now Sleeps the Crimson Petal", terribly doleful stuff.'

Gwen had boyfriends, with one or two of whom she had gone – so they said – nearly all the way; her men, Christina's, were all in books.

Gwen had boyfriends who took her to tennis-club dances and Blue Bird balls and then parked their cars down deserted lanes and chanced their luck.

'I was in love with Sir Lancelot and Heathcliff and Mr Rochester,' she told Livingstone. 'For years after I should have been. I never even went a quarter of the way.'

Straight from Sir Lancelot to Max. Max was over thirty. He'd left heavy petting and sexual-intercourse-by-numbers behind years ago. He took her to bed and deflowered her before she had time to get anxious about it. He seemed sure and decisive. He could have been Sir Lancelot. It took her some time to find out that he wasn't.

'Perhaps I envied Gwen her reality, but I don't know . . . There seemed to be no magic. I wanted magic.'

But she'd told him all this before, and discovered that, as she had been when young, so had he: an idealistic youth, confident of finding – out there, beyond the world of books – those characters within them that had fired his imagination: sorceresses, *belles dames sans merci*, pale Pre-Raphaelites with yards of spun-gold hair and milk-white bosoms. He had said, and so did she, oh so proudly: 'I am a romantic.' Being a romantic made all the disappointments, if not worthwhile, then just about bearable. Up to a point.

He would never cease to be one, she knew that. He loved soft autumn afternoons, assignations, illicit picnics, twilit partings, postcards of Botticelli's Venus on the back of which he could write: 'Oh my heart! L.' She watched him biting into a ripe fig, caught the seeds that spilled from it upon her own finger and brought it to her mouth, tasting him via the fruit. It was up to her – she knew that also – to convince him of the possibility that the substance could be, ultimately, far more satisfactory than the shadow.

She'd put new batteries in the radio. The Adagio from *The Four Seasons'* 'Autumn' played quietly, appropriately, in the background. She liked Vivaldi, but he wasn't keen. 'If God were to ask me if there was anything wrong in Paradise,' he said, covering their nakedness with the quilt, 'I might ask for a different soundtrack. But that's all.'

'Your only quibble?'

'Mm-hm. And that's probably only because to be human is to find it necessary to quibble.'

'You can't still be human,' she said. 'In Paradise.'

Under the quilt she explored the terrain of him: here the jagged appendix scar, there the repaired cartilage; a patch of non-pigmented skin on his thigh (it had appeared suddenly during adolescence; he thought he had leprosy), the luxurious chest hair that narrowed to a fine line as it traversed his belly before spreading out again to form a dense pubic thicket. So much of him she knew that was unknown to the rest of the world; so much that she didn't. More, in some ways, than Louise. Surely? And in others, infinitely less. Never would, could, know as much. Louise. Would America be far enough?

'So it's Paradise?' she said. Her mouth was beside his ear, she had only to whisper.

'Isn't it?'

'Not for me. Not yet, anyway.'

'Oh look,' he said, raising himself upon an elbow, pushing hair out of his eyes in order to read her expression. 'Is it money? Are you short? Is that why you wanted to do all those calculations? I can let you have some . . .'

He started to reach out towards the bedside table where he had put his wallet. She stayed his hand. 'No,' she said, 'it's not money. Well – not yet, it isn't. It's this place. Or rather, it's me, I suppose. I'm terrified at night, of staying in, of going out and coming back again. I know it's ridiculous.' (No, not *that* ridiculous: big house, empty, rich neighbourhood, deserted after dark – Paradise, for burglars, muggers, rapists. And he should know that without me having to tell him.)

'I'm unused to being alone. I never thought about it before-hand. Somehow I just supposed that we'd be together from the beginning. Stupid of me, I know: to act without consulting you and then to expect that you could just up and leave at a moment's notice. So I know I've only myself to blame, but it doesn't help to tell myself that at night when I'm scared stiff.'

He was still turned from her, reaching for his wallet, so she couldn't see his face. What would he say? Would it be: 'Oh my darling, I can't bear to think of you here, alone at night, your heart beating twenty to the dozen, your breath caught in your throat, your ears straining to identify every sound'?

He didn't turn back to face her. He swung his legs out of bed and got up and started to pull on his underpants. What he actually did say was, 'Look, Christina, I told you before, this place is like Fort Knox. And if you *were* to hear anything that could even remotely be considered as suspicious, all you have to do is pick up the phone and dial 999.'

'The phone's in the other room,' she said, ridiculously.

'Then buy one of those extension leads.'

He had put his underpants on back to front. He cursed and

started to rearrange them. She said, 'When, actually, will you be moving in?'

'I told you – everything's topsy-turvy at present, with this American trip in the offing.'

He had somehow contrived to get both legs into the hole intended for one. In other circumstances, it would have been funny.

'I know about that. I'm just asking you for a straight answer to a simple question. When? You see, if I just knew that, it would help. A bit like counting the days off the calendar when you're in jail.'

He'd finally conquered the underpants. He'd have managed the trousers too, except that the zip stuck an inch from home. She relented in her determined inquisition and offered help, but he refused it and fought with the fastening until they both heard an ominous ripping noise and she retreated, snubbed. No doubt Louise would be able to repair it, to put in the correct strategic stitch before she took wing for America. However little else there was to recommend her, she could at least *sew*.

'You're not going?' she asked, as he picked up his wallet and keys.

'Yes,' he said. 'And please don't look at me as though this comes as a total and terrible shock. I *told* you the score right at the beginning. I'm stealing time as it is.'

She put on her dressing gown. Tarts must feel like this, she thought: used and then left. But no, tarts were probably anxious to see the back of one client because they had another one lined up. Tarts were paid for their time. She remembered his hand going out towards his wallet and, momentarily, in the room warmed by their passion, she went cold. She didn't want to ask the obvious question. There were different interrogative Latin constructions, weren't there, available for use, depending upon whether you expected a positive or a negative response? 'Num' you used at the beginning of your sentence, or 'Nonne'. You said either, 'Are you not coming back?' or else, 'You'll be coming back, of course, later on?' She chose the latter form. And the briefest glance at his face was enough to tell her that she had picked the wrong alternative.

He shrugged on his leather jacket. 'Why don't you invite somebody round?' he said. 'To keep you company.'

To stay calm, that was the thing. She put on her slippers. She said, 'You haven't answered my question.'

'What *was* your question?'

Not to allow expression to her agitation, that was the trick. 'The date,' she said, 'the day you're going to move in here. I need to know.'

He was ducking down so that he could see to comb his hair in the mirror that was adjusted to her height. He continued to comb as he said, 'Well obviously it isn't going to be before the week after next, is it?'

'That's when she leaves?'

'Yes.'

'What day?'

'Wednesday.'

'Then we could say the – what – today's the eleventh – the twenty-third or the twenty-fourth?'

She kept her gaze steady. If you were prepared to issue ultimatums, then you must not allow yourself to be seen as anything but adamant in your determination to stick by them.

She thought he was going to say, 'Christ!' but instead he said, 'Christina,' or else changed it into that. He said, 'Christina, what's with all this third degree?'

'Not third degree at all. Just the need to know how many days – how many nights – I've got to get through before we're together. Wednesday, the twenty-third?' she said. 'Or, failing that, Thursday, the twenty-fourth? I can rely on that, can I?'

She sounded as though she were dealing with some not-entirely dependable tradesperson, as though she were attempting to ascertain a delivery date for a carpet or the exact timing of a Gas Board visit.

And that was not how she intended to sound. For once, she spoke before thinking; she said, 'You *do* intend to leave her?'

The question that was never going to be asked, asked.

He put his comb back into his pocket and, at last, turned to face her. He nodded. And then he said, 'I'm not very brave, you know.'

She was aware that he was telling her that he was unlikely to be able to see her over the weekend, but she was scarcely listening; she was thinking only of the nod and, on the strength of it, making out a shopping list in her head and at the top she was writing: 'Wine, several bottles, only just expensive enough not to be poisonous.'

If alcohol was necessary for getting her through the next twelve – or thirteen – days, then, for the next twelve days, or nights – or thirteen – she would become a drunk.

A postcard arrived from David. She picked it up from the letter-box on her way to work. It said, '! Letter to follow. D.' She wouldn't have bet her last five pounds on the likelihood of that letter ever arriving, but at least he had acknowledged her, at least he had not consigned her to that hell of shunning, undoubt-edly deserved by women who put their own happiness before their children's welfare.

It raised her spirits, helped to speed her to the bus-stop en route to her appointment with Hilary Roberts and her introduc-tion to the world of employment.

She had thought ahead sufficiently to equip herself with a timetable, but that couldn't tell her – as the rest of the queuing passengers did – that the 8.37 was rarely on time and that, to be certain of getting into town for nine, you should aim for the one before. It was obvious that Dr Roberts had been waiting for a while and not very patiently by the time she reached the Polytechnic.

A pointed glance at her watch, and then she said, 'Just *about* time to let you have a dekko at the computer room, if Sid's there, before I take you down to The System.'

Sid wasn't there and the door was locked. 'You'll just have to sus it out for yourself sometime during the week,' Hilary Roberts said, as they drove towards the business area of the city where the office was located. 'It's a bit of a dump,' she said, as they came to a halt outside an exceedingly Victorian-Gothic edifice that rose, anachronistically, between the plate-glass and concrete façades of its neighbours from which it was separated by narrow garbage-filled alleys: the Prudential Insurance and the DHSS.

Once, Christina supposed, it must have been devoted to a specific function, purpose-built, as a shipping office or an educational institute perhaps. Now the docks fell, one by one, into desuetude and the vast graffiti-daubed comprehensives produced savage armies of illiterates, and buildings such as these, outliving their purpose, were divided into small units and let out on short leases to firms and organisations destined, for the most part, to cease to exist before the leases expired.

They proceeded up the stone stairs to the third floor. No doubt the neighbouring buildings were close-carpeted, equipped with lifts and underfloor heating and air-conditioning, but they wouldn't have solid oak carved banisters or vaulted ceilings, they wouldn't have Dutch tiles or stained glass windows that filtered the morning light so that it decorated the pitch-pine floor with jewel-coloured lozenges: sapphire and topaz, amber and jade.

'It's due for demolition. About time too, in my opinion.'

Well, that figured. The world of squandered working lives and government-sponsored illiteracy could not afford to donate space to non-profit-making Victorian craftsmanship, however ornate. 'A dump,' Hilary Roberts called it, and she undoubtedly spoke with the voice of the people.

She purported to represent their views, at any rate, she and her fellow sociologists, sending out their minions to thrust clipboards under the noses of innocent passers-by, randomly sampling their representative populations, designing their questionnaires and weighting their responses to adjust for bias, translating the yeses and the nos into computer language and correlating their variables and then announcing their conclusions to the world: most married couples between the ages of twenty-five and forty perform the act of sexual intercourse two and a half times a week; Northern women tend to wear a D cup and their corsets are a size larger than those worn by their Southern sisters; there is a higher incidence of mental illness found among those born under the first three astrological signs of the year than in any other group . . .

'And?' she remembered asking Livingstone when she was feeling particularly demoralised, when nobody's theory seemed likely to explain mankind's universal will to destruction, and the asking of little questions seemed so pointless: corsets! astrology! incidence of conjugal relations!

She thought of this as she paused for breath on the second-floor landing. How easy it was to lose heart. Or to mock. But how else were you to approach the massive problem of ferreting out some meaning from an inscrutable universe? The voice of the people had to be built up, phoneme by phoneme, from the evidence presented by what might be considered pointless little enterprises such as that which she was about to undertake. She straightened her shoulders as Hilary Roberts ushered her into The System office, attempted to look eager, enthusiastic and capable as she was introduced to the two full-time employees with whom she was to liaise.

'Christina, Colette; Kenneth, Christina.'

She registered little initially, beyond the fact that Kenneth was tall and stout and Colette was small and thin.

'Both of them have been with The System since it started, but Colette's leaving at Christmas.'

Colette looked up from the typewriter, lifted her hands momentarily from its keys and made a regretful little moue. She was older than first glance had led Christina to believe. Little thin women often looked younger than their years; closer inspection was required to reveal the particularly gnome-like way in which they aged.

Not that Colette was gnome-like. She was small and proportionately scaled with sleek golden hair that fitted cap-like above a large-eyed, smiling, cat-shaped face: only the network of fine lines around her eyes and mouth hinted at an age retreating from thirty rather than progressing towards it.

'Between them, they're responsible for the day-to-day running of the office,' Hilary Roberts said, with a distinct air of lady of the manor deigning to acknowledge the existence of the tenants and congratulating herself on her democratic stance.

'Ken organises our card-index system, arranges the job and resource exchanges, and liaises with the media *vis-à-vis* advertising and so forth.'

'Answerable only to God and Dr Roberts,' Kenneth said, in response to this role-description and laughed. He had a loud, sycophantic laugh.

'Colette,' Hilary Roberts continued, 'is our secretary-cum-telephonist-cum-general-dogsbody – and performs all three jobs most efficiently, I might add.'

'Only until Christmas,' said Colette, with that same coy grimace.

'Oh my God, is that the time!' said Hilary Roberts, pretending to consult her watch. 'I'll have to dash.'

She dug into her tote bag and produced a sheaf of photocopied pages. 'This,' she said, 'is the membership list. If Kenneth will explain the filing system, then you can make a start on compiling your sample.'

To be chosen according to age, area and occupation. To be interviewed and asked to complete a questionnaire, the conclusions drawn from which would not only go some way towards answering a small part of the larger question to which the Interpersonal Relations Project addressed itself, but also supply information to the board of the Standish Trust, who were growing restive on the subject of whether continuing to fund The System would be a practical proposition.

'It may seem a trivial bit of research: asking old dears how they feel about someone who's agreed to mow their lawn in return for getting their ironing done,' Livingstone had said, when he'd first drawn her attention to the job vacancy, 'and it's only temporary, but these things sometimes have a habit of extending themselves into permanent posts.'

Livingstone: he'd stolen a couple of hours on Sunday afternoon. There had been no treats this time, no loaves of bread or flasks of wine. Just a rather perfunctory act of sexual intercourse followed by a cup of coffee. He'd been all togged up: suit, silk tie, and had been very careful to fold every garment neatly after he took it off. He said they had relations of Louise's expected that evening, come to wish her *bon voyage*. Attired thus (she was used to seeing him in jeans and leather jacket) he seemed somewhat distant, unfamiliar. Even in bed. She kept catching sight of his folded shirt on the chair: a very pretty, paisley-patterned shirt. Soon, she thought, I shall be able to buy him shirts; previous presents had always had to be books – they didn't attract attention, he could have bought those for himself.

Buy him shirts and iron them for him too. As soon as she acquired an iron.

'And this,' Kenneth was saying, 'is the cross-referencing code.'

His pale fat fingers were shuffling through the index, selecting a card here, a card there, as he explained the symbols thereon. He stood close to her, his belly, which was slackly confined in its striped rugby jersey, pressed up against her arm. She was conscious of a faint but unappetising body odour which hinted, faintly but unmistakeably, at sweat-stained underwear, unwashed socks, spaces between the teeth of combs clogged with large greasy flakes of dandruff.

She tried to suppress her distaste. He was some mother's – neglected – son and, contrary to the impression given by Colette, younger than she'd taken him for: no more than mid-twenties,

77

she thought, stealing a glance and noting a beefy complexion, prematurely thinning hair and eyes of a startlingly bright china blue that seemed capable of a disconcertingly unblinking regard.

'Leave you to it then,' he said, and crossed the room to answer the phone. He moved with that over-emphatic jut of the pelvic bones usually adopted by the heterosexual male when attempting parody of the non-heterosexual male. A gait ill-suited to someone of his size and girth. She heard him say, into the telephone receiver, 'Oh, it's you, Robin. I'd almost given you up . . .'

There followed one of those irritatingly baffling conversations that are characterised by one party – the party at your end – making monosyllabic responses. Christina listened for a while, but apparently Robin was doing all the talking so eventually she turned her attention to the card-index and, shyly semaphoring a request to steal a corner of Kenneth's desk, began to copy out names and addresses.

Her interviewees were to be selected according to the traditional methods of stage-sampling: divided first into categories according to age and sex. She worked quickly, sorting, rejecting, allocating. She was halfway through when it occurred to her that she'd forgotten about location – for all she knew the members of her carefully-selected sample were all huddled together within one of the city's twenty-three postal districts – and she had to scrap all she'd done and start again from scratch. Roll on the twenty-third, she thought, or the twenty-fourth – for undoubtedly she was suffering the effects of the morning after the night before. How ludicrous it was, she thought, to have to swallow alcohol simply because of its temporarily narcotic effect. She would have been better off begging a few Mogadon from the doctor; but the doctor was Max's doctor and Adam's, and she couldn't face the thought of explaining her changed circumstances to anybody else. Not yet. Although there was one person to whom they must be explained, one area in which her natural tendency to procrastinate must be suppressed, and that was school.

'Iron', she wrote, and 'keys' (to be copied), in the margin of her discarded sample, and 'Headmaster' and then raised her head and took a surreptitious look at her companions. Kenneth had concluded his conversation with Robin. Since then he'd taken a call from a woman who needed her garden rubbish removed, and one from a man with a fridge to give away in return for a

Black and Decker workmate. Now he was, spasmodically, totting up some figures – in the intervals between tussling with the *Telegraph* crossword clues. Colette had continued to type like an automaton, never raising her eyes from the page she was copying. No wonder that Hilary Roberts extolled her efficiency.

However, now, precisely on St Nicholas's stroke of one, she slammed back the carriage on her typewriter, screwed the top on to her Tippex and looked up and smiled and enquired whether Christina would like a sandwich bringing from the bar across the road and if so, what sort.

Christina chose cheese. Kenneth opted for ham and two jam doughnuts. They boiled the kettle for coffee and cleared a space on the other end of Kenneth's desk. It was quite cosy. And although she had not warmed instantly to either of her colleagues, it was early days yet, and unfair as well as irrational to draw conclusions on such brief acquaintanceship.

Colette unwrapped her lunch: cottage cheese and lettuce on wholewheat crispbread, a low-fat yoghourt, an apple and a phial of artificial sweeteners.

'Are you on a diet?' Christina enquired.

Colette's face went pink. Her sweet smile became sweeter and wider. She reminded you of that sort of child who always did the Shirley Temple impressions at concerts. Jumbo had encouraged Cousin Gwennie to be that sort of child: showing her off in frilly frocks to his country-club cronies, had even, one Christmas, persuaded her into a pair of red tap shoes and introduced her as part of the cabaret, performing 'The Sun Has Got His Hat On' to the inebriatedly maudlin delight of the audience. But Gwen had grown up and quickly learned to say, 'How utterly ridiculous,' to such suggestions in tones of stunning hauteur.

'Not *that* sort of diet,' Colette said. 'Not for losing weight.'

It was just about excusable to look coy if you were seven years old and singing 'The Sun Has Got His Hat On' in front of an audience fuelled by alcohol to a pitch of indiscriminate child-worship. After that, the effect was fairly nauseating. Colette looked down at her crispbread. The delicate pink glow spread downwards to her neck and up to her forehead. 'I have to be careful what I eat now,' she murmured. 'Got to get lots of vitamins, the doctor said. Course, there are my pills.' And she indicated an array of bottles that stood next to the Tippex. One of them bore the inscription: 'Pregaday'; light dawned and

Christina realised that all the subtle hint-dropping, the eyes-cast-down, Dora Copperfield demureness, had been a deliberate ploy to encourage her to ask the obvious question: 'Are you expecting a baby?'

Kenneth just about got the chance to lower his eyelids and mutter, 'You *could* say that,' and then Colette began to speak and continued to speak, through the crunching of crispbread and the spooning of yoghourt and the sipping of coffee. She told of the miraculous gift of this pregnancy after twelve years of marriage, of her delight and her husband Don's delight, of her conscientious regime of diet and exercise, of her midwife and her obstetrician and the list of babies' names that were being assessed for suitability, of the christening mugs and silver teaspoons already purchased – although it didn't do to tempt fate, did it, when you had a very narrow pelvis and an inhospitable womb?

Christina, who had belonged to the reticent school of pregnant women and had always welcomed a similar reticence in others, could do nothing but nod or shake her head when response seemed to be required. Kenneth munched solidly through his jam doughnuts; one got the impression that he had heard all this before, many, many times before.

'So you see,' said Colette, drawing in sufficient breath to fuel the next part of her discourse, 'I have to take every precaution. Don didn't want me to work *this* long, but it says in all the books that, providing you look after yourself, it's all right to continue until the sixth month. Anyway, I want to be able to get nice things for the baby. Have you got children?' she asked. 'Did *you* work when you were pregnant?'

But she was not interested in a reply. She was off again: talking about scans and epidural anaesthesia and Ostermilk.

She continued to talk, even after they'd cleared away the debris of their lunch and resumed work. She prattled on to a background of the typewriter's staccato rhythm: tests, screening, the pros and cons of home versus hospital confinement. Christina was struck by the contrast between Colette's delighted anticipation and her own bewilderment and apprehension all those years ago. She thought: what a difference it must make, what advantages must attach, to being a wanted child, like the foetus that was being carried so carefully within Colette's pelvic girdle, rather than one that was jolted accidentally into existence and had to fight for survival against odds that ranged from indifference and lack of welcome all the way through to vinegar-soaked Beecham's Pills.

Eventually Colette ran out of steam, but not before Kenneth had taken himself off into the outer office where he was to be observed engaging in a game of draughts with the black girl from Community Relations who'd come down to use the photocopier. And not before Christina, beset anew, as a result of all this baby-talk, with pangs of guilt-ridden anguish, had decided that she must expend some of her ever-dwindling resources on a gift for Adam, to be presented to him on his next visit, as evidence that she really wasn't a bad mother.

7

Adam was due on Wednesday. Before then, by the end of Monday afternoon, she had made a start on her sample. Most of Tuesday morning was spent on the phone, attempting to fix up a few initial interviews. She found that the membership list with which Hilary Roberts had supplied her was a not entirely accurate document. Many of those whose names appeared on it had opted out, or moved on, or died. And that was quite apart from the problem of persuading some of those who hadn't to allow her entrance to their homes and an hour or so of their time. After a while she began to feel like an unsuccessful double-glazing salesman. Most of Tuesday evening was spent in trying to revise her original list to exclude the dead, the vanished and the unwilling-to-be-interviewed. She was doing this when Livingstone rang. He said, 'I'm sorry, love. I'm stuck just off the M62. The car's packed up and I'm waiting for the RAC. God knows when they'll arrive. If I can make it before it gets too ridiculously late, I will, but don't count on it. Look, love – I've no more change . . .'

And then the phone had gone dead. She'd replaced the receiver, suspecting it was highly unlikely that she'd see him that night, but was able to face this prospect with a reasonable degree of equanimity. She looked up from her work and discovered, to her pleasant surprise, that it was eleven o'clock already.

Having an occupation – that explained it; that, and actually knowing that there was a date: if not the twenty-third then the twenty-fourth, after which the inebriated nights and the hung-over mornings need never happen again, not unless she wanted them to.

On Wednesday morning she set off for one of the city's most distant suburbs in order to conduct an interview. First, she boarded the wrong bus and then she got lost, even when she was on the right one.

Back in civilisation, she went to W. H. Smith's and bought an *A to Z*. 'Can't you *drive*?' Hilary Roberts had asked incredulously during their initial meeting, as though the inability to drive marked one as a complete social inadequate.

She also bought Adam a record, remembering a desire being expressed and hoping that between its expression and the acquisition of its object, his musical tastes hadn't moved on.

'Yes,' he said, when she gave it him that afternoon. 'Thanks,' he said. 'Great.'

He sat on the very edge of the sofa as though ready to spring up from it at a moment's notice. He placed the record in splendid isolation on the cushion beside him. 'What's the matter?' she said. 'Didn't I get the right one?'

'Oh yeah,' he said politely. 'It's just – well I've got it already. Well, Parkinson has. I taped it.'

'Give it back to me then. Let me change it. Which one would you like?'

'Oh no,' he said. 'No. It's OK.' And picked it up and clasped it tightly as though she was about to wrest it from him by force.

Of course, sometimes – as Gwen's Daddy, Jumbo, used to say, when Gwen was leading him a merry dance – you couldn't do right for doing wrong.

'How's your father?'

He'd shrugged and pretended to be reading the back of the record though, as far as she could tell, there *was* no writing on the back of the record.

She couldn't blame him. For an answer to be forthcoming, she'd have needed to be more specific, and such specificity was out of the question. She didn't mean: how's your father in terms of his ulcer or the yield on his share certificates or whether or not he's managed to avert the management-union dispute that's been looming these last few weeks; she meant how's your father apropos his reaction to my departure? Does he mention me? And if he does, is it solely for the purposes of vilification?

She couldn't expect Adam to answer those sort of questions. 'Couldn't you stay, for a meal?' she asked instead.

But, of course, there was his guitar lesson. And his desire to avoid Livingstone, though Livingstone was so late that Adam could well have eaten and left before his arrival.

The car had had to be garaged. Usually, when that happened, he borrowed Louise's, but Louise was much too busy at present to be deprived of it. He had to rely on public transport, and she knew what that was like . . .

She was beginning to.

Although the *A to Z* and a few bus and train timetables helped to make Thursday morning less of a disaster in terms of wasted time than Wednesday had been. She got a good interview too. And another one, in the afternoon. On the way home she stopped at the launderette and fed a machine with her washing. As she stooped to empty her bag, she caught sight, within one of her folders, of a message written on the margin of a page: 'Iron', it said. She'd forgotten, and the shops were now closed.

It also said 'Headmaster' on that margin, but that reminder was now redundant, that subject had been dealt with. She'd actually remembered to broach the subject to Adam. She'd said, in a studiedly casual manner, 'Oh, by the way, I must make an appointment to come to school and see Mr Whatshisname, your headmaster. I know it'll be a bit embarrassing for you, but it'll be even more embarrassing if I don't.'

'There's no need. Dad went to see him.'

'Really? When?'

'One day last week. Thursday. Friday. I forget.'

There was a price sticker on Adam's record. He began to pick it off, devoting all his attention to the activity.

'Are you sure?'

'Course I am.'

'And everything's all right at school, is it? Getting on OK with the work?'

He had his O Levels in June. So far, there had been no indication that he wouldn't take them in his stride, perhaps do very well. David had always been the one who gave overt cause for concern: slipping from the high-flying top of the class to the bottom in the space of a few terms, reluctantly producing reports that told of wasted talent and squandered potential. Adam had, throughout his school career, occupied a safe sort of second favourite's position in whatever stream he was placed.

'Yes?' she prompted.

'Yes!' he replied. 'Stop going on, will you?'

Looking for something to worry about, that was her trouble. As if there wasn't enough.

That was Wednesday. On Thursday she folded her unironed washing and on Friday went into The System office looking somewhat crumpled and Colette, a favourer of crisp white Peter Pan collars and creaseless, pastel-coloured, acrylan cardigans (who now knew that Christina was a *femme sole* of very recent vintage) asked if she wanted to borrow the little travelling iron that she, Colette, had won at the bingo in her pre-pregnant days, before her husband had been made redundant and she could still afford to go.

'I'll bring it in on Monday.'

'Thank you. Thank you very much.'

Monday the twenty-first. On Wednesday, the twenty-third or Thursday, the twenty-fourth, there would be two lots of washing and Livingstone would probably not take kindly to the idea of crumpled shirts.

Meanwhile, Friday the eighteenth – a lovely day: blue sky, balmy breeze, sun still surprisingly potent – she'd spent the afternoon on the Wirral. She'd interviewed a redundant executive and a couple of youths on a council estate where the major recreational activity was reputed to be the smoking of heroin. 'Smack City' they called it. The youths, Sammy and Rob (who offered unskilled painting and decorating, not really in exchange for anything, but just for something to do), talked of the problem. 'Kids as young as thirteen on it round here,' they said, their thin, sly, pinched-featured faces momentarily alight with moral indignation.

Oh Adam, she thought, Adam, take care, as she always did whenever she was faced with an example of the pitfalls – increasing by the minute – that lay in wait for the young, the unwary, the vulnerable. She had never thought: oh David, never feared for him in the same way, despite his teenage escapades. There was within him, she believed, a central core of steadiness that would save him from courting disaster. Besides, David had never had an absentee mother.

She was thinking about these things on Friday evening: wondering how reliable those frightening statistics that linked the broken home to any and all of the social ills actually were when the entryphone buzzed. She picked up the receiver and said, 'Honestly, your memory!' (She'd had keys cut for both Adam and Livingstone – although Adam had, symbolically perhaps, left his behind. She'd forgotten 'Iron' and almost forgotten 'Headmaster' but she'd remembered 'Keys'.)

'You'd forget your head if it was loose,' she said. He was famous for his absentmindedness: keys, gloves, items of clothing mislaid all over the place – once he'd left a manuscript, his only copy, in a taxi.

But there was no reply. However many times she said, 'Hello?' or even 'Hello!' there was still no reply, so she was eventually obliged to put the phone down and go downstairs.

There was an envelope in the letter-box, a long white rectangular envelope, very full, that hadn't been there when she came in. She hadn't switched on the hall light but that which filtered from the landing allowed her to read the name on it, her own name, and to recognise the hand that had written it.

She sat down on the bottom step of the stairs.

'I do love you. You know that?'

Last words?

They'd had the ring of last words when he'd spoken them just before taking his leave of her the previous evening. She'd brushed it aside, that feeling, just as she'd brushed everything else aside, everything she didn't want to hear, everything that might have given her pause in her headlong, headstrong, pursuit of what she wanted.

She'd known, known for days, hadn't she? Didn't need to have it spelled out. Perhaps that was why, although she took the letter from the box at about eight o'clock, it was almost nine before she opened it.

She'd only risen from the stairs because eventually her leg went into cramp. She went back to her flat and put the envelope, face up, on the coffee table and sat and gazed at it for a very long time. Then, suddenly and all in a rush, she tore it open and took out the several sheets that it contained and tried to read them, tried to concentrate on processing the information that they contained, sentence by sentence, consecutively, in the normal way, but found it impossible. Disjointed words and phrases jumped out at her: 'railroaded', 'without warning', 'loyalty'; her eyes and her brain seemed to be seriously out of sync, so that she moved on to the next paragraph before properly assimilating the intelligence conveyed by the one before.

'You never gave me a chance,' he'd written. 'You just went

ahead without either consultation with, or concern for anybody else.'

'I love you, Christina,' he'd written, 'but you must understand that I can't just up and walk out on her at a minute's notice. Not now of all times. She needs support.'

'I've torn up a dozen letters before this one,' he'd written. 'I've been writing them all week. Every one of them sounded as though it had been written by the worst kind of shit. But then, perhaps that's what I am.'

She turned the pages over, one by one, until she reached the end of the letter and saw, with the worst shock of all, the name 'Alan' written at the bottom.

'Alan'? She'd never known an Alan. Alan belonged to everyone else. Alan belonged to Louise.

She'd never known a Livingstone either, come to that. Only her version of him: no more real than Sir Lancelot or Mr Rochester. There'd only been a fantasy, dependent upon collusion: 'How would it be if . . .?'

She went into the kitchen and took one of the one-and-a-half-litre bottles of cheap red wine that she'd bought and opened it and drank from it. When the room at last began to whirl and she became aware that sometime, a long time ago, the station that the radio was tuned to had ceased to transmit and she was now hearing only white noise, she thought that perhaps she ought to lie down before she passed out. She staggered into the bedroom, pulled back the coverlet from the bed and saw a stain on the sheet below, memento of their last lovemaking.

Their last lovemaking. You ought not to make love for the last time without knowing that that was the case. Had she known, she would have extended each embrace until she'd extracted every atom of sweetness from it. Had she known, she'd have torn him limb from limb, bitten his sun-browned flesh till the blood flowed.

She watched her tears dropping on to the quilt, watched the droplets fall, spread, become absorbed into the fabric. And then she read the letter for the first time, in its proper sequence. Her tears mingled with the wine. *Lacrimae Christina. Lacrimae Christinae?* A classical education, once and long ago; what she'd learned from it forgotten, pushed out of her memory by the press of everything that had come after: birth control pills and dry-cleaning tickets and school forms to sign and sports shoes to buy and plumbers to ring and carpetlayers and orthodontists; hands to be held, tears to mop, pre-natal vomitings and post-natal stitchings, peace-keeping missions on Breton beaches, tons of dust to be shifted, mounds of clothes to be washed, hundred-weights of potatoes to be peeled.

Once, there had been a girl who wrote an essay on Kierkegaard and won a prize for it. She drank and she cried for that lost girl, for what she might have become. If her mother hadn't chanced to be placed next to Max's mother in the hospital bed, if her pituitary gland hadn't triggered an inappropriate ovulation. She wondered if somewhere, in some different dimension, there existed a coterminous universe, where the lives that might have been were being lived out – all of them infinitely more satisfac-torily, she was certain, than their actual, real counterparts.

Not that you could call this reality, she thought, chasing the black words that seemed to career across the white paper as if it were they that were drunk. This was nightmare. The only difference being that there was no prospect of waking up.

On Saturday afternoon he didn't bother with the entryphone. He used his keys. He did, first of all, tap on the flat door but then, receiving no response, opened it. Then he reached around and placed the keys on top of the bookshelf. Such a short period of possession, she thought. Waste of time having them cut, she thought. She thought, I cannot bear this.

'Can I come in? Do you want me to come in?'

She couldn't instantly find her voice. She made a gesture that could have meant anything but which he chose to interpret as invitation. He skirted her – as Max had so recently skirted her – and stood at the opposite side of the room, awaiting her response.

'Why the letter?'

She scarcely recognised the faltering squeak that issued from between her lips as being the sound of her own voice. Not that his was a model of either resonance or audibility; she had to strain to catch what he said.

'I thought it would give me a chance to explain myself, coherently. You can't always do that, face to face.'

Quite. Take the much-rehearsed parting scene with Max, for example. Trouble was, you had to rehearse blind, as it were. It was like playing dummy whist: the reactions of the absent protagonist could no more be vouched for than the identity of the cards that might be contained within the floating hand.

Plus which, of course, as soon as you wrote anything down, be it lies, rubbish or ravings, it attained a kind of spurious validity.

'Can I use your loo?'

He was a long time in the bathroom. It gave her the opportunity to recall that letter. It was, as he'd said, a coherent piece of work, irrefutably logical and sufficiently representative of his authentic voice to convince her that it was a failure of nerve, due to unpreparedness, that was responsible for his backing out at the last minute.

It would have been possible to read the letter and believe what she read. But with the end of self-delusion had come the inability to cushion the blow by opting for the least painful explanation: he *was* going to leave, but then he found he couldn't. Instinct told her – had been telling her ever since the beginning of October, had she only been willing to listen – that the intention had never existed.

'Sorry,' he said when he came back.

Sorry that he needed to pee? He'd said sorry so many times in the letter that perhaps the habit had become ingrained. He stood looking like a spare part, apparently waiting to be asked to sit down. Well, she wouldn't break down and give vent to screaming hysterics, injure him, kill him, kill herself, but she certainly wasn't going to be polite. After a moment or two he sat down anyway, sat and regarded her interrogatively, supplicatingly, evidently willing her to wipe her eyes and join with him in a gentleman's agreement: we had a love affair and now it's over and so let us part, as friends.

But no: those were not the terms of the truce, not according to the letter. The letter had said that, fundamentally, there were two reasons for his inability to join her – just yet – on a permanent basis: one of them – the main one – being that Louise, far from being better able to do without him now that her career was taking an upturn, needed him more than ever.

(Oh yes! Delicate little Louise, requiring round-the-clock, year-long, life-long protection. Probably as tough as old boots, if the truth were known.)

His second reason: place their relationship on a proper footing, make it licit and announce it to the world and, well, in time there would be little to distinguish it from those that they had rejected in its favour; in time, they would become Max and Christina, Alan and Louise.

And that, she supposed, was what underlay the interrogative regard: the need to know whether she could possibly accept – for the time being anyway – the status quo: afternoon assignations, figs, champagne . . . He knew it was a lot to ask . . . She foresaw a lifetime of love in the afternoon. In time, of course, passion would wane, sexual vigour decrease. What would they do then: drink tea, discuss their aches and pains, play bridge? Would he continue to assert that his marriage was a desert and these visits represented, for him, trips to the oasis? Would he, when Louise died and she asked him whether he couldn't, now, move in with her, plead the excuse of age and weariness for staying put?

For, whether he realised it or not, his two reasons cancelled each other out. He couldn't say, on the one hand, that coming together in a conventional relationship would spoil the magic and, on the other, that he had every intention – one day, once Louise had developed enough self-confidence to make his support unnecessary – of joining with her in a conventional relationship.

'Did it make any sense at all – the letter?'

'Perfect sense.'

'People always talk about the impossibility of accepting only a part of somebody else. But what if it's the best part? After all, you and me, well it was only one element of the situation, wasn't it? It did occur to me to wonder which was the stronger: the push to leave Max, or the pull towards me. I know you wanted a new life, a life for yourself. Obviously, sometime, you'd have made the break anyway. You took this flat off your own bat as soon as you were sure of the job, you were intending to bring Adam with you . . .'

At intervals throughout this speech he had left pauses for interjection. She hadn't responded but now she couldn't not speak. She said, 'No, I wouldn't have left, not to nothing. I haven't the courage. And if there hadn't been you, I'd certainly not have left Adam. And as for the flat – well, I simply couldn't afford it.' She said, 'Do you know how I managed to get together the deposit? I saved it up out of the Family Allowance.'

A hit. A very palpable hit. He looked away and said, 'Don't make it more difficult than it is.'

'Do you think it was easy for me?'

'Eas*ier*. Perhaps.'

He couldn't weigh *every* word before he uttered it, yet spontaneity was dangerous. She saw him draw back as though expecting attack, although he had no acquaintance with that side of her nature, had never been enlightened about the times that Max's silences had provoked her to violence.

Neither of them knew the other's private, domestic self, those aspects that, from his point of view, were best kept well out of sight when it came to successful part-time relationships.

He got to his feet and walked to the window and parted the muslin curtains. How ridiculous, even for a fantasy, white muslin curtains! You'd need to be washing them every five minutes. Because he had his back to her she couldn't tell what he was saying at first and had to ask him to repeat it. She was looking at the nape of his neck, the width of his shoulders, those beloved old second-skin jeans. He should have worn a suit for this errand and called himself Alan.

'What did you say?'

'I said perhaps we'll both have a clearer idea, after I get back.'

She said, 'I don't think my ideas are in any need of clarification.' She said, 'When you get back from where?'

'From the States.'

'What!'

'When I get back from the States.'

'But I thought it was Louise who was going to America? I thought – you said – why didn't you *say*?'

'I did say. In my letter.'

'You didn't. You bloody well didn't.'

'I did.'

She ran out of the room and across the hall and into the bedroom and opened the drawer in the bedside table and fished out the letter. (Had she thought that by concealing it from sight she might have caused it to dematerialise?)

'Where?' she said, running back, brandishing it. At the foot of the last page it simply said the name of a stranger: Alan.

Another stranger: Livingstone, turned from the window and said, 'Turn over,' so she did and read there: 'I've decided to go with Louise to America. She's a bit daunted at the thought of managing it on her own. And, quite honestly, I think it might be the best thing for us: a break, so that we can get everything into perspective.'

'How long?'

'Six weeks.'

'But what about your book, your research?'

'I've enough notes to keep me occupied until I get back. And I can work in a hotel room as well as anywhere. Besides, I'd like to see New York again. I was there for a year, you know, in '70. On an exchange. I imagine that it must have changed more than somewhat since then . . .'

It was then that she lost control. She threw his letter to the ground and then an ashtray. There being nothing else immediately to hand, she was obliged to cross the room to the bookcase for further ammunition. Thud, thud, thud, they went as they hit the wall opposite: *Questionnaire Design and Attitude Measurement, Readings in Social Psychology, This Side of Paradise.*

And after her anger had subsided, she debased herself, grovelled, literally, wet the carpet with her tears, appealed to his integrity, his concern, the – whatever it was that had grown between them since that touch of his hand on her shoulder, appealed to his self-interest, his lust, his vanity, *anything* that might respond to entreaty. At first he kept his distance as though afraid that propinquity might lead him into temptation, but eventually he reached out to her and took her in his arms and allowed her tears to wet his sleeve and she knew that, for all the response that was transmitted, she could have been a troubled stranger. Even Max, who no longer loved her, and with good cause, would have done as much.

❧ 8 ❧

And then, on cue, the weather changed: the dawning of Sunday morning was totally obliterated by fog. At least they said so, later that day on the radio. At dawn she had still been stuporous. But it persisted. When she finally came round at midday and looked out of the window nothing was visible beyond the shrubbery. It gave her a curious disembodied feeling, as though the grey fog were really water and the house marooned on an island in the centre of it.

The quietness, such a prominent feature of the neighbour-hood, was intensified – if you could talk about an intensification of silence, if you could describe a lack with a word that implied more.

By focusing on such pedantic and irrelevant details: the quality of the silence, whether the colour of the bedroom carpet was nearer to green than grey, how many steps there were on the way down to the front door to bring in the milk (a message for the milkman: 'I shan't be increasing my order. In fact, I'll probably be cancelling it altogether'), she might just be able to propel herself through the actions appropriate to a normal life, a normal day: the emptying of her bladder, the filling of the kettle, the spooning of coffee.

Or, alternatively, by taking the overview, by fixing her mind on the state of the world: Ethiopian famine, nuclear threat, incurable sexually-transmitted diseases, it might be possible (as Livingstone had suggested) for her to put the event into perspec-tive: there was this man and this woman, both of them old enough to know better, but they had an affair anyway, and the woman, seizing upon it as an excuse to leave a husband she'd married in error when she really was too young to know any better, had attempted to set up a home for them. Unfortunately he, the lover, had got cold feet at the last minute.

Or was astute enough to realise that what worked for a few hours a week might not work full time.

Whichever, when you boiled it down, it wasn't very important in the general scheme of things. Not when you could switch on the television set and see swollen-bellied African children with legs like twigs and eyes colonised by flies, not when you could open a newspaper and read about madmen with access to buttons which, if pressed, could obliterate half the world, not when hoardings warned you that by indulging in indiscriminate sex you could be signing your own death warrant.

But she had no television set, she hadn't yet ordered a newspaper to be delivered and, in view of the fog, it was highly unlikely that she would catch sight of a hoarding.

She washed herself and dressed herself and collected the bottles and took them down to the bin. Fog or no fog, she would have to go out as soon as the off-licence opened to replenish her stock. She needed an anaesthetic at hand for when the pain arrived.

She went into the sitting-room, prepared to pick up everything she'd thrown at him the previous day, but the floor was clear. He must have picked up the missiles and replaced them before he left. When he left she'd been prostrate upon her bed.

The unexpected tidiness allowed her to move on to her next project, which was the working out of various sums concerning her financial future. The problem was: she couldn't get the figures to add up to the same total twice in succession. Though she knew that no matter how she shuffled them there was no possibility of balancing her salary against her expenditure and not coming out with a number that had a minus sign in front of it.

But she persevered: covering pages with columns of addition and lines of multiplication, long after she realised the futility of such efforts. At least while thus engaged, she wasn't concentrating – to the exclusion of all else – upon hopes dashed, plans thwarted, foolishness made manifest.

And then it was opening-time. There were three off-licences within walking distance and she divided her custom between them, because she was worried that patronage of just the one might result in her being marked down as an inebriate. Although even if she was noticed, why should anyone care? She was a stranger in a strange place: rootless, faceless, status-less; she could walk the streets invisible.

That evening she could, at any rate. The fog had lifted, briefly, in the afternoon and the sun deigned to reassert its existence by diffusing a little' five-watt radiance through the catarrh-coloured sky, but by six o'clock it had dropped again, as densely as before; she had to feel her way along the garden walls until she reached the junction of Queen's Road and Lancaster Avenue. Passing the station, she saw that there was a notice advising passengers that, due to adverse weather conditions, the trains would be unavoidably delayed. Usually they said, 'Operating difficulties', which meant anything from a driver not having turned up for work to a body on the track. There was a particular stretch of the line popular with would-be suicides: easy of access, intersected by un-manned crossings, not too far from where she lived.

Where she used to live.

And where could she live now, after the end of the month?

'Can't we leave it in abeyance?' Livingstone had said. 'Keep this place on, at least for a while?'

'While you make up your mind?'

'While we get things sorted out. If I pay half the rent for the next month, until after Christmas, say? I reckon I can manage that. It is pretty expensive though, isn't it?'

After Christmas, presumably – in the event of his mind having been made up to stay with Louise – she would be expected to move out to an address more in keeping with her new status, financial and social.

'Will you give it some thought? I'll ring you, of course, before I go.'

'Don't.'

'No?'

'No.'

The illuminated sign of the Spar shop: 'Open Eight Till Late', boon to those in need of alcoholic anaesthesia, came into view. She entered and took from its shelves two large bottles of red wine. On the other side of the aisle a tramp person was selecting cider and sherry. 'White Lightning' they called that mixture when it was spiked with meths, sat with their bottles concealed in paper bags in St John's Gardens, occasionally telling the pigeons to fuck off, or the passers-by, or the Town Hall clock. How warily she had always skirted them: they were another breed, a different species. She wondered now how many of them had had their hopes dashed, their plans thwarted, their hearts broken, and embarked on the road that led to the bottle in the bag and the bench in the Gardens by way of two large bottles of supermarket red wine.

She took hers home and set about emptying them, impatient for the alcohol to take effect.

'I'll ring you before I go.'

'Don't.'

'No?'

'No.'

But that had been yesterday and before the impact of his decision had fully sunk in. Now the telephone had acquired a personality, sat on the shelf so smug, taunting her with its silence. At first she unplugged it and put it in the hall, but then it occurred to her that should he try to ring, she would never know about it, so she brought it back again and, after a while, she picked up the receiver and dialled his number, but it rang and rang until even she was obliged to concede that there was no one there to answer it. She hadn't planned as far ahead as what she might have said if there had been.

Planning ahead seemed, now, completely beyond her capability. All she could do was to pray that, somehow, she might be equal to sorting out the mess she had got herself into. If you don't like your life, they said (everybody said because, these days, everybody was an expert), then change it. So, after all the years through which she'd trudged with her eyes fixed on the ground just slightly ahead of her feet, unwilling to acknowledge anything outside her small sphere of existence, she'd done just that: looked up, stepped out, risked the gamble. And what had she received for her pains but the severest form of chastening?

'Please,' she prayed to whoever there might be out there who was prepared to listen, 'let me survive these next few days, weeks, months, not only in terms of emotional equilibrium but practically. Give me the clear-sightedness – and sufficient financial independence – to enable me to make some kind of a viable existence for myself. Failing that: if it's a choice between being partly kept as a part-time panorama and returning ignominiously to Winchester Road, then give me the strength and courage to choose wisely.'

Financial independence depended upon getting up in the morning and going to work. Work hadn't seemed so terribly important until now. Now it was all she had left and though her first instinct, when the alarm finally penetrated her stupor, was to stagger to the phone and ring Hilary Roberts and plead illness, she knew that if she were to succumb to that first instinct then she would be lost, might as well equip herself with a brown paper bag and book her seat in the Gardens.

The fog was as dense as ever. She covered her mouth with her scarf and tried to brace herself for what she might expect to contend with for the foreseeable future: bus queues full of people barking like sea lions, the stealthy transformation of a familiar landscape into a shrouded no-man's-land where every dimension seemed different from the way that normal illumination disposed you to experience it.

Kenneth was a victim of the prevailing virus: coughing like a consumptive, blowing his nose with foghorn blasts, projecting gouts of mucus into the wads of lavatory paper that served him as handkerchiefs. He should have stayed at home. Except that home was, she gathered, a room in some sort of hostel and unlikely to offer much in the way of invalid-nursing. She tried to keep a precautionary distance between them.

Colette had decided upon total precaution. At nine-thirty she rang to inform them that she wouldn't be coming in because of the fog, because of the climate of contagion that prevailed on public transport, and because she detected a slight but sinister tickle at the back of her throat. To take chances would be foolish. She was about to launch into an account of the effect of rhinoviruses upon the unborn foetus – Christina could hear a note of enthusiasm entering the quacking sounds that issued from the telephone receiver – when Kenneth slammed it down and cut her off in mid-quack.

'There's all this to be typed up,' he complained, brandishing a sheaf of that week's record of exchanges. 'Trust her to pick her moment. I don't know why she doesn't just shut herself up inside a glass case till it's all over . . .' He sneezed explosively over the typewriter keys.

'I'll do some if you like.'

On balance, she felt that she'd prefer to take her chances with

Ken's pestilential presence rather than attempt a trek through the fog to the far-distant address of Mrs Violet Mason, who was meant to be that morning's interviewee. And when she checked inside her briefcase she found that she'd forgotten to bring in her tape-recorder, so there was no alternative.

Kenneth fought a battle with martyrdom and won. The lure of pulling his chair close to the gas fire, equipping himself with the newspaper, several yards of lavatory tissue and his Vick inhaler was not to be resisted. Anyway, it wasn't possible to sneeze, on a regular basis, and type.

She wasn't a very good typist, and the machine was electronic and kept the location of most of its functions a closely-guarded secret and, by ten o'clock, she'd produced only one relatively-error-free page, but she knew that it was essential to occupy herself. Otherwise, she might have been tempted to cross the room and lift the telephone and dial the number that she knew as well as her own. Better.

Two days she had: to resist the temptation or succumb to it. Two days, and a lifetime in which to regret her decision.

At twelve o'clock, by which time Kenneth had read the paper front to back and then again in the reverse order, and she'd ruined several more sheets of A4, Hilary Roberts dropped by.

'Just dropped by,' she said, 'to see how you're getting on.'

Kenneth sprang to his feet, beamed, displaying neglected teeth, and made a gesture towards the kettle and the coffee jar. But Dr Roberts shook her head (and her earrings of a size normally to be found fastened through an African native woman's nostrils). A flying visit only. She lit a small cigar and unwound a scarf, which vied in length with Kenneth's mucus-mopping lavatory paper, from around her neck. Today, together with the tribal earrings, she wore a large long spiv overcoat and those sort of clumpy black leather ankle boots that look as though they are issued only upon prescription in orthopaedic clinics. Christina, familiar by now with the flying-ace look, the militant lesbian format, was at a loss to conceptualise this motley ensemble.

'Oughtn't you to be interviewing?'

'Yes, but it's an old dear and she's got this flu. I've had to postpone. And Colette's off ill as well.'

Oh to learn to lie without the inevitable accompaniment of the blush. Better to be like Colette and blush all the time and then it wasn't possible to distinguish the ones which were prompted by mendacity.

'It's a swine, isn't it?' said Hilary Roberts, flicking ash irritably over the papers that Ken had hastily spread on the other side of the desk to make it appear as though he was working. 'Gavin's got it. I've left him in bed with a bottle of Benylin. My chap,' she said, in response to Christina's politely interrogative glance.

Well of course. There was bound to be one. Hilary Roberts would know how to hold on to a man – if she wanted him.

'I'll let you get on then,' she said. 'But don't get into the habit of doing other people's jobs. And, in future, try to have a contingency plan, another interviewee lined up in case the original has to be cancelled.'

The rebuke was accompanied by the sweetest of smiles. Normally Christina would have gritted her teeth and swallowed back retort; today she had neither the spirit nor the self-esteem to do more than lower her eyes in acknowledgement that she deserved reprimand.

At least the rest of the day would be surveillance-free. Lulled by the gas fire's hissing and Kenneth's catarrhal snortings, Christina slept, dreamed that the events of the weekend had been a dream and Livingstone, laughing, was opening his arms to her, and woke sobbing.

'What's up with you?' Kenneth enquired unsympathetically. 'It's lunchtime. Are you going for the sandwiches?'

In view of the state of his health, she had no option but to wipe her eyes and nod her head. Perhaps obeying the precept about feeding a cold, he requested a shipping order: sandwiches, rolls, jam doughnuts and slices of gâteaux. She hauled them back and he started counting out money to pay her.

'You'll have to owe me twenty pence. I haven't got enough change.'

'Oh no, no,' he said, digging into each of his pockets in turn, unearthing odd, fluff-covered coppers. 'I like to get things straight as we go along. Otherwise you never know where you are.'

But the coppers didn't amount to enough to make up the discrepancy. He started to sort through the petty cash tin, effecting small exchanges. His over-meticulousness began to get on her nerves. 'Oh for God's sake,' she said. 'It's only twenty pence. You can let me have it back tomorrow.'

He winced. 'Please,' he said, 'don't blaspheme.'

It was a rebuke as deliberate as that delivered by Hilary Roberts, but without the accompaniment of a smile, however phony. She stood, mouth agape, hand extended to receive the moist pennies that he'd been clutching, remembering the various little signifiers that she'd noticed without bothering to analyse: the way his lips moved before he bit into his jam doughnut – obviously he was saying grace; the phrase that brought to an end his telephone conversations with Robin: 'God bless'; the glimpse she'd caught of the conclusion of a letter he'd been writing: 'Your brother in Christ, Kenneth.'

She closed her mouth and then opened it again to say, 'I'm sorry, I didn't mean to offend you,' and took her sandwich to the far side of the room and hoped that that would be the end of it.

Of course it wasn't. She might have known. There had been a cue for Colette that prompted her to launch into 'Pregnancy – Its Course and Disturbances, With Special Reference To Elderly Primagravidas'; there was a cue for Kenneth and she had inadvertently provided it.

'Thou shalt not,' he said, 'take the name of the Lord thy God in vain. It's something I try to live by.'

'I didn't realise you were – ' Religious, she'd been going to say, but thought that sounded a bit crude and patronising, so amended it to: ' – a church-goer.'

'Oh, it's rather more than that,' he said smugly.

There was a pause during which she realised he was going to tell her how much more than that it was.

'Church-going's one thing. Receiving Jesus into your life is quite another.'

She blushed. The hairs rose on the back of her neck. She was as embarrassed as if he'd admitted to some appallingly deviant behaviour, as horrified as she used to be when cowardly Max sent her to the door to deal with the Jehovah's Witnesses.

It was unlikely that the mere eating of a sandwich could protect her from his evangelical fervour so she picked up his discarded newspaper and hid herself behind it. Come back, Colette, she prayed, come back quickly. At least the experience of pregnancy could be shared, if not their attitudes towards it.

'There comes a time in your life,' Kenneth was saying, 'when you can no longer continue to live in the way that you were living.'

His cheeks were mottled with darker patches. His eyes were bright, tranced. She shook out the newspaper – it was the local rag – and saw that the City Council had decided to defy the government on the issue of rate-capping.

'It happens to all of us. I daresay it's happened to you.'

A tobacco firm was closing one of its local factories and a man who was about to be made redundant from his job there had won seven hundred and fifty thousand pounds on the football pools.

'A crossroads, when we become aware that there's something missing in our lives,' said Kenneth. His voice had taken on a kind of monotonous crooning quality; she hoped he wasn't going to start to speak in tongues.

There was a sale at the do-it-yourself shop. Three local hairdressers' apprentices had dressed hair so effectively in a national competition that they had won themselves a trip to Majorca. A prominent local citizen had died.

'That's what happened to me,' crooned Kenneth. 'That's when I invited the Lord Jesus Christ into my life. And I've been comforted beyond measure.'

If only it could be that simple. The religious life was well known for providing consolation for the lovelorn.

She stared at the paper. She saw that Mr Ernest Conway, MBE, a prominent local citizen, one-time proprietor of the city's oldest-established printing works, ex-councillor, former chairman of the board of governors of Bishop Latimer's School and captain of the Links Golf Club . . . She skimmed through the list of honours and achievements until she reached the end of the sentence: '. . . died on Saturday at The Cedars where he had made his home for the past twelve years.'

'We're a fairly small group still,' Kenneth said. 'Just Robin and I and a few other committed people . . .'

Mr Conway, a widower, the newspaper report said, left one son, Mr Maxwell Conway, who had taken over the running of the family firm upon his father's retirement.

'There's a Bible study every Tuesday evening,' Kenneth said, 'followed by an informal discussion. Everyone is made welcome . . .'

The funeral, it said in the newspaper, was to be held on

Wednesday morning: a service at the Anglican cathedral followed by interment. She scrabbled through the paper until she reached the Births, Marriages and Deaths. It was at the top of the list, there being no As or Bs. 'Conway,' she read, 'Peacefully, at his home, aged 87, Ernest Robert, beloved husband of the late Isabel, dear father of Max and grandfather of David and Adam . . . Enquiries to Messrs Hewlett and Hudson.'

She threw the paper down and moved across to the telephone. Kenneth repeated, 'Everyone is made welcome. Everyone.'

Her phone rang and rang. *Not* her phone, *theirs*. Adam was, presumably, at school, and Max at work. She dialled his office number. An unfamiliar voice answered her. (She remembered that old Mrs Thing had been due to retire.) She was informed that Mr Conway was not, at the moment, available.

Probably attending to the funeral arrangements. She stood with the telephone receiver in her hand, feeling deflated rather than relieved, as those who have nerved themselves to perform some unpleasant task and found their attempt frustrated usually do.

Still, she couldn't *not* get in touch. However little love was lost between them. His father was dead and she must, if not offer comfort (not a great deal of love had been lost between *them*: the Conways, father and son; visits to The Cedars, a plush retirement home in Cheshire, had usually been at her instigation), at least acknowledge the fact.

'Have you been listening to what I said?' Kenneth asked in a somewhat peeved tone. Inviting Jesus into his life didn't seem to have improved his temper. Of course she didn't know what it had been like beforehand.

'I'm sorry. I've just found out that my father-in-law has died.'

That was a mistake. The number of scriptural references applicable to bereavement seemed legion – and Kenneth seemed to be acquainted with each and every one.

At three o'clock she took a bus to the Comprehensive and waited outside the gates until half-past, when she was almost submerged by the tide of pubescent humanity that surged through them. Adam was with Parkinson. If looks could kill, she thought, seeing the expression that came over his face as soon as he saw her, she'd have been dead on the pavement.

'I'm sorry. I tried ringing home but there was nobody in.'

He muttered something out of the side of his mouth and Parkinson shambled away.

'About your grandfather . . .'

'Not *here*,' he said through gritted teeth.

'Look, Adam, I'm not feeling very well and I've had a hell of a job getting here. The buses are crawling . . . If I can't talk to you here, let's go back to the flat.'

'I told Dad I'd be home early. I'm supposed to be getting a suit. For the funeral.'

'Well, then . . . There's a café, isn't there, in the Concourse?'

'I think it shuts on Mondays.'

But it was open. They drank bitter lukewarm coffee and she told him about seeing the announcement in that morning's paper and he shrugged and said, 'Yeah, well. Borrowed time, really, wasn't it?'

She hadn't expected grief. Neither of the boys had seen him often enough, of late, for any sort of bond to be reinforced, even supposing one had been forged in the first place. And it hadn't. Ernest Conway had never felt disposed to adopt a conventional, benign, grandfatherly role. According to Max, playing a fatherly role had stretched him to the limit.

'I'm very sorry,' she said to Adam.

Though she wasn't. She'd always considered him to be a monstrously selfish old man – old even when she'd first met him, his chief concern being that his income should allow him to live in comfort and pamper his afflictions. For, like Max, he'd been over-anxious about his health: arthritis had plagued him, and high blood pressure. Gallstones he'd had and, though an abstemious man, gout. Sebaceous cysts there'd been, requiring surgical removal, and ulcerated varicose veins. Whenever she thought of him it was as a heavy-set, grey-faced old man in a dingy-coloured frayed cardigan, lowering himself creakily into a wicker chair on the verandah of The Cedars, opening his mouth mainly to complain about his digestion or his bladder or his bowels, enquiring querulously whether 'those boys' (his grandsons) needed to run around quite so boisterously, whether, indeed, they'd needed to bring them in the first place.

If men grew to resemble their fathers (though Max had been a mother's boy), then perhaps it was as well that she wouldn't be around to witness his old age.

But where *would* she be?

'Is your father very upset?'

Mother's boy he might have been, engaged for most of his adult life in a power struggle with 'that contrary old bastard' who'd hung on grimly to the reins of the firm's government long after he was capable of running it efficiently (so often Max had nearly, but not quite, told him what he could do with the business – caution had always prevailed), but your father was your father and reactions to a parent's death not always predictable.

Again Adam shrugged. A give-nothing-away gesture probably appropriate as a description of his father's undoubtedly buttoned-up reaction to the news. A family trait: Max translated all his pain and hurt and disappointment into irritability and various sorts of obsessive behaviour, just as his father had taken refuge in illness. Neither of them had seemed able to express themselves either spontaneously or directly (and perhaps the same was true of Adam). David, thank God, was different.

As if in telepathic response to her thoughts, Adam said, 'Dave rang. He's coming over for the funeral.'

There was a pang of jealousy: he couldn't ring *me*, but she suppressed it. She said, '*You're* going as well?'

'Yes,' he said, surprised that she'd asked. She didn't want to indulge cynicism, but wondered if the funeral happened to coincide with a double Maths period or some other, equally resistible, lesson. Or had Max recognised the need for a public display of family unity and insisted? She suspected that one of the causes of the distress that had been provoked by her leaving was the realisation that what had been kept determinedly private must now become common knowledge; he'd rather have endured misery than admit to the world that his marriage had failed. It was a measure of the ill-feeling that was directed towards her that, now, he preferred to let it be known that they were separated, when a phone call could have ensured her presence at the funeral and silenced the speculative tongues.

A girl cleared away their empty cups and then began to swab at the table with a dirty cloth. Adam zipped his jacket, reached down for his case. 'Better get off,' he said.

'Just a minute. There's something I have to say to you.'

He looked up to the ceiling and down to the floor, he inspected the red checked tablecloth and the glass ashtray, he read the fairly unappetising menu and then rubbed at a mark on the plastic wallet in which it was encased, while she tried to pick the words appropriate for telling your son that the lover you'd left him for had now left you.

'Oh Adam, it isn't that I want to drive a wedge between you and your father, it isn't that at all. I just somehow thought that . . . took it for granted . .'. I miss you terribly . . .'

'Gotta go.'

She saw from the look on his face that she'd be unwise to push it. Besides, how could he abandon his father now, in his hour of need? She wanted to say, 'I'm bereaved too. It doesn't necessarily take a death to confer that status.' She said, instead, 'Will you tell your father I'll ring him?'

But she didn't. She didn't ring anybody. Her hand went out towards the instrument a score of times during the two days that were left to her before Livingstone was due to leave, but, for a long time, she desisted. Tuesday evening was terrible; she paced the floor. 'I'll ring you before I go.' 'Don't.' 'No?' 'No.' Surely he'd realise that she couldn't possibly have meant what she said? Surely he couldn't leave her for six weeks without checking that she was safe and well?

'I'll ring at eight,' she told herself, and then, 'I'll ring at nine.' In just a few hours' time she wouldn't be able to ring at all. She felt that if she could just hold out until – say – eleven, then the desire would evaporate, the temptation be conquered. She paced and she drank. She could feel her skin prickling and her heart thudding. She was sweating freely. It wasn't stress that short-ened your life, she suspected, but ambivalence.

At five to twelve she dialled his number and got the engaged signal. She got the engaged signal at one-thirty too and again at two-fifteen and knew that he must have taken the phone off the hook. Then, despite herself, she fell asleep and stayed asleep until the alarm awoke her at seven-thirty. And found that, during the hours of sleep, something had happened, some kind of resignation process must have been at work and the impulse to contact him had gone temporarily into abeyance. Before – as long as she knew there was a date to look forward to: the date he was due to move in with her – she had been prepared to cross the days off the calendar quite patiently. Was it that now she was willing to do the same thing, to count off the forty-two days that must elapse before he returned from America and discovered – or not – that absence had been the begetter of fondness?

At nine she rang the Poly and spoke to Hilary Roberts' punk assistant, told her to relay a message to the effect that, due to a death in the family, she wouldn't be coming in to work today. At eleven she left the house. As she walked down the drive she thought she heard a phone ringing and raced back, but by the time she'd got indoors it had stopped. Or had only been ringing in her imagination.

The fog was patchy but, at its worst, worse than it had been the day before. Surely planes would be grounded? The buses were only just about running; she'd intended to go to the cathedral, but thought, at this rate, it would be all over bar the shouting by the time she arrived, so decided instead to make straight for the cemetery. Staring out of the bus window, as it made its agonisingly slow progress to the suburbs, she was reminded of those sort of vampire films that featured graveyards with their own (apparently) microcosmic climates: characters walked out of bright sunshine into a zone of endless twilight where, at critical moments, shreds of drifting fog obscured the doings beside or within the burial plots.

Those fictional conditions prevailed in the real-life cemetery (the real-death cemetery?): one minute you could see to the farthest landmark on the horizon, the most distant of the granite memorials, the next, it was difficult to discern the features of the weeping cherubim that marked the grave next door. People disappeared and reappeared with a disconcerting suddenness. The volume of the presiding cleric's voice waxed and waned as though he were speaking through a faulty microphone. She took refuge behind an angel's wings and, from this vantage point, spied upon her family.

David, she saw, was desperately in need of a decent haircut. His hair was that curly untameable sort that requires the regular attention of a skilled barber if it is not to resemble that of an aborigine caught in the middle of an electric storm. At least he'd had a shave. So had Adam, judging by the sticking plaster on his chin. Probably quite unnecessarily. Part of male perversity: when they didn't need to shave, they wanted to; as soon as shaving became necessary on a regular basis, they didn't want to.

And that didn't just apply to shaving.

The fog rolled across the fields, obliterating everything in its path with a flannel-like opacity. And then, as the coffin was lowered into the ground, it lifted and she saw Max – head bowed, hands folded in front of him – biting his lip and blinking his eyes. The relationship between himself and his father might have fallen short of the ideal, but the loss of a parent made you face up to the chilling realisation that you could no longer take refuge in childishness. Her relationship with her own parents had also been far from ideal – they had always given her the impression that they congratulated themselves upon having adapted astonishingly well, considering that a child of the menopause was the last thing they had bargained for – and yet their deaths had devastated her, had driven her, panic-stricken, towards the haven represented by Max's outstretched arms.

Suddenly he looked up and straight at her. She saw that Adam had noticed her, and David too. And others: distant relations, slight acquaintances. She heard that unmistakeable rustling that issues from people turning simultaneously to one another to point out some item of mutual interest, heard the low featureless murmuring typical of the exchange of scandalous information.

Max leaned forward and gathered up a handful of loose earth and scattered it on the coffin. It hit the surface with a peculiarly – and appropriately – dead sound.

The boys, respectively blushing and grimacing, followed suit. Others queued to copy them. And then the assembly began to disperse. She walked back to the chapel where the cars were parked, turned and watched them approaching her, three abreast: the family from whose bosom she had wantonly excluded herself. As Adam and David caught sight of her they began to slow down. Max carried on walking, up to her and past her, without acknowledging her presence by the slightest altera-tion in his expression or the merest gesture. He carried on walking until he reached the foremost of the waiting limousines and then he got into it. She stood rooted to the spot. It was cold but her face burned with the humiliation of so public a rejection. 'What you are doing is unforgivable,' Max had said, that last day, when she'd made him beg, only so that he might suffer the humiliation of rejection.

She turned from a battery of curious stares as other people reached the cars. Until now she'd always believed that 'unforgiv-able' was an adjective applicable only to other people's behaviour;

it came as a shock as disorienting as when the fog lifted unexpectedly to reveal all that it had obscured, to discover that the mere fact of who she was in relation to him was no guarantee, any longer, of special dispensation.

9

'Fucksake,' David said. 'It's not such a big deal.'

She hushed him, imagining that if his language were overheard, those overhearing it would be as shocked as she pretended to be.

'No need to make a crisis out of a drama,' David said, helping himself liberally from the bottle of wine that sported a label so obscure that it was either extraordinarily good or fearsomely bad – Christina had not yet tasted it.

'It's the other way round, isn't it: a drama out of a crisis?'

'Well, whatever. I just don't see the need for all the histrionics. It's not so uncommon, is it? I read somewhere that one family in five is now headed by a single person. It's the traditional nuclear family, you know: two adults, two and a half kids and a gerbil, that's in danger of ceasing to be the norm.'

Having her own argument reinforced did not make it seem any more convincing. The mere reduction of undesirable social phenomena to statistics did nothing to cancel out their undesirability.

'It's not me. It's *him*. You saw him. He walked past me as though I didn't exist.' (And so, taking his cue, had Adam. Only David had stopped, glanced from them to her and then said, 'Look, I've got to go to this post-funeral thrash thing, but I can meet you afterwards.' 'Come to the flat,' she'd said. But he said it was a bit far and he hadn't much time. Couldn't they make it somewhere more central? So they'd compromised at Klosters.)

'Do you call that rational, civilised behaviour?' she asked him now. 'Do you think there was any need for it?'

'Pride, innit? I mean, the guy thinks he has a point.'

She took up her glass and drank from it. The wine tasted of fruit and earth and iron filings and she was no nearer to appreciating its quality, or lack of it, than before. It was a complimentary bottle, sent over at Gwen's instigation, therefore unlikely to be actually poisonous. On the other hand – knowing Gwen – it was equally unlikely that she'd miss the chance to combine an expansive gesture with getting rid of an item from an unpopular line.

'And Adam? You might think your father has a point, but there was no need for Adam to follow suit.'

'I don't think the silly old sod's got a point – well, not one to justify acting like a drama queen. *He* thinks so, I said. It's all right this, isn't it?' he remarked, enthusiastically draining the bottle. 'Will she send another one over, do you think? Is she getting to be less of a miserable old cow in her old age? Adam?' he said, in response to her prompting. 'Oh, he's just acting monkey to the organ-grinder.'

'Is he?'

'Yeah. It's his normal cut-off-his-nose-to-spite-his-face routine. He takes after the old feller in that respect. Perhaps spoiled children are all alike. It's your own fault, you know.'

He said it so earnestly, obviously quite unaware of the offensive smugness of his tone, that it was impossible to take offence. 'It doesn't help to be told,' she said, smiling.

And he smiled back. 'Fair enough,' he replied and stretched out his legs and kicked over a stool. She saw Gwen, who had come into the bar to consult with her manager, glance across with a very sharp look which did not waver until he'd clumsily righted it.

'These places are designed for dwarfs.'

In restoring the stool to upright order he'd almost sent an ashtray flying.

'So I should be all right,' she said. And he said, at the same time, 'So you should be all right.' And they laughed together. He'd been so much taller than her for such a long time that it had become a standing joke. Because of his size she had found it difficult to continue to treat him (as she continued to treat Adam) as a child.

'It's so good to see you.'

He had a way of divesting everything of any melodramatic overtones. In his company, she felt that there wasn't anything so terrible that it couldn't be coped with, overcome: faithless lovers, unforgiving husbands, unnatural sons.

'Posh, this place, innit?' he said, examining the ashtray, which was green and gold like everything else and fashioned in the shape of an ivy leaf, so elegant that smokers might be deterred from depositing ash in it. Perhaps this was intentional, Gwen being as rabidly anti-smoking as only a recently cured addict can be.

She nodded across at them and spoke to the manager who, apparently as a result of this conversation, brought them over another bottle and two dishes of lasagne. 'A lovely wine,' he said, busy with a napkin at the neck of it. 'One of Mrs Swallow's best.'

So. Humbled further by having to admit to herself that she possessed a palate incapable of distinguishing between the choice grape and its inferior relations, Christina raised a hand in Gwen's direction as a sort of belated recognition of a generosity above and beyond the call of duty. For probably, in Gwen's view, generosity had been amply demonstrated by allowing David into Klosters in the first place: he looked as though he might be more at home in a cardboard box under Charing Cross arches.

'M'dame,' murmured the manager, so young and self-consciously handsome and discreetly up-to-the-minute in terms of trouser-bottom width and cuff-buttons and hairstyle. David looked at him in disgust, but refrained from comment. She remembered him telling her about being approached in a bar when he was younger by a homosexual and how he'd been so quick to reassure her that her worried reaction was quite unnecessary: 'It's OK. All you do, if they ask, is say, "I'm not gay."'

How simple it was. And if only it applied to every other aspect of a relationship: 'I'm sorry, I'm not gay/capable of deep feeling/tough enough to cope with rejection.'

David ate his lasagne rapidly and with relish. And then he ate hers. Even though he'd just come from a table that no doubt groaned with post-funeral meats. 'It's sound, this,' he said. 'Did that peculiar old bird cook it? Is she still around?'

'Corky? Oh yes.'

'Is she as weird as ever? Always looked to me like someone who might chew baccy.'

'On the subject of chewing,' she said, fixing him with that sort of cautionary maternal eye that says: Come on now, calm down, you're getting silly, 'I hope you're feeding yourself properly.'

It was impossible to tell whether he had lost or gained weight. For that, it would have been necessary for him to remove the baggy army-surplus shirt and the outsize holey sweater and the designed-for-Primo-Carnera greatcoat.

He pulled his aren't-over-protective-mothers-a-complete-pain-in-the-arse face, and then he said, 'They've opened a great new kebab house near us. They've got this sign on the wall: "Knapkins, five pence extra."' He bent and wrote it on one of Gwen's, which was linen and would cost considerably more than five pence were you to be obliged to replace it.

He regaled her with similar anecdotes: the solecisms committed by the anxious-to-integrate members of ethnic minorities who composed, in the area where he lived, the majority; the impressive, but somehow sinister, orthodoxy of those more anxious to retain their own cultural identity: the Fundamentalist Muslims, the Hassidic Jews. It was only when the manager placed a portion of cheesecake at his elbow and he turned his attention to that, that she was able to steer the conversation in the direction that, however unappealing, she knew it must go.

'You're not upset then?'

If loss of appetite characterised the condition, then he was not upset.

'What about?'

'About the separation,' she said patiently.

'Separation? That's a polite way of putting it, isn't it? I thought you'd waltzed off and left him. That's what he says.'

'What else does he say?'

'Not a lot. I asked him why you'd gone – '

He paused while he took another mouthful and chewed and swallowed it and she wondered if any shred of loyalty had survived her desertion.

' – and he said about some bloke. Is that right?'

'There was,' she said, staring at her hands which were clasped in her lap. 'There isn't any more.'

And realised that, now she'd said it, she could no longer continue to believe that it wasn't true.

'And you were going to – set up with him?'

'*I* thought so.'

Being of that unworldly turn of mind that leads you to believe that life is like a certain sort of book: that, having put up with your unsatisfactory lot for the requisite number of years, you were then rewarded with a happy ending.

'So what you gonna do now?'

'I don't know. What do *you* think I should do?'

'God, don't ask me. It's your life, isn't it?'

Yes, it is, but it's out of control: my lover has rejected me, my husband won't even acknowledge my existence, I can't afford to keep my flat on, and the only way I can ensure a few hours' sleep at night is to drug myself with alcohol.

Gwen came across to inform them that Klosters was now closing and, loath though she was to turn them out, she had the licence to consider.

'How are you getting on with your studies, David?' she asked. It was not so much a genuine enquiry as Gwen in condescending mood, but David, unlike Adam, who'd flush up and stare at the floor, was a match for that. He smiled cheerfully and said, 'They're going OK, I think. At any rate, I'm on to joined up writing next term.'

Gwen was hazily aware that this response was more in the nature of cheek than friendly quip. The voluptuous curves of her mouth disappeared as she drew her lips tight against her teeth, the pupils of her eyes narrowed to cat-like slits. 'Well I wouldn't know about that,' she said. 'Some of us,' she said, changing pronouns to emphasise her displeasure, 'never had the chance.'

The way she said it made you think that it was lack of opportunity, not lack of intellect, that had excluded her from higher education.

She turned from them to bestow a proprietor's smile of recognition upon a departing customer: a trainee estate agent with a smart suit and unlimited prospects, as different as could be from this scruffy creature; she'd seen them more well-groomed asleep on park benches.

She turned back. 'How long are you staying?' she asked. 'How long do they let you out for?'

David's eyes sparkled. He enjoyed a bit of bare-knuckle sparring as much as Gwen did. 'Parole note expires at midnight,' he said. 'Not that I'd really be missed. I'm only wasting the tax payers' money, after all.'

Christina felt bound to interject before there was open warfare. 'How long *are* you staying?' she asked. Perhaps she could just afford to take him out for a meal tonight. Greek. He liked Greek. She didn't, but that was of no consequence. And besides, Greek was cheap.

'I'm off now. Well, as soon as I've picked up my bag and said *ciao* to the old feller.'

Gwen moved away, failing to suppress an unpleasant little smile. Christina felt deflation as a definite physical sensation, as though a vital structural part of her anatomy had been removed and all the rest had caved in. 'Do you have to?' she pleaded.

'We do have lectures and stuff, you know. I can't sag off indefinitely.'

'One *day* can't make much difference.'

'Don't go on,' he said, snappishly for him.

'I thought you might have had time for a word with Adam, try to make him understand. He's so very hostile.'

'Little jerk,' David said, and yawned widely. 'He'll grow up. I expect. Although he's taking a hell of a time about it.'

'I can't wait for him to grow up,' she said, and thought: *how* will he grow up?

'I'll write to him,' David said, 'if it'll make you happy.'

She nodded. She could do no other. But she knew that it was about as likely as Livingstone changing his mind, as Max offering her forgiveness, as the proprietors of the kebab house becoming faultlessly fluent in English.

'It's dead simple actually,' the punk girl said. Her vermilion Mohican projected from her shaved dome. Not a hair of it stirred, not a strand detached itself from the moulded perfection of the structure as she leaned over Christina's shoulder, punching keys, awaiting response, tearing off sections of print-out as it came tumbling forth, with an insouciance typical of those for whom technology holds no terrors.

'I think that's where you were making your mistake,' she said, 'right at the beginning, when you were logging in. Mind you, the bugger's always on the blink. We need new equipment. Whole bleedin' lot's about ten years behind the times.'

Today she wore a bracelet formed from a padlock and chain. It made a noise like an old-fashioned horror film soundtrack whenever it came into contact with the keyboard. When she gave the paper-feed a thump – as she frequently did, stating that technological progress was no bleedin' use if it was sabotaged at every turn by mechanical failure – there was a sound reminiscent of a hundred hauntings.

'Right, well, if you've got the hang, I'll get off.'

The punk girl, whose name was Jinx (surely it wasn't, Christina thought, any more than Corky's was Corky?), had said that computers weren't really her bag. Nevertheless she demonstrated an enviable command of the knowledge required to make them work.

'Can't you hang on just till we see if it's doing what it should?' Christina pleaded. Though this was only a preliminary, hypothetical run-through, she felt as nervous as a bride at a wedding rehearsal.

Jinx glanced at the clock. 'Well, awright,' she said. 'I'm meeting my bloke at half-four though, so I can't piss about too long.'

She hitched up her tight little leather skirt and perched herself on the edge of a table. She wore the sort of black fishnet stockings that used to feature largely in fifties' films involving French tarts.

'Mind if I 'ave a fag?'

She rolled one with a sleight of hand almost as impressive as that demonstrated by Corky (whose expertise had probably improved ten-fold since taking up residence with Gwen: smoking was meant to be restricted to her own room, but Corky could have a fag rolled and lit and concealed in a cupped hand behind her back before Gwen's nose had started to twitch).

The computer terminal made mysterious groaning noises as though it was about to bring forth, which indeed it did: great screeds of flimsy paper spewed out of it, curled over and flopped on to the floor. Christina started forward to detach sections of the print-out, but Jinx shook her head: leave it, she said, until it was finished, otherwise she might have to spend the rest of the day trying to figure out the order in which it had arrived.

Eventually the paper-feed stuttered to a halt and together they tamed the torrent of print. 'Thanks very much for your help,' Christina said. 'I expect you think I'm awfully dim.'

'Nah. Better, innit, than having to ask Our Leader?'

Christina thought she meant Stanley, the official computer-room technician who appeared to hate computers, and computer-users, and females, but most particularly female computer-users, and rarely responded to queries with anything more enlightening than a grunt from behind Page Three. But she didn't. 'Herr Doktor Goebbels,' she said. 'Hilary.'

'Ah.'

'She can be really tight,' Jinx said, picking a hole in her fishnet. 'A real pain.'

She looked to Christina for corroboration of this opinion. 'Well,' Christina said diplomatically, feeling that, whatever her attitude towards Hilary Roberts, old acquaintance at least ought to prompt a measure of loyalty.

'Weren't you at college together or something?' Jinx said. 'Was she always the same? Or did she get to be like it after the kid died?'

'Which kid died?'

'She had this kid apparently. It got meningitis or something gruesome like that and died. She went a bit potty afterwards – well, you would, wouldn't you – even her? She comes over all peculiar now if you even talk about kids for any length of time. Poor old Gav can't even have his at the house. He has to visit them on the sly.'

'Gav?'

'Her bloke, Gavin. Humanities. Little weedy feller, looks as though he's only got one in him and that one's holding him together. But he's got about two dozen kids – well, five or something. He's divorced and they're with their mother and old Hil threatens to throw a wobbly if he wants to bring them home for their teas even. Bloody 'ell,' she said, glancing up at the clock. 'Is that the time? I'll get battered.' She grabbed her chain-festooned leather jacket and ran, knock-kneed, towards the door. 'See ya, Chris. Don't go mad and tear paper.'

The machine had disgorged another length. Carefully, with regard for order and precedence, she detached it and folded it. Well fancy, she thought, as she gathered and folded, fancy Hilary Roberts having a child and losing it. She remembered the Beecham's Pills in the college bathroom and the tears and the fear and the guilt over a child that didn't exist. Just one of life's little ironies, presumably, a dress-rehearsal for the real thing.

Stanley stuck his grizzled head round the door. 'I'm locking up now,' he said, 'so you'll have to move yourself. My oppo's not due on till six and I'm not leaving you in here.'

It was the greatest number of words that he'd addressed to her at any one time, although he managed not to look at her once while he was doing so.

'Let's be having you then,' he said.

She was quite impressed: he had taken charmlessness almost into the realms of art form; it must have involved years of practice. 'I'd finished anyway,' she said haughtily, gathering up her paper and stuffing it into her briefcase.

There was mist this evening rather than fog: the street lamps were haloed, every outline blurred, the pavements shiny as wet-look PVC. She'd been wearing a wet-look PVC mac the first time she'd met Max: a terrible, tasteless garment, cracked at the seams, sporting huge silver buttons – it was the fashion. Despite the fashion, Max must have found her attractive. He had walked with her along the hospital corridor and down the stairs. When they'd reached the car-park he'd offered her a lift. Being a well-brought-up girl she'd refused, but it was winter then and dark and such a long drag to the bus-stop, so the next night, when he'd offered again, she'd accepted.

No one to offer now. She must walk alone down the hill, through the centre of the town and into the after-hours stillness of the deserted business area. Every Thursday evening there was a full meeting for members of The System; the flu epidemic had meant cancellation for the last couple of weeks, but now the flu epidemic was on the wane and life had returned to normal and part of normal life was Christina's attendance at these meetings so that she could observe and note down the pattern of interpersonal relations that prevailed.

Anticipating a healthy attendance, she had brought a very large exercise book in which diagrams of group structure and performance, of decision-making hierarchies and amounts of dominant and submissive eye contact could be set out. But the room was not crowded. Seated around the table were Kenneth, Colette (in her capacity as taker-of-the-minutes; Don didn't like her coming out of an evening now she was getting on – you know – blush, moue, grimace; it wasn't a very nice area, this) and half a dozen others, some of whom she'd met briefly in passing or spoken to on the telephone, others who were complete strangers.

Introductions were performed. Here were: John and Norman, Maureen and Linda, Jim and Klaus and, last but not least,

Robin, the Rev. Robin, with whom Kenneth shared so many long and intense telephone conversations.

'How nice,' he said, bending to look intently into her face as though first acquaintance could yield evidence of her private self if he looked hard enough. His hand was warm and slippery. He reminded her of a cross between Uriah Heep and Mister Spock (the alien, not the child-care expert) what with his insinuating damp handshake and the shape of his ears, which tapered, pixielike, in miniature replication of his head, which also tapered gradually to a halt and, with its loosely-woven, coarse-stranded covering of hair, put her in mind of a coconut.

'Kenneth has mentioned you,' he said, and Kenneth looked up and they exchanged a smile. They wore matching rugby jerseys – Robin was obviously the sort of clergyman who believed in mufti whenever possible – the only difference being that his was cleaner.

He and the others composed the (self-appointed) committee of The System, being those of the membership who bothered to turn up and who had therefore, by default, come to regard themselves as being in charge.

This informality extended as far as lack of agenda: if someone had a point, he or she raised it. The Chair alternated, from week to week, between members. Consequently, a combination of weak Chair and loud voice could result in one pet topic being debated all night long.

But tonight was something of a crisis meeting. By the end of the six-monthly funding period the Standish Trust had to be persuaded to renew its financial backing: there was rent to be paid, and wages, advertising costs and printing. The very existence of The System was at stake and they couldn't afford to fart about, as Norman said. He was a very big man with a very loud voice who thenceforward appointed himself leader and hunted out a piece of chalk and wrote 'Business' on the black-board in big letters, underlined it, ordered Colette to copy it down, and then proceeded to outline a list of subjects for discussion, six in all, but each so full of sub-sections and extra clauses that the chance of debating them within the space of two and a half hours seemed very slim indeed.

These impressive gestures having been made, the meeting then degenerated into what, Christina suspected, was the usual free for all. Norman had a loud voice and wanted to discuss, principally, The System's main project: clearing a council-donated area of wasteland and transforming it into a landscaped garden. (Norman was, by trade, a landscape gardener.) John (who worked for Norman), a young man with a vicious squint and the sort of stammer that meant that his sentences were always finished for him by whoever happened to be the least patient member of any group he was part of, supported him. As did Jim, who had come straight off shift and still wore his bus-driver's uniform. But Klaus had a loud voice too and he wanted to concentrate upon the performance of the resource-exchange scheme (the cornerstone upon which, after all, the organisation was founded) and Klaus had the support of Maureen and Linda, middle-aged twins distinguishable only by the different-coloured plastic slides that held swathes of thin hair off their broad vacant foreheads and allowed the residue to fall forward over the opposite eye *à la* Veronica Lake.

Robin had the loudest voice of all and used its stentorian powers to drown out everyone else while he picked up on the most niggling, tedious details of whatever happened to be under discussion. Robin, nit-picking, hair-splitting, logic-chopping, in that resonant, round-vowelled, just-gargled-with-port-wine voice, Robin, employing his though-I-wear-a-dog-collar (but only when obliged to) I'm-just-an-ordinary-bloke-like-you tones of persuasion, was sufficient to bring on a very severe headache. Christina found two elderly and dubious-looking aspirins at the bottom of her bag and swallowed them down when the meeting adjourned for coffee. Mostly she tried to shut out his droning by concentrating on adorning her diagrams with intricate doodling – they needed some adornment being, in the main, sadly lacking in complexity: three dominant nuclei: Norman, Klaus and Robin, each with its attendant satellites.

Satellite singular, in Robin's case: Kenneth was uncharacteris-tically quiet, speaking when called upon to do so but otherwise lost, it seemed, in admiration. He hung on to Robin's every word, his eyes followed Robin's every pulpit-theatrical gesture. Lovelorn, Christina would have supposed, though Robin was, apparently, possessed of wife and children: he had offered their services as horticultural labourers in Norman's garden.

Only once did Kenneth venture an unsolicited comment: they had been discussing the intransigence of the resources committee of the City Council. Klaus was all for refurbishing a disused café near the Pier Head and using it as a base to attract youngsters to the scheme – young blood was very conspicuous by its absence. A couple of juke-boxes and a pin-table machine were all that were required. (Christina saw Robin shaking his head ruefully: all the pin-tables and juke-boxes in Christendom could not attract young people to anything that smelled of community service; if they were that way inclined, they did it anyway.) The Council however refused to allow the building to reopen as a café, the relevant regulations having changed. No doubt it would be left to rot and they'd end up demolishing it. Typical, everyone agreed. 'And they have the cheek to call *us* barmy,' Kenneth said.

She didn't know whether he meant Us The System or Us The Ratepayers, or a different Us altogether.

After coffee (pink hairslide Maureen made it, green hairslide Linda cleared it away), Christina was prevailed upon to deliver a brief account of the progress of her work to date. She did so, though there was nothing much to tell; the technical details of pilot study and questionnaire construction would hardly satisfy their desire to know whether the scheme stood a chance of surviving. She thought, as she spoke, it's a wonder that I have *anything* to report. But, somehow, she was managing to go through the motions, had done two more interviews that morning, one with a tongue-tied school-leaver who didn't appear to have an opinion about anything, least of all non-profit-making transactions, the other with an unemployed accountant (she had thought that of all those least likely to be casualties of the recession, accountants would be top of the list, wondered if schizophrenia might be a limiting factor: his eyes darted, his hands trembled, he spoke of 'them').

It was swiftly becoming apparent that membership of The System fell into three categories: there were the constitutional joiners of any organisation formed, there were those who used it on a purely practical basis: having their gardens dug or their gas fires exchanged for two-speed electric drills, and there were those – in the main social inadequates – who looked to it for provision of everything that normal society withheld from them: friendship, status, a sense of belonging.

'Nothing definite to tell us yet then?' Norman enquired.

'Not really.'

'Oh well,' he said and ploughed on to the next sub-section of

Clause Four. By the time they'd reached Any Other Business, Colette had filled pages with her neat shorthand notes, a great many resolutions had been proposed, including a higher budget allocation for advertising and the organisation of some sort of social event which would combine recruitment with fund-raising, but not one definite plan of action had been agreed upon. Consensus was only reached when it was suggested that the meeting be brought to an end.

Maureen and Linda folded their scarves, schoolchild-fashion, across their chests and tucked them into the waistbands of their navy-blue, accordion-pleated, polyester skirts, picked up their leather-look handbags and left, assuring each other that they were in plenty of time for the bus. 'Heaps of time, bags of it,' said Jim-the-bus-driver with the sort of condescending jocularity adopted by one in the know. Norman gave John a lift home in his Range-Rover. Robin and Kenneth put on their matching anoraks over their matching rugby shirts. Robin's wife was providing a little light supper. Would Christina care to join them? Christina politely declined and then pretended to be deep in conversation with Colette on the subject of epidural anaesthesia.

But fascinating though this discussion was, Colette was obliged to tear herself away from it. The meeting had finished late and Don would be freezing to death out there. She'd told him time without number to come up and wait in the office but he was so shy . . .

'Are yez right then?' enquired the cleaning woman, rattling her mop in the bucket in an aggressive fashion. 'I've not got all night.'

She waited impatiently for them to go. The state of it! her look said: that daft little pregnant one acting like the Virgin Mary with knobs on, taking a fit if you so much as pulled your ciggies out of your pinny pocket, threatening to report you. As if nobody had had a kid before.

If she'd seen the way that Colette's husband enquired after her welfare as anxiously as if his last sighting of her had been a good deal less recent than a couple of hours ago, she'd have been even more scathing.

'This is Don,' said Colette superfluously, when she had finished reassuring him as to the non-recurrence of her backache and legache and digestive disturbances. 'My husband,' she said, in the manner of Cinderella introducing the Prince.

Though there the comparison ended. Don was short and squat and unpleasing of countenance. It was as if all his features had undergone a slight but significant shift away from symmetry: eyes a few centimetres too close together, too little space between lower lip and chin, too much from upper lip to base of nostrils, the end of his meagre moustache projecting fractionally further beyond one side of his mouth than it did on the other. He wore a prep-schoolboy's navy-blue belted gaberdine raincoat and a flat cap, quartered and topped with a button, which reminded Christina of a hot-cross bun.

She tried to correct this increasing tendency to judge by appearances: asymmetrical features, hair like coconut matting, complexions resembling badly-hung beef – none of these physical defects had anything to do with what lay beneath. Or vice-versa. You had only to take Max, or Livingstone. Or even Gwen: exterior like a ripe peach; bite into it too enthusiastically and you could break your teeth on the stone.

'We go up here for the number seventeen,' he was saying, in his timid little voice, Colette's husband, Donald Donaldson. She'd marvelled at his parents' lack of imagination, but Colette had explained that there'd been no responsible parents, unimaginative or otherwise; he'd been taken in, nameless, by a Catholic orphanage and the Fathers had christened him.

They stood at the corner of the street: the Donaldsons, arms around each other's waists, bound for the bus-stop, Christina headed for the train. (The bus passed nearer to the flat than did the train, but the walk from the station involved more brightly-lit streets.) 'Any luck with the job-hunting?' she asked. He'd been a van-driver for the Imperial Dry Cleaners, Colette had said, but had been laid off. He had his Heavy Goods, Colette had said, emitting a little glow of pride in his achievement, but jobs like that demanded long-distance travel and he refused to consider it while she was – you know.

He shook his head and looked at the ground as though his lack of employment could be attributed in some way to lack of effort rather than being a consequence of living in a deliberately and systematically job-starved area of the country.

They trod carefully away, shoulder to shoulder, hip to hip. Peculiar, they might be, odd-looking, but at least they had each other. And that was surely preferable – so long as you were content with oddness and peculiarity – to wending your solitary way home, past the pub on the corner where you and your lover had sat together on so many occasions, exchanging the sort of eye contact that didn't need to be analysed but transmitted messages more effectively than any amount of verbal communication.

This pub, that corner, those streets – a dozen popular songs testified to the fact that, however much she vowed to pull herself together and try to get on with her crippled life, the pain would persist.

She walked blindly, automatically, and found that she'd reached the ticket-barrier in the station. At the same instant it dawned on her that she'd left her briefcase behind. And her briefcase contained not only the computer print-out and the notes that she'd intended to type up when she got back to the flat, but also her train ticket.

The cleaning woman would, surely, still be in residence, however cursorily she attended to her duties? She was, reading the *Star* with her feet up, a mug of tea at her elbow and a cigarette smouldering in a polish-tin lid. She glanced scornfully across at Christina, waited until she'd ascertained that the case was no longer beside the chair where she'd left it, allowed her to panic: cheque book, banker's card, oh-my-God, and then produced it from some hidey-hole with the sanctimonious assertion that some would lose their heads were they not attached, and yon bag was but a quarter of a hour away from being deposited with the busies at the Bridewell.

Vicious old cow, thought Christina, running down the stairs and slamming the door behind her. The sweat of panic lay sticky on her skin, her pulse beat twenty to the dozen.

How dark it seemed, darker than before. She tucked the case under her arm and set off down the alley. There were steel caps fixed to the heels of her boots. They gave her footsteps a precise, confident ring. Beware, they said. Don't try it, they said, just don't you try it. Or did they simply betray the presence of a lone woman in a dark deserted place?

There was a sound from a doorway. And a dark shape that, amoeba-like, changed its outline as she approached it: loomed, expanded, receded and contracted. To proceed or retreat?

Adrenalin was being pumped in great spurts through her bloodstream, her heart was bursting beneath the onslaught of its accelerated rhythm, but the logical, decision-making part of the brain was paralysed, condemned her to frozen passivity.

The shape put forth a flurry of protuberances, separated, became two entities, emerged from the doorway and went on its way, slightly less entwined, as a young man and a girl. She walked behind them, pent-up breath escaping from her lungs in a great audible sigh, pulse rate decelerating, erected body hair slowly beginning to relax. It was obvious that a grip – and a very firm one at that – was needed if she wasn't to turn into a complete nervous wreck.

~ 10 ~

Janet Holloway said, 'We got this garbled story from Alison Harrington, but you know what she's like. Why on earth didn't you *say*? We could hardly believe it. You *are* a dark horse.'

Felicity Munro (the one who'd been having lunch with Christina when Louise Livingstone passed by their table) said, 'Max hasn't said a dicky-bird. We only knew from Alison Big-Mouth Harrington and somebody seeing this housekeeper-woman going into your house. Peter saw him the other night, Max, said he looked very down in the mouth. You can't help feeling a bit sorry for him, can you, whatever the circumstances?'

So go round there, Christina thought, wipe his tears, Hoover his carpet.

But she couldn't afford to indulge more than the odd fleeting negative feeling towards them in view of the fact that she was seeking their help. It had taken her hours to pluck up the courage to ring them in the first place: friends, she called them: Janet and Felicity, but they weren't the sort of friends you had when you were young, the sort with whom you formed a bond of loyalty so strong that it seemed inconceivable that a mere man could be the agent of its betrayal. At some point, down the years, she had lost the knack of friendship; perhaps it was due to her natural reserve, perhaps it was because Max had never encouraged gregariousness. At any rate, Janet and Felicity were really no more than propinquitous social acquaintances and she could hardly expect them to fall over themselves to offer assistance.

Would they have done so anyway, even if they had been the firmest and fastest of bosom-buddies? She had offended against their code, demonstrated the weakness of the cement that held people together as couples, brought home to them their hypocrisy: they would complain forever about how dissatisfied they were, but when it came to *doing* . . . They were conventional women, conservative, scared. And she knew that nothing existed between them that could be remotely compared to male solidarity: never would a relationship with a man be put in jeopardy for the sake of demonstrating moral support for a woman friend. There was a kind of grudging admiration to be detected in Janet Holloway's tone; Felicity Munro came across as covertly disapproving, but their responses to her plea were identical (though the excuses differed: *so* sorry, but – unfortunately – they found themselves unable – at this particular time – to offer her shelter for the week or so she needed it to allow her to look for alternative accommodation).

'I've my mother-in-law arriving on Monday,' Felicity said. 'God help us all. You don't know how lucky you are in that respect. Well, were . . .' Janet expected the decorators.

'But tell me,' each of them said. 'What's *happened* . . . ?'

She held the telephone receiver at a distance from her ear while first, Janet, and then Felicity, jabbered on. With her free hand she sought for paper and pen in order to write to the landlord giving notice.

She made out a cheque for the rent and did some more sums, but this time the totals always tallied no matter how often she totted up the figures, and the totals meant going into the bedroom that had been destined for Adam but, now, would never be inhabited by him, and dragging down her suitcases from the top of the wardrobe and confronting the inescapable fact that, within a week or so, she must pack her belongings into them and transport them and herself to another address. She was in a mess, wiped out – not only emotionally, but financially too. 'Landing on your arse,' Jumbo, Gwen's father, would have called it. 'Up shit creek without the proverbial,' Corky would have said.

'Gwen,' she said aloud to herself, and then she said, 'Max,' and then she sat down on the edge of the bed and juggled the two names around in her head like ping-pong balls. If she had been loath to ring Janet Holloway and Felicity Munro then how very much more reluctant she was to ring Gwen, who would say, 'I told you so,' longer and louder than anyone else.

And Max? And Winchester Road? There were things she had left behind, things she needed – whatever and wherever her eventual destination might be and lie; he couldn't deny her those.

126

She bought the local paper. The rooms she could afford were, she saw, located for the most part in areas where she would prefer not to live. All the same, she rang four of the advertised numbers. Two of the rooms had been taken; she got no answer from the third, and the fourth brought forth a query as to whether she was in work because, the sharp female voice informed her, 'I don't take DHSS cases.'

'I am not a DHSS case,' she said. An impecunious case, a neurotic case, a hopeless case even, but not yet a case totally dependent upon the state. She put the phone down anyway. Pursuing the matter seemed to demand more energy than she possessed.

Just as she had put off ringing Livingstone until it was too late, so she procrastinated with regard to contacting Gwen. Or Max. It was Tuesday afternoon before the decision was made, and the decision was made by tossing a coin. Gwen. Or Max. Tails. Tails three times. Max, then.

She went straight from work. She took the train. And, already, the landscape seemed unfamiliar. Ten years at the same address and, for a moment, she couldn't remember which way the gate opened, or at which side of the door the bell-push was situated. There was a clump of scabious still blooming in the garden. Baby Adam had planted those seeds, opening his plump fist and broadcasting them with such reckless abandon that she'd doubted whether any would germinate. But they had done. And grown and bloomed and thrived.

Baby Adam, who had clung to her hand, crying, 'Don't leave me.'

It was Adam who opened the door to her. Her legs went weak with relief.

He was dressed for outdoors: the Farah trousers and the Ben Sherman shirt, the Nike trainers and the Lyle and Scott pullover, the regulation bright red woollen scarf tucked into the black kidskin jacket.

'Hello darling,' she said. And then, apprehensively, 'Where's your father?'

'Had to go back to the works. They've a rush order on and there's a union dispute about manning or something.'

'When will he be back?'

'Dunno.'

'Well can I come *in*?'

He started zipping and buttoning his jacket. 'I was just going out,' he said doubtfully. 'It's my guitar lesson.'

'Well, before you go, perhaps you can let me in so that I can wait. I'm not going to steal the silver.'

He shrugged and then flung open the door wide enough to accommodate a harem of estranged wives. 'I'm off then,' he said. 'Oh, by the way, I can't make it tomorrow. We've got this rehearsal for this school concert crap. See you.'

'Adam!'

He was halfway down the drive. He came to an abrupt and histrionic halt. '*Yes?*' he said, with the emphasis of one whose patience is being sorely tried.

'I'll probably see you later, when you get back.'

'Shouldn't think so.'

'Why not?'

'Going out again.'

'Where?'

'Out.'

'Adam! Be careful.'

But he was gone – and it was only then that it dawned on her that he wasn't carrying his guitar case – down the dark, privet-lined street, towards . . . the malevolent Parkinson? Girls? Discos? A pub? Smack City?

Don't even *think* it, she told herself. When David was Adam's age he'd taken to lighting joss sticks in his bedroom and anointing himself with patchouli, assuming that it disguised the faint but unmistakeable musty-sweet aroma that was exuded from his pores and lingered in the atmosphere. Max had threatened to throw him out and, as an assertion of his autonomy, David had climbed on to his motor-bike and roared down the road and stayed away for two nights, the two longest nights of her life, during which she'd had to be forcibly restrained from ringing the police every hour on the hour. (They'd been civil enough but so aggravatingly calm on being informed that he was missing: lads, Mrs Conway, they'd said, went missing all the time.) During the afternoon of the third day, the gesture having been made, he'd returned and apologised.

But Adam wasn't David. And then was not now.

She moved through the house, trailing a hand across the surface of this table, that sideboard (dustless, she saw), lifting a vase that they'd brought back from Greece, riffling the pages of

Jude the Obscure that lay open on top of the bookcase, opening drawers. She was in Adam's room, about to start rummaging, when she heard the sound of a car turning into the drive. In her anxiety to get downstairs before he found out that she'd been snooping, she knocked a beaker full of pens off the desk and had to crawl round the carpet retrieving them. By the time that Max had opened the front door she'd only succeeded in reaching the second-from-bottom step of the stairs and had forgotten to turn off the upstairs lights.

His expression of alarm was replaced by one of extreme distaste. He nodded to himself and said, 'Adam.'

'Well you didn't seriously think that he'd refuse his own mother entry to the house?'

'I didn't think that his mother would have the brass neck to come round here. Though I don't know why I thought that. I wouldn't put anything past you.'

He had not closed the door behind him. Now he opened it wider. He said, 'Well now you've seen whatever it is you wanted to see, I suggest you get going. If you don't mind,' he said, the door in his hand, in the manner of a floorwalker at Lewis's politely informing a lingering customer that the store was about to close.

'Please. I've got to talk to you.'

She waited. When he made no move but stood with one hand on the doorknob and the other pointing out into the night like some Victorian paterfamilias ejecting a disgraced skivvy, she said, 'If you want me to leave, you're going to have to put me out. And I'll make sure the whole neighbourhood knows about it.'

She had no doubt that lace curtains must have been twitching all the way along Winchester Road as she approached the house – well, at least, fully-lined velvets and Habitat blinds and – in the case of the Harringtons, who were renowned for their lack of taste – Dralon.

Max hesitated for a moment and then closed the door. 'Whatever it is,' he said, 'get it said and go. I'm busy.'

'Do we have to stand here?'

Reluctantly, he led her into the sitting-room, sat down primly, knees together, on the sofa, but made no move to take off his overcoat.

'Well, what is it?'

He spoke as though she would have a list of queries drawn up, ready to be presented for his deliberation, much in the way that the union representatives, from whom he'd just returned, had put forward their case. She suspected, from the look on his face (a layer of irritation underlying the layer of irritation attributable to her presence), that they'd won. Or reached a compromise more advantageous to workers than management. It was a bad time to have chosen for confrontation. But then that went for any time at all.

She saw a little spasm of pain cross his face, knew that these combined irritations were causing his digestive tract to respond by releasing great floods of acid to aggravate his ulcer. Who comforted him now, she wondered, if he awoke in the night in pain? Who steamed fish for him and soft-boiled his eggs and stirred pudding rice into milk?

Though she'd never been much of a nurse and it was hypocritical to pretend otherwise. Mostly she'd feigned sleep when he'd woken groaning and clutching at his stomach, and her timing of soft-boiled eggs was not always accurate and she forgot to stir the rice pudding so that an indigestible skin formed on its surface.

He was tapping his foot impatiently, picking imaginary specks of lint from the sleeve of his coat. It was the same coat that he'd worn for the funeral. 'I'm sorry,' she said, 'about your father.'

'You didn't come here just to tell me that?'

No. She searched his face for just the slightest hint that there might be the chance of some give in his rigidity. Vainly. He would regard even the faintest of conciliatory gestures as a demonstration of weakness.

'There are some things of mine that I wanted to collect – well – arrange to be collected. Obviously I can't carry them all myself . . .'

Those were the words that emerged when she opened her mouth. They were not the ones that she had intended to speak. Those words: 'Max, I made a mistake and I've landed on my arse, I'm up shit creek. For the sake of our shared twenty years – let's not call it love, let's not call it anything, but just acknowledge that travelling through two decades together must mean something – reach out a hand and help me; just a hand, that's all'; those words refused to offer themselves up for articulation.

Max said, 'Couldn't he give you a lift then? Or has he got fed up with you already?'

Perhaps somebody had talked: Janet Holloway or Felicity Munro, but that was of no consequence. Better, in a way, if he knew already, ought to make it easier.

But for the life of her she couldn't spit out what she wanted to say. She had to listen to him asking what these things were that she needed and, in response, recite a list of articles that, if she were never to clap eyes on them again, wouldn't cause her a moment's regret.

'And when do you intend to collect them?'

'Whenever it's convenient. Anyway, there are other things to discuss, aren't there?'

'I think we can leave that to the solicitors.'

She heard herself saying, 'Why?' and him replying – as if from a great distance – 'I like to know where I stand.'

'And what about Adam?' she said. She was clutching at straws and she knew it.

'What *about* Adam?'

'It's him I wanted to talk about to you.'

'Talk to you about,' he said, pedantic to the last.

'Oh, does it matter, for God's sake?'

'Yes,' he said, suddenly savage, 'it does matter. It matters to express yourself correctly, do things properly. That's what people like you can't or won't understand. Nothing matters to you, does it, except for your own immediate gratification? You go through life, creating havoc. You think that just because you're you you've some special dispensation to mess up other people's lives with absolute impunity. "Does it matter?" Yes, it matters, because most of the misery in the world is caused by you and your sort.'

'My sort! What about your sort: your cold, grudging, dog-in-the-manger sort? Mean, mean-minded and mean-spirited . . .'

But he was retreating in order to advance: 'Concern for Adam?' he was saying, quietly, mockingly. 'So concerned that you'd abandon him for the chance of an illicit screw with somebody who wanted you, apparently, for that and that only. What happened: found out you were frigid, did he?'

'Frigid?' she shouted. 'What do you mean by that? Just because I didn't want to sleep with you doesn't make me frigid. If you must know, I stopped sleeping with you because you were mean even in bed. You even begrudged sharing your pleasure. Were you afraid that I might get something out of it?'

'As a matter of fact,' he was saying, 'it came as something of a relief to me when I didn't have to go through the motions any more.'

He accompanied the remark with a smile of such unalloyed nastiness that her hand went out automatically to reach for something that could be thrown to wipe it off his face. It found the Greek vase. Her intention was to smash it into a jigsaw on the parquet, but her aim being poor, it landed on the edge of the rug and rolled to rest, quite intact.

He continued to smile, reached down and picked it up and replaced it on the table. He was calm again, cold. She could rage till she fell down in a fit, but he wouldn't rise to the bait. He said, 'Obviously, we can't use the same solicitor, so I suggest you get yourself another one. And now, if you don't mind, I'm expecting an important call . . .'

'*Very* well-bred.'

That had been Jumbo's verdict when Max came to seek from him permission to marry his niece. 'Polite,' Jumbo had said. 'Nice manners.' It went some way towards softening the blow of finding out that the child in his charge was expecting another one.

'I like to know where I stand,' Max repeated. He said it very politely. But wherever that might be, it was, most emphatically, no longer beside her. 'I'll always be here, always,' he'd said, the polite young man, during that insane time after her mother died. 'I'll never leave you, never,' he'd said, when she'd been counting the ever-increasing days of overdue menstruation on the calendar and biting her knuckles.

Only the politeness remained; the young man was dead. The degree of her culpability in the matter of his demise was a moot point; the fact remained that he no longer existed. Politely, he held out her handbag towards her and she felt that there was no logical option left to her but to depart.

Somebody said, 'If you can't afford the rent on your flat, why don't you sub-let part of it?' But a phone call to the landlord established the fact that sub-letting was forbidden. On Wednesday afternoon she cut short an interview in a run-down suburb: shops boarded-up, mis-spelt graffiti everywhere, and went to inspect a room in the near vicinity. All the way home she thought about it and shuddered. It made not the slightest difference when the voice of reason told her that thousands of people lived like that, in rooms furnished with cracked enamel washbasins and chipped two-ring cooking stoves and a meter that devoured fifty pence pieces in exchange for providing a meagre glow of heat, rooms where cat-swinging talents would be tested to the full. She derived no comfort from that knowledge.

But a room like that was all she could afford. Unless she sued Max for maintenance. And she didn't want to do that. Did she? It had all the connotations of yet another irrevocable step. It meant solicitors, divorce proceedings. Didn't it?

She gazed unseeingly out of the bus window. She didn't want to be divorced. Not now. Not now there was no Livingstone. Did she? He might still come back to her. Mightn't he? And she certainly couldn't/didn't want to go home again. Wasn't that the case?

These internal debates were as devoid of resolution as any Thursday meeting of The System's self-appointed committee. But alternatives, she discovered, have a habit of dwindling if procrastination is practised for long enough. She walked down the drive towards the front door. She glanced towards the shrubbery (not because she was afraid of assailants lurking there – it was still light, and only after dark did the fear get a grip – but because she still entertained the forlorn but unquenchable hope that, one day, Livingstone would step out from behind it, his pockets full of sun-ripened fruit, his lips sweet with promises of constancy). She saw neither loiterers with evil intent nor lovers come to pledge themselves; she saw a couple of tea chests which, upon closer inspection, proved to contain those items that she had listed to Max as being the reason for her visit to Winchester Road.

She picked them up, one by one, and replaced them: books, photographs, a pair of flared denim jeans, her grandmother's tea-pot. *The Secret Garden*: 'This prize is awarded to Christina Carroll for good conduct, December 1956'; her Student Union card; her parents' wedding photograph; old Family Allowance books, empty of counterfoils, keys that fitted locks long forgotten, combs and brushes and tarnished powder compacts and jars of Christmas-gift bath crystals, underslips that dated from when skirts were short and when they were long and suspender belts minus suspenders, cheap jewellery and scent of a nose-wrinkling pungency that the boys had brought back as presents from their school holidays. 'Orphaneers' the child David had called them.

Every last fluff-covered article had been cleared from the back of every one of the drawers in those great heavy chests and dressers and tallboys: stubs of lipsticks and depleted matchbooks and 1974 diaries and passport photographs of such ancient vintage that she could scarcely recognise herself; the wedding anniversary gold bracelet and the ring with a glass bead in it ('Is it a diamond?') that the young Adam had won for her in an amusement arcade in Morecambe; her graduation photograph, a book of Green Shield stamps and a voucher to reclaim the cost of one packet of Fairy Snow – he had cleared her out completely.

Hallowe'en. Colette, it was, who looked at the calendar and identified that day as such. Kenneth was preparing himself to read from the Scriptures to the congregation during the following Sunday's All Saints service. They heard him practising: in the loo, or proclaiming to the photocopier. He broke off to rebuke her. 'A stupid heathen belief,' he said. She ignored him, shivered affectedly. 'They get up to all sorts on Hallowe'en round our way,' she said. 'Even worse than normal. Make sure you lock your door,' she told Christina, undoubtedly deriving great satisfaction as the secure are apt to do when cautioning the vulnerable to be on their guard.

'If you believe in all that twaddle,' Kenneth said, 'what's the point of locking your door?'

Had it not been for Colette, she'd never have registered the significance of the date beyond its being the beginning of the countdown to when she must leave the flat. She'd simply have taken her normal alcoholic precautions whilst checking the evening paper and ringing the numbers of the rooms to let. Or, perhaps, she might even have attempted to brace herself to do without the alcohol because there was a chance that alcohol might bring on her period and she wasn't sure that she wanted it to be brought on.

Six days late – this was the first time that she'd acknowledged the fact. Acknowledgement would have meant taking a stance and, in common with every other aspect of her life, she didn't know whether the absence of a period (and all that it entailed) was what she wanted to be the case, or not.

'I always wanted sons.'

They'd always been careful. Pretty careful. Well, to be exact, less careful than they might have been, had they been younger. Fertility waned, did it not? 'I'm thirty-nine,' she reminded herself. 'It is unlikely that only a slight carelessness during that last act of love could have resulted in conception.' Unlikely, but possible.

She found herself walking slowly up staircases, choosing half a pint of milk at lunchtime instead of her usual coffee, working out a date some nine months hence. It used to be the oldest blackmail trick in the book. Twenty years ago when, shame-facedly, she'd had to admit her predicament to Gwen, Gwen had said: 'Did you do it deliberately?' Reliable contraception and easily obtainable abortion and an alteration in social attitudes had changed all that: no man would now feel obliged to marry the woman he'd impregnated. But if it was a man whose wife was barren, who'd always wanted sons . . .? By Christmas, when he was due back from America, she'd be going on for three months, long enough to consider her condition as an established fact, not long enough to make termination of it either difficult or dangerous.

That evening she typed up her interviews, she ate her usual boil-in-the-bag, individual meal, she washed up her plate, she rang up the only two rooms to let that sounded like feasible propositions (the first one had gone and the second was intended solely for male occupation: 'I only take gentlemen') and then, instead of reaching for the corkscrew, as was normally her wont at this time of night, she sat for a long while, gazing into the gas fire's flame, wondering if life or fate or whatever it was could possibly – a second time – have engineered her future by means of making her pregnant.

Her reverie was rudely interrupted by the buzz of the entryphone. She was jerked back from what might be to what was. She jumped a foot and then, as she crossed the room to answer it, she stopped being startled and scared and apprehensive and began to feel a new, unfamiliar sensation and remembered that its name was hope.

There won't be a word of recrimination, she thought, I'll just let him talk and when he's finished I'll say: 'Come on up,' and it'll be just as I meant it to be, after all.

'Yes?' she said, in a mouse's squeak of a voice.

'Go fuck yourself, missis,' said the voice at the other end.

She slammed the phone down and retreated from it as though threat could emerge, physically, along the wire and through the wall. 'Lock your door,' Colette had said. It was locked. But it was only a door, no more unassailable than any other, and outside it somebody uttered obscenities.

The phone buzzed again, continued to buzz. Ridiculously, listening to that seemed less bearable than hearing the message that it heralded. A minute or two of it was all she could stand and then she moved towards it on trembling legs and picked it up and another voice said – shouted – it made her eardrum cringe: 'Fuck off, cunt!'

They were down there, behind the shrubbery, where first Livingstone had stood and then the tea chests, youths, out to cause mischief, their viciousness as unspecific as their obscenities were spontaneous. She turned off the light and looked from behind the edge of the curtain and saw movement among the still laurels.

A door between them and her, a stout door. Silly kids, harmless. The phone buzzed again. And again. She could have lifted it off the hook, she could have rung the police, except that fear had immobilised her. She crouched in the middle of the carpet, hands clasped around her knees, each breath having to fight for its existence against the competition of a thundering heartbeat.

And then, suddenly, fear was superseded by rage. She raced across the room, tore the receiver from the hook, screamed into it: obscenities as foul and fouler than those directed at her. The ease with which they fell from her tongue would have horrified her, had she been in her right mind.

But she wasn't in her right mind. She continued to shriek and curse long after she was aware that her persecutors had fled, moved on – youths have low boredom thresholds and short attention spans: at some point there had been a scuffling and then the sound of feet running on the gravel.

She opened the window and hurled her imprecations at anyone who might be listening: at the screeching owls and all the other nocturnal creatures responsible for her night-time persecution. She screamed and yelled and banged her head against the glass. And then she turned and picked up the ashtray and threw it against the mirror and wondered, crazed as she was, whether she had intended to choose, from amid the wreckage, a long jagged sliver of glass that could be drawn across the blue veins at her wrist, couldn't quite figure out whether she'd meant to turn her anger upon herself, whether it was she or everything that wasn't she that was to blame.

Fear, rage, and then suddenly there was nothing but a total weariness. She flung the fearsome splinter away and stretched out on the sofa, drifting in and out of sleep. At seven-thirty a pain awakened her, a pain low down in her pelvis, the sort of pain that is indicative of the onset of menstruation. She relinquished her last shred of hope. At eight o'clock she cleaned up the broken glass and at nine she rang Gwen.

PART TWO

At Gwen's

1

Max used to complain about being disturbed by her cries whenever she woke from a nightmare. 'For God's sake!' he'd groan. 'It's three o'clock!' he'd moan, failing (or refusing) to recognise that she needed reassurance, that adult night-terrors can, sometimes, be as intense as those of childhood.

Well, there would be no complaints now – there was nobody to complain about the noises she made. If indeed she had made a noise; awake, there was no sense of reverberation, no clue as to whether the dream's silent scream had been vocalised. She scrabbled at the side of the bed for the light switch, her panic increasing as it became apparent that there *was* no light switch. And then she remembered that the light switch *here* was located above the bed and she found it and snapped it on just in the nick of time, before whatever it was that had migrated from the dream to hover in wait in the darkness could pounce.

Her surroundings, thus illuminated, came as a shock: furnishings unfamiliar, dimensions awry. The opposite wall, instead of presenting a matt mushroom Anaglypta'd surface, was papered in a dark blue regency stripe; there was a rod with velvet curtains hanging from rings where she'd expected nets, and silver frames enclosing photographs of strange faces on a many-mirrored dressing-table which reflected the only satisfactorily-identified entity in the room: herself.

The green eye of the digital clock winked out the time: three forty-five. She had slept then for just twenty minutes before forcing herself awake to avoid the nightmare's conclusion. She shifted her position and two books fell and hit the carpet with a thud. She reached down for one of them and opened it at the page where she'd left off. It was an extremely large paperback book, so tightly stuffed into its cover that, when you reached the middle, the first word of every line disappeared into the binding. Not that it mattered much. There were so many other words, arranged in such brain-numbing patterns of banality, that these omissions proved not to be particularly detrimental to the story: an Indian prince, an orphan, war, flight – and the obligatory bout of sexual gymnastics introjected whenever the narrative began to flag . . . She'd chosen it, together with its companion, which sported a cover depicting a sort of composite wife of Henry VIII, from the unappealing contents of Gwen's bookcase as being the likeliest candidate to send her to sleep.

But it had failed to induce more than a superficial drowsiness, beneath the surface of which her mind raced and her nerves twitched. The green eye of the clock winked constantly: three forty-five, four, four-thirty. In two hours there would be the fire-engine blare of Corky's alarm, her feet on the stairs, the reverberating slam of the front door as she set off on her jogging, and then returned to perform what she called her Swedish exercises, followed by her noisy ablutions, her fry-up, and the grinding sounds of the bull-nosed Morris being backed out of the garage. At that point, Christina felt, with a prophetic certainty, sleep would arrive but find itself thwarted by Gwen's morning salutation, her proffering of the weak, heavily-sugared, suitable-for-invalids cup of tea, her not-so-subtle-as-she-supposed sweeping glance to check that all was as it should be: no spills on the carpet, smears on the mirror, evidence of nocturnal rummaging.

All was not as it should be. Christina bent to pick up the pseudo-historical novel and felt a familiar warmth and fluidity between her thighs, drew back the quilt and uncovered a fresh, brilliant stain of menstrual blood despoiling the pristine surface of Gwen's Country Diary of an Edwardian Lady poly/cotton bottom sheet.

There was no point in ransacking her suitcases. They contained neither Tampax nor towels nor anything that could be hacked at with nail-scissors to provide a temporary substitute. (She'd felt that to furnish herself with sanitary protection before the event would be to tempt fate; she knew now that neither temptation nor the refraining from it could make the slightest difference.) She would simply have to lie very still, her night-dress bunched between her thighs, and wait for the morning and Gwen and her ill-concealed distaste.

But the flow proved to be too profuse for that. Sheer necessity drove her down to the kitchen before the clock had winked seven-thirty.

Corky was at the kitchen table, mopping fragrant juices from her plate with a crust of bread and reading last night's *Echo*; it was still too early for her *Sun* or Gwen's *Telegraph* to have dropped through the letter-box. Her lips moved, keeping pace with the rate at which she read, indicative not, Christina felt, of limited intelligence, but rather from habit: part of a cluster of symptoms, bred out of solitariness, that included talking to oneself out loud – which she also did occasionally.

The radio played; one of those young professional broadcasting voices: flattened vowels and slovenly diction, gabbled with manic cheerfulness as it introduced a record. 'Caterwauling bastards!' Corky said, without rancour. 'Shut your racket!' It seemed that the radio, like the newspaper, provided her with continual fuel for complaint. By way of greeting, she passed the middle section of the *Echo* to Christina for her inspection and, presumably, corroboration: 'Would you look at that Nancy Reagan! Sick woman, wouldn't you say? There isn't a picking on her. Be like going to bed with a hatrack. Not that he does, I shouldn't think. Past all that, surely?'

Presumably there were no fry-ups for Nancy Reagan. Corky soaked up the last of the grease on her plate with her bread, retrieved the newspaper, gave the photograph one final scathing glance and flicked over the page. If Arthur Scargill or Nigel Lawson was over the page he would probably provoke a similar outburst.

Fascinating (and welcome, in that it did away with the necessity for formal greeting) as this without-preamble statement of prejudice might be, Christina was in no position to enter into either an exchange of views or a confirmation of shared bigotry: she had stained the bedsheet, she was now in grave danger of staining the floor. 'Do you perhaps, by any chance, happen to have . . .?'

Corky, sleeves rolled up to display muscular forearms, feet shod in size eight training shoes, fixed her with an uncomprehending stare. (If Nancy Reagan wasn't a very sick woman but simply of a physical type inhabiting the extreme end of the ectomorphic scale, then Corky was an archetype of mesomorphology.)

It was difficult to think of her in association with things

gynaecological, but Christina forced herself to try. 'My period has started,' she said, 'and I've nothing . . .'

Corky jerked her head towards the ceiling. 'Airing cupboard, second shelf,' she said. 'I'll make you some tea.'

In the bathroom Christina took out the packet of Kotex (Gwen's, presumably) and tidied herself up. It was a split-personality bathroom: one part frothing with flowered shower-curtains and frilled bath caps, aromatic with oils and powders and unctions, the other spartan in its accoutrements: a tooth-brush in a plastic beaker, a pumice stone, a tube of Steradent and a tartan flannel precisely folded, steaming still. One almost expected to find a cut-throat razor. Except that Corky would, no doubt, favour the retention of body hair for warmth.

She favoured strong tea. You could almost stand the spoon up in it. But strong tea was sometimes what was required, when your nerves were twanging like harp strings and, however sternly you told yourself that you must buck up, you couldn't shake off the sensation of putting out a foot to take a step that wasn't there.

'You look a bit peaky. Ought to get some good grub down you. Don't suppose you've been bothering over much? There's some brains in the fridge. Fancy 'em on toast?'

It was impossible to suppress the shudder. 'Good for you, brains,' said Corky, chidingly. 'Anything like that: liver, tripe, sweetbreads . . . When I was a girl, if I was a bit off-colour, they'd give me the beestings to drink. That's the best.'

'Beestings?'

'First milk after calving. Blood in it. I used to be like you — squeamish, kicked up a fuss.'

A childhood on, or near, a farm somewhere. And that was all anybody knew. Even Gwen. 'Close,' Gwen said. 'Very,' and accompanied this terse criticism with one of her mega-sniffs.

But the sort who don't tell are very often the sort who don't ask. And for this relief, Christina was truly thankful. It was Corky who had come to pick her up the day before, who had humped her trunk and her cases down to the car and, rather scornfully, shaken off attempts at assistance. She had made only two comments: the first when they were on their way downstairs: 'You don't think you might be better off staying with a friend, perhaps?' What she meant was: You know Gwen is going to make a meal out of this and you'll end up feeling six inches tall?

What could she have said in reply: I have no really close friend to turn to? I'd rather put up with Gwen's condescension than allow some acquaintance to know what a fool I've made of myself? She'd said, 'I'm afraid that wouldn't do. They all live in or near Winchester Road. It would be embarrassing – apart from the gossip . . .'

'I know,' Corky had said. 'You'd be the talk of the washhouse. Fair enough,' she'd said, and heaved the trunk into the boot of her car without any noticeable effort.

'If you're all right then,' she said now, 'I'll get off. Oh, you could take Her Ladyship's tea up to her, if you wanted. Take these as well, would you?'

'These' were a pile of letters and small parcels that had just dropped into the box behind the door. 'It's our birthday today,' Corky said, inspecting them. 'We're forty. Can't be sure exactly how we're going to take it.'

She mouthed 'forty' soundlessly as though it was a word too obscene for utterance. Women like Gwen would, Christina supposed, be profoundly agitated by such landmarks. So much more to lose. In the way of looks at any rate. Not that she'd suffered dramatically yet. She was still extremely attractive. For a forty-year-old woman.

She placed the cards and the parcels, together with cup, saucer, milk and sugar on a tray, reflecting upon the different circumstances of their respective entries into the world: if she, Christina, had arrived in 1946 to a less than rapturous welcome, then her cousin Gwendoline must have been the most wanted baby of '45. They said that Jumbo, who was getting on a bit and who had almost despaired of issue, had come whooping through the gates of the maternity home; that night, he'd cracked more bottles of what he called The Widow with his cronies than anyone cared to remember.

Gwen preferred Krug to Clicquot. There were three bottles chilling in the slate-shelved pantry ready for that night's dinner party, Corky said. Together with the cake that she had baked and iced. She would be cooking the meal too but, she told Christina, wild horses wouldn't drag her to the bunfight.

'Why not?'

'Why not? Sit round yacking with that Queenie Goldsmith and that dozy husband of hers? I'd sooner catch clap.'

And Christina could imagine what Gwen would say: 'Corky?

Oh you know Corky. Much happier in the background. Quaint, isn't it?' And she'd produce the laugh that sounded like the rattle of a charm bracelet, and you might never guess that Gwen too was happier that Corky preferred to stay in the background.

'Who else is coming?' Christina asked, pouring Lapsang Souchong, cutting the crusts off the toast and arranging it upon the Spode plate.

'That vet feller and that Edward crony of hers from the bank and the Goldsmiths – he runs an estate agency, she's one of those little-girly types, forever flapping her eyelashes and talking in a daft voice. They've got no kids. You very often find that they get like that: women with no kids and too much money.'

Gwen hadn't. But then Gwen had been Daddy's Precious Little Girl at a time when it was, presumably, appropriate for her to be so.

'Gwen. Gwen! I've brought you some tea. Happy birthday.'

Beneath a down quilt so plumply stuffed that it probably shot off the end of the tog scale, all that was visible of Gwen was a gloved hand (special night gloves, impregnated with skin food) and half her face. Her eyelid twitched, there was a deep sleep crease in her cheek and a thread of saliva glistened at the corner of her mouth. Christina looked away; it was unfair to take advantage and, besides, that sleeping vulnerability disconcerted her, so great was the contrast with Gwen's controlled, powerful, waking self.

The rapid eye movements grew more rapid and then ceased as Gwen woke and blinked and frowned and yawned. The movement disturbed the bed's other resident: a large, long-haired, dirty-white cat that had been all but buried in the quilt's deep folds. It rose and stretched and flexed its claws and sneezed and then trod delicately towards Gwen and began to butt its head against her arm.

Gwen querulous: 'But I was going to bring *you* tea,' became Gwen adoring. She pressed her thumb against the cat's pink nose leather, gently ruffled the fur behind its ear. 'Good morning, little man. Hello Boysie. Who's beautiful? Who's beautiful *then*?'

It began to make a noise in its throat reminiscent of an outboard motor and grinned at her. It had a wide gangster's face with a scar between its yellow eyes that gave it a slightly quizzical look. Suddenly it bent its head and savagely investigated some parasitic infestation in the fold of its thigh before jumping off the bed with a display of feline grace analogous to a sack of potatoes hitting the ground.

'He wants his breakfast,' Gwen said. 'Open the door for him, would you?'

Christina complied and Muffin (for such was his – its – name, although Gwen mostly called him Boysie) thumped his way downstairs. He was a stray. They'd found him foraging in the dustbins in the yard at the back of the wine bar, his head a mass of festering sores. Bite you as soon as look at you, Corky said. Gwen had adopted him, had his wounds attended to and his testicles removed and brought him home where he had adjusted himself smoothly to a regime of top-of-the-milk and feather quilts and excessive pampering. 'Child substitute,' Corky said, sneering. But you'd have expected Gwen to have chosen an aristocrat: a velvet-coated Siamese with china-blue eyes, rather than a grizzled tom whose instincts might have been cut off in their prime but whose spectacularly insalubrious habits persisted.

Gwen sipped her tea. 'I thought you'd have taken the opportunity for a lie-in,' she said crossly. Like most natural organisers, she accepted the thwarting of her plans with a bad grace.

'Couldn't sleep.'

No need to mention the sheet. Not yet, if at all.

'Sorry I haven't a present for you . . .'

Gwen read her cards and opened her parcels: a box of chocolates from Charbonnel et Walker, a phial of *Opium*, a silver bracelet, a silk scarf. 'Oh, lovely,' Christina said, stroking its surface, admiring the subtlety of its design. 'From Miriam Jones,' Gwen said, unimpressed. 'I wonder where she got it? Simpson's, do you think? If so, I can change it. Grey's just not my colour. Makes me look washed out.'

She laid it aside with the rest: small-fry gifts; the big stuff, the serious presents would arrive that night.

'Tonight,' Gwen said, 'I'm giving a little dinner party. Miriam Jones rang up yesterday to say that she's got to go down to Cheltenham – her mother's ill, so at least it won't mess up the numbers now that you're here.'

'You're inviting me?'

'Well naturally.'

If I'd had forethought, Christina reflected, I could have invented a previous engagement; if I'd used my brains, I'd have remembered that November 2nd was always the signal for beacons to be lit and rockets to be launched and general rejoicing to take place. But forethought had never been her strong suit, and her brains, when it came to avoiding uncongenial situations, were of so little use that they might as well have been removed and eaten on toast for breakfast.

'Well naturally you're invited.'

Gwen drank her tea, gazed at the opposite wall, displaying a deliberately neutral expression, but irritation was detectable in the set of her jaw, the little sigh that she gave, and you knew that she had scant patience with those who stood around with faces like wet weekends. 'If the wind changes, it'll stay like that,' Gwen's Daddy, Jumbo, used to warn, jovially, referring to Christina's expression. 'Cheer up,' he'd say. 'It might never happen. There! That didn't hurt, did it?' he'd say, his clowning having finally coaxed a reluctant smile out of her.

He'd been a kindly man, sympathetic, a trait that Gwennie had not inherited. She sighed and inspected her fingernails, obviously deriving great satisfaction from their opalescent symmetry. 'Oh what a mess!' she said. 'However did you get yourself into such a mess?'

It was a genuine query as well as being a judgemental statement. Gwen did not realise how thin the crust was that separated some people from the most glutinous of messes: an unwary foot in the wrong direction and there you were, in it up to your neck, up shit creek without the proverbial.

Only some people though. Not people like Gwen. And that wasn't entirely due to the insulatory, duck-board effect of a healthy bank balance.

'I didn't deliberately set out to create it.'

Gwen, looking sceptical (and who could argue that she hadn't every justification?), got up and put on her peignoir. 'What are your plans then?' she asked.

'Plans?'

'Yes, plans. Sorting yourself out.'

What possible set of circumstances could there be that might prove unamenable to being sorted out? Thus it was in Gwen's philosophy.

'Well . . . I thought . . . if I could hang on here for a while . . .'

Hang on here, sheltered from the storm, head in the sand – or under the duvet, safe from all those threats that I suspected might be lying in wait for me as soon as I shook off my protection.

'Hang on until I can find somewhere else, somewhere not quite as expensive and a bit less isolated . . .'

Gwen was contorting her face in order to remove her night-cream, her nose almost pressed to the mirror. She was in a transitional stage between hard and soft contact lenses and the spectacles which had been acquired to bridge this gap were, more often than not, appropriated by Corky who couldn't be bothered to get a prescription made up for herself.

'If I were you I'd swallow my pride and salvage what I could from the situation. You've been a fool, certainly, but you don't have to remain a fool. Get round there, make him realise why you strayed in the first place. Mind you, if you'd asserted yourself from the beginning, you'd never have needed to stray.'

You could have them eating out of your hand, men, Gwen said, if you went about it the right way. Even Max. But a different kind of intelligence was required from the sort necessary for the achievement of gold stars and scholarships.

'After all,' she said, 'you're at the age now when the chances of finding an unattached man aren't likely to crop up all that often.'

You seem to find plenty, Christina thought, and you're nearly a year older than I am. But she knew that, apart from the proximity of their birthdates, there were no other grounds for making a valid comparison.

Gwen came home early from Klosters. Corky too. They devoted themselves, respectively, to beautification and cooking. They were totally absorbed, as only those who regard their occupation with deadly seriousness and boundless respect can be. Christina riffled through the contents of her suitcases, rejecting frock after frock, skirt after skirt. What did it matter anyway, she thought, why should she care what Gwen or the Goldsmiths or the Edward crony from the bank or the vet chappie with the Adam's apple thought about her?

Her hand fell upon the Louise Livingstone jersey. Well, why

not? No longer any point in feeling embarrassed about wearing a garment designed by one's lover's wife when he was no longer one's lover.

It suited her. She could tell by the slightly startled expression on Gwen's face when she walked into the sitting-room. Mr Goldsmith seemed to be staring at her very fixedly too. With one eye, at any rate. Then she realised that one of Mr Gold-smith's eyes – the one that did the staring – was made of glass.

'My cousin,' Gwen said, presenting her to the assembled company and the assembled company accorded her just enough attention to weigh up the amount of attention that *needed* to be accorded to her, and then resumed their conversations.

'You spoil me,' Gwen was saying as she unwrapped their gifts: from the vet: a Royal Copenhagen plate to match her collection of Royal Copenhagen plates; from Edward: a porcelain cat to match her collection of porcelain cats.

'Oh how sweet!' she said, holding up the latter so that everyone could admire it, turning it this way and that. 'Doesn't it remind you of Muffin – a little?'

Any resemblance to any cat, living or dead, let alone to Muffin was, Christina thought, purely coincidental. There was a little silence and then the vet said, 'Why perhaps he does – a little.' He was miffed, you could tell, that Edward had had the perspicacity to go for the cats rather than the Royal Copenhagen. But he did have one indisputable advantage. 'I've been meaning to ask you,' Gwen said, placing the ornament gently on the mantelpiece, 'about Muffin's injections. Isn't it time for his boosters? Oh, and there's also that sore patch on his tummy. You remember – you gave him the cream? It doesn't seem to be clearing up properly . . .'

The vet – Mr Flynn, Quinn – an Irish name, Christina thought, not having registered it properly in the flurry of introductions – cast a cold eye in the direction of Boysie whose slumber was briefly interrupted by the apparent necessity to scratch at a flea (Mrs Goldsmith, seated next to him on the sofa, attempted to move farther away) and then smiled warmly, if insincerely. 'Don't worry,' he said. 'We'll sort him out.' He leaned across to address the object of their concern directly. 'You're a magnificent specimen, aren't you?' he said. Boysie, too tired or too idle to proceed with his scratching – the movement of his hind leg became feebler and feebler until it ceased altogether – gave him one brief disdainful glance, yawned and then went back to sleep.

Gwen could have talked cats all evening, but mindful of her duties as hostess, turned from the avid gaze of Mr Flynn, Quinn – O'Byrne, possibly? – avoided the even more avid gaze of Edward from the bank and brought Mr Goldsmith's good eye into contact with both of Christina's. 'My cousin,' she said, 'is looking for a flat. Perhaps you'll be able to help her.'

'Hutch up, Queenie,' said Mr Goldsmith, moving along the sofa so that Christina came within his field of vision. Hutching up meant that Queenie had to decrease the distance between herself and Boysie and whatever parasitic life he might be supporting, but she obligingly complied. She was a fair, blood-less woman of indeterminate age with thin legs and a compulsive nervous giggle.

'What   er, what – er sort of bracket were you aiming at?' asked Mr Goldsmith. He breathed heavily when he spoke. So many men did. Christina wondered if it was to do with them having more and thicker hair up their nostrils. Taken aback by the indelicacy of the question, unsure of where the brackets would be likely to start and end, she sought for an answer that would neither expose her as an ignoramus nor stigmatise her as a pauper. 'Well,' she said eventually, 'modest, you know. To begin with.'

'Nice little development at Badger's Green,' he said. 'Sixty, thereabouts.'

'Sixty flats?'

'No,' he said, puzzled at her mistake. 'Sixty thou. Mortgage facilities available, of course.'

While Christina's mind was boggling, Queenie swallowed down the last of her current handful of cashew nuts (for a thin woman she could certainly shift what Gwen called the 'nibbles'). She dabbed at the corners of her mouth and then dusted her hands and said, 'Perhaps Christina wasn't thinking of paying that much, Daddy.'

'Daddy?' repeated his wife; he was rambling still about mortgage facilities and underfloor central-heating and timber frames and hardwood cladding and energy-saving devices.

'Mm!' Christina said, and 'Mm?' She doubted that the area in which Daddy operated touched, even peripherally, upon the abomination of desolation that was known as furnished accommodation, where energy-saving was usually interpreted as a rolled-up coat jammed at the bottom of the door and a window covered in polythene to keep out the draughts.

She said, 'Mm?' and 'Mm!' and covertly watched Gwen who was wearing black. ('I am in mourning for my fortieth birthday,' Corky had murmured earlier, and Christina had been surprised at this evidence of erudition, having had Corky marked down – in as much as she *could* be marked down – as one whose acquaintanceship with learning and culture had always been of the most distant sort.)

A bell rang. It was Corky's signal that the first course of the meal was on the table. But as they rose to adjourn to the dining-room, another bell rang and this was the front doorbell and it wasn't until Gwen had answered it and allowed admittance to some male person with an unfamiliar voice, that Christina's pulse rate went back to normal.

(Every time a doorbell rang, every time a telephone shrilled: at work, at Gwen's, she still found it impossible to suppress that forlorn but flaring hope.)

The caller: a sandy-haired man with spectacles, had brought a present for Gwen. Gwen, unwrapping a rather stylish terracotta plant-holder, said, 'How on earth did you know? Oh, you're a wicked man. I'm really cross,' and almost brushed her lips against his cheek and divested him of his overcoat and then went into the kitchen in search of Corky, saying, 'Of *course* you must stay. It's no trouble at all. I thought you were away this weekend or – naturally – I should have invited you.'

The faces of Edward and the vet did not immediately register pleasurable surprise; indeed, it could be said that they looked positively glum. 'Millward,' Edward said, and then looked down at the highly-polished toe-caps of his shoes. The vet nodded, and Mr Goldsmith said, 'Evenin'.' Only Queenie made gestures of welcome and did what Gwen ought to have done, which was to introduce him to Christina: 'This is Stephen Millward. He's our accountant.'

The kitchen door closed upon a little burst of altercation (one could imagine how gladly Corky must have received the news of another mouth to feed at this late stage) and Gwen rejoined her guests with the air of one who has just delivered instruction to an entirely subservient menial instead of having made a heartfelt plea to a recalcitrant partner.

'Do sit down, everyone.'

A chair was brought for Stephen Millward and placed opposite to Gwen's so that his gallantry might be rewarded by having the delightful spectacle of an unimpeded view of her beauty. Christina was placed between Mr Goldsmith and the vet: Milligan, perhaps? Between the static orb and the hyperactive thyroid cartilage. Though the vet, having Gwen on his other side, mostly presented to her the back of his arm and his shoulder-blade. Only when Gwen rose to attend to the serving of the pheasant did he turn and acknowledge her existence. She soon wished that he hadn't.

'Gwen mentioned your – situation,' he said. He pushed his face close to hers when he spoke and spoke quietly. She got the impression that he considered that what was being said was not fit for public consumption, that she, as a marriage-breaker, a woman in flight, ought not to flaunt her 'situation' but could only expect to have it discussed, *sotto voce*, in sombre tones.

'There's no chance that you might get back together?' he said, as though enquiring of a terminal patient the possibility of remission.

A few weeks ago she would have answered him meekly, expressed regret that she had dared to upset the matrimonial applecart, but something was changing. Action, so long deferred, had triggered some long-suppressed anger.

'There's no chance at all,' she replied, concentrating fiercely upon the removal of the little splintery bones from her meat. 'Although it's absolutely no concern of yours.'

Of course she regretted it as soon as she'd said it. If you were willing to risk self-assertion then you had also to be prepared for calm rebuttal of, or dignified indifference to, the reactions you might arouse. But she was a novice in the matter of speaking her mind and could only, alternately, seethe inwardly and die a thousand deaths beneath the weight of his contempt, which was tacit for the most part, but put eagerly into words when the conversation turned to the subject of children. How precious they were, he declared, how much he and his late wife had rejoiced in their family life (and here the thyroid cartilage vibrated so violently that you trembled lest it should break free from confinement, burst through his neck and land on his plate).

How incomprehensible, he declared, were the motivations of those who wantonly sought to sabotage the institution: the wilful, the frivolous, who acted with no thought but for themselves; how much of the blame for the disaffection of youth might be laid at their door – well, you could draw your own conclusions, couldn't you?

Edward from the bank clenched his jaw to disguise a yawn. He was annoyed, having just succeeded in steering Gwen on to the subject of Swan Hellenic cruises when this pronouncement was made. Mr Goldsmith cleared his throat very loudly and thoroughly. Queenie made pleats in the tablecloth and adopted the half-witted expression that those who are pretending to be so absorbed in their inner thoughts that they have missed what has been said are wont to adopt. Gwen, alert to the slightest nuance, continued to smile but her eyebrows moved a significant millimetre towards her hairline and she urged Stephen Millward to refill the glasses.

When he reached Christina's she covered it with her hand. Such a joy: not to *have* to drink – although Mr – O'Brien, Donleavy, Joyce? was certainly doing his best to drive her to it. After a moment, Stephen Millward desisted from plying her with wine, but did not immediately switch his attention away from her. 'That's a beautiful – jersey, is that what they're called still, these days? My daughter tells me I'm twenty years behind the times when it comes to ladies' fashions.'

'I call it a jersey. But then I'm probably twenty years behind the times too.'

He wasn't as old as Mr Goldsmith or Edward or the terrible Mr – O'Casey, Synge, Wilde? He was nearer her own age. Perhaps his memories would be her memories: *Sunny Stories* and dancing to Chris Barber and his Jazzmen and the same passage of Virgil to be translated for the scholarship exam. But there was another face that interposed itself between hers and his and there was no way that she could make the template fit the reality, however much she needed the morale-boosting attentions of a man perspicacious enough to realise – albeit unconsciously – that if ever a woman needs a compliment, it's when she's wearing a garment designed by her ex-lover's wife.

'Stephen,' said Gwen. 'I'd like you to taste this cheese. It was sent to me by Sylvia Moorhead – you remember Sylvia Moorhead? She moved down to Somerset when Howard retired;

they're running a little antiques business now. Well, this is a sample of one of these new-fangled cheeses, apparently. She sings its praises, but you know what an idiot Sylvia can be . . . Finish your cake and try a little.'

He was recaptured and Christina was cautioned to remember her place with a sharp look. All the men were there for Gwen; surely that was understood?

It was the carrying in and cutting of Gwen's birthday cake that had steered the conversation towards children. Mr Goldsmith had remarked, jocularly enough to disguise any lack of gallantry, upon the paucity of candles. Queenie had giggled and said, do you remember when you were a child and required to blow out your candles with one puff and how you never had the breath for it? And Edward from the bank had recalled singeing the front of his childish curls during just such an attempt, and then Mr – Reagan, Kennedy, O'Houlihan? had launched into his encomium: the blessings of family life, and the selfishness – nay depravity – of those who saw fit to undermine it.

'It's made too easy for them these days, that's the trouble. Why, we could all have thrown in the towel some time or another, I'm sure . . .'

'Oh come on, Eric,' said Stephen Millward. 'Think of all those poor wretches who used to be chained to each other for a lifetime, all those kids who couldn't be legitimised. You wouldn't want us to go back to that, surely?'

'Think of all those kids whose lives are blighted because their parents decide that they can't be bothered to make a go of their marriages,' said the vet. 'Think of them.' Annoyance appeared to have caused all his features to compete for first place in the rush to inhabit the centre of his face: small sea-pebble eyes beneath tufty brows, a pursed mouth, a hawk nose, all set within acres of mottled forehead and cheek and chin. 'That's the trouble,' he said, 'nobody does think of them.'

Corky had been prevailed upon to come in with the birthday cake. Having ignited the single candle preparatory to its extinguishment by Gwen's gentle expiration, she now stood, coffee pot in her hand, waiting her opportunity to make a getaway.

'My late wife had a cousin who left her children to run off with a vicar, of all people,' the vet was saying. 'Those kids – well, my wife used to say it broke her heart to see them – Aah!

Aah! A-aah!' yelled the vet, Mr – *McTavish*, that was his name; she'd suffered a touch of Gaelic confusion.

The coffee was piping hot. You'd have thought, wouldn't you, Corky said afterwards, that the silly sod would have had the sense to keep still? Waving his arms about like that! Was it her fault if he'd jolted her elbow as she was filling his cup so that he'd received a bit of a scald on his thigh? Could have been worse. A few inches higher and he'd have been damn glad, considering he was so fond of kids, that he'd already fathered some.

Across the table, Stephen Millward looked at Christina solemnly and then winked. It came as quite a surprise to discover that – amid all the hostility – it just might be possible to identify the odd ally.

2

Gwen wouldn't give her a key. *That* would have implied expectation of a long residence.

Lack of a key meant that, should Christina mistime her return to the house between the daily woman leaving it and either Corky or Gwen coming back, she was obliged to take shelter in the porch.

She calculated wrongly on the following Tuesday evening. After ringing the doorbell until it became quite evident that the house was empty, she had to wait among the potted geraniums, watching the windows steaming up and the street-lighting switching itself on, illuminating small discrete areas between the overhanging branches of the horse-chestnut trees. In one of these pools of light, opposite Gwen's house, a man stood motionless. She was too far away and the light was too dim for her to be able to distinguish more than the height and the build of him. It was his stillness that struck her: as though he had willed himself into a lack of animation so extreme that he might be taken for part of the scenery.

Perhaps he was casing the joint: this sort of area and these kinds of dwellings: elegant Georgian town houses set around a garden in a quiet tree-lined square, must be high on burgling lists. If that was so, then he was on a hiding to nothing: Gwen's house was fitted with intruder alarms and infra-red traps at any and every point where the most resourceful of burglars might attempt to effect an entry; you couldn't open the lavatory window without alerting the local police station.

There was the sound of gears grinding and tyres squealing on wet tarmac and Gwen's Volvo made its erratic entrance into the square and came to a halt outside her gate. 'What on earth are you lurking in there for?' she asked, as soon as she spotted Christina.

'What else can I do? If you'd lend me a key . . .'

'There isn't a spare, and I don't like handing over keys to those cutters. You never know what they might do . . .'

'Take it to one of those while-you-wait places. You can watch them there.'

'Oh yes, yes. I don't think it will be necessary, actually . . .'

They continued to debate the issue until they were inside. Christina looked back briefly over her shoulder but the man was gone.

On Wednesday morning, on the way to work, she dropped a letter to David into the post-box at the corner of the square. Next to the post-box was a telephone kiosk. Typical, she thought, that an area like this, where every house was certain to have a phone, should be provided with the public variety, whereas in the run-down districts where she had sought accommodation there was rarely one to be found, not even one that had been vandalised.

She'd looked at two bedsitting-rooms during her lunch break on Tuesday, and then told Gwen that they weren't suitable. To Corky – from whom a certain cordiality seemed to emanate – she'd confided the extent of their unsuitability: 'Either they're clean and you'd go mad with claustrophobia, or else they're like caverns: freezing cold with that sort of brown and red aborted-foetus wallpaper and cookers that look as though they were used for prehistoric fry-ups and haven't been cleaned since.'

'Why don't you try farther out?' Corky had asked, applying Swarfega liberally to her hands and arms; the Morris had needed an oil-change and, as always, she'd had a tussle with the sump-nut. 'Cheaper there,' she'd said, 'in the suburbs.'

'But what I saved in rent I'd spend in fares. And then there'd be travelling time. If I'd learned to drive . . .'

But even if she'd learned to drive she couldn't have afforded a car.

'Where did *you* learn to drive? In the army?'

Corky, dripping oily green lather all over the quarry-tiled floor, had nodded. Christina got the impression that she gave you the answer you were expecting to hear, whether it was the truth or not.

She had written to David asking if *he'd* written to Adam. (It was the necessity to find a place where she might, at least once a week, entertain Adam that motivated her to search for accommodation; he would find every excuse in the book for not visiting Gwen's house. Otherwise, all her instincts were to remain where she was: safe, warm, comfortable.)

'Answer this *please*,' she said out loud as she dropped the letter into the slot. And then she noticed that the man standing in the telephone kiosk was staring at her. She stared back at him, but he stared her out, was still staring when she turned from the letter-box. Had it not been for the soundproofing effect of the glass, she might have remarked sarcastically that he'd know her again.

Might have. She'd acquired a measure of boldness, but perhaps not enough for that.

On Thursday evening, walking back from the bus-stop after The System committee meeting, she'd heard footsteps behind her. Following her? She couldn't be sure, knew only that as her pace quickened, so did that of the footsteps. At last, within sight of the house, she'd plucked up the courage to look back over her shoulder and had caught the merest, edge-of-the-eyeball glimpse of a figure disappearing around the corner of the little railed garden that formed the fourth side of the square, the *cul* part of the *cul-de-sac*. Though it was only vehicular traffic for which there was no thoroughfare: narrow lanes ran each side of the garden, leading into the main road.

Had she seen someone, or was she imagining things? Had the ghoulies and ghosties and lurkers-in-the-shrubbery followed her from Swinburne Court to Lansdowne Gardens? Or was her mind cracking under the strain?

And if she *wasn't* suffering from delusions, was this the same man? And, if so, why was he watching her, following her? Was he a private detective, set on her tail by Max? Redundant, surely, now?

The next evening, when she got in from work, she said, 'Have either of you noticed a man hanging round here, staring up at this house? I'm sure it's the same one, and I'm sure I'm not imagining it. You're always worrying about burglars, Gwen . . .'

But Gwen drove everywhere, and Corky's jogging usually took place too early in the morning, surely, for even the most dedicated caser-of-joints to be abroad?

It wasn't the best time to raise the subject anyway. Gwen and

Corky were in the middle of a row and in the brief time that Christina had enjoyed their hospitality she had come to realise that neither sense nor reason was to be got from either of them when they were engaged in one of their rows.

The cause of the quarrel remained a mystery. By the time that Christina entered the scene the hostilities were well under way. She'd walked into the sitting-room where Corky was watching *Blankety-Blank* with the volume turned up unnecessarily high and Gwen was petting Boysie with the sort of extravagance she usually displayed when she wished to demonstrate how very much more pleasure she derived from the cat's company than Corky's.

Boysie squirmed and grinned like a crocodile. 'Oh, who's so-o-o sweet?' Gwen enquired of him. 'Who is his mama's best little lambkin boy? Who's beautiful?'

Corky had turned her head just enough to display an expression of unmingled contempt. 'They'll put you away,' she said, 'if you carry on like that.'

Gwen had ignored her, continued to stroke beneath Boysie's outstretched chin. Both of them had ignored Christina and both glanced across at her when she spoke with looks that suggested she had no right to interpose herself between them and their animosity.

'What man?' Gwen said, irritably, as Corky left the room, declaring to the atmosphere at large that she'd get well out of the road before Gwen's little lapdog arrived. (Edward from the bank was expected, to collect Gwen and take her to see Tony Bennett in cabaret.)

Gwen crossed the room and tweaked a curtain and looked out as though the man would, obligingly, be there and make his presence known. 'I can't see anybody. Well, except for Mr Frobisher taking his dog for a walk. I think you're suffering from your nerves. I think you ought to get them attended to.'

She went back to her chair and took a mirror from her bag and became lost in rapt contemplation of her beauty.

Corky came back, ostensibly in search of the newspaper, but actually to deliver herself of further insults. 'Mirror, mirror on the wall,' she said, 'who is the fairest of us all? Don't answer that.' And, 'I love me, who do you love?' And, 'Much longer, and you'll crack it.'

'I thought you'd gone. I thought you were going to see that stupid film, the one that's so popular with little boys.'

Rambo she meant. But it was an ill-judged and unwarranted criticism: Corky usually went to the cinema every Friday, unless they had a special party booked at Klosters, irrespective of what film was showing.

'Changed my mind. That's all right, isn't it? I am allowed to stay in the house.'

'Oh yes,' Gwen said sweetly. 'Just so long as you remember whose house it is that you're staying in.'

Corky's complexion assumed the hue of weathered brick, and Christina, realising that her warnings of imminent break-in were likely to fall on deaf ears for a good while yet, left the room.

Perhaps Gwen was right. Perhaps she was seeing things. Perhaps you could reach a stage of mortal anxiety when even the most innocent actions and events could be translated into evidence of threat. What else could it be, when you fled from danger towards safety and then found that the terrors had kept company alongside you?

Corky came out into the hall. 'What's up with you?' she said. 'You look like a dying duck in a thunderstorm.'

The doorbell rang. 'Suffering Jesus,' she said. 'Get out of *his* way for a kick-off. D'you fancy a drink?' and she accompanied this invitation with a head-jerking gesture up the stairs.

Christina did not fancy a drink, but the chance to penetrate Corky's domain – hitherto absolutely out of bounds – was too tempting to be refused.

Corky paused in her ascent to look over the banisters and down upon the defenceless cranium of Edward from the bank. His bald spot looked scurfy and he'd made a futile attempt to disguise it with a few carefully-arranged strands of hair. 'Did you ever see such a dozy creature?' she asked, rhetorically. 'I wish I was a pigeon. God help us,' she said. 'If she isn't messing about with young lads that have scarcely gone into long pants, it's moonstruck old creeps that're practically ready for their pensions.'

But still younger than you, Christina thought, still nearer in age to us, Gwen and myself, than you are.

She panted her way up the stairs, trying to match Corky's pace. The calendar might bear witness to the proximity of bus-passes and pension-books but in terms of physical fitness she put them all to shame.

Her door was locked – twice: a deadlock latch had been fitted as reinforcement to the already existing mortice. 'I like my private things *kept* private,' she said with a meaningful glance. Knowing that, for Gwen, anything placed behind lock and key exerted an irresistible fascination (Christina remembered kirby grips being taken to cupboards and drawers during childhood visits to relatives), one could only wince at the thought of the row that must have been sparked off by this particular bit of joinery.

The locks were turned. Christina had expected she knew not what: army-barracks-functional? The unmistakeable whiff of blanco and dubbin? What she saw was a cosy attic room with a sloping ceiling, lit by dormer windows, with a goatskin rug on the floor and a bright scarlet horse-blanket bedcover and embroidered scatter-cushions and easy chairs and a tapestry footstool.

'Sit you down,' said Corky, and took a bottle of whisky from a cupboard and poured two generous measures and settled herself in front of the fire, pulling up her skirt to allow its warmth direct access to her knees. 'It's my arthuritis,' she explained. 'Always worse when it's damp. Always get the pain in winter, no matter how much exercise I take. You can't halt the clock altogether. That's what Her Ladyship'll find out one of these fine days. She's wearing well up to now, but it'll come, choose how many pots of cream she coats herself with. It comes to us all.'

Because she did not want to enter with Corky into an anti-Gwen alliance – though, to do her justice, Corky rarely said behind Gwen's back what she wasn't prepared to say to her face – and to avoid making an issue of her disinclination, Christina got up and wandered round the room, inspecting the ornaments, which were mainly souvenirs by the look of them: brass ashtrays and chains of elephants linked trunk to tail, layered Isle of Wight sand in glass containers, a plastic model of the Eiffel Tower, castanets and paper knives in the form of daggers mass-produced in Toledo, miniature panniered Majorcan donkeys and Palestinian camels and Catalonian fighting bulls, curly-toed Turkish slippers and apothecary-jar-coloured mock-Venetian goblets, doll-sized Dutch clogs and German beer steins – clearly there wasn't a package tour from which Corky had not hauled back a memento of the most tasteless sort. Perhaps it was a good job that they *were* behind lock and key, hidden from view; Gwen would hardly have allowed them to be displayed among her own ornaments that had been mostly purchased in accordance with expert advice.

Never had she been in a room – seemingly crammed with personal effects – that exuded such a strong odour of impersonality. Even the silver cup on the mantelpiece was inscribed with the legend that it had been awarded to the best fat goose in the show.

'Oh that!' Corky massaged her knees. 'I won that at school. It was during the war. You couldn't get silver cups for love nor money. Somebody donated it. They were going to have it reengraved but they never got round to it.' She picked it up, breathed on it and polished it with her sleeve. 'Yes,' she said, replacing it on the shelf, 'I've taken some stick over the years on account of that.'

'What did you win it for?'

'Sports. Best all-round athlete.'

She refilled her glass, felt behind the clock and produced her tobacco tin and began to roll herself a cigarette. 'Nowadays,' she said, 'it would be more likely to be for the best fat goose – size I'm getting to be.'

'You were always athletic then? When you were in the army?' Christina asked, noticing as she did the odd, shutter-like effect that you saw in Corky's eyes whenever she was obliged to answer a direct personal question.

'I did a bit, yes. Drink your drink.'

Interpreting this as a signal that hospitality was about to be withdrawn, Christina did so and put down her glass and moved towards the door. But Corky sat still and said, 'Can you keep something under your hat?' and took what appeared to be a photograph album from the shelf beneath her television set.

Christina had expected family snaps, was disappointed to find that the album was actually a scrapbook, filled with cuttings referring to the marathons and fun runs that had been organised in recent years and which had attracted such a huge amount of public interest. She looked at limbless persons and paraplegics urging their wheelchairs across finishing lines, at Jimmy Savile jogging along with a cigar in his mouth, at mock waiters and bunny girls and Mickey Mouses rattling their collecting tins as they ran. Corky watched her as she turned over the pages, then she pursed her lips, nodded her head and winked. 'Just don't let on to Madame Fanakapan, will you? I can do very well without her sarky comments.'

'Let on? About what?'

'Going to enter, aren't I? Going to put my name down.'

'But . . .' Christina said, and then thought of the wheelchairs and the funrunners and those whose aim was to collect money for charity. But Corky had the glint of naked ambition in her eye. She would not be running for fun or charity, but to win. Or, at least, to be seen as a serious contender. The road, shortening now, that led towards the pension-book and the bus-pass would not be taken at a leisurely stroll but rather breakneck, at the gallop. One could only admire her courage. Or deplore her recklessness.

Lovingly, she smoothed her press-cuttings, closed her album and stowed it away. And then the expression on her face changed abruptly from a sort of dreaming fondness to an intense and narrow-eyed regard. 'What were you saying earlier on?' she asked. 'About some man hanging around?'

But Christina was ceasing to believe in the uncorroborated evidence of her senses. If someone else saw a man, then there was a man; if they didn't, then there wasn't. And what was the point of voicing her fears only to be mocked and told that she was going round the bend?

She said, 'I thought so, but now I'm not sure. Like Gwen said, my nerves are bad and I'm seeing things. It's being alone in that house – and all the rest, that did it, I suppose.'

Corky drew in a great lungful of smoke and exhaled it steadily in a long stream from her nostrils. 'Shook you up a bit, didn't it?' she said.

'Yes, a bit.'

Corky gave her knees successive brisk bouts of massage and then pulled down her skirt. (She wore a skirt as often as she wore trousers, but it was Corky in trousers that you always pictured in your mind's eye.) 'Time,' she said. 'That's the thing. Hurts as much, but matters less. In time. But you'll know that.'

Christina nodded, knowing only that if everyone said so then it must be so.

'Not that there's one worth losing a minute's sleep over. I expect you know that as well. Another drink?'

Christina shook her head. She was aware that there was a certain sort of covert consensus arrived at between women at a particular stage of their lives on the subject of the absolute unsatisfactoriness of every member of the male sex, but also an agreement that, for various reasons: financial, emotional – less often sexual – they must be put up with. She couldn't imagine reaching this point of view and even if she did, couldn't understand why it should make her feel happier and less likely to lose sleep.

Corky got up and refilled her glass. 'Talking of hanging about,' she said. 'I've seen your lad, the younger one, a few times now in town during the day. Mooching around. Shouldn't he be in school?'

'Oh, it's all right. Nothing sinister. The teachers are on strike and I believe they have a lot of cancelled lessons. I expect he goes into town for something to do.'

Said so nonchalantly that Corky could never have suspected her disquiet. Even if he was, genuinely, at liberty, rather than playing truant, shouldn't he be at home or in a library, revising for his exams? Mooching suggested a kind of directionless progress, a dangerously unoccupied state in which any passing temptation might be difficult to resist.

She managed to speak to Adam on the phone without having to do it via Max. When she said, 'You *are* going into school as you should be, aren't you, Adam?' he said, 'Yeah, course I am when we've actually got a lesson to go in *to*. Most of 'em get cancelled.'

'Won't this affect your exam work?'

'Dunno. Dad said he's going to arrange some private tuition or something.'

Well then *that* was all right, wasn't it? But acting on the very slight suspicion that it wasn't, she rang his school, pretending that she'd mislaid the note with the date of that term's parent-teacher meeting. 'Oh dear,' the secretary had said. 'I'm afraid it's been and gone. A couple of weeks ago. The next one, for the Lower Fifth, isn't until March 20th, after the results of their Mocks have come through.'

Bloody Max! Keeping it from her. Bloody, vindictive Max, who thought he could cancel her out as the mother of his sons as well as his wife. She was tempted to ring him (always assuming she got the chance to speak before he put the phone down on her); it seemed such a long time to have to wait – until March – to find out whether she was panicking unnecessarily. For that was what he would accuse her of, as he had done so often in the past. He'd also accused her, equally as often, of adopting too *laissez-faire* an attitude towards life's more urgent dilemmas; no balance, he'd said, that was her trouble, no satisfactory equilibrium.

And it was in this sort of atmosphere, in the chilly aftermath of the rows that had followed upon those sort of accusations, that Adam had spent his formative years. How typical was this? Scarcely? Very? If the latter, as the break-up of one in three marriages would suggest, then how come parents didn't produce monsters all the time rather than just now and again? Or, at least, long lines of the emotionally crippled, columns of the incurably damaged? Human resilience was beyond human understanding. As was human vulnerability. *And* what determined one rather than the other. Somehow, she suspected that all the socio-psychological research in the world would never uncover the reasons. Or the psycho-sociological research, for that matter.

On the subject of which, her own, rather more mundane attempts to understand human behaviour were proceeding at a slower rate than Dr Roberts found satisfactory. Christina submitted to a telling-off. Jinx, sorting notes in the outer office, distorted her expression into a series of leering grimaces as a gesture of solidarity. 'Dr HE Rhubarb' it said in scrambled letters on the desk. Christina averted her eyes, strove for composure.

Not only was the interviewing behind schedule, but the recordings of interpersonal relations were vouchsafing precious little enlightenment. Christina appeared to be failing to elicit the concealed motivations that underlay the obvious clusters and caucuses of group function; the quality of her participant observation told of either too little participation or insufficiently keen observation. Or both.

There had been a meaningful pause, during which Christina had realised that Hilary Roberts' bad humour was prompted by something more than mere personal animosity: the data amassed so far seemed to be refusing to fit her theory, and there is nothing more frustrating than to face the prospect of the slaughter of a beautiful hypothesis by an ugly fact.

'Aren't the members putting in some work on the garden project this weekend?' she asked.

Christina nodded.

'Then perhaps you might see your way clear to turning up there for a while at least. We need to start getting some results. And quickly.'

The point was taken. On the following Saturday morning, equipped with notebook and pen and two sweaters, Christina presented herself for general labouring duties at a patch of derelict land on the south side of the city.

Surprisingly, a fair number of people had turned up to offer their services. Perhaps it was simply a reaction against the fogs of the past weeks, a siren-luring to outdoors and exercise occasioned by a spell of warm weather that, falsely, hinted at spring. Norman was there, and Jim and John, Klaus and the Twins, Kenneth and Robin and, among a few other unfamiliar faces, a woman who turned out to be Robin's wife.

She was exactly what you would have expected of an evangel-ical curate's wife. (Why did life, with such dreary predictability, confirm one's most pessimistic expectations, Christina wondered; why couldn't Robin's wife have looked like Joan Collins?): plain, dowdily-dressed and exuding that air of irrepressible cheerful-ness that might induce the depressed to contemplate the compet-ing attractions of suicide. Her children, equally plain, all three of them, and extremely glum, had been brought along to swell the ranks. 'Even the tinies can do their bit, can't they?' she said, their mother: Joyce, her rosy, pug-featured face lit with that all-can-be-well-with-the-world-if-only-we-all-try-jolly-hard radi-ance that results from excellent health, unquenchable optimism and a somewhat blunted intelligence. 'Tab,' she called, 'Tab, Tabitha!' attempting to engage the attention of the smallest child who had taken off a mitten for the purpose of a thorough investigation of her left nostril, 'Out, please, at once! Dorcas, put on Tabitha's glove. Simon, find her a little trowel and she can do a bit of digging in the borders. You'd like to plant some sweet little flowers, wouldn't you, Tab?'

Tabitha stared vacantly, sniffed up the bogey she'd almost succeeded in dislodging and, inertly, allowed her hand to be rammed back into its mitten. Norman, who was striding around self-importantly, determined to let everyone know that only he was qualified to issue instruction, caught the tail-end of this remark. 'Sweet little flowers,' he repeated derisively. 'In Novem-ber! Which sweet little flowers would those be? Dear, oh dear!'

And he shook his head and affected mirth at being lumbered with such a bunch of horticultural ignoramuses before clapping his hands together and then cupping them, megaphone-style, and shouting through them: 'Now then! If I can have your attention.'

The company was divided into twos according to the principle of immediately prevailing proximity (Kenneth, who had obviously wanted to be with Robin, was standing closer to red-pixie-hooded Linda and, as a result of this pairing, prepared to sulk) and allotted their tasks: digging, weeding, ground-clearing, fence-dismantling, depending upon their sex and/or physical capability. Christina and Joyce ('Oh, *jolly* good,' Joyce said, beaming, in the manner of a member of the fourth form whose best friend has just been chosen for the same rounders team) were provided with a wheelbarrow and instructed to remove unearthed stones and transport them to where Kenneth and Linda (whose equality in terms of girth and bulk and strength cancelled out the gender difference) waited to sort out the ones that could be used for a rockery.

The pair of them performed this task with an extremely bad grace. Blue-pixie-hooded Maureen had been paired with Klaus and had seized the opportunity of this advantage to the full: much girlish laughter was to be heard. Linda's sulking was quite as accomplished as Kenneth's. 'You're a proper pair of Dismal Desmonds,' Joyce said, digging the heels of her wellingtons into the rutted ground in order to brake the wheelbarrow which, Christina noted with grudging admiration, she pushed with the strength of ten.

'Didn't succeed in persuading yours to lend a hand then?' Joyce asked, grunting with effort as she hauled large lumps of stone over to the barrow. The colour of her face had turned traffic-light red and perspiration poured from it.

'Mine?'

'Your son. You've got a son, haven't you? I'm sure Ken mentioned you had a son. Thought you might have brought him with you. Young lads usually have lots of excess energy to be worked off. Only use it doing something they shouldn't, otherwise.'

'. . . I've seen your lad . . . a few times in town . . . during the day . . . mooching around . . .'

'Of course,' Joyce said, wiping her dripping nose on the back of her glove, 'we haven't reached that stage yet. Ours are still merely a nuisance with chicken-pox and whatnot and not wanting to go to bed and so on.'

They scraped away, her children, the three of them, silently and morosely, with hoes of varying sizes, at a patch of earth intended for a rose bed.

'They're very good though, I must admit. On the whole, you'd hardly know they were there. And each one takes care of the next.'

At that moment, beyond Joyce's field of vision, Simon hit Dorcas on the ankle with his hoe. Whether this was accidental or deliberate was impossible to tell. Instead of yelling, Dorcas, in turn, applied her hoe to Tabitha's ankle, an assault which provoked, not noise and tears, but instead a moon-faced stare and a resigned moving out of harm's way. The eerie, silent-film quality of their antipathy made one shiver. Joyce, unaware, continued, 'However much we moan, we wouldn't be without them, would we? And they certainly couldn't do without us.'

Couldn't they? Oh to be as certain as Joyce of that fact.

'Oh well,' she said, 'mustn't shirk or the job'll never get done.' Unaided, she hefted a stone which looked to be equal in weight to a sack of coal into her wheelbarrow. 'We must get to know each other,' she said, in a tone which brooked no argument and which so unnerved Christina that she begged a respite from duty, pleading exhaustion: 'This flu, you know, takes it out of you.'

'I never get flu,' Joyce said. 'I don't have the *time*.'

Joyce's enthusiasm and industry were not typical of the spirit of the group. Most were beginning to flag by the time they were called together for a mid-morning drink. Christina sat on the edge of a garden roller, balanced her notebook on her knee and wrote: 'Norman is enthusiastic, but in his role as site-foreman apparently doesn't think that he ought to participate in the labouring. John works doggedly enough, but Jim talks more than he works and distracts the others. Maureen is flirting with Klaus. Linda is watching Maureen flirting with Klaus and therefore attending only spasmodically to the task in hand. Kenneth has the air about him of one who is due, at any moment, to stamp his foot and burst into tears.'

Later, she would attempt to translate all this into some sort of diagram. She didn't know how, exactly, but she'd think of something.

'Budge up,' Joyce said, claiming a space on the roller. 'Whew,' she said. 'Soon warms you up, doesn't it, a bit of running around?' She had taken off her anorak and, as Christina had suspected would be the case, released a heady scent of perspiration from beneath the armpits of her sweater. Onions, Christina identified as being its main constituent, onions and wet sheep.

Suddenly shrieks were heard. Investigation showed that they were being emitted by Joyce's children who, in the course of poking behind a crumbling brick wall, had unearthed a cache of hibernating snails.

The shrieks were occasioned not by horror but delight. And here, for the first time that day, was to be observed the true spirit of cooperation: Tabitha dislodged the snails from the crevices in the mortar where they had secreted themselves, Dorcas arranged them in an orderly heap on the ground, and Simon lifted his hoe above his head and smashed it down upon the cluster of shells thus assembled.

'Oh dear.'

Joyce ran across to the scene of the carnage. Robin was doing the same from the opposite direction. 'No, no,' she heard him say, and then, predictably, something about God's creatures. Simon let his hoe fall once more upon the few intact shells that were left, Dorcas scraped mangled remains from the sole of her wellington boot, Tabitha returned to investigating her nostril. Then they allowed themselves to be arranged at Robin's knee: he had squatted, the better to impart to them whatever parable he considered appropriate for the occasion. There might well be one concerning the undesirability of the wholesale slaughter of snail colonies.

Kenneth would know. He took Joyce's place on the roller. The reek of one sort of sweat was replaced by odorous gusts of another. He warmed his hands around his Bovril mug. 'Little horrors,' he said.

He must be really out of sorts. Joyce had confided earlier, during one of their journeys to the skip, that Ken was marvellous with the kids, got on with them like a house on fire. 'No qualms,' Joyce had said. 'No qualms at all.'

Whatever that meant.

'Proper discipline, that's what's lacking,' Kenneth said, blowing vigorously across the surface of the Bovril. 'As if you can *explain* everything to kids,' he said scornfully.

No response, beyond the odd corroborative grunt, seemed to be required. Sidelong, she studied him, the entire unappetising bulk of him: his hair, lanker than ever due to dampening with the perspiration of effort, looked as though it had been cut with a knife and fork. His cold had bequeathed him a couple of weeping sores each side of his upper lip and patches of scurfy skin around his nostrils.

Nevertheless, some mother's son who had once, difficult though it was to imagine, been a child as young as Robin's children, who now, Christina saw, had been induced to put their hands together and bow their heads and, presumably, pray for the souls of departed gastropods.

'Oh *no*,' Kenneth said suddenly. He slammed his mug down on the roller so hard that Bovril splashed over his knee. And hers too.

'What's the matter?'

She followed his gaze. At the far side of the land, between the gate stumps, there stood a man, very still, looking across towards them with exactly the same kind of fixity of attention that had been directed at Gwen's house.

She blinked her eyes rapidly in the attempt to get a clearer focus. Was it the same man? *Could* it be? Or was her mind disintegrating? *Did* mad people know they were mad? If their delusions were sufficiently bizarre then it was conceivable that they might just suspect that something was amiss, but a man was a man, and this one was still there.

Kenneth peevishly dashed the rest of his Bovril to the ground. 'Trust him,' he said. 'Pushing himself in where he isn't wanted.'

But Robin, who had, by now, concluded the prayer meeting and risen to his feet, obviously wanted him. The expansiveness of his gestures as he strode towards the gate-posts suggested that there wasn't a soul in the world he wanted more. His greeting travelled across to them faintly through the still air: '. . . *so* pleased . . . *knew* you'd try . . . meet some of the others.'

'Who *is* it?' she enquired of Kenneth, who was staring gloomily at the ground and picking savagely at one of his cold sores. She peered intently in the man's direction. Perhaps he was taller? Or broader? Or fairer, than the man who had gazed at Gwen's house from the shelter of the trees, through the glass of the telephone kiosk, around the corner of the gardens?

'Don't ask *me*,' Kenneth said, and winced as he detached a crust from his sore and exposed the weeping surface beneath.

'He's got a room in the house where I live,' he said at length and grudgingly. 'He's been to Robin and Joyce's a couple of times. Worming his way in.'

Obviously evangelical zeal was no match for the plain, ordinary, common or garden, green-eyed monster: Robin, Christina felt, would accord to the newest member the greatest amount of attention. Which was how it should be, from the point of view of gaining converts.

But not from the hero-worshipping point of view. Or the close friendship stance. Or the being-in-love position. Kenneth kicked at the roller with his heels. 'Robin's too trusting,' he said. 'Too ready to see good in everybody.'

She refrained from commenting that this was, surely, a *sine qua non* of the clergyman's function. Nothing that she said could have helped anyway.

'I won't forget *your* face in a hurry,' she had told herself when the man had stared at her through the windows of the telephone box. But she had. Or, at least, had not remembered it well enough to be certain that the face that now came, increasingly, into clearer focus was one and the same.

No particularly distinguishing feature, that was the snag: average height, average build, medium colouring; wearing a pair of trousers and an anorak such as are worn by possibly seventy-five per cent of males between the ages of sixteen and sixty. She watched him as Robin moved with him through the garden performing introductions, tried to superimpose *that* face upon this one, to make the template fit. It *could* be him. And then again . . .

'Of course, you know Kenneth, don't you?' Robin said. 'And this is Christina. Christina, meet Murray, a member of our congregation.'

He nodded towards her. There was no flicker of any corresponding recognition, nothing to suggest that she had been the subject of his surveillance over the past week. She stared at his face, longer than was strictly polite. It was a not-unattractive face: high-cheekboned, square-chinned, with a lock of pale hair falling across a broad forehead and, for a moment, she was aware of a certain familiarity about it (above and beyond the familiarity of supposing him to be the watcher in the square), but for the life of her she couldn't think who it was he reminded her of.

'Murray Pearl,' Robin said. 'I've been trying to persuade him to join our little band for weeks.'

For the first time the merest hint of an expression flickered over the young man's face and there was a slight movement of his upper lip. He might have been suppressing a smile – or a sneer.

'Well,' said Robin and engaged in hand-washing gestures, 'this won't buy baby a new bonnet. Let's go and see what plans Norman has for us, shall we?'

They walked away. Kenneth kicked the roller again and winced as he jarred the sole of his foot against the unyielding cast-iron surface. 'I wouldn't trust him,' he said, in the tone of one who considers it his public duty to issue a timely warning, 'as far as I could throw him.'

'Why's that?'

She was coming to the conclusion that her initial assumption had been wrong. She had been led astray by the stillness of his stance, the fixity of his gaze. Any average-looking man, standing thus, staring in that way, would probably have filled the bill.

Kenneth was shaking his head in the manner of one who could reveal earth-shattering secrets, had he a mind to do so. 'Too close for my liking,' he said. 'Never lets anything drop about himself.'

But neither did Kenneth. At least, he never volunteered information. And she was all in favour of reticence, if the alternative was unremittent disclosure.

'And *smarmy*,' Kenneth said. And then he said, 'Oh!' in alarm, because Joyce, having crept up behind him unnoticed, had clapped her hands over his eyes.

She found this antic extremely amusing. She chuckled and chortled and said, 'Honestly! Your face! Anyway, time to get back to work, you shirkers. The garden won't dig itself.'

Her enthusiasm was not contagious. It wasn't long before watches were being consulted and a tacit consensus arrived at that it was time to break for lunch. A pub lunch – to Christina's surprise; though she wasn't sure why she had supposed that inviting Jesus into your life led inevitably to excluding alcohol from it. 'A pint and a ploughman's,' Robin said expansively, employing one of his man-of-the-people gestures: look, no uniform, and no teetotal nonsense either!

Unfortunately the Brickmakers' Arms was one of the few remaining hostelries yet to be gathered beneath the banner that proclaimed: 'Let's tart up our pubs and attract families rather than allow them to remain mere watering holes for serious drinkers.' It featured not carpets and French café curtains on rings and brass hanging lamps and an overwhelming choice of exorbitantly-priced bottled German beers, but seating covered in cracked leatherette through which the padding protruded and lino worn patternless and nicotine-coloured fixtures and fitments and an ancient barmaid whose brave attempt at a cleavage made one think of the skin covering hens' thighs and the possibility of contracting pneumonia.

Neither were there any ploughman's lunches to be had. The culinary fare on offer was restricted to a pile of limp sandwiches and a few rather pallid meat pies.

She stood at the bar, next to Murray Pearl, and the landlord, typically, chose to serve him first. There was a certain sort of landlord (most of them, if truth were told) who, if confronted with a hundred women at his bar and one man, would choose to serve the man. Christina seethed. 'The lady is before me,' Murray Pearl said, to her surprise.

Pretending not to notice Joyce's frantic gesticulations, she carried her gin and a pie to an empty table in the corner of the lounge bar. A door led from this room into the porch where Simon and Dorcas and Tabitha, excluded from entry despite Robin's entreaties, had been deposited to consume their crisps and lemonade. Faintly distorted through the figured glass though their actions were, she saw that Simon, having eaten his own, had appropriated Dorcas's crisps and Dorcas had remedied this theft by stealing Tabitha's.

She lifted the barely-cooked pastry from her pie to reveal indigestible chunks of pale meat reposing in an orange-coloured jelly and quickly replaced the covering, in the manner of one who has inadvertently raised the lid of a coffin long overdue for burial.

'Have one of these.'

He stood at the other side of her table, Murray Pearl, offering her one of his wrapped sandwiches.

'These'll probably only make you ill. That looks like it could kill you.'

He continued to hold the sandwich towards her. He said, 'I got a couple, but I find I'm not all that hungry. Mind if I sit here?'

Having accepted his sandwich, she could hardly reject his company. She made an accommodating gesture, and he placed his glass, that contained either some gin concoction suitable for a tropical verandah or else plain lemonade, on the table and pulled up a stool.

For a time they ate and drank silently, but she was not the sort who could tolerate silence for very long. She took a swig of gin, abandoned caution and said, 'Excuse me, but don't I know you from somewhere? Your face seems awfully familiar.'

'Where?'

'Sorry?'

'Know me from where?'

'Well, that's it – I don't know. Around, I suppose. Do you live anywhere near Lansdowne Gardens?'

With a fastidious gesture he edged a sandwich crumb into the corner of his mouth. He said, 'Is that near the park?'

'Yes. On the far side. Between the park and South Road.'

'No,' he said, and sipped what was, judging by its innocent vanilla-like smell, just lemonade.

'Oh yes, of course,' she said, remembering, 'you live in the same place as Kenneth, don't you?'

'That's right.'

He wiped his mouth and set the crumpled paper napkin neatly on the centre of his plate. Then he produced a tin and a packet of papers from his pocket and began to make a cigarette with gestures as accomplished, as precisely functional, as those of Jinx or Corky.

When it was finished and lit, he drew upon it hungrily and then, regarding her quizzically through a plume of exhaled smoke, said, 'You're not one of Robin's lot, are you?'

'No,' she said, horrified that anyone might assume this to be the case. 'No, I'm attached to the Social Sciences Department at the Poly. We're doing a project involving The System: interpersonal relations, how people view each other in this kind of situation.'

'And how do they?'

She was brought up short by his question. He regarded her keenly through the perfect smoke ring that floated upwards from his steadily-held cigarette. She said feebly, 'Well I'm not sure yet. I've not been doing it for very long. Besides, I'm only the research assistant, the dogsbody. I just collect the data. It's other people who draw the conclusions.'

'Didn't think you looked like one of Robin's lot,' was all he said and then he swallowed the final inch of lemonade that was left in his glass and extinguished his cigarette and excused himself to visit the Gents.

Joyce was having hiccoughs. They sounded histrionic but were probably genuinely uncontrollable. Robin had thumped her on the back. Kenneth had dropped a key down the neck of her sweater. Now she was attempting to sip water from the side of the glass furthest away from her mouth. 'I guzzled my – hic – Coke,' she explained, raising her head from this messy and ineffective operation. 'Oh I say,' she said, spotting Christina's glass. 'You *are* – hic – hitting the bottle, aren't you? Don't want you falling down drunk on the job this afternoon – hic.'

If Christina had done so, it would have left only four of them (not counting the children) to proceed with clearing the site. Some people had justified their departure with excuses; the rest simply didn't return.

Robin said, 'Oh well,' in the philosophical tone of one accustomed to human frailty, but Joyce was incensed. 'Well really!' she said. 'Well – hic – really! They might – hic – have said!'

Her eructations had ceased to be amusing and were now starting to irritate. 'Have you tried holding your breath?' Kenneth asked testily, as though the idea of forever might not have been far from his thoughts.

'Tried it. *And* drinking water upside down. And drinking it through a tissue. Tried them all – hic. Hic!'

The spasm transformed itself into a scream as a half-brick came flying past her, its trajectory allowing for scarcely any margin of error.

They turned, agog. Murray Pearl, a distance away, was wiping brick dust from his hands. 'A shock,' he called. 'Usually does the trick.'

'I expect a fractured skull would do the trick as well,' Kenneth said. 'You could have killed her.'

Murray Pearl only smiled and shook his head.

Joyce looked rather pale, but the hiccoughs had stopped.

'It *was* a bit reckless, surely?' Christina murmured later to Robin, who was helping her to sort out the gardening equipment.

Robin ran a hand across the top of his coconut-matting hair, a gesture he used often when giving due consideration to another's opinion, however misinformed.

'Perhaps if any of *us* had done it, yes,' he said. 'But I believe Murray is something of an expert in judging distances. Shot for the army, I believe, at one time.'

Christina thought that shooting for the army was a prerequisite for being in it. Robin patiently explained himself with greater clarity: Murray Pearl had been in the army and had distinguished himself at target-shooting. Obviously one would feel a great deal more confident if someone with that sort of expertise, rather than just any old body, chucked half a brick in close proximity to one's wife's left ear.

In the gloaming, at the far end of the plot, Murray Pearl uprooted privet, working methodically and rhythmically.

'Has he left the army then?' she asked Robin.

'Yes,' he said. 'So sad, people's circumstances, aren't they?'

Were they and *what* were they? But she hadn't time to get the questions out before he had moved on, to explain the principle of equal distribution to Simon who was dividing a packet of fruit gums between himself and his sisters at the expected ratio of two to one, but in favour of himself.

3

Her days acquired a pattern. She moved through them like a sleepwalker, conducting interviews, sitting at the computer terminal and translating responses into numbers on charts and dots on graphs and then reporting to Hilary Roberts who scrutinised these preliminary analyses, suggested modifications, urged keener attention and demanded more rapid results. On Thursdays she attended successive and equally inconclusive meetings of The System. On Wednesdays, after school, she met Adam in the Concourse café. ('Is everything all right?' 'Course it is.' The time he could spare for these meetings seemed to dwindle as the weeks went by.) At the weekends she looked for a room, but as Christmas drew closer, what little enthusiasm she had waned even further. Christmas at Gwen's might be something of an ordeal, but it was infinitely preferable to Christmas alone.

Gwen coopted her to assist with the decorating of Klosters; the existing staff, decimated by illness, was direly in need of augmentation. 'Flu viruses!' Gwen said. 'They're just too anxious to succumb, some of them, if you ask my opinion. It's all a question of attitude. Some of us have to soldier on regardless.'

So Christina, together with those few on Gwen's payroll whose white corpuscles were efficiently fighting off infection, had mounted a pair of stepladders with a packet of drawing pins and a card of Blu-tack and patiently awaited instruction from the young man with gold highlights in his hair and trousers that sheathed his tight little buttocks like a second skin, whom Gwen had called in to supervise the decoration.

As befitted one with highly-developed aesthetic sensibilities he was prone to displays of temperament. 'Oh no!' he'd cry in tones of lamentation more in keeping with the chorus of a Greek tragedy than as a reaction to somebody hanging a streamer crooked. Occasionally, aggravated beyond endurance by the clumsiness of his labour force, he'd climb the ladder himself to fiddle with this bit of tinsel or that bauble until it met with his approval.

He *was* good though. It *did* look effective. Not particularly Christmas-y, but then Christmas-y was usually considered vulgar: glitter and cotton-wool and inaccurately-drawn stage coaches. What he had created: festoons of golden garlands, swags of tinsel and clumps of glossy green baubles, giant filigree snowflakes and rosettes of white ribbon, might be considered appropriate for any occasion from a Barmitzvah party to a Chinese New Year, but was, nevertheless, a work of window-dressing of the highest order.

Even Gwen couldn't fault it. 'It's very nice indeed, Jason,' she said, as he dusted off his hands and lifted his lilac suede blouson jacket and his cashmere scarf from the back of the chair. 'If you'd like to come into the office, I'll settle up with you.'

As they walked away, she looked back over her shoulder and called to Christina, 'If you want some lunch, you'd better come and get it now.'

There was a tray laid for two in the office. 'You don't want wine, do you?' Gwen said. 'I don't usually bother at lunchtime.'

Well, yes, I do quite fancy a glass of – well, Frascati or something of that sort – would go quite nicely with these scallops in cream, Christina said, in her head, while pouring herself a tumbler of water.

Gwen sat down gingerly. Somebody up there doesn't like me, she thought, lowering herself on to a cushion, else why should they send down the two afflictions in tandem? Haemorrhoids had long been an intermittent penance, a cross bravely borne, but haemorrhoids and *candida albicans* at one and the same time seemed like some malevolent supernatural being's idea of a bad joke.

'What's the matter?' asked Christina, as unable to ignore the grunt of pain when *derrière* made contact with cushion, as Gwen was unable to stifle it.

'Thrush,' Gwen said. She wouldn't have admitted to piles on pain of death.

'What a nuisance. They say that wearing tights can do it, don't they? Or using bath-salts.'

Or sex. But she wouldn't have dreamed of putting forward that suggestion. Nuns could get thrush.

Gwen concentrated on her scallops. 'Mm,' she said. *She wouldn't have dreamed of admitting what she suspected was the cause of the trouble.* She felt pretty certain that it was a legacy from the night she'd reluctantly acceded to Edward's demands, and she was livid. It wasn't even as if she'd derived any enjoyment, let alone satisfaction, from the activity. Edward, allowed his way, had scarcely acknowledged, beyond the odd clumsy caress, that the flesh at which he thrust himself, to the accompaniment of a great deal of unmelodious moaning and groaning, belonged to another human being and was entitled to a reciprocal degree of consideration. Though he wasn't aware of it yet, Edward had enjoyed, with her, his first and last sexual encounter. Better to enter into a relationship which involved nothing more than mutual admiration with a young man in a lilac jacket. Or there was always the possibility of the serious cultivation of Stephen Millward.

'Are you going into town this afternoon?' she enquired of Christina and, without waiting for a reply, continued, 'If you are, you could get me some things. I can't possibly spare any more time for Christmas shopping. I've made a list.'

The list was a long one. And disturbingly vague. In essence it was Gwen's list of people for whom she felt obliged to buy presents without thinking enough of them to care how suitable those presents actually were: most of the staff of Klosters, extremely peripheral social acquaintances.

'Oh and you could pick up my watch from the mender's,' Gwen said. 'And I've a handbag on order from George Henry Lee's . . .'

Christina had another two flatlets to see at the weekend. She felt that – however unsuitable they might be – she would be highly inclined to like them.

On December 22nd she rang Livingstone's number. She had intended to put the phone down as soon as he answered, her purpose being solely to ascertain that he was back. But when a voice said, '987 4327, Stephanie Lewis speaking,' she forgot her original intention and said, 'It was Alan Livingstone I wanted.'

Mr Livingstone (landlord) was still in America. He was not

expected back for a couple of months. Could she, Stephanie Lewis (tenant) take a message?

She walked away from the telephone kiosk feeling stunned. At the back of her mind had been the idea – hazy and unformulated though it was – that, by Christmas, everything would be all right.

She made her way back to Gwen's, past giggling revellers and gift-laden commuters, shop windows full of fairy lights and blow-up Father Christmases. In the square she was waylaid by a group of carol-singing con-merchants who rendered the first few bars of 'Good King Wenceslas' and then demanded money, only just without menaces. No wonder you never had them at your door these days, she reflected, as she meekly paid up: they didn't need to bother, they could earn as much from highway robbery.

She told Gwen about it when she got in. 'Then you're a fool,' Gwen said, as if that fact – of which she was already cognisant – required further emphasis. 'I sent them off with a flea in their ear. Did they pester you, Jason?'

Jason, wonderfully decadent-looking in designer black leather that drew its inspiration from Hell's Angels but interpreted it in terms of thirties' Berlin transvestite chic rather than dirt-track sweat, shook his head and smiled as if to imply that urchins of that sort would recognise class when they saw it and be too over-awed to approach.

He'd come over in his cute little customised Alfa to deliver some more of the decorations that were to enhance the one or two soirées that Gwen had organised for the odd moment she would have free during this traditionally hectic period in the restaurateur's calendar. What, Gwen wondered, were Christina's plans?

What indeed? She thought of Christmases past. Max's firm always had a party. Each of them, in different ways, had found it an embarrassing ordeal: Max because letting his hair down and pretending to be one of the boys caused him actual physical pain – his ulcer always played up dreadfully afterwards, Christina because she was quite unable to reconcile the Max who exchanged pleasantries with his employees and danced with their wives and who, on one never-to-be-forgotten occasion, had been induced to lead a pack of roisterers in the conga, with the Max who grumbled endlessly about his workforce and criticised everything about them from the way they combed their hair to the knots in their shoelaces.

She wondered how he'd coped this year, how he'd explained away her absence, couldn't imagine anything, this year, inducing him to lead them in a conga.

No husband, this year, no lover either but, ever-hopeful, she rang David and actually managed to speak to him, only to be told that he wasn't returning until Christmas Eve and even then, well, he had his own friends just as Adam did.

She would see them, briefly. They would exchange presents. She would kiss their respective bristly and downy cheeks and plead with them to spare her just a little more time. They would explain, at first patiently and then less patiently, that they had lives of their own, that (in David's case), much as he would like to stay, he had promised Ben or Dan or Jane or Kate, that there was this party or that concert; Adam, if questioned as to his destination, would merely say, 'Out.'

What alternative did she have to attendance at Gwen's dinner parties, to enduring whatever insults Mr McTavish with the Adam's apple cared to fling at her?

Just one, it seemed: to take up the open-ended invitation that had been issued repeatedly by the Perrots, Joyce and Robin, and which, now that the season when we celebrated Our Saviour's birth, when we publicly reaffirmed our oneness with the Lord Jesus, approached, had become more specific: a party the night before Christmas Eve for all the gang and anyone else who cared to join in. 'You know us,' Joyce had said. 'It's always open house with us.'

She had been reminded of Jumbo, who also kept an open house. His hospitality had consisted of card schools and bottle upon gleaming bottle of liquor and big fat Havana cigars for the big fat men who accepted his invitations (and women who took their clothes off sometimes, Gwen had reported, women who could be spied through a gap in the concealing curtain, peeling off elbow-length black satin gloves and several, progressively-scantier, brassieres to reveal large bosoms usually well past their pert and jutting prime; the big fat men, Gwen had reported, had appeared to be entirely unmoved by the spectacle of all this liberated flesh, and continued, unblinkingly, to pour from bottle to glass, to puff on their cigars and tap their playing-cards against their thumbnails).

The Perrots' hospitality would be somewhat different, Christina supposed, would remind her of those teenage parties that hadn't been much to her taste even as a teenager. It was necessary to dwell upon the alternative horrors: Gwen condescending, Mr McTavish hissing insults, before she could bring herself to convey to Joyce, via Kenneth, that she would be delighted . . .

'And what about you, Colette?' she asked, as they packed up their belongings in the office. 'Will you be spending Christmas with your family?'

For some reason she imagined Colette as issuing from a large extended family, all of them living in close proximity to her home: a council house on an outlying estate which – such was the incidence of unemployment among its residents and so extreme their inability or reluctance to pay their debts – was known locally as Dodge City.

'Haven't got any family,' Colette replied. 'There's only me and Don. For the present, at any rate,' she said, and passed a protective hand across the bump that had only recently begun to proclaim itself beneath her smocks when she stood sideways. 'Never had a family,' she said, and went on to explain that she had been brought up in a Catholic orphanage, the female equivalent, presumably, of that inhabited by the infant Donald Donaldson. Like him, she had been abandoned to the care of others at a very early age, parents unknown.

'Have you never tried to trace them? Either of you?'

Colette clicked the cover on to her typewriter. 'How could we trace them?' she said. 'Don was left on the doorstep of the Home, and they found me in the Ladies' toilet at the bus station. There's nothing you could start tracing from. Anyway,' she said, 'best left alone, if you ask me. Never know what you might find.'

Pass the parcel, they'd played (the prize reposing in the middle, which Christina had had the misfortune to win, turned out to be a little book entitled *Onward to Glory*, the autobiography of a deep-dyed-sinner-turned-evangelist. There was a picture of him on the back: West Point haircut, blinding smile, Nuremberg rally eyes).

Choruses, they'd sung, interspersed with carols. Someone called Audrey, who had an advanced case of acne, played the piano. It was obvious that whatever her degree of accomplishment, it had been achieved by hard work and owed nothing to any natural talent. To this thudding accompaniment they sang 'Hark the Herald Angels' and 'I Saw Three Ships' before moving on to tunes for which only Christina and Murray Pearl didn't know the words: 'Just as I am, without one plea, oh lamb of God, I come'; 'What a friend we have in Jesus, all our sins and griefs to bear . . .' Hearts and souls were put into the singing of these choruses. The vocalising of highly-charged emotion made up for the accompaniment's lack of brio. Some of the party began to jump up and down. At one point a voice was heard to utter, 'Jesus, my saviour!', its timbre recalling the sound of utterances made in the course of sexual transports.

After the choruses they played a game in which each person had a card with a name printed on it pinned to his or her back and was then encouraged to guess, by means of indirect questioning of other guests, this bestowed identity. The names were all biblical: Joyce was Martha; Christina, unable to guess herself despite much suggestive giggling, proved to be Delilah; Murray Pearl was Lazarus.

Then there was a quoting contest: Robin read out passages from the New Testament and marks were awarded to those who could successfully identify the source. For Christina, an exception was made in terms of an exceptionally easily-identifiable passage. Because of this, she scored two marks. The winner, Audrey, scored forty-four. Murray Pearl scored nil. As did Kenneth, who sat through this competition with the sort of expression on his face that suggested he could answer correctly if he wanted to; he just didn't want to.

Subsequent to this game, someone suggested the one with the balloons – which were in plentiful supply among the streamers criss-crossing the cracked plaster ceiling and hanging, looped, from the shabbily-decorated walls of the Perrots' sitting-room. At this point, Christina enquired as to the location of the lavatory and excused herself.

Strip-poker, they used to play, sometimes: Jumbo and his dour party-guests and their female companions, Gwen had reported. Late at night in the close-curtained cocktail bar – but only when Gwen's mother was away; Jumbo was a respectful husband and a devoted father and he'd have been devastated if he'd discovered that it was Gwennie's habit to tiptoe round the rose-garden and peep in at the french windows. Once, Gwen had reported, she'd seen a woman totally naked except for her peep-toed sandals. As she watched, one of the fat men had taken the naked woman's hand and rubbed it slowly across the front of his trousers. Gwen, who needed the lavatory anyway, had almost wet herself. Her breath had misted up the window so that, in order to witness the next, enlightening phase of this debauchery, she'd had to wipe it clear with her sleeve, just in time – to her chagrin – to see the man and the woman leaving the room.

As she climbed the Perrots' staircase, which was strewn with the small broken pieces of plastic that so often betoken a household containing more children than can be effectively regulated, Christina thought that a bit of an orgy might not have come amiss as an alternative to the frantic and determined juvenility of this evening's activities.

The Perrots' bathroom was as huge and cold and spartan as the rest of their house. Christina suspected that the water that ran from the hot tap would be cold. It was. Cringing, she rinsed her hands beneath it. Verdigris stained the basin, there was a ring round the bath and the plug was tied on with a piece of string. A similar piece of string was attached to the lavatory chain to bring it within reach of a child's grasp – though it appeared that the last child who'd emptied its bladder hadn't made use of this facility.

In the world of salvation and redemption which was the Perrots' domain, none of these details would matter. Cleanliness, in Joyce's view – if ever she thought about it – would not come next to godliness but be seen, in its extreme form at least, as a highly-neurotic preoccupation. Presumably Robin abluted every morning and shaved his narrow chin with this blunt blade and cold water, and didn't mind a bit. Max would have had a triple fit.

She whiled away her unnecessarily long stay in the bathroom by imagining super-fastidious Max married to not-so-fastidious Joyce and came to the conclusion that in the ensuing battle of wills it would be hers that would prevail, simply because none of his stratagems: sulking, nagging or silence, would succeed in penetrating the carapace of insensitivity that protected Joyce's inner self from hurt. 'You are a Dismal Desmond,' she'd say, failing to notice his pallor, the tic beating in his cheek, the grey desolation of his gaze. If Joyce had been married to Max, she'd either have tamed him or driven him totally mad.

Joyce was in the hall, carrying through a tray of mince pies. She dropped a couple on the floor and, presumably considering herself to be unobserved, bent to pick them up. Christina looked down over the banister rail upon her beam end which was clad in a pair of those dark-green, too-short, Crimplene slacks, sizes sixteen and eighteen, that hang in such depressing rows in chain stores as an awful warning to all but the most determinedly youthful of women of what the approach of middle age may actually entail.

'Enjoying yourself?'

The mince pie plate was thrust beneath her nose. 'Give us a smile then,' Joyce prompted, baring her teeth in an unnervingly wide example of that which was to be imitated. 'Come on Murray,' she shouted, having spied him at the far side of the sitting-room, also guilty of failing to display enjoyment. 'Come over here and chat to Christina. The pair of you look as though you need putting into a sack and shaking up.'

'Eat up! Drink up! Cheer up!' exhorted Joyce Perrot, stepping backwards and joggling someone's elbow so that a glass of punch got spilt on the floor. She mopped at it with her handkerchief. 'Never mind,' she said. 'It'll all come out in the wash.'

That seemed very unlikely: that there would be a wash for it to come out in. It was possible that the carpet had once boasted a vivid pattern, but that must have been long ago and however thorough their scrutiny of it, Christina's and Murray Pearl's, it did not yield up more than a blurred intermingling of threads, the pile worn flat, the original hues faded with age and obscured by dust.

Eventually they raised their faces and their eyes met. Murray Pearl's eyelid moved almost imperceptibly, but moved all the same: a wink, a wink indicating complicity. 'What a bunch of prats!' was the message conveyed by that wink. 'Just look at them!' it said. She looked: towards Robin who was distributing punch into an assortment of cups and glasses, towards Kenneth who was leaning against a bookcase with a pamphlet in his hand, looking excessively Byronic, towards Tabitha who had, illicitly, come downstairs to join in the revelry and stood sucking a piece of soiled blanket and plucking the sodden fabric of her pyjama bottoms away from her crotch while various persons patted her on the head and offered her titbits and, because it was the festive season, generally spoiled her in a manner usually reserved for rather more winsome children.

She looked and was very tempted to wink back, was as pleasantly surprised as when she'd discovered, during Gwen's dreadful dinner party, that she had an ally in Stephen Millward.

'How's life in Lansdowne Gardens then?' Murray Pearl said.

'Oh, all right, I suppose.' She took a drink of the noxious punch both for something to do and because she thought it might supply sufficient Dutch courage to get her through the rest of the evening.

'They're big houses, those, aren't they?' he commented. 'Are they in flats?'

'No. I live with my cousin. She owns the house.'

'Is that the one who runs the wine bar?'

He raised a hand and pushed a lock of hair back from his forehead. She was instantly reminded – but too faintly to be able to identify the source – of somebody else who made that identical gesture. 'Yes,' she said. 'How did you know?'

'Oh' – he motioned with the hand that held the medicine-measuring vial containing his punch. 'Ken said.'

She wouldn't have expected there to be any communication between them, in view of Kenneth's antipathy towards him.

'I just thought,' he said, 'maybe they were in flats. I'm looking for a flat.'

'So am I,' she said. 'Not easy, is it?'

He shook his head. 'I didn't realise just how difficult it would be. I haven't really got the hang of it yet, flat-hunting. Well civilian life generally. If you hear of anything,' he said, 'that won't do for you but might do for me . . .'

'Yes,' she said, 'certainly. Yes, Robin said about you being in the army . . .'

He nodded. 'Yes I was. Welsh Guards. Until last year. Until the accident.'

He gestured towards his leg. She couldn't see anything wrong with it, but perhaps the army was very strict about physical fitness. Perhaps that was what Robin had meant about it being very sad.

Audrey perched herself upon the piano stool and started to bang out some preliminary chords. The company grouped itself in a corner. Somebody led Tabitha to the front. A damp patch steamed on the seat of the chair she'd vacated.

Perhaps Gwen's party might not have been *too* awful after all, Christina thought. Comparatively. And then she thought of the parties at which, even now, Livingstone and Louise would, no doubt, be enjoying themselves, and a wave of desolation engulfed her to the extent that she could scarcely speak coherently when she finally cornered Joyce in order to make her excuses and leave.

'Are you weak and heavy-laden, burdened with a load of care?' they were starting to sing as she went upstairs for her coat. When she came down she saw Murray Pearl zipping himself into his anorak.

'You off too?'

She nodded.

'It is a *bit*, isn't it?'

'*Just* a bit.'

'Not much up your street then: God-bothering?'

'Not really, no.'

'Nor mine either.'

At the gate, they both paused, each trying to anticipate the direction the other would take. From the house they could hear: 'Praise the Lord, praise the Lord, let the people rejoice,' sung fortissimo.

'This way?' he said.

She nodded. '. . . to God be the glory, great things he has done.' Audrey must be standing on the loud pedal.

He walked along with her towards the bus-stop. She felt slightly apprehensive. *Could* she be sure that his were not the footsteps that echoed hers when she returned to Lansdowne Gardens after dark? (Still there, occasionally, either in reality, or in her head. She took no chances these days, but started to run as soon as she got off the bus.)

And if they were those same footsteps, was it safer to have them walking beside you than behind you?

A wind had sprung up. It made moaning noises as it was trapped in the passageways between the houses, caused the small limbs of trees to creak unnervingly.

Or was he after her, in the more popular sense of the phrase? Was that possible? A man more than ten years her junior? Attracted to a woman who, since October, had ceased to think of herself in terms other than being somehow deserving of universal rejection? The idea was disconcerting. Not to mention absurd. Wasn't it?

The lights of the bus appeared through the gloom. He raised a hand in farewell and carried on walking.

$$\backsim 4 \backsim$$

She rode to the terminus where she had to change buses. All the way there she was thinking: not only am I prey to paranoid delusions; now I'm falling victim to the nonsensical notion – traditionally attributed to sexually-deprived women of a certain age – that any man who addresses more than a couple of words to me is expressing something more than common politeness.

'Chris! Hey, Chris!'

There were two persons standing in the shadow of a corner formed by the adjacent walls of the cut-price cosmetics shop and the Burger Bar; the girl had to step out and wave before Christina recognised her as Jinx.

'Christina! What you doing out after dark?'

The staider of those who waited in the bus queue in front of and behind Christina exchanged looks.

'I'm on my way home,' she said. She saw the hostility in the ordinary, average, unremarkable faces around her. That Jinx and her companion, resplendent as peacocks, should attract such animosity simply because they looked different made her angry. It was for this reason that when Jinx said, 'Oh don't go home yet, come and have a Christmas drink,' she refused only twice and changed the third potential refusal into an acceptance.

'This is K,' Jinx said, of her companion. K said, 'Hi there,' and inclined his Mohican towards her. It was, if anything, more rigid in its construction, more breathtakingly symmetrical in its design, than Jinx's and its colour veered slightly more towards the rose madder end of the palette. Otherwise they matched each other in every detail, from their, respectively, right and left-handed wrist-padlocks to the spider's web tattoos on the backs of their hands and the spurs attached to the heels of their cracked black Charlie Chaplin boots.

Christina walked beside them, in the shadow of their splendour, through the night-time city. They walked towards the docks, along cobbled jiggers, beside deserted warehouses and garbage-strewn wastelands, past sleazy clubs where men with mean expressions and heavy shoulders talked quietly together, ignoring the shrill sailors in drag who drank port and watched the door with a hunger they couldn't disguise. Through convoluted concrete walkways they went, up spittle-besmeared steps and along vomit-spattered alleys, beneath viaducts scrawled with the despairing messages that still retained a vestige of humour: CHEAP HEROIN – MAGGIE'S ANSWER TO UNEMPLOYMENT, messages that dated from the gentler times that had permitted the luxury of just one satisfactorily-identified enemy: NO POPERY; DOWN WITH KING BILLY, and messages stark in their proclamation of vicious intent: EVERTON PAKI-BASHERS; KILL THE WOGS.

They passed the entrance of one pub. And another. And a third. Christina paused at the door of the fourth. Jinx shook her head. 'Christ, no,' she said.

They explained: that there were pubs which they could freely enter and pubs where they would be subjected to constant harassment if not outright ag. There were pubs where grievous bodily harm would be the penalty for seeking to exchange their money for liquor.

'Go in there,' K said, nodding towards the apparent Dickensian cosiness of the fourth pub, 'you're asking for a smack in the mouth. Try The George, eh?'

Jinx nodded and they crossed a derelict courtyard and turned into a narrow thoroughfare where a man emerged from the shadows and plucked at Christina's elbow.

She jerked herself free and scuttled from him in alarm. But Jinx and K had paused to listen to the message that, although disadvantaged in this respect by the absence of most of the teeth vital for clarity of diction, he was attempting to convey.

'Feller,' he was saying. 'Down there – middle of the road – can't shift him.'

They walked on to where, prostrate in the centre of the highway, there lay something that looked, at first glance, to be little more than a skeleton in an overcoat, but proved, on closer inspection, to be an actual living breathing human being exceedingly the worse for drink, apparently incapable of raising its bones from the tarmac and propelling them towards the safety of the pavement.

'Gunna get run over,' the toothless man proclaimed. 'Won't shift. *I* can't shift him.'

In terms of drunkenness, he was obviously well away but still reasonably distant from the stage of paralysis reached by his companion, who now, vaguely aware of being the centre of attention, raised his grey head (his face being as grey as his hair) and emitted a feeble giggle.

K bent over him. 'Where you from, chief?' he enquired. 'How d'you get here?'

The skeleton man raised a hand that could have been used as a teaching aid in an anatomy lesson and waved it towards the pavement. The not-quite-so-drunk man pointed out a sort of nest that had been made there, fashioned from old coats and cardboard boxes. 'He's from there,' he said, as though, for the purposes of identification, this was an address as satisfactory as any other.

'Well, you can't stay there, can you?' K said. 'But, for sure, you can't stay here either. Come on then, pal. Let's have you.' And he leaned over and lifted the man and set him down among his coats and bin-liners and boxes.

'We can't leave him there,' Jinx said. 'He'll freeze to death.'

'Pigs'll find him before that,' K said.

Restored to his proper resting-place, the skeleton man suddenly achieved a measure of lucidity, raised himself and beckoned. 'God bless you son,' he said. And then a mad light danced for an instant in his dead eyes. 'I hate you,' he said. Then he coughed and spat and said sadly, and with a kind of dignity that totally transcended himself and his surroundings, 'You know what I mean, don't you?'

'Yeah,' K said, stepping back and shaking himself so that all his chains and beads hung symmetrical. 'I know what you mean.'

In the pub at the bottom of the alley they were served drinks without either let, hindrance or the slightest indication that their appearances could be considered in any way out of the common. They bought tall pints of dark beer and hailed others of their ilk and said, 'You what? Ah come on, it's Christmas,' when Christina requested a small sherry.

'You look,' Jinx said, leading the way to a little room at the back of the bar where a few unmatching hard chairs were set around a scarred table and a fly-paper hung from the cracked parchment shade of the single central light bulb and a couple of crones drank Guinness in the corner, 'like you could do with a good strong drink. You look like you just been to a funeral.'

'No,' Christina said. 'It was a party actually.'

Christina described its nature to her, explained that, being unable to take any more in the way of come-to-Jesus jollity, she'd left before the end.

Jinx hooted at the idea of a prayer meeting masquerading as a party. 'Why d'you go?' she asked.

K had arrived at their table bringing for Christina a small sherry *and* a pint of beer. He waved away her demur. 'You're all right. Got me Giro this morning. Month's money cos of Christmas.'

'Well?' Jinx repeated. 'Why did you go if you knew it was gonna be a bunch of bible-thumpers with their brains shot away?'

She tried to explain: that she had gone to that party to escape being obliged to be present at another: that hosted by her cousin which was likely to be attended by a bunch of equally – if differently – awful people. Briefly, she explained Gwen and the circle of her acquaintanceship within which she, Christina, felt so utterly, so generically, out of place.

'Roll us another,' K asked of Jinx, having finished the cigarette which she'd manufactured earlier. She obliged. For a while they watched her expertise in silent admiration. Then K turned his attention to Christina and said, 'You wanna knock that on the 'ead double-quick. In my opinion.'

'I would,' she said, 'if there was anywhere else to go.'

'Stacks a places to go,' he said. 'What d'you want? Buck House?'

'No. Just somewhere that's clean and warm and doesn't look as though cockroaches might crawl from under the skirting-board as soon as the light goes out. Somewhere that doesn't have a loo that's shared with people who've never been taught elementary personal hygiene. Somewhere that you don't run the risk of getting raped or mugged or worse whenever you put a foot outside the door. That's all.'

It was an unusually long speech. For her. Usually she wasn't given the opportunity to reach the end of a speech of that length.

Usually Gwen interjected, or Hilary Roberts cut in, or Colette started talking about episiotomies.

'And all that's more important than having to put up with the grief your cousin gives you?' asked K.

She considered. It was and it wasn't. She felt, at least, safe at Gwen's. Out of place, but safe. And who could say that there would be anywhere she'd actually feel *in* place?

They urged her to drink up. They wanted to catch another pub before closing time. Christina thought that, at this point, she had decided to make her farewells and then her way home, but found herself walking between Jinx and K back along the alley that was now empty of dossers; even the cardboard boxes had gone: only the shards of broken bottles remained.

They passed Klosters *en route* to their destination. Peeping in as the doors opened and closed behind groups of fashionably-dressed young persons, they saw what a frightfully good expensive time everyone seemed to be having amid the golden garlands and the silver snowflakes and the discreetly positioned green-shaded spotlights beneath which complexions had a cast reminiscent of fish in an aquarium. Very sleek fish. 'Go on, yer posing prat!' said K of a young man in a pink suit with one of those haircuts that look as though they derive their inspiration from long contemplation of a scrubbing brush, who was leaning over a girl with silver eyelids and a rapt and/or mesmerised expression and being heavily sincere. 'Klosters!' K said, and shook himself so that all his chains rattled together menacingly. 'Is that the place you make for when you want to go on the piste, or what?'

He nudged Jinx and repeated the joke. Both she and Christina were incapacitated with a mirth out of all proportion to the wit of the remark and staggered against each other, giggling. The doorman put his head out of the entrance and said, 'Clear off, will you!'

There was a small amount of ritual locking of horns: 'What if we won't?' 'Then I'll make you, pal.' 'Oh yeah? You and whose army?' 'Fuck off, scumbag, and take your slags with you.' But time prevented them from prolonging it for too long. Even licence extensions granted for Christmas must run out sometime.

The second pub seemed to be – in Christina's intoxicated view – a carbon copy of the first: the same rickety bentwood chairs, the same corpse-hung fly-paper, even the same two old ladies sitting in the corner drinking stout. Perhaps it *was* the same pub;

perhaps, in their slightly staggering progress around the city centre, they had described a full circle. Except here, other punks, who had merely acknowledged their presence in the other place, joined them. She was introduced (if you could put such informal exchanges under the heading of introduction) to Person and Jimmy L and Horror Bull and Rocks, who raised their glasses to her and then returned to the subject under discussion which was marriage and why anyone whose brains weren't shot away entirely should wish to subscribe to such an outmoded institution. A girl called Jan, it appeared, was about to plight her troth to a young man called Bonzo. It wasn't even as if she was up the stick or anything. Not that being up the stick was sufficient reason for taking such a step. Not like in your day, they said in kindly tones, displaying infinite understanding of that punitive, hypocrisy-ridden dark age in which she had been unfortunate enough to grow up.

'He went to a building society,' someone said disgustedly. 'And she went to the Council.'

Someone else had even seen *her* looking in at the window of Boodle and Dunthorne.

It was as bad, they agreed, as those weekend Hellsies, who cut the lawns in front of their semi-detached houses during the week and went to work as clerical assistants in the Civil Service.

Their chagrin was genuine, their sense of betrayal acute. Obviously their codes of behaviour were every bit as rigid and rule-bound as those prevailing in that conventional society they affected to despise.

Time passed and their voices, though boomingly loud, seemed to come from afar. Their faces seemed huge and hugely decorative, adorned as they were with intricately-crayoned patterns. K was talking about a club, but her reception of his signals was faulty and his voice faded in and out as the vicar's had done on the day of Max's father's funeral. 'Sup up,' somebody said, and she politely obliged and then her elbow slipped off the edge of the table top and there was a tremendous degree of vertigo involved in trying to get to her feet. It appeared that they were moving on because the night was young and there was still a lot of serious drinking to get through.

She could feel the hairs stiffening on the back of her neck and nausea rising in her gullet. She managed, by means of some judicious swallowing and standing very still, to resist the impulse, but decided that perhaps a taxi ought to be requisitioned to take her home, although that was a misnomer if ever there was one – she felt more at home among this collection of weirdly attired, menacing-looking youths half her age than she ever would at Gwen's. 'Jinx,' she said, 'K,' and started to try to tell them what a great bunch of people they were, but the words seemed reluctant to leave her mouth and Jinx was making the sort of soothing noises indicating that comment was unnecessary, and by then the taxi had arrived and they helped her into it and that was the last thing she remembered until the sound of Gwen's hysteria brought her back to consciousness.

'You'll feel better if you can get it up.'

Such was Corky's advice, as she held a bowl beneath Christina's chin. Christina couldn't have agreed more, but all her attempts to do so produced only bouts of painful retching.

'How is . . . ?' she asked, feebly inclining her head in the direction of Gwen's bedroom.

'Two sleeping pills,' Corky said tersely. 'See to the biggest part of the day, I reckon. Would be today of all days, wouldn't it? Busiest night of the bleedin' year. I'll have to get going soon, choose how many policemen and RSPCA inspectors we've got calling. You can see to 'em, can't you? See to her too?' she asked, looking at Christina in a way that suggested that a demonstration of lack of moral fibre, at this juncture, would not be appreciated.

'Where is . . . ?'

'Garden shed. Covered with a bit of sacking. She doesn't know. Told her I was burying it straightaway, but they've got to *see* it, haven't they? Stands to reason. Are you feeling any better now?'

Christina closed her eyes and then opened them again gingerly. 'Not a lot,' she replied.

'That's what it does for you, getting pissed,' Corky said, with a confidential wink. 'Here, drink this. It'll either kill you or cure you.'

'This' was an orange-flavoured Vitamin C tablet which was dissolving in water. Christina sipped at it. As she sipped, questions rose to her lips concerning blurred memories of the night before that were only now, after the morning's high drama, beginning to surface. 'The taxi?' she asked, having no recollection of tendering her fare, having no recollection, for that matter, of having been asked for it. Although, apparently, the taxi-driver had assisted her to the door before handing her over to Corky who had carried her up to bed.

'I paid it,' Corky said. 'You owe me two-seventy. I think he was bunging it on a bit. Good job it wasn't tonight, it'd be twice the price,' she added, Irishly.

There had been odd lucid moments. She remembered Gwen on the doorstep calling the cat, remembered her taking a step sideways so as to place the greatest amount of distance between herself and Christina. 'Thank God my guests have left,' she'd said, and then opened her mouth and sent her muezzin's cry: 'Muffin, Muffin!' resounding across the quiet square.

'You get off to work,' she said to Corky now and screwed up all her courage to drain the glass and swung her legs sideways and out of bed and cautiously raised herself into a sitting position and was reassured to discover that life at this angle was just about supportable.

'Back as soon as I can,' Corky said. 'Ta-ta for now.' But she lingered. 'Funny business, eh?' she said. 'Kids, do you think?'

'Could be. Certain sorts of children seem to go through phases of sadism.'

Although she had a suspicion that 'phase' might not be appropriate to an explanation of the psychopathology of the thing, and perhaps certain sorts of children grew up to be certain sorts of adults.

Gently, she levered herself upwards. Added to her physical discomforts was a certain amount of psychological stress. Had she made a spectacle of herself the night before? At the time, the drunker she became, the stronger had seemed the affinity between them: she and her companions; neither the age difference nor the gulf separating their lifestyles had seemed to matter too much. At the time, she had been conscious – if only vaguely – of enjoying herself for the first time in ages.

But now, this morning, alcohol poisoned her bloodstream and foetid gases erupted from a disturbed digestion and her head pounded and whenever she remembered how she had come to be in such a state she was overcome with embarrassment. This morning she was once again a middle-aged woman with no place to belong, burdened with an inescapable sense of loss.

Though, as such, not unique. In one respect, anyway. She paused outside Gwen's bedroom door and heard the sound of heavy, regular breathing. Reminiscent of Boysie's. Of how it used to be. Because now he would breathe no more.

The policeman and the RSPCA inspector arrived almost simultaneously. She led them through the house, out of the kitchen door and towards the garden shed, indicated the piece of sacking on the shelf and stood aside, squeamishly, while they tweaked it away to expose the stiffening corpse of Boysie with his throat cut – not quite from ear to ear, as the expression had it – but as near as dammit.

'This morning?' the policeman said. 'Found on the doorstep? What time?'

'Oh, before seven.'

Gwen had called and called the night before but he hadn't responded. Which was unusual for him because since he'd been castrated he was more likely (as Mr McTavish put it) to reach for his slippers at night than for his overcoat. Corky, in between ministering to drunken house-guests, had had to persuade her to leave it and get to bed. Gwen had been reluctant. She had a peculiar feeling, she told Corky, that something was wrong.

And that was why she'd risen at the crack of dawn this morning and gone downstairs to see if he was back. She'd chastise him – the little monkey – for ignoring her entreaties, before gathering him to her breast and kissing the top of his scarred head and opening him a tin of Whiskas.

He was back all right, laid out neatly on the doorstep, face upwards; the blood on his breast beginning to congeal. The scream she'd emitted had brought Corky hammering down the stairs at a speed that would have qualified her for marathon running at Olympic level. The scream was such that it had even penetrated Christina's stupor.

The RSPCA man let the sacking fall back over the body. Sheer sadism, he reckoned. Were there many children in the area? He asked because there was no precedent. In this area cats were usually stolen for their fur – unscrupulous manufacturers produced gloves from it, or because they were valuable: show cats. Whereas anyone could see that Boysie was – had been – merely the commonest, least attractive sort of domestic moggy.

'We'll enquire,' the policeman said. 'See if there's been any similar incidents. We tend to get a spate of them, now and again. Silly kids, usually. Right, Jock?'

Jock agreed. They watched these videos, kids: people drilling holes in other people's heads, ripping their throats out; gore by the gallon and guts by the yard, and then they tried out their own experiments on anything that couldn't fight back. Personally, he'd bring back the birch.

That morning, Gwen wouldn't believe that Boysie couldn't be revived. Not for ages. Though Corky kept stressing the fact, perhaps not as tactfully as she might have done: 'Dead as a bleedin' doornail.' Gwen kept saying, 'Send for Eric McTavish, please!' To which Corky had replied that although she knew vets were required to undertake long and arduous training, she was pretty certain that their resultant expertise did not include the performing of miracles.

Gwen woke up at three o'clock. Christina sat by the side of her bed, alternately proffering Mogadon and thinly-sliced smoked salmon sandwiches, recognising that, beyond this, she could offer no help, that there were no short cuts along the long road of recovery from bereavement.

Without make-up, Gwen looked both older and more child-like. She stared at the sandwiches. 'He loved smoked salmon,' she said, at last.

'And prawns,' Christina ventured, hesitantly.

'Oh yes, prawns. And if we had Dover sole he used to jump on to the dining table. Do you remember?'

They agreed that Boysie, whose diet when first discovered had consisted of dustbin-scavengings, had rapidly developed a gourmet appreciation for the most expensive of culinary delicacies.

'Do you remember how he'd practically swallow them down whole, the prawns, when I held them out to him? He was so greedy, wasn't he?'

He *was* greedy, Christina agreed, hoping that she'd also managed to imply that it was in the nicest possible way.

'But so *sweet*. Even at the beginning, when he used to bite so much, he'd look at you straight afterwards as much as to say: "I know I'm a naughty boy, but I just can't help myself." Do you remember?'

Christina nodded, although this pre-dated her arrival. 'Love-bites,' Gwen had called them, according to Corky. 'Love-bites!' Springing at you and sinking his fangs into the fleshiest part of your calf or, sometimes, even biting the hand that fed him. Assaulted once too often, Corky had placed her foot fairly and squarely in the region where he'd once had balls and booted him along the hall. He hadn't bitten anyone since.

'A real personality,' Gwen said. 'Not like those awful pampered Siamese of Monica Stone's, forever screeching and tearing the curtains to pieces. I used to tell her that, these days, a pedigree is just something to appeal to the snobbishness of a pet owner. Actually, all this in-breeding produces is inferior stock: those cats of hers are neurotic. You could never say that about Boysie.'

Well you could, but Christina would refrain from doing so.

'Never *have* said it.'

Gwen corrected herself and wept afresh. When the worst was over she wiped her nose on her peacock-printed, lavender sheet and said, 'Do you remember how playful he was? I've watched him sometimes chasing his tail . . . There are some photographs . . .' She heaved herself out of bed. Dozens of crumpled, tear-sodden balls of tissue tumbled to the carpet in her wake.

They looked at photographs of Boysie eating his dinner, Boysie attacking the red flower of a gladiolus, Boysie digging a latrine and then filling it in. Christina listened to the anecdotes that accompanied each of these pictures and stifled her yawns.

'You think I'm a fool, don't you?' Gwen said suddenly. 'You think I'm a silly woman who ought to have had some children to worry about, don't you?'

Christina shook her head. Having to worry about children was a penance she wouldn't wish on anyone.

'Corky does. She's always sneering. I don't know why. You'd think, from the superior way she carries on, she'd had tribes of them and years of experience. Well, anyway, Boysie *wasn't* a child substitute; he was a cat. If I'd wanted a child I'd have had one. I could have done.'

'Then why?'

It came out barely above a whisper, Christina being torn between avid curiosity and not wanting to know.

'Didn't want any,' Gwen said simply and raised a frighteningly naked face and looked at Christina and there was a moment of honesty between them, the like of which had not occurred before and would probably never happen again.

'I never could see the point in having them just for the sake of it. Not fair. On anybody. A pet's different. A pet doesn't ask for more than you've got. Oh why?' she said. 'Why should anyone *do* such a thing?'

As the reason for that was not given to humankind to understand, any sort of useful reply was impossible. Christina concentrated instead on attempting to supply comfort: Boysie had, at least, enjoyed a short time in his otherwise miserable existence secure in the knowledge that he was loved and cherished; Gwen must seek to remember him as he had been in his heyday: well fed and cosseted, learning to display affection spontaneously, learning that life could be more than a word and a blow.

Gwen, courtesy of another pill, was once again asleep when Corky returned.

'A whisky?' she suggested, reaching for the bottle, and then saw the expression on Christina's face and remembered and said, 'Sorry, perhaps not.'

But she continued to fiddle with the bottle top. 'This – man,' she said. 'Do you reckon he could have had anything to do with it? This man you reckon you've seen hanging around here?'

Suddenly she stopped fidgeting and unscrewed the cap and poured herself a large drink and downed it and then poured another.

'I've no idea. I haven't seen anything lately. Why, have you?'

'No,' Corky said, and turned round so that you could see all the little red veins in her cheeks, like worms, that were always emphasised by the drinking of alcohol. 'No. What makes you ask that?'

'No reason particularly,' Christina replied. 'I just thought, from the way you said it, you might have seen something too.'

'Well I haven't,' Corky said. Then she had another drink and she seemed to relax a little and she said, '*I* reckon it's kids. Little bastards.'

She looked across to Christina as though desirous of having her opinion corroborated. Perhaps, tough though she professed to be, Boysie's death had upset her. Perhaps she too was looking for comfort.

But Christina had done her stint in that area. There came a time in the life of every hangover when its demands for total immobility in a supine position with the eyes tightly closed must be met. She went to her room and locked her door and lay down and fell into a depth of unconsciousness from which the reporting of an epidemic of cut throats might not have aroused her.

ᵔ 5 ᵔ

Everyone seemed glad when Christmas was over. At least this was the inference to be drawn from the sentiments expressed at the first new year meeting of The System. Even Joyce seemed subdued. Perhaps praising the Lord so long and so loudly had tired her out. Only once did she venture a comment and then it was to reprimand Kenneth, who was chairman, for his ineptitude in bringing the meeting to order.

Kenneth flushed darkly and glared at her. Obviously there had been a falling-out between them. 'If looks could kill,' Christina hummed under her breath, echoing the refrain of a record that, years ago, David had played until the grooves were worn smooth.

She thought of David while Klaus droned on about a new plan for interesting the public in The System. She thought about Adam too. On Christmas Eve, after she had phoned the Gold-smiths and explained in low, death-in-the-house tones, just why Gwen would be unable to attend their little get-together, David and Adam and a girl called Jools who was David's current sexual partner or platonic companion – obviously girlfriend was a very unfashionable phrase, if the derision he evinced when Christina used it to describe her was anything to go by – had arrived to exchange gifts and compliments of the season.

She was a large girl with a lion's mane of bronze-coloured hair tied up in a chiffon scarf *à la* comic charladies in pre-war West End revues. She'd sat with a proprietorial hand upon David's arm, arousing all the traditional mother-in-law reservations and irrational antipathies within Christina's breast, not least because she kept looking at her watch. They were going to a party. Or rather, parties. Different ones: she and David to a club, Adam to a friend's house. Christina's heart sank; she knew about those sort of parties, where parents went out in all innocence and came back to find copulating bodies in their bed, drunks laid out flat on their lawn and more damage to furniture and fitments than could have been inflicted by a demolition squad.

'David,' Jools had said, pushing his cuff back to look at his watch, 'hadn't we better be going?'

She was staying, it appeared, over Christmas. Not only was she staying; she was cooking the Christmas dinner too, although all the preparation had been done by the woman who functioned as a 'sort of housekeeper', and whom none of them seemed capable of describing beyond the fact that she was 'clocking on' and was 'a sort of widow, or something, I think'.

Whoever she was, she'd need to be super-efficient: calm, sure-handed, confident, one of those women that you saw walking steadily through the thronged Saturday-morning streets carrying cakes in square white cardboard boxes tied up with string. They always managed to keep a controlling finger on the knot and the box never split or buckled so that when you got home you discovered that you had a sorry mashed mixture of jam and cream and shattered meringue.

'David,' Jools had said, not wheedlingly this time but in tones of command, so they had made their excuses and left.

And she hadn't seen them since. David had gone down to Bristol to stay with Jools' family; and Adam left for a school skiing trip.

She tried to fix her attention upon the meeting, but it would have taken a superhuman effort of concentration to follow its tedious and halting progress. She wondered idly if the symbols that Colette was inscribing so conscientiously in her notebook actually bore any relation to what was taking place. It was Colette's last meeting. 'I'll type these up,' she said, 'and post them on to you. Oh, by the way,' she said, 'while I think on.' She took a small folded piece of paper from her bag and handed it to Christina. 'We'd like you to come for your tea on Saturday. I've drawn you a map and put down the times of the buses. If you get the five to three it'll get you to ours about half-past. Don'll walk you back to the stop afterwards. Round our way, it can be – not very nice, what with the kids and that.'

Christina looked at the paper. The map, for its purpose, was meticulously over-detailed, and there was a bus timetable pro-vided that would allow for an improbable margin of unpunctuality. She felt that, given this immaculate organisation, she had little option but to accept.

Not only had Colette made sure that Don would escort Christina to the bus-stop afterwards, she'd obviously prevailed upon him to meet the incoming buses and, as Christina had missed the one that she'd intended to catch – despite (or perhaps because of) all those maps and timetables – obviously he'd been waiting some not inconsiderable while.

You'd never have guessed it from his demeanour, which suggested that he could wait all day without giving expression to any symptoms of impatience. He even seemed surprised by her apology, as though he would not presume to expect that anyone should accord him the courtesy of being on time.

They walked through a warren of avenues and closes and drives: you thought of cherry blossom trees and curving gravelled driveways, of smooth lawns and tennis clubs and parish halls; what you actually saw were patches of scrubland covered in canine faeces and squashed lager cans and crisp packets that had been used to contain glue; front gardens clogged with rusting bicycles and exploded mattresses and tyres and defunct fridges and cookers; rows of shops, boarded up, except for the odd, skimpily-stocked, unhygienic-looking grocery store; wandering mongrel dogs afflicted with mange, given to long and pointless bouts of barking; snotty toddlers and scuffling teenagers whose conversation, when you came within earshot of it, seemed to consist of little more than a core structure involving the present indicative active tense of one verb: 'to go', the adjectival form of another verb: 'to fuck', and two inaccurately-applied nouns: 'cunt' and 'dickhead'.

They turned the corner of Jasmine Avenue into Primrose Close, skirting an electricity sub-station upon which someone had mis-spelled 'Remember Munich '58', bypassing a group of youths who were taking it in turn to rev a huge shiny Japanese motor-bike. 'They can't manage to pay the rent,' Gwen said of the people who lived in areas like this, 'but you take note of the number of motor-bikes and video recorders and microwave ovens that you'll find behind their front doors.'

You could just about make out that, once upon a time, the front doors in Primrose Close had been painted by the Council in bright primary colours. Most had been neglected to the extent that now the natural colour of the plywood showed through. The contrast between these and the oak (or Philippine mahogany, to be precise) that was sported by number thirty-seven couldn't have been more marked. Varnished to a high gloss, it was, and embellished with a doorbell and a letter-box and a lion's head knocker in lacquered brass. The windows were double-glazed and behind them could be seen the scallops of ruched satin curtains. The front of the house was adorned with a kind of crazy-paving of stone cladding. The front garden was actually crazily-paved in ice-cream colours: pink, yellow, pistachio. Three gnomes sat on toadstools and fished into a tiny pool. A handkerchief-sized patch of lawn was edged with a neat border of rock plants. A window box showed evidence of life in the green tips of crocuses that were pushing their way towards the light.

In fact, the contrast between number thirty-seven and its neighbours was total. A gardenia on a dung-heap, Christina thought, a technicolour film when you'd expected only black and white. Don Donaldson followed her gaze and allowed himself a little self-satisfied smile. 'We're buying ours,' he said quietly, as one who – though too modest to blow any sort of trumpet – has recognised himself among the descriptions of the typical membership of a property-owning democracy.

'Isn't it difficult?' Christina enquired cautiously. 'Now that you're out of a job?'

'I've got my redundancy money,' he said, a trifle edgily, she thought, as though he preferred not to be reminded of this unsatisfactory state of affairs. 'There's bound to be something,' he said, 'before we need to start worrying. Course the baby – getting ready for it – is costing us a lot.'

The baby was now apparent as a definite bump that preceded the rest of Colette when she opened the back door. She delivered only the mildest of rebukes: 'Nearly given you up,' and then she looked down markedly at the door mat upon which, after Don had finished an unnecessarily vigorous sort of soft shoe shuffle, Christina felt obliged to wipe her perfectly clean shoes. In fact, there were two door mats: one outside the back door and another inside the threshold. There was also a small piece of carpet midway along the kitchen floor. By the time one had traversed these precautionary stepping-stones to reach what Colette called the lounge, it was improbable that there would be any scrap of objectionable matter still adhering to one's feet.

The rooms of council houses tend to be small. Number thirty-seven, although on its way to becoming a privately owned residence, did not differ, in this respect, from any other. The 'lounge' could just about have accommodated the minimum of furniture usually required for comfort and convenience; the Donaldsons had filled theirs to almost absolute capacity. Tea was set out upon one of those long low tables that have what resemble enormous lace paper doyleys pressed between two layers of glass, but to reach it one was required to negotiate an obstacle course: in addition to the normal household furnishings there were nests of tables, a large hi-fi stacked in a unit, two patchwork leather pouffes, a magazine rack, a wrought-iron telephone table, a wickerwork chair that resembled the Peacock Throne, a bamboo construction in the shape of a serpent, in the coils of which were tucked various potted plants, a standard lamp with a huge circular satin shade, a cabinet that housed the television set and video recorder, and a set of shelves upon which were displayed a large onyx table-lighter, two soapstone book-ends (minus books), an imitation Tibetan temple-bell, a posy of artificial flowers and a photograph commemorating the Donald-son nuptials. Christina banged her hip-bone and barked her shin. Presumably a great deal of practice was required before you could move around without causing damage to either the furniture or your person or both.

'The teapot, Don,' said Colette, urging Christina onwards, around the furniture, towards a Dralon-covered armchair, in the manner of an air-traffic controller coaxing a plane along the runway. 'And don't forget to hang up your hat,' she called after him, explaining to Christina, who'd finally made it to base, that he often forgot and left it on the bottom step of the stairs and then of course stood upon it. He'd been very untidy, she explained, as she handed Christina a china plate and a matching paper napkin, until she'd taken him in hand. Christina held the plate very carefully beneath each sandwich and piece of teacake that she consumed and thought – as she'd once speculated on the conjunction of Max and Joyce Perrot – of a double act comprising Max and Colette. Were perfectionists better off together, in that it meant that other people were spared, or would that be as disastrous as the pairing of – say – quick-tempered people?

The idea of Max inhabiting this doll's house parlour, crammed with mail-order furniture and adorned with chain-store art was too bizarre to be entertained for very long. 'You're terrible snobs,' David had once said, when she and Max had been somewhat less than enthusiastic about a particular friendship of his: that formed with a boy who hailed from the city's most notorious council estate.

Was she a snob? Snobbery was surely Gwen, to whom the looking down the length of her nose came as naturally as that self-satisfied expression she adopted when she was primping herself. Gwen and her friends. And she had friends, Christina had discovered, of a sort that made Mr McTavish the vet seem, by comparison, a perfectly charming fellow. Some of them had arrived on New Year's Day. They had driven over in what they called 'the Roller'. They wore a great deal of very large, very golden, gold jewellery – both the men and the women. Scores of small slaughtered animals, and the hides of larger ones, composed their outer clothing. They were new money: restaurateurs, owners of health clubs and retirement homes and leisure centres. They talked golf and Marbella and yachts and dropped names that might have impressed Christina had she not been so far behind the door when it came to keeping up with current celebrities.

Perhaps snobbery was endemic in the human character. Perhaps everyone needed someone to despise. Colette was talking about her neighbours. They were a rough lot, she said. They were also deeply envious of those who worked hard to realise their aspirations; why, the little paling fence that Don had erected to demarcate their front garden (none of the other houses bothered about demarcation: rubbish just flowed willy-nilly from one garden into the next) had once been quite deliberately smashed.

'They just want to drag you down to their level,' said Colette. 'And they bring their children up to be exactly the same.'

She smoothed her smock across her bump and rubbed at the calves of her legs which, she said, were prone to cramp. These last weeks seemed as though they would go on for ever, what with the backache and the insomnia and the heartburn and the tiredness. Though of course they'd be taking her into hospital early, as a precaution. It was policy to take you in early so that they could keep an eye on you if you were over thirty-five and it

207

was your first baby. At this point, Christina actually began to listen. 'You're not over thirty-five, surely?' she said. 'I'll be forty in July,' Colette replied. 'We'd nearly given up hope,' she added, while Christina was assimilating this astonishing news.

Suddenly Colette started to her feet and manoeuvred her way across the room and pulled aside first the white figured net and then the green ruched satin curtain and then rapped on the window pane. 'Don!' she cried. 'They're at it again!' And Don rose to his feet too and, sidestepping the chairs and the tables and the writhing bamboo serpent, made his way to the door.

'In the front garden,' Colette explained. 'Pretend they've kicked their ball in there when you go out to them.'

There was a burst of jeering from outside as Don attempted to clear the trespassers from his property. The chanting of some scurrilous epithet became louder and more insistent and then diminished in volume as the chanters dispersed. Christina wondered why on earth the Donaldsons hadn't sought to buy a property in a slightly more salubrious district and then remembered that, as sitting tenants, the council would be charging them a purchase price much lower than the actual market value of the house.

'Don!' called Colette, when he came back. 'Fetch us down the baby things, would you? I want to show them to Christina.' Obediently, he went upstairs. There was a Pavlovian quality about his response to her every request that was disconcerting to see.

He brought down coats and jackets and nightdresses and mittens and bonnets and bootees. They were exquisite: faultless knitting and tatting and smocking and crochet and drawn-thread work. The nuns had taught her, Colette said. She'd started knitting and sewing and embroidering years ago, soon after she got married, assuming that pregnancy would occur quickly and spontaneously, never dreaming that she would have amassed this huge layette before, finally, after endless visits to the hospital and endless prayers to Sts Theresa and Teresa and the Holy Virgin – and, in the end, St Jude, patron saint of hopeless cases – the test came back positive.

Covertly, Christina glanced at her watch. Until she could, legitimately, plead the need to set off to catch her bus, they chatted desultorily. Don, needless to say, was to be present at the birth. He had been accompanying Colette to the ante-natal classes since the very beginning. These days, fathers were encouraged to take an active part in a child's upbringing, and it made a bond, didn't it, if the father actually saw his child being born?

Perhaps it did. The presence of fathers in the labour ward had not been the fashion when Christina's sons came into the world. Max had arrived, with purple gladioli, when all was clean and neat and tidy; he'd probably never made the connection between the swathed Baby-Jesus infant in its crib with the pain and the sweat that had brought it forth in gouts of blood and mucus.

Children came into the world messy, and the mess always seemed to spread to fill the space available. In three months' time the Donaldsons' cluttered palace was due to become a good deal more cluttered – if that was possible.

Gwen called into The System office to say that Corky had left a cheque book behind that morning and as she, Gwen, had an appointment for her annual check-up at the BUPA clinic in Manchester and was running late already, could Christina please oblige her by delivering it to Klosters?

It was as much of a command as the directive to do her Christmas shopping had been, but this time, at least, it was couched as a question. Gwen was in a mellower mood these days. Her thrush had subsided, her haemorrhoids had shrunk, and she was setting about her cultivation of Stephen Millward: a gradual process; she knew better than to rush it.

'I've got an appointment myself at lunchtime actually,' Christina said.

'Oh, please! It won't take a minute. I'd be *so* grateful.'

And she'd produced the melting smile which she usually employed for getting her own way – but it was also for the benefit of Kenneth, and Murray Pearl, who'd come into the office behind her. She was never able to resist the temptation of an opportunity to dazzle any man, however obvious it was that he wasn't worth the effort.

'Is that your cousin who has the wine bar?' Murray Pearl asked, after she'd gone.

'Yes.'

'Nice place she has, isn't it? I had a meal there over Christmas.'

'Can we *help* you?' Kenneth enquired frostily.

'Joyce asked me to drop these in.'

'These' were raffle tickets. A bring and buy sale was to be organised to raise funds for The System, date and venue yet to be arranged – as was the bulk of its organisation – by Kenneth, a fact which contributed to his testiness. Perhaps he'd have been even testier had he not been in love.

Being in love not only made his uncertain temper even less predictable (one minute he was complaining about the burden of extra work and Dr Roberts' failure to replace Colette, the next he was gazing into space with a foolish smile on his face); it had also led to a radical change in his appearance. Gone were the laddered rugby jerseys and dilapidated training shoes and baggy-crotched jeans. Now he wore a suit and a tie and a pair of leather shoes. The suit had wide lapels and a cinched waist and flared trousers (and made you think of the days when shoes had Cuban heels and shirts had long pointed collars and 'Tie a Yellow Ribbon' was top of the hit parade), and the tie was kipper-shaped and suggested a late seventies' vintage, and the shoes resembled those elastic-sided Chelsea boots without which no self-respecting sixties' Swinger would have extended a foot out of doors.

She had not long been left in ignorance concerning the reason for this dandification. Like many another, he could not resist the temptation to mention the beloved's name. Once, Robin's name had been forever on his lips, Robin's opinions cited as criteria for every decision. Now it was Janet. Janet said this and Janet said that; every word that dropped from her lips was a pearl of wisdom, every action she performed a symphony of harmony and grace. Janet, it seemed, was not a born-again Christian, so Kenneth ceased to be one forthwith.

Christina concluded that his bouts of bad temper were due to the fact that feelings were not yet reciprocated. She tried to augment the information already in her possession: namely, that Janet worked in the advertising department of the local daily paper and that was where Kenneth had met her. A copy of an arts magazine left lying around the office had provided the opportunity. He'd once mentioned his fondness for the ballet. She'd flicked through it and said, 'I see the Festival Ballet is coming to the Empire in February. You'll have to take Janet to see it. That's if she likes the ballet?'

'I don't know,' he'd said, without raising his eyes from the paper in front of him. 'I haven't asked her.'

'You *are* actually going out with this Janet, are you?'

He'd kept his eyes fixed on the desk and said, 'Well, not actually going *out*, no.'

'Oh? Why's that?'

It was a little akin to pulling the wings off flies, but he'd been so gratuitously unpleasant to her of late that she couldn't resist the impulse to get her own back.

'She's very busy. Her mother's been ill. And she's doing this degree with the Open University.'

It struck Christina that Janet was fortunate in having at her disposal a fair number of excuses to fob off the attentions of unwelcome suitors. After all, what sort of a girl could possibly be attracted to Kenneth Little, in his bizarre conglomeration of yesterday's fashions?

On the other hand, if one thought in terms of there being a league table of attractiveness, then it was a well-known fact that people tended to choose their partners from within the same division.

'Perhaps she doesn't realise just how keen on her you are,' she'd said. At this, his sullen expression had been slowly transformed into one that suggested a cautious curiosity to hear what she had to say.

'It's just as easy to underestimate someone's feelings as it is to overestimate them. Perhaps you should go all out and declare yourself.'

'You think that would be a good idea, do you?' he had said in a grudging sort of fancy-*me*-asking-*you*-for-advice way.

'I haven't a clue,' she'd replied brusquely, suddenly appalled at the sadistic streak within her that urged him towards making an even bigger fool of himself than was already the case.

Her lunchtime appointment was with a man she'd met during the course of her interviewing, a man who renovated old properties and let them off in flats. He didn't have anything vacant at present, he told her, but promised to let her know just as soon as he did. She decided to take his word, to discontinue her searching. Particularly as Gwen had stopped dropping hints to the tune of wasn't it about time she found herself some alternative accommodation. Perhaps Gwen felt that in view of the peculiar goings-on it was probably all to the good that the house should be occupied continuously: she and Corky were often out in the evenings, Christina rarely.

One decision made: a small achievement. She pulled on the gloves that Adam had brought her back from Les Arces – another reason to be cheerful, surely? – and made her way to Klosters.

'About time too,' Corky said ungratefully when the cheque book was handed over to her. She sat down and cleared a space on the table and began writing cheques at a tremendous rate and tearing them off and ramming them into envelopes. 'Albert!' she called across the kitchen. 'You might as well make yourself useful. For you're damn all use here today. You can take this lot to the post-box.'

He came waddling across from the sink where he'd been attempting to wash dishes with one hand. His right arm was in a sling. 'I'm not doing so bad,' he said truculently, demonstrating his dish-washing techniques with his good arm.

'Perhaps you can manage to wash up,' Corky said, 'but how're you going to dry them, you daft bugger?'

That stumped him, furrow his square wide brow as he might. 'Dunno,' he said eventually. He looked down at the bunch of letters that Corky was thrusting towards him. 'You've put that stamp on upside down,' he said. 'That's an insult to the Queen, that is. They won't deliver it.'

'Don't talk so wet,' said Corky, 'and get going, before I lose my temper.'

But that seemed to have occurred already.

'What's he done to himself?' Christina asked, as Albert reached down his overcoat and trilby from the specially-positioned hook beside the back door and donned them with a display of the highest sort of dudgeon of which a dwarf is capable.

'About half a dozen over the eight last night, apparently,' Corky said. 'Usual result: tumbled from top to bottom of the staircase where he lives. Wonder he didn't brain himself. Not much use to me, is he?' she said. 'One more stunt like that and he gets his cards. He's starting to pull them a bit too often. A few months back he disappeared to the boozer after lunch and came back here just before Dozy Dick locked up.' (Dozy Dick was the previous manager whose services Gwen had been obliged to dispense with because he was making too-obvious sheep's eyes at her.) 'Somehow he missed Albert and the daft little sod fell asleep in here with a fag in his hand. If it hadn't been for that Richard coming back on duty early, the whole place'd have gone up in flames.'

Albert, buttoned up and ready to go, called across the kitchen to Christina: 'What's the latitude of Murmansk?'

Corky spun round on her chair. He departed.

They drank coffee in silence. As Gwen's piles had shrunk, so she had become less irritable. But Corky seemed to be making up for it. There was an untypical edginess about her behaviour these days: when making pastry she was miles away; if you rode as a passenger in her car you had to repeat your every comment, so abstracted did she seem. Her marathon-running – despite the bitterness of the weather, she now ran morning and evening – didn't seem to afford her much satisfaction. Even the early-morning tea-drinking sessions that she and Christina still shared seemed less cosy than of yore. The comments that were snorted out from behind the *Sun* were more likely, nowadays, to refer to doings closer to home than those perpetrated by toadying cabinet lackeys or turncoats or CND Commie-sympathisers. It used to be much more relaxing, Christina remembered, when she was merely required to murmur assent to comments about Arthur Scargill's hairdo or Nigel Lawson's uncanny resemblance to the elderly Oscar Wilde.

Of course she might have known that a day that started off well, a day when she'd woken, for once, without the sensation of having a ten-ton weight on her chest – a day like that was bound to be harbouring a nasty surprise. There was an envelope for her on the hall table when she arrived back that evening. After a moment's perusal of its contents, she noticed that her hands were shaking. She noticed it in the most peculiar way: as though there was Christina-the-observer watching, at a distance, the reactions of Christina-to-whom-it-was-happening.

'What's the matter?' Gwen said. She had photographs spread out on the table in front of her. The idea was to remove the Swallow ancestors from their elegant silver frames and put in their place the images of Boysie that could no longer be treasured within the confines of an album but demanded display.

'It's a divorce petition. I think.'

She had difficulty in making the connection between those names: Maxwell Ernest Conway and Christine (Christine!)

Conway, that had been typed into the spaces left blank for this purpose on the printed form, with the people they purported to represent.

Gwen compared a photograph of Boysie snoozing with one of Boysie alert, made her decision and began to trim the edges of the latter to fit the frame she'd selected for it. 'What did you expect?' she said. It was necessary to cut off Boysie's toes to make him fit, but the alternative was a new frame and, deep and sincere though Gwen's grief was, it hadn't blinded her to the cost of acquiring antique silver frames.

Not this, Christina thought. Illogical, perhaps. But not this, not so soon.

'I told you ages ago, didn't I? You'll need to get a solicitor.'

'But why?'

'Why? For a settlement to be sorted out,' Gwen said, very slowly and distinctly as though addressing an imbecile.

'But I'm the one who's guilty. I committed adultery. I walked out on him. What settlement would I be entitled to?'

'You never admit liability,' Gwen said, as though discussing a motoring accident. '*Your* solicitor will want to know what *drove* you to commit adultery, what *forced* you to leave the matrimonial home. He's going to try to establish provocation, or mental cruelty.'

'You mean – fight it?' Christina said. 'Go to court and listen to barristers tearing us to pieces?'

She shuddered. Gwen said, 'If that's what it takes, yes. Being thin-skinned gets you nowhere in this world. Oh drat it!' she then said, having discovered that, in order to be made to fit the frame, the picture of Boysie would not only have to be lopped off at the feet, but dismembered around the ears as well, and that the extent of this Procrustean damage would probably make her wish she'd forked out for new frames after all.

'Unlikely it'd reach that stage anyway,' Gwen said. Perhaps if she juggled the photographs around – put Boysie recoiling in terror from a stuffed mouse into this frame, and Boysie marooned halfway up the apple tree in *that* . . .

'How do you mean?'

'All the horse-trading'll probably take place before ever it gets to court. An agreement will have been reached and the judge will just have to rubber-stamp it.'

Christina turned the page. 'It says here that the custody

arrangements for the dependent children will have to satisfy the court before a decree can be granted.'

Perhaps that might be her chance: to persuade them that Adam needed a mother as much and more than he needed a father.

'I expect they'll just ask Adam who he prefers to live with, and then check that Max is a suitable person and can provide him with a proper home – that sort of thing,' Gwen said. 'You'll have to – whatsit – arrange to have him compromised. If you want to make it seem that he isn't a fit person.'

What did she mean? Dancing girls and topless models and orgies in their quiet suburban avenue? Evidence that Max frequented massage parlours, misbehaved himself in men's lavatories, printed porn? Rack her brains as she might, she couldn't think of anything of that nature. She could list pages of traits that, in her view, made him an unsuitable person to have custody of a child, but they weren't the sort of characteristics to which a court would object.

Anyway, those traits might not be nearly so noticeable nowadays. The judge: His Honour Justice Whatever-Whatever, might well discover that Maxwell Ernest Conway was a different kettle of fish entirely when not being provoked by his wife (Christine).

Corky came in from her run during the silence that fell between them while Gwen was wondering whether she could remedy her too-enthusiastic photograph-trimming by inserting some sort of backing material into the frame, and Christina was pondering the question of whether a decree of divorcement was valid if it mis-spelled your Christian name.

She sank heavily on to the sofa, stretched her legs straight out in front of her and dug the heels of her (slightly muddy) training shoes into the pale carpet and began to wipe her face with her handkerchief. 'Oh, I see I've interrupted a meeting of the Cat Adoration Society,' she said, glancing across at the photographs. She then, quite deliberately and solely for the effect that it would have upon Gwen, blew her nose vigorously, not directly into her handkerchief, but into her handkerchief via her fingers. Gwen, who had been prepared to ignore the earlier sally, could not ignore so marked a display of provocation. She closed her eyes. 'Must you?' she said.

'Must I what?'

Corky shoved the handkerchief back into her pocket and looked from one to the other of them. 'Has somebody died?' she enquired, wide-eyed.

Gwen began to collect together the unframed photographs. 'Christina has just received her divorce papers,' she said evenly. 'So you'd hardly expect her to be dancing a jig.'

Corky had discovered that if she kicked her heels against the pile of the carpet hard enough, little crescents of half-dried mud could be dislodged from the cleats in the soles of her shoes. She proceeded to do this, rhythmically. 'Why not?' she said. 'That was the object of the exercise, wasn't it? Given that she left him because the marriage had fallen to bits, I would have thought that divorce was the logical thing.'

'She left him,' said Gwen, averting her eyes from the despoiled carpet by the most tremendous effort of will, 'because of – other circumstances. As you well know.'

'You mean she left him because of that other feller who bottled out when it came to the crunch? You mean now she doesn't want a divorce after all?'

'Circumstances are somewhat different now, yes,' Gwen said.

'Oh come on. If you start dishing it out, you've got to be prepared to take it,' Corky said and banged her feet so that a shower of little clods flew into the air and on to the carpet.

'Will you *stop* it!' shrieked Gwen.

'I *am* here,' Christina said.

Afterwards, when Corky had stridden (a participle of the verb that Christina had never before had occasion to employ, but no other word could accurately describe her progress) out of the room, and Gwen had ignored Christina's advice about leaving the mud to dry before attempting to remove it from the carpet and had, therefore, created more of a disaster area than had existed in the first place, and they were both on their knees beside a bucket of soapy water and a vacuum-cleaner, Christina said, point-blank, 'Whatever's the matter with Corky these days?'

'Oh she has these phases,' Gwen said, rubbing vainly at the spreading grey stain.

'There seems to be something on her mind. She talks to herself an awful lot lately.'

Christina's bedroom was directly beneath Corky's. It could be disconcerting, until you realised what was happening, especially when the talking seemed to consist mainly of the uttering of curses.

'Oh I haven't time to try to find out what goes on in her head,' Gwen said. She leaned back on her heels. 'I expect I'll end up having to call in the professional cleaners . . .'

She clicked her tongue against her teeth in exasperation. In her opinion people's heads could be sorted out a good deal more easily than ruined carpets. More cheaply, anyway.

❦ 6 ❦

All of a sudden, Corky bucked up. On February 1st Christina woke to the strains of 'Guide Me O Thou Great Jehovah' being rendered fortissimo as Corky carried up the tea and then stayed to chat about her morning run: a seal washed up on the beach, a car wrapped round the bollards at the bottom of the hill, another body on the railway line neatly separated from its head by the 6.23. (You could always estimate the extent of Corky's good humour by the gruesomeness of her anecdotes.)

And from then on cheerfulness seemed to be the order of the day: now she attended closely to your conversation and waxed Gwen's car without being asked. Now her puff-pastry rose to its former mouth-watering, feather-light heights and Albert was given the day off to go to Carlisle to compete in the North of England semi-final of the Quiz League; she even provided him with a packed lunch. Now she always made a point of removing her running shoes outside the back door and banging their soles together to free the cleats of impacted mud.

It was just a pity that the event which probably explained this transformation was that responsible for precipitating Gwen into a mammoth attack of sour grapes.

'Look, would you rather I didn't?' Christina asked for the umpteenth time, and Gwen said again, 'You're a grown woman, aren't you? It's up to you who you go out with. If you want to be bored to death all evening that's your funeral. Why should it concern me?'

'Well, I thought perhaps . . . with you not seeing so much of Edward these days . . . I thought perhaps you and Stephen . . .'

'Well you thought wrong,' Gwen said. 'And by the way, did you know the back of your hem's coming down?'

Christina pinned it up. She wanted Gwen to issue a veto, to

say: 'Hands off, he's mine.' It would absolve her from the need to make a decision.

She'd been cutting through the station on the previous Monday morning. Murray Pearl was standing at the barrier of the London platform, carrying a holdall. She tried to attract his attention but there was too much noise and confusion and he disappeared from view.

'Oops! Where's the fire?'

Turning abruptly, she had barged straight into Stephen Millward. She'd dropped a folder. The papers that it contained were scattered all over the pavement and he bent down to help her to pick them up. A film cliché, like that other one that Livingstone had brought to life: the lover waiting in the rain for his beloved, a bunch of freesias in his hand. Significant moments.

But there is nothing more dissatisfactory than sharing a significant moment with the wrong person. A man with a round face and spectacles and sandy hair and a pleasant smile stooped to gather up her notes, and Livingstone was in America.

This particular cliché depended on the man, having restored the woman's belongings to order, then asking her to join him in a drink. It was too early for a drink; he suggested a cup of coffee instead, and because the alternatives were so unattractive: supermarket own brand instant with chicory at The System, in the company of Kenneth who'd either be mooning or glowering; best quality, freshly-ground Kenyan at Klosters – but the price to be paid there was Corky's foul mood, she accepted.

They went to the Adelphi. The coffee was good. They chatted cautiously while they drank it: he was a widower, he had a daughter who'd just finished college and started her first job as a food technician. She'd gone to London. He missed her. His sister kept house for him. He'd met Gwen at some function to do with the Chamber of Trade.

'She's quite a lady, isn't she,' he said, 'Gwen?' To which Christina could only politely nod her assent.

And then, when their cups were empty and there was no more coffee left in the pot and she got up to leave, he'd carried the cliché through to its logical conclusion by asking her if she'd care to accompany him to the ballet on Saturday evening.

'There's nothing between Gwen and me,' he'd said. 'Not like that.'

But she'd wondered if Gwen was of quite the same opinion.

'Very shallow, I thought,' Gwen said. 'Pleasant enough, I suppose, to make up the numbers at a dinner party, but beyond that . . . A bit of an eye to the main chance too, I gather. Thought Monica Stone's husband had left her very well provided for and was never off the doorstep. When he found out that wasn't the case, it was a different story.'

Christina put on the Louise Livingstone jersey, but experienced such a piercing pain upon doing so that she took it off again. 'Well there's no danger of his falling prey to any such misconception with me,' she said.

She made flippant remarks not just because she derived satisfaction from Gwen's annoyance, but also to disguise her nervousness. She needed a manual, one entitled, 'How to Go Out with a Man', for she had forgotten the ground rules.

'I feel I'm doing wrong,' she said to Corky.

'Why's that? You're separated, aren't you? You'll soon be divorced. He's widowed. What's wrong with that? And don't fall for all that guff that Titty Fa-la's putting about: him being a gold-digger and so on. She's only saying that because she's had her nose put out of joint.'

She walked away, humming to herself. When she was halfway up the stairs Christina heard her saying, 'Ruptured, yet on top of the world!' It was an exclamation she was apt to use when she was in an exceptionally good mood. At least I'm making someone happy, Christina thought, as she flicked unenthusiastically through the rest of the clothes in her wardrobe.

A new life. She kept repeating the phrase as a taxi bore her to the hotel where they'd arranged to meet. And how could you build yourself a new life if you weren't willing to meet people, go places, knights errant being highly unlikely to knock at Gwen's door on the off-chance?

He was sitting in the corner at the far side of the piano lounge. He saw her before she spotted him and got up and crossed the room to meet her. 'Don't look so worried,' he said, leading her back to a sofa. Oh God, she thought, is that to be the way of it: the kindly, slightly patronising protector of vulnerable women?

But wasn't that what she wanted?

Perhaps there'd be a moment where rapport would suddenly establish itself. After all: all those months when Livingstone had been nothing more than a name on a door, a red pencil despoiling the neat margins of an assignment, and then – between one heartbeat and the next – he had undergone some invisible transformation and changed into the object of her desire.

An elderly woman wearing a long dress and a spangled snood walked to the piano, sat down and began to play 'Night and Day'. She played very histrionically, dropping her hands on to the keyboard from a great height, tossing her snood, moving a dramatic profile from side to side. After a moment, Christina put down her drink very carefully and dared to raise her eyes to meet those of her companion, found that he too was attempting to stifle hysteria, remembered the wink across Gwen's dinner table, the feeling she'd had that he was on her side.

'Reminds you of those Hollywood films about Franz Liszt,' he murmured. 'She even looks like Franz Liszt.'

'More like Max Wall – about to launch into one of the Hungarian Rhapsodies.'

'That hair – yes!'

Tacitly, they decided that perhaps they should leave before they might be asked to leave – other people appeared to be listening enraptured.

In the foyer they released their pent-up mirth. He blew his nose, wiped his eyes. 'Sorry about that,' he said, helping her on with her coat. 'I didn't bargain on *that* sort of cabaret.'

She wasn't sorry, not at all. She could imagine how stiff and stilted their encounter might otherwise have been.

He took her to the theatre bar instead, which was so crowded and noisy that they weren't able to do much more than try to interpret each other's odd exchanged pleasantries. Judgement would have to be reserved. She knew only that he was attentive, genial, and had succeeded in doing what she had not thought possible: which was to make her laugh.

He had bought good seats and it was an impressive production – not that she was in any position to make valid comparisons: Max had never cared for the ballet and she and Livingstone had had so little opportunity to be together in the evenings that when they did manage to meet it seemed a waste not to spend the time in bed. Besides, appearing together in public places was fraught with danger.

She must not think of Livingstone. She fixed her eyes, and tried to fix her thoughts, upon what was happening on the stage. Trouble was, what was happening on the stage was a girl mourning her faithless lover – and, oh, that music! An invitation to wallow.

She tried to resist it. She tried very hard. She thought she'd succeeded. After the performance he took her to a quiet pub where they discussed the ballets they'd seen and the ones they'd like to see, the difficulty of actually getting to see any in the provinces, the cultural scene generally and what their preferences were. 'Not piano-players particularly, I take it?' he said, smiling.

She smiled too and said, 'Night and Day – you are a one.' It was what Max used to say, years ago, in a previous lifetime that had included shared laughter.

'Beg your pardon?' said Stephen Millward.

'Just something my husband used to say.'

Well that *was* a good start, wasn't it: bringing up the subject of your estranged spouse on your first date with another man? Just about top of the list of taboo subjects, she supposed.

Not that it would apply to him. He – having been separated from his wife by death rather than dishonour – would not feel the need for any such delicacy.

But he said only, when Christina felt obliged to enquire, 'She died three years ago. Sometimes it feels like yesterday and sometimes I can hardly remember what she looked like. Until I see Lucy – that's my daughter – and then it hurts like hell. You have sons, haven't you? Easier, I imagine, than bringing up girls.'

She was disabusing him of this notion when the landlord called time. They left the pub and walked up the hill to where he'd parked the car. He offered her his arm. It was a street lined on one side with rather seedy small hotels. How reassuring it felt to have a man walking protectively beside you on the outside of the pavement . . .

Suddenly a glass fell – apparently from the sky – and shattered into a hundred pieces not six inches away from her. Instinctively, she ducked, flung a hand across her face. 'What the hell!' said Stephen Millward.

Groups of people appeared from nowhere, enquired as to her welfare. 'Could have knocked you unconscious,' they said. 'Could have killed you.' Feet scattered the fragments of glass – it had been a heavy beer mug that fell – across the pavement. 'You want to call the coppers. Could have brained you.'

She was trembling uncontrollably. The glass had apparently

fallen from a window in one of the hotels, fallen on her side of the pavement – so much for male protection. Stephen Millward was deep in conversation with a man who stood at the door of the hotel. This man was apologising profusely. She caught the sentences: 'We've an Irish rugby team staying here,' and 'I'll go up and warn them to cool it. I'll call the police too, if you want . . .'

She shook her head. She had thought, for one mad moment, that the missile had been aimed specifically at her, but it was, after all, merely a random accident, result of roistering. She was still trembling though. Stephen Millward came up close and put his arms around her.

To comfort, only, nothing more, but she recoiled from him as violently as if he'd attempted assault.

'I'm sorry . . .'

She'd been aware of the height of him, the breadth, the smell of him, saw his face in close-up – and they were all wrong, would never, ever, do.

Abruptly, he withdrew his hand from her shoulder, a hand sprinkled with freckles, tufted with sandy-coloured hair, a hand that she could not but compare with another: slim, brown, long-fingered, the hand that had touched her and brought her to life.

He drove her back to Gwen's, switching on the car radio to mask any awkward silences. A nice man. Or, at least, *seemed* to be. Worth finding out if he was, surely? She knew that she could make it obvious to him in a variety of subtle ways that she would welcome another invitation. And then she would have a nice man: presentable, considerate, rich enough to show her a good time (as Corky put it) and, more to the point (most to the point, Gwen would say), available; a man to escort her home, so that she need not tread fearfully through dim alleyways or listen to the footsteps that mimicked her footsteps and imagine some threatening presence, some baleful eye, watching her every movement.

A few words, one gesture – all it would have taken to convey to him her willingness to be considered long term rather than short. She was incapable of making it. She sat shrivelled into herself as he brought the car to a halt and said that – apart from that one unfortunate incident – how very pleasant it had been. He turned towards her and she felt every muscle stiffen at his approach. He touched her lightly on the back of her gloved hand. 'Chin up,' he said.

To be alone, you needed to be strong. Or mad. She hurried to get the door open (Gwen had relented and had a key cut for her) although he waited gallantly to see her safe indoors. In her case, madness seemed a much likelier possibility than strength.

$$\backsim 7 \backsim$$

Sharon Mary Theresa Donaldson was an eight-month baby. Among the post that waited in the wire basket behind The System office door on Monday morning was an envelope containing the regulation stork-and-bundle card and a message to the effect that Colette and Don were happy to announce the arrival of an addition to their family.

Kenneth held it between forefinger and thumb, at the greatest possible distance from himself, as though it had been some unsolicited obscene communication. 'Praise the Lord for that,' he said, in a thoroughly irreligious manner. 'Perhaps she'll change the record now.'

'I doubt it. It's the beginning, not the end.'

'Do you think it's a hint that we'll be expected to buy something for the wretched thing?'

'It is the usual custom.'

'Oh is it?' he said. 'Well I can't. I'm skint. And even if I wasn't, I don't see why I should have to fork out just because she feels the need to have kids. At her age!' he said disgustedly.

Small wonder he was skint; he'd been flinging money away recently like water. The motley collection of sixties and seventies garments that had replaced the torn rugby jerseys and baggy-crotched jeans had, in turn, been replaced by clothes that, though no less cheap and shoddy, were slightly more *à la mode*. He had visited a hairdressing salon instead of his usual barber and the result was a cross between bouffant and crew-cut with the hint of a quiff – probably the best that could be achieved given the unpromising raw material. At his instigation, every day for a fortnight, flowers had been delivered to the desk of Janet in the newspaper office. Sometimes he called in to present chocolates or a corsage in person. At least the telephone calls with which he bombarded her were free: being paid for jointly by the Standish Trust and, indirectly, the taxpayer.

He doodled around the edges of work-sheets and business letters and advertising copy. When you looked you saw that all the doodles had as their starting point, their focus and centre, the name 'Janet'; he worked out complicated numerological equations assessing their two names for compatibility. He bought horoscope books so that he could find out how they compared astrologically. He equipped himself with a pack of Tarot cards and spent hours shuffling them and dealing them and bemoaning the proximity of the Alchemist to the Nine Cups or the Seven Florins.

Janet lived on the Wirral. He bought Saveaway tickets so that he could take the train over there and, from the cover of a convenient bus shelter, gaze at her family home.

And the result of all this ardour, all this searching for omens, the chill bus-stop vigils? One minute he was the picture of gloom, lower lip clenched between his teeth; the next, the sun had come out and blazed forth from a cloudless sky and he sat staring vacantly at the opposite wall, a smile on his face.

Obviously, he was either being given a very cynical run-around (gifts welcome, donor definitely not) or else he was subject to periodic bouts of inordinate self-delusion. Christina felt like ringing Janet herself and begging for an absolutely unambiguous statement of intent.

She thought of this later that morning when Kenneth, having spent an hour or so half-heartedly updating the mailing list, leaned back in his chair and yawned and stretched his arms above his head. 'Have you finished with that phone?' he enquired. 'If you have, I might give Janet a bell before she goes on her break. Sort something out for tomorrow evening.'

He ambled across the room. Even his gait had changed. Gone the camp mincing; now he moved with the studied deliberation of Clint Eastwood when he was deciding whether to shoot someone.

He had a drawling way of talking to match. Christina almost expected him to say not, 'Please can you put me through to Janet Poole,' but 'Shit!' or 'I need a shave,' or 'Gimme a whisky.'

There was a moment or two when that screwed-up expression which contradicted the ambling and the drawl gave way to a vacuous smile as the tones of the beloved were transmitted into his ear. What she was saying banished it immediately. 'No,' Christina heard him say, and 'Oh no,' and 'But . . .' before she felt it would be politic to leave the room.

She spent ten minutes in the Ladies' cloakroom washing her hands very thoroughly and combing her hair until she could see the marks of the teeth in it and putting on lipstick and then, having no other means available for gilding the lily and bored with her own reflection, returned reluctantly to the office.

He was standing by the telephone where she'd left him, his hand still on the receiver, though she had the feeling that the conversation had been concluded some time ago. There was a fixity about his stare and his head was cocked slightly to one side as though he was listening to something that would be inaudible to anyone else. 'Are you all right?' she asked. His gaze swivelled towards her and he started to form words but before they found utterance his eyes had slid upwards in their sockets and the sound that was meant to accompany the words emerged as a brief but piercing cry and then he teetered for a moment before falling forward full length on the floor.

It must have lasted a minute or two from start to finish: his seizure, but it seemed like hours. By the time she'd collected herself and moved towards him with the hazy notion of ramming something between his clenched teeth, or loosening his collar, it was over: the rigor had ceased, his breathing had quietened, his face returned to its normal colour and the only thing amiss was the dark staining of the cloth of his trousers that spread from his crotch and down his thigh.

Slowly he gathered himself. She saw that where there had been froth at the corner of his mouth now there were flecks of blood.

He sat down heavily. 'Shall I call an ambulance?' she said. 'Or at least your doctor?'

He shook his head. 'No point,' he said. 'Forgot my pills, that's all.'

'Oughtn't you to go home? If only . . .'

To take off your wet clothes, she'd been going to say, before changing her mind. And he knew she'd been going to say it. He put his head in his hands and started to cry.

'Oh look here . . . It can't be that bad.'

He sobbed uncontrollably. His face glistened with tears. They dripped from his chin and through his fingers. 'You said,' he finally managed to stutter.

'*I* said?'

'You said . . . I should . . . keep trying . . . with Janet . . .'

So she had, but then she was no expert on human relations. Surely he must have realised that?

Colette's baby looked not so much small and delicate – as befitted a premature infant – but very old indeed.

'There *are* kiddies like that,' Mae Somebody, a godmother, confided to Christina with a confidence that suggested a lifetime's bearing of children, though it turned out that she was actually *Miss* Mae Somebody and had had everything removed at an early age. 'They look as old as the hills when they're born,' she said. 'It's only as they get older they look younger. Give her time,' she said, 'she'll be as right as ninepence.'

Which did not go down too well with Colette who presumably considered her to be as right as ninepence already.

The other godmother was Sister Mary Benedict, who not only looked old but was old (the likelihood that she would be around to monitor her namesake's spiritual progress for very long seemed remote; one simply hoped that God's grace would allow her to last out the christening ceremony), and the godfather was Don's ex-boss.

'I thought they only yelled when the priest put the water on their heads,' he whispered to Christina who was standing next to him. 'I'll not be expected to hold it, shall I? To tell you the truth,' he said, 'I can't think why Don asked me to be godfather. I'm not a practising Roman and though he worked for me a number of years, he always kept himself very much to himself. Never one of the lads.'

He excused himself, pleading a prior engagement, from accompanying them back to the Donaldsons' to partake of a celebratory tea. A sturdy young nun came to collect an over-tired Sister Mary Benedict and take her back to the convent. The rest of them returned to Primrose Close where food was distributed on the kitchen table – with the baby's carry-cot taking up space in the lounge, there wasn't room for five adults to circulate in there. They couldn't do much circulating in the kitchen for that matter, but there were fewer ornaments in danger of being dislodged.

'She's a pair of lungs on her all right,' Father Fagan said, extending his glass for a refill. 'She'll make a good Everton supporter,' he said to Don, but Don only smiled pallidly, not being a football fan, and after that there was a rather embarrassing pause and you could see the priest weighing up the conversational hard-going against the inferior and limited amount of drink – he was one of your modern clerics: a pint in the pub with the lads and a singsong on the coach to the cup-final and a follow-your-own-conscience approach to contraception, and found it difficult to relate to the more introverted and taciturn of his flock.

'I didn't know it was the time it is,' he said, consulting his watch. 'They'll be hammering down the doors of the youth club by now. Many thanks,' he said, and gave a blessing almost on the run – if being on the run had been a possibility within the crowded confines of the Donaldsons' home. 'Priests!' Miss Mae Somebody said scornfully. 'They have a great life. I myself,' she said, 'don't have a lot of time for them.' Father Fagan had eaten only half of his Viennese whirl. She contemplated it for a moment and then shrugged her shoulders and picked it up and polished it off. Eating after a priest ought to be safe enough; left-footers, at least, seeing as they didn't even pass round the chalice but kept it all to themselves.

It didn't seem right that Sharon Mary Theresa, born of staunch Catholics, should have non-religious persons for two of her godparents. No wonder she wailed. All through the ceremony and during the journey homewards she had maintained a ceaseless yelling; now both rhythm and volume had increased. 'Have you thought of giving her a dummy?' Christina asked eventually.

'Oh no!' Colette replied, in horrified tones. 'The health visitor says that it'll stop soon of its own accord.'

'I don't think you need to follow their advice slavishly,' Christina said cautiously, remembering one of that ilk who had diagnosed Adam's infant acute bronchitis as a mere sniffle and recommended maximum fresh air during the coldest March on record. 'I think trial and error is probably the best way to cope. If it works, do it, that sort of thing . . .'

Colette looked unconvinced, as well she might if she'd known the extent of Christina's parental shortcomings. It had been Max who'd overruled her cry of 'But the health visitor *said*,' and bundled Adam into blankets and driven him to the hospital where they suspected pneumonia and gave him sulphonamides and oxygen.

'I want to do it properly,' Colette said firmly. 'She'll settle down. She has to learn.'

It was almost as if those words hit the right button: the crying ceased in mid-spate, there was an irritable hiccough and then silence. For a minute they held their breath. But then Colette, rather than expressing relief at the respite, said, 'Oh dear, it's the wrong time. I'm going to have to wake her up in half an hour for her feed.'

Then she said, 'Come up to the nursery and see the presents.'

There was Christina's christening spoon and Sister Mary Benedict's white leather-bound missal and Miss Mae Somebody's plastic feeding bowl which looked as though it ought to have DOG printed around its rim, but the rest: the silver mugs and rosaries and holy medals and photograph frames ready to contain images of the child at every stage of its development, had been, Christina suspected, purchased by the Donaldsons themselves.

Colette sank down into the nursing chair, closed her eyes for a moment or two and allowed expression to an infinite weariness. Then she said again, 'She'll settle down. She has to learn. If you give in to it they just play up all the more. That's what the health visitor said. She has to learn who's boss right from the start.'

The health visitor had said so. To argue would have been a waste of breath. It seemed safer to turn the conversation in a direction where controversy was less likely to prevail. 'Do you think you'll be coming back to work? Everything's gone to pot since you left.'

Colette shook her head. There was the maternity grant and the benefit for eighteen weeks. Surely, by then, a job would have materialised for Don, one that didn't involve his absence for days at a stretch? A mother's place was with her child. Suddenly she clapped a hand to her forehead. 'Oh, those notes I promised to type up for Dr Roberts! Tell her I haven't forgotten them. It's just that I get a bit tired and forgetful . . . Why, how do you mean, it's gone to pot at work?'

Christina explained: Hilary Roberts' failure to provide them with a replacement, Kenneth's lovelorn state. She described his seizure and the fright it had given her, not having been fore-warned of the possibility.

'I knew he took fits,' Colette said, 'but I thought they were just – like mild ones, you know; he'd go off for a bit – vacant, like. I didn't know he threw bad ones. Course, they often have them, don't they?' she said.

'Have what? Epilepsy? Who does?'

'Mental people,' Colette said, and yawned as though she found the subject somewhat less than fascinating.

'Didn't you know?'

'No, I didn't know. What's wrong with him?'

Nothing now, presumably. He was supposed to be cured. Discharged into the community. (Unfortunate phrase, Christina thought, made one think of sewage.) 'Normalised' as the social workers called it. Resettled into one of those hostels that were meant to act as staging-posts for those who needed to find their feet. It was the policy of the Standish Trust (which had been set up to fund, among other things, halfway houses for ex-mental patients – hadn't Christina discovered that in the course of her research?) to find jobs for such people.

The baby started to cry again and Colette rose slowly to her feet.

'At least you won't have to wake her up for her feed,' Christina said encouragingly.

Colette looked at her watch. 'But that's not for another ten minutes,' she said.

8

In the kitchen of Klosters, Albert sat with *The Encyclopaedia of Dates and Events* on his knees and closed his eyes and chanted the order of the battles of the Crimean War: '1854, Alma, Inkerman 1855, Sebastopol – oh, now then, I've missed out Balaclava . . .'

Then he did the same for the Hundred Years' War and the War of Spanish Succession.

Corky said, 'When's this bloody thing finish?'

'February 28th. Finals at Berwick-on-Tweed.'

'Thank Christ for that. Perhaps we'll get some peace then. You sound like a bleedin' demented parrot.'

But when he asked her if she'd hear him while he recited the films of Humphrey Bogart (his specialist subject), and the colours of the national flags of the major nations (his understudy for a fellow team-member's specialist subject), she complied good-humouredly and cuffed him quite kindly and called him 'Cloth-head' when he mixed up Bulgaria with Italy.

'I suppose you're going to need another day off?'

He paused a moment in his recital: 'Rumania, vertical, blue, yellow and red . . .' and nodded, 'Netherlands, horizontal, red white and blue.'

'What do you win – *if* you win?'

'A trophy.'

'Well don't go filling it with champagne. We had enough trouble with you last time.'

He giggled. Last time – after the semi-finals, the police had picked him up for standing on his head at midnight on St George's Plateau (at least, they'd told him that's what he was doing – all he knew was that he had a bruise the size of a gull's egg above his ear).

'And if you lose – don't go drowning your sorrows.'

'Oh we'll beat 'em. No danger. Wipe the floor with 'em.'

Corky put down *The Encyclopaedia of Dates and Events* and *The Films of Humphrey Bogart* and *The Flags of All Nations* and said, 'Which reminds me – isn't it time you did the same for this one? You could eat your dinner off it. And I don't mean because it's so clean. There's no chance of you getting down on your hands and knees and giving it a scrub, I suppose?'

Christina thought of Don Donaldson, down on his hands and knees, picking up crumbs from beneath the kitchen table when she and Colette came downstairs on the day of the christening. Colette had told him to make them a cup of tea and they'd drunk it to the tune of Sharon's incessant screaming. Colette had concentrated on the face of her watch. When the full ten minutes were up, and not a moment sooner, she'd gone to heat a bottle of baby food.

Then she had to run outside to disperse a bunch of kids who were climbing on the back fence and Don took advantage of her absence to test the temperature of the milk upon the back of his hand, lift the baby from her cot, settle her upon his knee and fit the teat of the bottle into her mouth.

There had been a couple of minutes' peace while Sharon sucked and Don stroked the few fronds of hair that surrounded that still prominent and pulsating fontanelle and Christina looked on, thinking that, despite their respective lack of attractiveness, they made quite a pretty picture. Then Colette had returned and snatched the child and told him to stick to what he was good at.

Washing the dishes, picking up crumbs from beneath the kitchen table – nothing more than that, apparently. 'He's so clumsy,' Colette explained. 'He'd have her dropped on the floor before you knew it. Now come on, madam,' she said to the child, who appeared to have lost interest in the bottle and was flailing her tiny limbs from side to side like a stranded starfish.

At least she had the spirit to be angry; her father simply stood watching, as though he had no hope of being allowed any closer involvement in his daughter's upbringing, as though he had resigned himself already to the role of spectator, the function of spare part.

Albert began to mop the floor, rather more enthusiastically than thoroughly. Corky said, 'So what can I do you for? Or did you just come in to bum a coffee?'

Christina had taken to using Klosters as her afternoon bolt-hole. She'd visit The System office, make her telephone calls as rapidly as possible and then leave and pick up a coffee at the wine bar before proceeding towards her interviews. The reason for this was that Kenneth melancholy was hard enough to take, Kenneth melancholy and apparently convinced that she was responsible for the break-up of his romance was impossible. Mostly she found the telephone switched to the answering machine and no transcription made of any subsequent recording. Usually the work sheets and exchange records were blank. He spent the greater part of his time, it seemed to her, chewing on the end of biros until he'd cracked the plastic of both outer and inner casing and flooded his mouth with ink, or else staring at the typewriter from which he hadn't even removed the cover.

It is not my concern, she told herself. I have quite enough on my plate without appointing myself monitor of Those Discharged Into The Community. That night's meeting of The System would, anyway, most probably bring to light the fact that he hadn't done a stroke for weeks.

It took her no time at all that evening to produce a diagram representing group interaction: it consisted of one target and eight arrows. Having done so, she volunteered to make the coffee in order to distance herself from the attack to which everyone except Murray Pearl (who was back from wherever he'd been) and Robin appeared to wish to contribute.

She could see Kenneth at the far end of the table. He seemed curled into himself: head bowed, arms clasped around his body; the snails assaulted by the Perrot children must have attempted just such desperate retraction. But at least they had shells.

'We've come here – most of us at great inconvenience, I've no doubt. I've had awful trouble getting a sitter . . .'

Joyce Perrot appealed to the company, but they were, to a man – and a woman – persons without dependants or attachments or reasons to draw them back to the domestic hearth.

'We've come here to discuss the bring and buy, set for two weeks next Saturday, and what do we find? That not only has the membership not been informed of the date, the press haven't been contacted, the handbills haven't been ordered from the printers. In fact, *nothing's* been done. Not a thing. I can't believe it. I cannot believe that the person responsible could behave this way. Not without a very good reason. Which there doesn't appear to be. Which leaves us to draw our own conclusions. I must say, sheer idleness would be mine.'

'Steady on,' Robin murmured, no doubt mindful of the cosy, matching-rugby-shirts threesomes of happier times.

'Steady on! I think I've been jolly restrained, considering . . . Well, I'll leave it up to the rest of you.'

Klaus spoke up. 'The job sheets are blank since two weeks,' he said. 'We made it a point of importance that job sheets should be kept up to date. We cannot have efficiency if the documentation is neglected. We cannot rely on the memory. Even one younger than mine.' And here he nodded courteously at Kenneth, recognising the age gap and presumable discrepancy in the number of brain cells. 'Running my shop, if I relied on the memory, I would very soon find myself in Carey Street. And my business,' he continued, 'is the traditional sort that involves money changing hands. When money changes hands we take care. Then, you understand, how much more necessary to take care when all is voluntary and no pecuniary gain involved.'

Linda and Maureen nodded vigorously, though you could tell that they weren't exactly sure what pecuniary gain meant. 'Why haven't you got the letters done, Kenneth?' Linda asked, straight out.

Maureen said, 'If he hasn't even written the letters, I don't suppose he's booked the hall either.'

His silence indicated that this was indeed the case. Norman, who had been uncharacteristically quiet, now made a statement which explained his uncharacteristic quietness. 'I've been jotting down some points,' he said, handing a sheet of paper to Jim who sat on his left-hand side. 'Read it and pass it on,' he commanded. 'Just some thoughts to toss around between ourselves while we drink our coffee. Where *is* our coffee?' he said and looked into the kitchen and clapped his hands together and shouted 'Chop-chop.'

By the time it was made and carried in, Norman's memo had reached Robin via Joyce. Joyce had read it, nodding her head vigorously, but Robin said, 'Oh come now!' and ran a hand through his coconut-matting hair. 'Isn't this going a bit far? After all, there's no real damage done, is there? A bit of communal effort . . .'

They stared at him wide-eyed and open-mouthed. They were

volunteers, generously giving of their time and energy; Kenneth was *paid* to do the job.

'All he had to do was write one letter and copy it,' Jim said.

'And stick the stamps on the en-en-en-en-envelopes,' was John's contribution.

'And ring up the *Echo*.' Linda glared at Kenneth and so did Maureen.

In the Ladies, Joyce passed water copiously and noisily. When she came out she said to Christina, who had taken refuge in there as befitted one who should remain impartial, 'I told Robin ages ago that he was unsuitable. Did you know, I caught him hitting Simon at Christmas? He said Simon had kicked *him*. It was a blatant lie of course. Simon just isn't that type. "I may not know much," I said to him, "but I do know my own child." I'm afraid I think he should be given his cards.'

The trait most typical of the Thursday meetings of The System was irresolution. But tonight decision was reached rapidly and almost unanimously: in the event of Kenneth's being unable to provide a satisfactory explanation for his negligence, a recommendation should be made to Dr Roberts that he be dismissed from his post. A show of hands in favour had been minus only those of Christina and Robin and Murray Pearl; Christina had no vote, Robin voted against, Murray Pearl had abstained.

Kenneth seemed not altogether aware that his livelihood was being balloted away. As the rest of them put on their coats and picked up their belongings, she tapped him on the shoulder and said, 'Are you OK?'

He didn't answer but, very deliberately, with a twitch of the shoulder blades, removed himself from contact.

'If you tell them you're sorry,' she said, 'I'm sure they won't give you the sack. You've put their backs up, that's all, by being so uncommunicative.'

The wall, had she addressed it, might have proved more responsive. 'Oh suit yourself,' she said, in the end, and went to get her coat. Her concern derived anyway not from compassion but guilt. Though even if she had mischievously encouraged him in the pursuit of love, such a small misdemeanour hardly warranted a crisis of conscience.

How swiftly everyone had dispersed. Earlier, a sliver of moon had cast some light, but now it was very dark. The lamp at the head of the alley wasn't working either. She began to walk towards the distant sanctuary of the Underground sign.

Afterwards, when trying to recall the actual sequence of events, she found that she couldn't: it had all happened so quickly. She had been aware of a great shouting and feet running and a hand clutching at her shoulder and she'd tried to turn round and, in doing so, lost her balance, teetered for a moment and then fallen heavily on to her knees. There'd been the agonising sting of gravel on raw flesh; it had sickened her; momentarily there'd been a swirling redness behind her closed eyelids and then she'd opened them and looked straight into the face of Murray Pearl.

'Are you all right? Sure? I'll see to him then.'

Slowly, and cautiously, she got to her feet. A few yards away Kenneth Little was engaged in what Colette would have called throwing a fit. Murray Pearl waded in through the flurry of jerking limbs. He went straight to Kenneth's top pocket and took from it a cylindrical piece of hard rubber which he forced between his teeth. He loosened his tie and dragged across a dirty old piece of tarpaulin that someone had flung into the yard and covered him with it.

'I think we'd better call the hostel. Come on, let's get you upstairs.'

In the office, the cleaning woman, who was smoking a cigarette and ticking off her bingo numbers, was roused to action. 'Make her a cup of tea, plenty of sugar,' he said. 'Quick!' The phone call he made must have communicated a similar urgency because it brought two people in a car to the foot of the alley before Kenneth had come round.

One of them was the warden of the hostel in which Kenneth lived. The other, his psychiatric social worker. They listened to Murray Pearl's account of events and then they all went downstairs again, and the cleaning woman followed them and, after a few minutes, scuttled back on legs surprisingly agile considering she never ceased to complain about the crippling varicosity of her veins, and reported that 'that barmy one, he's come to life, and one of the fellas has helped him up and give him some pills and put him in the back of the car. Sacred Heart of Jesus!' she said, looking at Christina more closely. 'You're as white as a sheet. What happened?'

Murray Pearl had said that Kenneth had looked as though he was going to hit her, before he'd managed to pull him away. She knew only that her shoulder hurt where he'd clutched at it, that her knees were bleeding and she was still feeling extremely shaken. The psychiatric social worker said that perhaps she ought to go to the hospital.

'Oh no!'

She had no desire to wait, endlessly, among assorted madmen and drunks in the casualty department, staring at the out of order notice on the coffee machine.

'Well, if you're sure . . .'

She nodded. 'What about . . . ?' she said, gesturing downwards to where Kenneth was, presumably, still in the back of the car.

He told her: Kenneth would be taken back to the hostel, pro tem, but it would, indubitably, be considered necessary for a re-assessment of his condition to be made. Up until now, during the two years since his release from hospital he had coped well, but a potentially violent episode such as this might indicate that re-institutionalisation would be the best thing.

'If you can wait here until we get back,' he said, 'I'll take you home.'

'I'll take her,' Murray Pearl said.

'Would you?'

'Sure.'

They rang for a taxi, drank hot sweet tea while waiting for it to arrive. Murray Pearl rolled a cigarette. 'I could have told them,' he said, 'that he was going round the twist. Should never have been let out in the first place.'

'Do you really think he *was* going to – attack me?'

'Dunno. But best to be on the safe side, wasn't it?'

He had come to her rescue. She hadn't believed that there was any such person left in the world.

'Shook you up a bit, didn't it?' he said, when they were in the taxi and he could see that she hadn't yet got her colour back. 'Stands to reason.'

'I've always hated walking down that alley on my own, always dreaded somebody springing out on me. Though I never expected it to be him . . .'

'You should have said.' He wound down the car window and

flicked out his cigarette stub. 'I'll walk you back on a Thursday, if you like.'

'Wouldn't you mind?'

'Why should I mind? No problem.'

He smiled. It occurred to her as he did so that she'd never seen him smile before. Well, perhaps life was not being too kind to him either. And perhaps sufferers needed to stick together. Once, she'd thought he was spying on her, and then she'd wondered if he was interested in her. She'd been wrong on both counts, so maybe another of her assumptions was wrong too: that there was no such thing as disinterested gallantry. After all, what other explanation could there be?

The social worker, whose name was Mr Stewart, told her that Kenneth had been committed to the local psychiatric hospital for observation. Eventually he would be transferred to the institution in Surrey where he used to live and where they were more *au fait* with his case history.

'Why did he move up here?' she asked.

'He thought that a complete break might be the best thing. A fresh start. Sometimes, of course, it can work,' Mr Stewart said.

She'd scarcely replaced the telephone receiver when it rang again. She was so taken aback by the identity of the voice at the other end that she didn't respond immediately. 'Are you *there*?' Max said.

'Yes, I'm here.'

'The headmaster – whatshisname – wants to see us. Apparently Adam's been faking sick-notes to cover his absences during the exams – you know, the Mocks. The headmaster thinks we should meet without delay to try to get to the bottom of it. I didn't tell him that it was a moot point whether you'd be interested . . .'

She twisted the telephone cord between her fingers. 'My fault,' she said. 'Isn't it? Bound to be.'

'Well that's for you to decide. Tomorrow evening,' he said. 'Six o'clock. I'll see you there.'

Anybody else might have offered to give her a lift. He had made sure that, whatever happened, she would remain aware of her separate status and the extent of her accountability.

*

When the school had been a grammar school the pupils had worn blazers with pocket crests and Latin mottoes. The headmaster had been a very imposing gentleman who sat in his study beneath a studio portrait of himself, which was hung just to the right of a notice-board informing you that he was only the latest MA Cantab in a line which stretched back to the school's foundation. Since the educational reorganisation, the school had come under the aegis of the comprehensive headmaster, who looked, Max said, more like Wigan Polytechnic than Jesus College, Cambridge.

Mr Stanley Phipps, who (and this would have caused Max immense chagrin, had he known) had as much right to append the title Cantabriensis to his name as any of his predecessors, sat on the front edge of his desk, swinging his legs. The bottom of his tie was stained, Christina noticed, as though it had fallen into his dinner at some time. She also noticed that he leaned forward a great deal in order to effect trust-making eye-contact. Pressures, he spoke of: some boys got worked up to a pitch out of all proportion to the importance of the exams. But they were often boys with a record of going to pieces, whereas Adam had always acquitted himself well.

Of course (and here he concentrated fiercely upon a mark on the knee of his trousers), there were pressures other than the scholastic sort, and this was, obviously, a difficult time for all concerned.

He picked up a sheaf of papers from his desk. These were reports on Adam's schoolwork since the beginning of the academic year. They were not good. In fact, to be blunt, they were very bad.

Max turned to Adam. 'Well, what have you got to say for yourself?' he enquired.

'But, pardon me, Mr Conway,' Stanley Phipps said, gently, reprovingly, 'pardon me . . .'

There were approaches guaranteed to turn recalcitrant schoolboys into incorrigible rebels, and Mr Conway's was one of them. He didn't exactly say this, but the implication was there. There was no need to call out the fire brigade, he said. All that was required was cards on the table. There was obviously a problem. Once it was identified, out in the open, then steps could be taken to remedy it.

A long and gentle inquisition produced only grunts or silences or monosyllabic replies of the least enlightening sort. Mr Stanley Phipps' initial expansive gestures dwindled, the informality of his approach was replaced by reliance upon the stricter and cruder code that experience and tradition dictated. By the time they reached the end of the interview he was back behind his desk, sitting very straight and saying that Adam realised, of course, that such deceit, coupled with truancy, could not be allowed to go unpunished.

He requested a brief private word before they left.

'It's not that uncommon, you know,' he said, 'all the botherations of adolescence surfacing, together with the perfectly natural apprehensions that attach to taking exams. Sensitive boys find it more difficult to cope. Your family problems occurring at the same time probably haven't helped. On the other hand, they might have nothing to do with it,' he said quickly; modern psychology stressed that the apportioning of blame rarely achieved anything but the elicitation of resentment.

'He's not on drugs, is he?' Max said. The chap had got his back up: taken a school with an enviable reputation and turned it, in the space of a few years, into a place whose name was a byword for lawlessness and illiteracy, and yet he had the nerve to stand there and preach to them about child management.

Mr Phipps began to smile. He had been asked this question – perhaps in a more roundabout fashion – by anxious parents on more occasions than he cared to remember. He said that it would be foolish to deny that there *was* a drugs problem but, as usual, the press had been guilty of wild exaggeration and caused a lot of unnecessary alarm. He did not believe that Adam's troubles stemmed from drug abuse. Unless they, as Adam's parents, had noticed anything . . . ?

They drove home in silence. They intended to remain calm, but it was difficult to remain calm in the face of such deliberate obdurance. Max, who started off calling Adam 'son', was soon referring to him as a bloody idiot. Christina found herself driven to a deplorable lack of subtlety: 'Is it simply because you fell behind with your work and were too scared to admit it? Don't you like the school? Or the subjects you're doing?' And, knowing it was fatal but unable to resist it: 'I knew there'd be trouble when you started consorting with that awful Parkinson.'

Most of the questions were obviously considered unworthy of

the effort involved to produce an answer. Some elicited a curt response: school was last, the subjects he'd chosen were last.

Couldn't he change his options? A bit late in the day, but not *too* late, if he was prepared to commit himself to serious effort.

The other subjects on offer were also last.

But her denigration of Parkinson produced reaction. He'd looked up and glared at her. 'Don't you insult my friends,' he'd said. 'They're *my* friends. Nothing to do with you.'

A deep breath, a new start. 'Is it the work that's beyond you? Can't you cope with it?'

A long incredulous stare. 'Course I can cope. It's a piece of piss.'

'Well then, why?'

'Is it because . . .' she said hesitantly, 'is it because of us?'

'Dunno what you mean.'

'Our separation. Is it our separation that's caused this falling-off in your work? Would it be different – would it help – if we weren't?'

She was aware as soon as she'd said it that it was a cowardly and despicable thing to say. As a small boy, she'd often bribed him, bought his good behaviour with the promise of deferred treats. It had been bad enough then: 'Be a good boy and I'll let you stay up late tonight, buy you a bike for your birthday.' What was the equivalent now: 'Be a good boy and Mummy will come home to live with you and Daddy again'?

'What *do* you want to do?'

'Wanna leave.'

Said clearly, unhesitatingly.

'You *can't* leave, you can't leave school unqualified. Your O Levels! Your A Levels! University!'

'Don't wanna go to university.'

'You'll regret it for the rest of your life,' Max said. If the lad had wanted to learn the business, to step into his father's shoes, fair enough, but he didn't.

'You can't possibly appreciate the repercussions of making such a rash decision,' Christina said.

'Your mother's right. What are you going to do? Live on the dole for the rest of your days? There are few enough opportunites for those *with* qualifications. What chance would you have with none?'

They stood together, she and Max, each relinquishing to the

other the next stage in the progress of the argument. 'Your mother is right.' How sad, she thought, that their brief unity depended upon trouble of this sort.

'I don't wanna go to university. I wanna leave. It's doin' me 'ead in.'

'Well you *can't* leave,' Max said. 'Not until July. The law insists that you stay until then at least. And, if I might be allowed to make a suggestion, you'd do well to make the best of it and get your finger out in the meantime.'

Adam said, 'Get stuffed,' and got up and ran out of the room and, noisily, up the stairs.

She made to follow, but Max held out a prohibiting hand and although that wouldn't have stopped her if she'd thought that anything could be achieved by going after him, she recognised the futility of such action and stayed put.

'What's your opinion?' she asked eventually, knowing that now they were alone, they would very soon adopt the usual hostile postures.

He scratched beneath his jaw. David did that, when perplexed. What a strange interweaving of the like and unlike there was, within the issue of a union. What modifications there were, and yet, now and again, a gesture or facial expression as identical as if it had been cloned. It seemed to her that David had taken the best from each of them. Pray God that Adam hadn't been endowed with the worst.

'I think it's just a phase,' Max said. 'I think he's been buggering about. Like David did at his age. Better now than later. I'll talk to him when he's calmed down a bit.'

'Perhaps if we were to try and organise something nice for his birthday . . .'

Another case of bribery and corruption but so what, if it got him through his exams?

'We'd thought of going away that weekend, actually,' Max said, carefully not looking at her.

'Oh,' she said.

He continued not to look at her in an even more studied manner. 'Heard anything more about the divorce?' he said, as though 'the divorce' was something self-generated that now proceeded quite autonomously.

'No. You?'

He shook his head. 'They take their time,' he said, 'solicitors.'

Perhaps this was so. She had not yet engaged the services of one to test the truth of this proposition.

'I believe it's nothing dramatic – the actual court thing,' he said.

'No?'

'More or less just a pronouncement, once the judge has satisfied himself that the children are being properly cared for.'

'Yes?'

Why did he keep going on about it? As though attempting to reassure her.

As if bent on confounding her expectations, he got up and poured himself a drink and offered her one. She shook her head. Much as she appreciated this suspension of hostilities, puzzlement as to the reason prevented her from taking advantage of it.

'Everything – all right, is it?' he asked.

'How do you mean?'

'You. Everything all right with you?'

She wanted to say: 'Oh yes, everything's just tickety-boo. I'm homeless, rejected, filled with self-disgust at my own foolishness and timidity and – to cap it all – last night a madman tried to take a swing at me.' But somehow she never could say to him what really mattered. She said, instead, feebly, 'I suppose so.' And then she said, 'Look Max, do you think you might be able to persuade Adam to see me more often? After all, there's nothing to be gained by hostility, is there?'

'You're suggesting I'm turning him against you?'

'No,' she said patiently. 'I'm not suggesting that at all. I just think that the more normal and civilised we try to make things, the better it will be for him. And if you were to make it clear that there isn't a contest between us for his allegiance . . .'

'I hope I've done that already. If he thinks otherwise, then that's down to you.'

She stood up. She said, 'Max, I'm a bad woman, that is to say, an adulterous wife and a deserting mother and, taken together, that *has* to add up to a bad woman. But I am getting my just deserts so you can lay off with the scourge for a bit, and let's try to concentrate on repairing some of the damage I've caused, because I did not become a bad woman in a vacuum, you know.'

He studied his gin for a moment and then drained his glass. 'All right,' he said. 'I'll see what I can do.'

'Do you think I should see him before I go?'

'Best leave well alone. He'll come round sooner if left to himself.'

She contented herself with a tap on his bedroom door and the calling out of a farewell greeting. There was a long silence and then a mumble.

Max was taking a casserole out of the oven where, presumably, it had been placed earlier in the day by the housekeeper. It smelled most appetising. In my day, she thought (and already it seemed as though her day was part of another, prehistoric era), casseroles were very dodgy propositions on account of Adam detesting vegetables and David going through a vegetarian phase and Max needing to be very careful not to aggravate his ulcer. Perhaps the housekeeper had a way with casseroles which got round all these dietary prohibitions.

'Do you mind if I ring for a taxi?'

He shook his head, hung the oven gloves neatly on their hook and reached down plates from the cupboard. 'I'd give you a lift,' he said, 'but as you can see, the meal's ready.'

She left him, looking the picture of contented domesticity, amazed at the change in him. Perhaps this had come about not simply because she'd left him. Perhaps his father's death had freed him of a few demons. Perhaps Adam's naughtiness had alerted him to the need to be nicer.

She'd almost reached Gwen's house before it occurred to her just why he was working so hard at being pleasant. If the court got wind of Adam's disturbed behaviour they might not be so anxious to give custody to the parent under whose control and guidance that behaviour was being manifested. And the only person likely to make certain the court got wind of it was herself via her solicitor.

'Bastard!' she said. She must have said it out loud because the taxi-driver turned to look at her. 'Oh, not you,' she said. Once upon a time she'd have been embarrassed beyond measure and tipped him hugely to divert attention from her confusion, but times changed.

∽ 9 ∾

Max sent her a note saying that he'd had a long talk with Adam, during which Adam had promised to mend his ways, to go into school and work hard for his exams, and to visit his mother on a more regular basis, the first of these visits to take place on Friday evening – if this was convenient, if that ghastly Gwen wasn't filling her house with her ghastly friends?

There was a postscript:

'Is it lack of funds that obliges you to stay with Gwen all these weeks?' he wrote. 'If it would help, perhaps it might be possible to forward some of the money that will be settled on you after the divorce. I'm sure that Adam would find it easier if you had a place of your own.'

A divorce settlement of a lump sum was envisaged, a once-and-for-all payment to be rid of her. Not so much an astute financial move, she felt, as the disinclination to maintain contact which the paying of regular maintenance might involve.

'Let me know,' he had written. She'd see him in hell first. It never occurred to her that it was possible both to take the money *and* blow the whistle on him in court, if need be.

She asked Gwen if it would be convenient for Adam to come round on Friday evening.

'Yes of course,' Gwen said indistinctly. She had on a face mask. When she stripped off the resultant membrane, it was supposed to take her wrinkles with it.

'You've not invited anyone round?'

'No. Stephen and I are going to a supper party at the Goldsmiths. Stephen Millward.'

Only her eyes were visible. But they conveyed an unmistakeably direct message. All the way to the Poly Christina pondered her possibly premature rejection of the gentleman in question.

246

She was alone and she was lonely, and she hadn't given him a chance, had nipped the relationship in the bud, knowing full well that Gwen wouldn't fail to take advantage of that kind of unforced error.

She'd been summoned to appear before Hilary Roberts to discuss the critical situation that now obtained *vis-à-vis* The System personnel, the non-existent personnel, what with Colette playing happy families and Kenneth confined to the rubber room.

'It's a damn nuisance,' she said, 'this whole business. I was *assured* by that Stewart chap that Kenneth was as sane as I am. Unfortunately, part of the deal with the Standish Trust is that we fill job vacancies with these discharged –' Lunatics, she'd been going to say, but amended it to 'people'. 'If they're suitable. Obviously we don't want to be landed with someone else who's going to revert to type. Surely the judgement of these so-called experts can't be totally off-beam all the time? I mean, I take it that a discharge into the community is not consented to without good cause? What about this Murray chap, the one who came to your rescue? He's not working, is he? And he's obviously no longer doolally, if ever he was. *That* would satisfy the Trust – *and* mean we don't need to waste time advertising.'

'Murray Pearl? Doolally?'

Hilary Roberts shook her head. 'Some sort of minor break-down, I gather, that meant the end of his army career – you know what the army's like: you can be subject to every weird psychological hang-up in the book as long as it makes you more aggressive, but one sign of weakness and you're out on your ear. Obviously he's perfectly all right. You should know that, of all people.'

Indeed. How unfair, she thought, that he might be tarred with the same brush as Kenneth simply because they'd shared the same address.

'Leave it with me,' Hilary Roberts said firmly. 'Do as much as you can, between you, and I'll try to sort something out.' She stacked papers together to indicate that the meeting was at an end. 'Will you ask Jennifer to come in?' she said.

'Jennifer?'

'Yes. Jennifer Weatherby.'

Jennifer Weatherby: it sounded like a girl who went to hunt

balls and got married to a merchant banker and had her wedding photograph in *The Tatler*.

'Oh, you mean Jinx?'

'Jinx!' Hilary Roberts said scornfully. 'Silly girl. Trying to be something she's not.'

Christina went through to the outer office.

'You're wanted.'

She picked up a notebook and went to answer Hilary Roberts' bidding: Jennifer Weatherby, full-time research assistant and part-time punk. Or was it the other way round?

'Do as much as you can, between you.'

Between whom? Did Hilary Roberts mean Norman, who'd stuck his head round the door one afternoon and said, 'Coping? Yes? Jolly good,' and disappeared again? Or Linda, who'd spent an entire morning filing her fingernails to fearsome points and bending Christina's ear with tales of Maureen's shameless pursuit of men? Or Jim, who'd put in an evening and succeeded in thoroughly de-sorting that proportion of the records that she'd managed to arrange into some semblance of order?

Between Christina and Christina, was what she had meant. And there was just too much work for one person to cope with. For a start, the phone never stopped ringing. Scores of people seemed to have old fridges they wanted to be rid of in return for a bit of gardening, or two-speed hammer drills in exchange for baby-walkers. A man offered a course of flute lessons to anyone who could mend his guttering. A woman who iced cakes was anxious to learn rudimentary Italian in time for her holiday. The problem was – and this was the reason for the scheme's general lack of success – that rarely could a match be achieved between these demands, most particularly when the work records, which might have disclosed the names and addresses of gutter-fixers or Italian speakers, were in a state of chaos.

And all this quite apart from the demands of her own job.

At eleven o'clock on Friday morning she flipped the switch that transferred the calls to the machine and left to do some very important shopping.

Gwen was off to her supper party at the Goldsmiths. Corky would be at Klosters. Christina had the freedom of the kitchen to cook Adam a meal. She bought a very expensive piece of fillet steak and some asparagus. She bought a strawberry flan and a slab of Wensleydale. She bought a melon and a bottle of wine. She bought ice-cream in case he'd suddenly gone off strawberry flan. It was wrapped in newspaper and the afternoon temperature wasn't much above freezing, but all the same she was anxious to get it home and into Gwen's freezer before it melted, so she wasn't too pleased to find her progress impeded by Don Donaldson.

He had been hanging about outside the office in the hope of catching her, she gathered. He had something to say. He cleared his throat and moistened his lips and fiddled with his belt buckle.

'What *is* it?' she asked. 'I'm in a terrific hurry.'

An effort was made. Could she possibly come round to see Colette? Colette would like to see her. Could she please come round?

'When?'

'S'afternoon?'

'No, I'm afraid that's impossible. I've a meal to prepare. How would it be if I gave her a ring?'

'We're not on the telephone,' Don Donaldson said, looking at his reflection in his shoes.

'But Colette used to ring up from home when she wasn't feeling well . . .'

'We're not on the telephone any more.'

'Oh.'

'We'd got behind with the payments for the pram . . .'

'Ah.'

There was a silence and then she said, 'What about tomorrow afternoon? I could probably come round then.'

He shuffled his feet. 'We go to the Kwiksave of a Sat'day,' he said.

'Some time next week then? When I've a free afternoon?'

He nodded his head reluctantly and, plonking his hat back on it, turned to go.

'How is Sharon getting on?' she called after him. 'Does she cry less now?'

He turned back to her. There was a brief spark of animation in his dull eye. 'She doesn't cry much at all now,' he said.

'Told you it would ease off, didn't I?'

It was gratifying to be able to display one's superior knowledge, even if it was only to someone as constitutionally inferior as Don Donaldson.

'And the job-hunting? Any luck?'

He nodded again. 'Start Monday,' he said.

'Oh? Good. What?'

'Haulage.'

'Oh,' she said. 'Isn't that long-distance? I thought Colette wasn't keen on you doing that.'

He shrugged. 'Got to,' he said. 'No option.'

She had told Adam to arrive at six-thirty, had timed the meal for seven. At half-past she telephoned the place that she still called home. There was no reply. At quarter to eight she tried again. There was still no reply. At eight o'clock she decided to turn off the gas beneath what were now vegetables with every vestige of life and vitamin content steamed out of them. The constituents of the strawberry flan had begun to subside, messily, into each other. The melon had been in and out of the fridge so often that its jaunty, yacht-sail decoration of orange and lemon slices had begun to wilt.

But the wine had certainly had every chance to breathe. Despairing, she poured herself a glass. And another. At quarter-past eight, when the doorbell rang, she'd drunk three-quarters of the bottle.

'Where on *earth* have you been?'

'Had my guitar lesson, didn't I?' He eyed the recesses of Gwen's hall suspiciously as though he expected the proprietor of the house to jump out at him.

Guitar lesson? On a Friday? At this rate, she thought, he ought to be able to play like Segovia.

'Well, take your jacket off,' she said, and urged him through to the dining-room. He looked at the table. 'Who are you expecting?' he asked.

'You,' she replied. 'Sit yourself down and I'll fetch the food.'

He gaped at it as though he'd never seen plates and cutlery before. 'I've eaten,' he said.

Well, of course. Naturally. What else had she expected?

'You eat,' he said politely, encouragingly. But her stomach, churning so long during the waiting, signalled its lack of appetite. She poured herself another glass of wine. He sat picking cat hairs off his trousers (Boysie was dead but his shed coat lingered on) and straightening the cuffs of his shirt. It was a very pretty, stylish shirt, paisley. 'New?' she asked.

He nodded.

Kidskin jackets and cashmere sweaters and paisley shirts – Max must have increased the budget set aside for clothing quite lavishly – to make up, presumably, for other deprivations.

'How's the teachers' strike affecting you these days?' she asked, attempting to grope her way, gently, through the darkness of forbidden territory.

'They aren't now, not so much.'

Assuming that you are in school often enough to be aware of any change, she thought. 'I expect it hasn't helped,' she said. 'I expect that, sometimes, it hardly seemed worthwhile going in.'

'Yeah,' he said.

'Everyone gets a period of feeling that they're really in the doldrums at school,' she went on. 'A feeling that they're going nowhere, not fast but very slowly indeed. I did myself.'

'Did you?'

'Mm. I hated the place: all that tedious routine and all those petty regulations and not having a clue as to what I wanted to do when I left . . .'

Only the last was true. When she was Adam's age her father had just died and her mother had started to be ill and school was a refuge: a place where security obtained and events could be controlled.

'Couldn't have been as bad as our place.'

For the first time she got the impression that what she was saying might be sufficiently interesting to divert his attention from the necessity to remove cat hairs from his trousers or to click the button on his watch so that it presented some sort of vastly complicated digital display informing him of the time in Bangkok or the amount of rainfall in Tierra del Fuego.

'What's wrong with it?'

'It's like prison. And it's run by a bunch of sadists. And those that aren't sadists are dickheads.'

'In what *way*?'

'Half of 'em are like Phipps – as thick as shit. The other half – it's all a big act. Like they're *comedians* or something, and you're their stooges. They really get a kick out of putting you down. There's this lad in the Lower Five Science set and he's got this awful stammer – it takes him about five minutes to get a word out – and that twat, Benson, the Biology teacher, mocks him.'

'So do you,' she reminded him gently. All the kids did. The same with the spastic boy and the grossly fat one, and so on.

'But *Benson* shouldn't, should he?' he said fiercely. 'He really *enjoys* it. He always makes a point of asking that lad a question if the answer begins with a "p" or a "b" because those are the words it takes him hours to spit out. He's a right bastard. And so's Delaney. And Watson.'

She strove to put faces to these names. All perfectly average-looking, adequately-civil men, as far as she could recall.

'Everyone feels that way about teachers. Granted there must be some who go into the profession because it gives them the chance to exercise their megalomania, but you lot aren't a bunch of angels and anyone can be provoked.'

'But they shouldn't be allowed! If they can lay down the law to us then they should be better than we are, not the same. Or worse.'

She felt that his fervour was laudable, if directed at the wrong targets, although bringing her deductive powers to bear on the search for the real targets was an uncomfortable process.

But at least they were talking. Communication was happening. He'd refused her lovingly-prepared meal but he didn't refuse to empty the bowls that she'd filled with Gwen's cashew nuts and cocktail savouries, nor did he turn up his nose at the wedge of decomposed strawberry flan that she brought in later. Talking, he ate them almost without noticing. And as long as they kept the conversation sufficiently impersonal, he was willing to converse. She should have been content with that. But he was her son and, sooner or later, despite herself, she would be obliged to address him as a mother rather than a debating partner. As ever, the moment came sooner rather than later, with a remark about David having evinced a similar distaste for school, and yet, in the final analysis, having turned to and buckled down.

She was aware of her mistake even as she spoke. What devil in her head put such clichés on her tongue? His face had been open, his tone exclamatory. He was being himself – however precariously integrated that entity actually was. Now he lowered his eyes and looked at his watch and muttered that he had to go and concentrated on cracking his knuckle joints while she blethered on about making efforts and sticking with it.

'How are you getting back? Shall I ring you a taxi?'

'Got me bike.'

He had the clips on his trousers and his leg over the crossbar and was halfway across the square before the sound of her farewell had died on the air.

She had absolutely no desire to visit Colette, but some sort of conscience pang (displaced conscience, the Freudians would say) drove her there the following Tuesday afternoon.

A wasted journey: Colette was on her way out as Christina reached the front gate. They talked briefly and uncomfortably (it was an eye-wateringly windy day and Colette's house, being on a corner, afforded no shelter).

'I'm just on me way to me friend's,' Colette said.

'Don asked if I'd call round. I'd have rung, but . . .'

'Sorry,' said Colette, and clicked the front gate behind her.

'How's Sharon? Where *is* she, incidentally?'

'She's with me other friend,' Colette said. 'For the afternoon.'

Such a flowering of friends where once there had been a dearth.

'She got over the constant crying then?'

'Oh yes. It was a phase. Like the health visitor said. Once they learn they can't play the old soldier . . . I'll have to get going,' she said, suiting action to words.

As she appeared to be walking in the direction of the bus-stop, Christina kept pace, looking at her sidelong. There was a slightly unkempt air about her: the impression being less of someone prepared to go out than of a person who, seeing an unwelcome visitor approaching the front door, flings on a coat and pretends to be going somewhere in order to avoid having to invite her in. Colette's hair was uncombed. She carried no handbag – and Colette, Christina would have sworn, was one of life's handbag-carriers.

Could her arrival have been considered so very unwelcome? However little we think of others, it is most galling to discover that they think less of us.

'Don's started his new job, has he?'

Colette was walking very quickly, and though she was a short-legged woman with not much of a stride, it was difficult to keep up.

'Yes. Monday. Went down to Felixstowe.'

'Don't you mind?'

She shook her head. 'No. I'm glad for him to be out from under me feet.'

They reached the corner of the street. 'I go this way,' Colette said, indicating the opposite direction.

'Well, take care. Perhaps when you get your phone reconnected – mended – I'll give you a ring?'

Colette nodded, gazing out over the expanse of concrete, furnished with a climbing frame and three tyres on ropes, that was dignified with the title of adventure playground.

'Oh,' Christina said, remembering a message, 'Hilary Roberts wants to know if you can let her have those notes you were typing. They're very important, apparently. She can't press onward and upward without them.'

'I've not quite finished it yet. It's getting round to it, what with the extra washing and ironing and getting up in the night and that, I never seem to have a minute. But I'll get it done. I'll get it done in the next day or two and let her have it.'

She seemed quite agitated. 'Don't worry,' Christina said. 'Take your time. I'm sure it's not that urgent.'

But Colette's attention had already wandered back to the playground where one child had mounted a swinging tyre and was kicking away another who had attempted to join him.

'You have all that to look forward to,' Christina said, following her gaze. But Colette didn't answer. Presumably the extent of her horizon was somewhere beyond the tussling children. The ultimate horizon, perhaps, Christina thought, as she waited in the bus shelter, trying to remain equidistant from a patch of dried vomit in one corner and a puddle of urine in the other, that which you felt must be waiting for you beyond all the peaks and troughs involved in your role as a procreating female: all the broken nights and grinding boredom, the fearfully hectic course of childish ailments, the morning sickness unto death, the endless round of supermarkets and school runs, the collecting together of the component pieces of Lego, the sewing on of Cub Scout badges and the writing of excuse notes for Games, the agony of post-natal stitchings, the thrush and the Trichomonas, the cystitis and mastitis and hormonal imbalances, the crimson blood, spotting and flooding or being absent when it ought to have flowed, the gynaecologist's cold instruments, the cysts and erosions, the phone calls at midnight from police stations, the letters from headmasters that began: 'Dear Mr and Mrs Conway,

I think you should know . . .', the locked doors and locked hearts, the worries when they were there and the worries when they weren't, the promises you made to yourself that one day, when you finally surmounted that final peak . . .

And found, no doubt, that it was a mirage, that every peak you thought was the last was followed by another, that the idea of a different horizon was an illusion. And perhaps it would be as well, perhaps it would mean that you'd not need to ask those two terrifying questions: 'For what?' and 'What now?'

∽ 10 ∽

Murray Pearl was duly offered Kenneth's job and accepted it with alacrity. He'd been looking for a break ever since leaving the army. His had been enforced idleness interspersed with temporary posts: doorman, storeman, barman. This was his first chance at a proper position.

And, within a surprisingly short space of time, he had introduced order where chaos had lately reigned: the work sheets were sorted, the filing system reorganised, the books brought up to date. Immaculately-legible records were kept of enquiries and requests and offers of exchanges. It began to seem no longer inconceivable that a match might be found between the man who could lay lino and the woman with a diploma in voice production. Now Christina did not need to take a deep breath before crossing the threshold in case she should be met with a sullen glare or a burst of paranoid muttering. Now there would be a hot, fragrant cup of coffee waiting and her needs anticipated in terms of addresses and telephone numbers. The office was run with an efficiency lacking since Colette left. She couldn't imagine why he hadn't been able to find a permanent job before.

'Not so easy,' he said, tipping out the contents of Kenneth's drawer: a dirty handkerchief, a pack of Tarot cards, a half-eaten fossilised Mars Bar, a clutch of savagely-chewed biros. 'You've got to get to the stage where you can show them what you can do. There's no chance of that if you never even make the interview. None of this is worth keeping, is it?' He stirred the rubbish with the tip of his forefinger. 'Shall I chuck it?'

In it went, into a bin-liner, together with the out-of-date membership lists and the broken stapler and the clogged Tippex containers and Kenneth's astrology books and Colette's empty pill bottles.

'Didn't the army help?' she asked as he went to work on the scarred and stained desk top with wax polish, meths and a duster.

'Not so you'd notice.'

He seemed reluctant to talk about his army career. It took a lot of worming out of him. 'No point dwelling on the past,' he said, taking a broom to the fluff behind the filing cabinet. (The cleaning woman was apparently unaware of the fact that rooms generally have corners.) Only gradually did she piece together the story of his recent past, the reason for his present circumstances and his eagerness to jump at some form of employment that might give him the chance to demonstrate that he was something more than discarded cannon-fodder.

And she could only attribute his reluctance to tell to modesty. For, it transpired, Murray Pearl ('What a funny name,' she felt emboldened to say after they'd been working together for a day or two. 'Not English, surely?' No, he had said, he'd been named after his adoptive father, a Canadian airforce pilot, now dead), Murray Pearl was a war hero. He had been waved off from the quay at Southampton to the tune of 'Sailing' and welcomed back by cheering crowds and a band playing 'Land of Hope and Glory'. He had been wounded at Goose Green and awarded a medal for bravery. Unfortunately, the wound: a bullet entering the back of his leg, had smashed his kneecap and rendered him unsuitable for subsequent military service. He had been discharged and seeking to find his niche in civilian life ever since the Falklands. Britain – traditionally a country willing to wave flags but unwilling to do anything but neglect those returning victorious from battles fought to keep it free – was, these days, as short on jobs as it was on its respect for heroism.

'Don't you feel bitter?' she asked him, as he arranged the stationery receipts into date-order and then hung a cute-cat calendar on the wall.

'Dunno. Suppose so. It was all I knew: the army. You feel lost when you're out on your own.'

He had drifted, she gathered, having no family left, no roots, drifted into the hostel, to Robin's congregation and thence to The System: in the hope of making friends, she supposed, and she was sympathetic, knowing how difficult that could be once you'd stepped outside (or, in his case, been forced to abandon) your natural social circle.

First she'd felt alarm, suspected him of being a dogger-of-her-footsteps. Then she'd been foolish enough to wonder if he was attracted to her despite their age difference: nothing to speak of between a man of forty and a woman of twenty-seven or so; insuperable, probably, the other way round. Now she began to feel maternal towards him (probably the result of her own children's making it plain that they could manage perfectly well without a mother): sewed him a button on, asked – while they were eating their lunchtime sandwiches – whether the hostel provided him with a proper cooked meal in the evenings, invited him into Gwen's for a warm before he undertook the return journey after he'd walked her home.

Twice, on successive Thursdays, he'd provided an escort service. It had been bitterly cold, but on both occasions he had refused her offer of hospitality, shoving his hands deep into his pockets, burying his nose in his scarf.

She wasn't sorry. Although they got on well enough, and she was deeply grateful for the protection of his company, she never felt entirely at ease with him. Sometimes he would laugh and joke and converse freely, but other times he seemed to be in a world of his own and long uncomfortable silences would develop between them. Then she would feel guilty that she didn't feel more grateful. Then she would watch him banging his hands together outside Gwen's front gate, and resolve to buy him a pair of gloves.

'Sure you won't come in?' she'd say, already closing the gate between them. He'd light a cigarette, narrowing his eyes against the flame, and shake his head.

'Don't linger then,' she'd say. 'Or you'll catch your death of cold.'

But sometimes he'd stay where he was, until she had unlocked the front door, gazing after her, rather enviously, she thought, as though he could imagine good-fellowship inside there, family life, a blazing fire at which he could warm his hands. She felt rather sorry for him then. Even though the reality would not have come up to his expectations.

Gwen's house was centrally-heated. And her only – reluctant – connection with a blazing fire occurred on the night of February

28th when Klosters went up in flames and the police came round to apprise her of this fact.

It was the same policeman who'd been sent to take details of Boysie's untimely demise. But on this occasion he was able to speak to Mrs Swallow in person. Before coming downstairs, she had taken off her eye-mask and her night-cream-impregnated gloves, put on her peignoir and her velvet high-heeled mules, combed her hair and rouged her lips. When the constable, after escorting her to the smouldering scene, returned to the station, he was inspired to remark that if he were into rich widows, then Mrs Swallow was exactly the sort of rich widow he'd wish to be into.

His sergeant, who'd also seen her – clothed, by then, wrapped against the chill night air in sable – had said, 'You? She'd eat you alive, son. No danger.'

For Gwen, in spate, was a sight terrible to behold. She had stood amid the wreckage, demanding to see an inspector, a chief constable, a director of public prosecutions, demanding instant investigations and incontrovertible conclusions as to the reason for her livelihood having gone up in smoke.

It was a very still, bitterly cold night with bright stars and a big pale moon. They stood outside, together with the few people who actually resided in the area and who had been awakened by the sound of the fire engines, contemplating the damage. The fire had been extinguished, but the smoke still hung in a pall, exuding amalgamated odours of burned wood and scorched steel and melted rubber and synthetic fibres welded together, flowing one into the other, fusing, mingling their toxic fumes. All that, and something else besides, for Klosters was no longer a wine bar, but a crematorium.

'What?' Gwen said, venturing too close and beginning to cough as the acrid smoke got into the back of her throat. 'Get back, lady,' a fireman said and, when she ignored him, physically removed her from the path of the ambulancemen.

'Oh my God,' Corky said. She'd started, from habit, to roll a cigarette but then, perhaps realising the tactlessness of the gesture, abandoned it. 'Oh my God,' she said, as the ambulancemen carried their cargo to the street.

Christina had automatically averted her eyes but now, forcing herself to look, saw that there was not a great deal to be seen: a red blanket on a stretcher with little more than a slight hump distorting its flatness – a dwarf, after all, does not occupy much space, even before being reduced to a cinder.

There was a sharp intake of breath from the huddled spectators. Corky turned a face as white as the moonlight in the direction of the departing ambulance, and then leaned forward and vomited copiously into the gutter.

The policeman who appeared to be in charge of the proceedings trod cautiously towards them across the rubble. 'No sense in hanging round here, ladies,' he said. He meant that now the casualty had been unofficially identified, they could go. The official procedure could wait till the morning.

The neighbours began to disperse. Gwen was escorted home in a police car. Christina rode back with Corky. 'What do you think happened?' she asked. A car full of jeering youths came careering past them, scraped their offside wing, wavered into the middle of the road, anticipated the lights and sped away in the direction of the Tunnel.

Normally, an occurrence of that sort, particularly one involving damage to her beloved car, would have caused Corky to blow a gasket, but compared with what had gone before it seemed scarcely worthy of comment. She contented herself with clicking her tongue against her plate and taking a hand off the steering wheel to shake her fist in the direction that the joyriders had taken. Then she said, 'I think he'd done the same as he did that other time. I think he got back from – where was it – Berwick-on-Tweed? and went celebrating and got pie-eyed and couldn't be bothered going home. I think he has – had – some way of opening that basement window and climbing in.'

The other windows were secured at night with grilles but the window in the basement was so little that only a very small child could have squeezed through it – a very small child or a dwarf.

'I think he probably lit a fag and fell asleep, or passed out. Fag fell on to a tea towel or a duster of whatever, smouldered . . . It doesn't take much, does it? It's why they tell you never to smoke in bed, not even a post-whatsit ciggie.'

She bared her dentures in the gruesome imitation of a smile. The sour odour of vomit lingered, was even more unpleasant than the stench of the smoke that clung to their clothes.

Gwen had immersed herself in the bath immediately upon ushering her escort policeman out of the door. She came downstairs, as fragrant as a rose. 'Phew!' she said. 'You reek!' and placed herself at a discreet distance from them.

They had expected drama, comparable to the sort that had followed her discovery of Boysie's corpse. She surprised them, helping herself to coffee, cutting a sandwich, exhorting them to buck themselves up and go take a shower. If ever there was anyone you'd have had marked down as placing a higher value on property than person, it was Gwendoline Swallow. And yet she serenely munched a smoked salmon sandwich and debated whether there was any point in swallowing a Mogadon when, in a few hours, she would obviously need to be up and doing, dealing with policemen and insurers and putting in an appearance at the morgue, if Albert proved to have no relative who could identify him.

'My God, you're taking it calmly, aren't you?' Corky said, running a hand through the nicotine-streaked front of her hair, newly contaminated with smoke.

'I don't think you're actually required to inspect the charred remains, are you?' Gwen said. 'I believe it's sufficient if you can identify anything they find on the body – a wristwatch or a ring or whatever . . .'

'I don't just mean the identification. I mean the whole thing. You must have been well insured,' Corky commented sourly. It was obvious that she was peeved at this role-reversal: she was usually the one who remained calm in a crisis while Gwen did the metaphorical equivalent of throwing up into the gutter.

'Well yes, the policy was up-rated not so long ago, as it happens,' Gwen said. She finished her sandwich and went in search of the cake tin.

'You didn't go round there yourself earlier on with a box of matches, did you?'

Gwen cut herself a sizeable wedge of chocolate fudge cake. 'I don't see why you need to be so obnoxious,' she said. 'And I can't see that there's anything to be gained by weeping and wailing and gnashing my teeth at this juncture. We don't know how bad the damage is, how long it's going to put us out of business, or anything else.'

'You were shouting your mouth off at the police loud enough.'

'Well you have to shout at them,' Gwen said, 'or else they really try to take advantage – when they find out that you're a woman on her own.'

The picture she conjured up was of a frail and languishing maiden, whereas – as the police sergeant had said – a woman of Gwen's ilk would devour the average unarmed male and display the same sort of relish with which she demolished her chocolate cake.

The police found a relative who agreed to be escorted to the mortuary and there identify a signet ring, engraved with the initials: 'AW', as belonging to his cousin Albert Joseph Wagstaffe. There was a medal too, that had withstood the fire's heat, but the cousin knew nothing about that. It needed the licensee of The George, Albert Wagstaffe's local, to throw light on the origin of *that*.

Gradually the details accumulated, the jigsaw was pieced together: the team from The George which had travelled to Berwick-on-Tweed to compete in the North of England finals of the Quiz League had been victorious, so the publican was able to report. They had won the trophy and each individual member had been presented with a medal. Albert Wagstaffe (specialist subject: the films of Humphrey Bogart) had been a member of that team. There had been a lot of drinking on the coach on the way back from Berwick, and you could have said that Albert was – merry; he got merry rather quicker than most on account of his size, one supposed: less capacity. Upon returning to the city, the majority of the team and its supporters had shared taxis back to their homes, but Albert had wandered off before anyone had the chance to offer him a lift. No one bothered overmuch: Albert always got – merry, after a quiz victory, and he'd never come to any harm before.

All this the publican of The George recounted to the coroner. Where his evidence ceased, that of Mrs Swallow took over: yes, it had come to her notice in the past that Mr Wagstaffe, who was employed by her in the capacity of dishwasher, had spent the night at his place of work in preference to returning to his home. And yes, there had, on a previous occasion, been evidence of his having fallen asleep – or whatever – allowing a lighted cigarette to drop down the side of his chair. On that occasion serious consequences had been averted by the timely intervention of one of her undermanagers. Albert Wagstaffe had been severely reprimanded and warned that any repeat performance would result in his dismissal. But – well – under the influence of drink, warnings tended to be forgotten, didn't they?

The coroner was impressed by Mrs Swallow's evidence. She spoke up, and what she had to say was brief and to the point. He was a gentleman of advancing years but that didn't mean that he'd ceased to appreciate a good-looking woman. Had the verdict depended solely upon what Mrs Swallow had to report, then he would probably have wound up the proceedings without further ado, but there were other findings, deriving from the investigations of the fire service and the insurance assessors, and these were not necessarily corroborative of the cause of the fire being Albert Wagstaffe in his cups, however persuasive the theory.

The findings of those aforementioned investigations could be summed up in a word, namely: petrol. Although it seemed that a great many words were required to explain the significance of that one, principally because the investigating bodies were not entirely in agreement about the amount or exact location of the inflammable agent involved: the fire chief reckoned that Albert Wagstaffe, slumped by the door, a bottle of rum at his side, drunkenly attempting to fill his lighter (a tin of fuel was kept in the kitchen for this purpose) and smoking at the same time, might have been sufficient to cause some tea towels (which were close by) to catch fire and that these, in turn, could have ignited the spilled liquor and a pan of oil on the stove (left uncovered, regrettably), with predictable results: the man from the Pru alleged that there was evidence that fibres of cloth found close to the door did not match those of the tea towels commonly used in the kitchen.

Conflicting evidence was common in cases of this sort. The coroner had covered his mouth with his hand to disguise a yawn. He couldn't disguise the rumblings of his stomach. It was nearly lunchtime and he was inclined, anyway, to the reductionist view. He brought in a verdict of accidental death, and the insurance company paid up and Gwen decided to take Stephen Millward up on his offer of a fortnight in Barbados while the builders got to work on Klosters. Albert Wagstaffe's remains were released for Christian burial or – as Christina and Corky, representative mourners, were informed by the cousin – to be precise: cremation, Albert having left no assets and the DHSS being required to foot the bill. Cremation was cheaper than buying a grave.

'Is your journey really necessary?' Corky murmured under her breath as they watched the casket sliding through the curtains towards the flames. Afterwards, they shook hands with the presiding priest and inspected the wreaths that were arranged in the little courtyard beside the chapel: 'In loving memory of Al – a great little competitor – from his mates on the team'; 'Deepest sympathy, J and M Johnson (Licensees), The George'. Corky blew her nose very thoroughly. 'Dozy little sod,' she said. 'Never took a blind bit of notice when I warned him.'

'Do you really think he was to blame?'

Christina had asked the same question of Gwen the night before she left for her holiday. Gwen had looked up from packing frilly-skirted swimwear and halter-necked sunsuits and layers of lace-trimmed lingerie into her Vuitton suitcase (single rooms had been booked, but only one of them might actually be used) and said, 'What other explanation could there be?'

She did not wish to admit that there was even the possibility of arson. Admitting that meant also admitting that somebody, somewhere, disliked her enough to want to burn her business to the ground.

Nobody disliked her that much – that she knew of. Nobody had cause. There'd been a spate of nuisance calls a few months ago; someone putting down their telephone receiver as soon as she picked hers up – she'd been about to negotiate to go ex-directory when they ceased – but many single women were subjected to harassment of that nature. And before that, there'd been Christina and her far-fetched tales of a man watching the house. But dislike to that degree? It was inconceivable. Even thinking about it, as Stephen said, was unwise; you could scare yourself half to death. Best to refuse to give credence to any such notion.

And Corky appeared to be of the same opinion. Who but Albert, she said, would be likely to be creeping round Klosters at dead of night with petrol and lighted matches?

'I haven't a clue. I was just thinking: first the cat and now Klosters . . .'

'Coincidence,' Corky said, 'that's all. You can link anything to anything else if you try hard enough,' she said, as they walked back to the car through the Garden of Remembrance. Late frost had blackened some of the ornamental shrubs: a great clump of Rose of Sharon was shrivelled and scorched. There wasn't a single tree in bud and it seemed inconceivable that winter would ever relax its grip.

'If it's as cold as this here, whatever will it be like in Scarborough?' Christina asked, turning her head from the direction of a clearing in the trees where a tall chimney was visible and, issuing from it, a plume of smoke. Though it was not necessarily Albert. Corky said that it was policy – perhaps in order to save fuel – to wait until they had a few before incinerating them.

'You call this cold?' Corky replied. The drip on the end of her nose contradicted her insouciance. 'At least Scarborough's bracing.'

Most of Klosters was a blackened ruin. Gwen had resisted her natural inclination, which was to monitor its rebuilding and refurbishment, and flown off to the West Indies. It made sense that Corky too should take a holiday. She had rung the proprietor of a boarding-house in Scarborough of her acquaintance who'd just returned from wintering in Fuengirola and who promised to open up a room for her, and she'd packed a holdall with tracksuits and sweaters and training shoes. Gwen might be content to lie back and be waited upon by little black boys, but she would use the time to get some practice in, would pound her way around the cliff-top paths of England's eastern coastline.

The enforced break would at least give her the chance to really test herself, to see whether her fitness was up to the demands that would be placed upon it early on the morning of April 20th in Greenwich Park.

The Morris was polished to as high a gloss as the hearse next to which it was parked. 'Can I give you a lift?' Corky enquired. She had her holdall in the back, having decided to leave directly the service was over. 'Polytechnic or office?'

'Office, please.'

'Did they find somebody for that barmy fellow's job then?' Corky asked as she drove out of the crematorium gates.

'Yes. We've got a replacement at last, thank goodness.'

'Bit of an improvement then?'

'Oh yes. He's very efficient.'

'Nice, is he?' Corky asked, glancing at her.

'He's all right. Much too young for me, if *that's* what you mean,' Christina said, flushing. Fat lot of chance there was to establish yourself as an independent spirit if even people like Corky, normally refreshingly free of stereotypical notions, felt it incumbent upon themselves to enquire whether you had some man in tow.

'Oh it's all the fashion these days, isn't it, younger men?' Corky said, waving a dithering old-age pensioner on across the zebra. The sight filled her with deep gloom. She'd received a letter from the DHSS last week asking if she intended to retire and claim her pension now that her sixtieth birthday was imminent. There had been a list enclosed of the entitlements for which a sixty-year-old woman might qualify.

It had made her see red. Entitlements! No wonder the country was riddled with scroungers, unwilling to get up off their arses and break sweat. She'd written them a very sarky reply, even though she suspected it would only be read by a computer in Newcastle-on-Tyne.

'All these actresses and pop-stars and whatnot,' she continued, as the old dear hobbled across the road (they *let* themselves get like that; it was simply a question of attitude), 'they all have their toyboys nowadays, don't they?'

Pretty disgusting to observe though it was when Gwen encouraged such attentions: all those fawning little undermanagers, dazzled by the promise offered by her ample womanliness.

Although little boys posed less of a threat than grown men with the wherewithal to offer holidays in Barbados and the experience to know best how to conduct a courtship. She'd placed her faith on that score in Christina, but might have known that the Christinas of this world were never a match for the Gwens.

Not that this had prevented her from expressing her disappointment. 'You've been a bit behind the door, haven't you?' she'd said. 'Could have got yourself a fortnight in the sun if you'd played your cards right. Mind you,' she'd said, 'what kind of a fellow is it that moves between one and the next like that? You'd think *she'd* have more about her, wouldn't you, than to settle for being second best?'

Christina had listened and then pretended to agree. If assuming that Stephen Millward was a rampant womaniser and Gwen lacking in seemliness made it easier for Corky to cope with her jealousy, then so be it. And it wasn't just jealousy that prompted the mockery, the denigration; there was also fear, fear that this relationship might turn out to be *the* relationship, that Stephen Millward might progress from being holiday companion to regular escort and so on, inevitably, to permanent fixture.

And where would that leave Corky? Many second and subsequent husbands were willing to accept an inheritance of already-existing children, or dependent elderly relatives, but she'd never heard of one willing to share his domestic arrangements with his wife's female friend.

PART THREE

Going Forth

~ 1 ~

In The System office, Murray Pearl beavered away, preparing for the postponed bring and buy sale, sorting through a selection of felted cardigans and cracked shoes that had been donated by the Ladies' Guild of Robin's church. Arriving to await Elizabeth McLaverty, erstwhile member of The System, who had already stood her up on two occasions, but promised faithfully to keep this appointment, Christina picked up a pair of patent leather winklepickers and thought: what a pity Kenneth is no longer with us; these would have been just the thing to wear with his three-button Italian suit.

Murray Pearl crossed the room and took them from her. He put them down carefully between a green glass urinal-shaped vase and a pot dog without a nose.

'Please don't mix them up,' he said sternly, shifting a pile of *Girls' Crystal* annuals from the floor to the desk. 'I've only just got them sorted out. I'm still trying to work out prices. What do you think?'

'I haven't the faintest. I suppose it's best to mark up and then people can always haggle. Not that I can imagine anyone in their right mind actually buying some of these things.'

A pencil-case with a broken catch, a moth-eaten college scarf, a chipped enamel saucepan with its handle insecurely riveted.

'You're not kidding,' he said, picking up a yellowed rayon petticoat as gingerly as if it were infected with anthrax germs and adding it to a pile of gruesome-looking undergarments.

'Do you want a hand with the labelling? Until my woman arrives?'

'No, you're all right,' he said, sitting down to cut adhesive paper into stickers. 'I can manage. You could put the kettle on though.'

She did so and then sat watching him work. For a while silence reigned, disturbed only by the snap of his scissors and the sound of his breathing. His cutting-out was sure-handed and neat and contrasted strikingly with his price-marking and handwriting. He made the same kind of heavy weather of it as Corky did when pencilling in the captions to the marathon pictures in her scrapbook. Then he said, 'I see the builders are starting to make headway with your cousin's wine bar. Rebuilding it differently, are they?'

'Yes. She's having some alterations made.'

A new bar had been planned and an extension to the kitchen.

'So it hasn't hit her too hard in the pocket then?' he asked, holding up a collection of 78 records for Christina's guidance apropos their value. She squinted at the labels: 'Amapola', 'In a Monastery Garden', 'That's What God Made Mothers For'. 'Oh, I don't know – fifty pee the lot? Gwen?' she said. 'I doubt it. Gwen's too astute for that. The insurers were a bit stroppy but they agreed to pay out eventually. Knowing Gwen, she's probably done very well out of it.'

'Antique records,' he printed, in uneven capitals, or would have, had not the last two letters of the first word been transposed. She resisted a Max-like impulse to correct him, given that the records weren't antique and few of the customers would be likely to notice anyway.

'Did her a favour then?' he said, labelling a boxed propelling-pencil (minus leads) with the title 'Unwanted Present'. 'Whoever started the fire?'

'Perhaps so.'

'What about whatd'you call her – Corky? She can't be too pleased about being laid off.'

'Oh, I don't know. It's given her the chance to do some training.'

She'd inadvertently let drop the fact that Corky had a place in the London Marathon. He'd seemed greatly impressed, asked about Corky's history in terms of sporting prowess. In answer to which, Christina could only reply that, apart from the display of a silver cup awarded to the best fat goose in the show, the pages of the book that composed Corky's past life were never open to inspection.

Unlike The System's, which were now fit to be viewed by the most critical of auditors. And not only had he organised the books, he'd resurrected and put into operation the plans for the bring and buy sale, he'd managed to extract the promise of free advertising from a local newspaper, cajole air-time from a radio station and, by means of the scrupulous chasing-up of inactive members and persuading them to resume their functioning, breathed life into the almost extinct nub of The System: the resource exchange. Now Hilary Roberts could walk into the office at any time, check the accounts, flick through the filing, read the reports and be assured that the efficiency displayed was genuine rather than adopted for the duration of her visit; now it began to be feasible that the Standish Trust, presented with evidence that the scheme was alive and kicking, might not after all withdraw its funding.

Though there were still hiccoughs. The day that Christina's interviewee failed to turn up was invariably the day Hilary Roberts chose to put in an appearance. And that day, by the time she arrived, it was obvious that Elizabeth McLaverty wasn't going to.

'Oh for heaven's sake,' she said, 'not *again*. I can't think what you must be saying to them to put them off,' as though there existed queues of interviewees waiting impatiently to propound their views until Christina dissuaded them from doing so.

'How much is this going to knock us off schedule?'

'Not much. Hardly at all actually. I'd booked the computer for tomorrow morning, but I can run the group performance data instead and try to catch up with this tomorrow afternoon . . .'

'By the way,' Hilary Roberts interrupted, 'has Colette Donaldson sent those notes yet? I tried to ring her yesterday but I got that sound that you get when it's been cut off. Haven't they paid the bill?'

'I gather they got into a bit of a stew financially, what with Don losing his job, and the baby – generally biting off more than they could chew.'

'These people!' said Hilary Roberts. 'I wrote to her a week or so ago but got no reply. Most unlike her. She used to be so conscientious. Anyway, if you're at a loose end this afternoon, perhaps you could go round there and collect the notes. I've a thing at Manchester this evening. I'll drop you off on the way.'

Christina thought: if you've a thing at Manchester this evening and therefore find yourself in the vicinity of Colette's house, why on earth can't you collect the notes yourself? Why involve me? Was it simply the imposition of a penance, or was Jinx's account of Hilary Roberts' aversion to babies – hitherto dismissed as exaggeration – perfectly accurate?

'I've to go back to the Department first to pick up some papers and Jennifer. It's mainly for her benefit that we're going.'

She explained as they drove to the Polytechnic. A paper on Social Deviance was being presented at Manchester and, as Christina knew, Social Deviance, or rather aspects of it, was the theme of Jennifer's research project.

Though an exposition of it in the company of Hilary Roberts was clearly not much to Jinx's taste. She got into the back of the car and sat gazing gloomily at her leopardskin-clad knees while her Leader spoke about Professor Bric-a-brac (or, at least, that was how it sounded to Christina), foremost authority on the pluralisation of social experience (in the phenomenological sense), who was delivering his ideas that night to an eagerly-anticipative audience. 'Bleedin' 'ell,' Jinx said, into her kneecaps.

She said, 'Bleedin' 'ell,' again when they entered the Donaldsons' estate. And with equal justification. Bathed in the fag-end of the grey daylight that characterised these relentless winter days, the sense of bleakness and ruination was all-pervasive.

Primula Road, Forsythia Crescent, Jasmine Avenue. 'This one,' Christina said. 'Here, the one on the corner, the one with the gnomes.'

'Good God! It looks like the Gingerbread House out of *Hansel and Gretel*,' said Jinx, marvelling at the ice-cream-coloured crazy paving, the ornamental pond, the mock-Georgian, bullion-set windows, the ruched satin blinds.

Which were drawn. In every window, upstairs and down. Nor did light shine from behind any one of them. From the look of it, the house was empty. 'Can you hang on for a moment until I see if there's anyone in?' Christina asked as she got out of the car. She had no desire to be stranded on the estate waiting for the hourly bus.

She pressed the bell and heard the chimes reverberating within the house (the first few bars of 'Tannenbaum' – at least one supposed it was 'Tannenbaum' and not 'The Red Flag', Colette having professed to be a staunch supporter of that political party which offered council tenants the opportunity to become property-owners within a democracy). She banged the lion's head doorknocker. She pushed open the letter-box and squinted through it into the hall where nothing at all was distinguishable in the windowless gloom. She even went round to the back door but rapping on that didn't produce any response and her view of the kitchen's interior was concealed by a blind.

'Fort Knox.'

A very fat young woman emerged from the back door of the adjoining house. Small children were attached to each side of her skirt. 'She's in there, you know,' she said. 'But she won't answer the door to anybody. Off her trolley, if you ask me. The woman from the Welfare's been a couple of times. Won't answer to her neither. Only time she does, it's to take the milk in. Doesn't even have to go to the shops. They've got a freezer, haven't they? Where's the kid though? *He's* been away all week . . . Due back tonight, or else my fella said ring nine, nine, nine. Mind you, *he's* not all there either.'

'What on earth is going on? Why are you hanging around when there's obviously nobody in?'

Hilary Roberts' voice preceded her around the corner of the house. Jinx who, one rather suspected, was not all that perturbed at the prospect of her encounter with Professor Bric-a-brac being delayed, came after.

'This lady says there *is* somebody in.'

The young woman nodded. 'She's in there all right. I see her sometimes peering round the curtains. I think she's gone funny. They do sometimes, don't they, if they're getting on a bit when they have their first kid? You never hear it now, the kid. Used to yell day and night. *I* reckon it's been taken into care. When they found out she's got a slate loose. If you ask me, she always did, snobby cow. Wouldn't speak to any of us round here. Too good for us. I told her once: at least my fella's in work. You wouldn't care if she had anything to swank about. Just because they're buying this house. My fella says you'd have to be mad to buy one a these. They're built wrong, seemingly. There's cracks all over the show. You'd have to be mad,' she repeated. 'That's what my fella said when we heard that the queer one had put in for a mortgage.'

There was no knowing how long they might have stood, transfixed by the mesmeric repetitiveness of her monologue, had not 'the queer one', namely Don Donaldson, been espied approaching.

He reached his front gate, paused for a moment, and then advanced slowly towards them. Hilary Roberts said, without preamble, 'Your wife has got some notes for me that are needed urgently and we can't get any response.'

He put a hand into his trouser pocket and brought out his keys and fumbled among them until he'd separated the one that fitted the lock on the back door.

The key turned, but to no avail. He kept on turning it. 'Oh, let me,' Hilary Roberts said eventually, driven to exasperation by the futile reiteration of his movements. 'It's bolted,' she said. 'I can feel it. Well, if it's bolted, there must be somebody in there.'

'Not necessarily,' Jinx said. 'She could have bolted the back and then let herself out at the front, couldn't she? Is there a bolt on the front door?'

Don Donaldson nodded.

'Well if that's on, she's in. If not, you can use your key.'

But this key was no more instrumental in effecting entrance to the front of the house than that which had turned fruitlessly in the lock at the back. Hilary Roberts paced the bounds, searching for evidence of an open window, but every one, as well as being obscured by drawn curtains, appeared to be securely fastened. 'Is it a big bolt?' Jinx enquired of Don. Struck dumber than usual, apparently with awe at the look of her, he shook his head. 'Then I think we should try to burst it open,' she said. 'You never know what might have happened. She could have collapsed inside there, fallen down the stairs, anything. Unless you wanna piss about waiting for the filth or the fire brigade or something?'

Heads that had been poked from other front doors were now being followed by bodies. A little knot of arms-folded observers had gathered on the opposite corner, did not disperse even when Jinx called across to them that the cabaret for tonight had been cancelled, right? *Right*?

The cabaret had been cancelled because just as they had hurled themselves at the door, the door had opened so that only the presence of a fairly high doorstep had prevented them from hurtling through to the hall, flattening Colette beneath their collective weight.

'Shit!' Jinx said, rubbing at her barked shin. 'You deaf, or what?' she enquired of their reluctant hostess. 'Shit!' she repeated, seating herself on the bottom step of the stairs and indulging a brief bout of agonised writhing.

'Colette? I've come to collect my notes,' said Hilary Roberts, whose single-minded ability to get her priorities right was quite awesome. Jinx, sufficiently recovered from her injury to raise herself from the staircase and test her weight on both feet, said, 'D'you mean to say you didn't hear all the racket, all the bell-ringing and banging on the door?'

She turned towards Colette, too quickly, and swept an ornament off the hallstand.

'I was asleep,' Colette said. She looked like a little doll: not a shining golden hair out of place, her cheeks pink, her pale blue eyes wide and expressionless.

'Christ,' Jinx said, 'you must sleep like the dead. Or else you're going a bit mutton. I'd put in for a hearing aid if I were you.'

There wasn't space enough for all of them in the hall. Christina and Don were squeezed up against the front door, Hilary Roberts was obliged to retreat into the kitchen. Jinx's Mohican caught the trailing leaves of a variegated ivy that hung suspended from a hook in the ceiling and sent the plant spinning every time she moved her head.

Colette seemed to make a determined effort to rouse herself. 'Dr Roberts,' she said, 'I've got your notes typed up. I was meaning to post them this morning but then I fell asleep. They're in the lounge. I'll fetch them for you.'

Easier said than done. A great deal of breathing in and flattening themselves against the walls had to occur in order that Colette could squeeze past to reach the lounge door, collect a folder and re-emerge.

'Right, thanks,' Hilary Roberts said. 'We'll be off then.'

'Bye,' Colette said, and allowed her lids to close over those china doll eyes, as though her intention, as soon as she was rid of them, was to go back to sleep. Christina moved past Don towards the door but he didn't make the necessary reciprocal movement to allow her to get to it.

'Oh do come on,' said Hilary Roberts. And Colette swayed a little, sleepily, and repeated after her, 'Come on, Don, let the ladies through. They haven't got all night.'

And then Don Donaldson drew breath deep into his lungs and

used it to cry out to the assembled company, the unheeding world: 'No!'

Not a cry so much as a howl; they could practically hear an echo. As its reverberation died away he turned to Christina and he said, 'Upstairs, make her go upstairs.'

And then he barged past the intervening bodies in order to grasp Colette by the shoulders and shake her, more and more violently. 'Hey, steady on!' Jinx said. And then Hilary Roberts, as befitted her status, took charge. She clapped her hands together and she said, 'Whatever is all this fuss about? Now come on, Mr Donaldson, get a grip on yourself!'

She interposed herself between them. 'Your wife,' she said, 'doesn't look at all well to me.' She put an arm around Colette's shoulders and began to urge her towards the stairs. 'Don't upset yourself,' she said. 'You're probably still very run down. A bit of a rest and you'll feel a lot better. Maybe you should start on a vitamin supplement regime. I started mine a few months ago and it's made a world of difference.'

As they slowly ascended the staircase she could be heard talking of oestrogen and progesterone, prostaglandins and essential fatty acid conversion. Men, she could be heard to say, didn't have a clue about the fine-tuning necessary for the optimum functioning of the femal hormonal system. Had Colette ever thought of attending a Well Woman clinic?

There was a moment when Don Donaldson remained motionless and then he moved more quickly than Christina had ever seen him move and took hold of her hand and tore up the stairs, dragging her after him. 'Make her open the door,' he begged of her. 'Make her open it.'

The door that he indicated was not locked. Christina moved past the two women, who had, by now, reached the landing, and extended a hand and pushed it open. She could feel Don Donaldson's breath on her neck. Even before she switched on the light and revealed the baby in its cot, even before she approached it and realised that it was not merely asleep, she heard him say, very quietly and mournfully, 'She's killed her. I thought she had.'

For a moment she stared down at the child: white, waxen, motionless. And then she was no longer in control of herself. She turned and she flew at him, hitting out: at his stupidity, passivity, docility, whichever combination of the three it was that had allowed the child to die.

'Bastard! Bastard!'

She screamed at him, hit him in the eye, the mouth, the ear. If Jinx hadn't leapt forward to restrain her, the bodily harm she was inflicting would have been a good deal more grievous.

Jinx had pushed past Colette and Hilary Roberts in order to go to his rescue. Hilary Roberts came after her, peering around them to see what all this new fuss was about. She saw. She stared goggle-eyed. And then she made a bleating sound. And then she fled, down the stairs and out of the front door and got into her car and was sitting there, with the doors locked, when the police arrived.

You felt, afterwards, that nothing could ever be the same again.

But the world continued to turn. A moon with a ghastly face rose as usual in the evening sky. Professor Bric-a-brac was welcomed with sherry and rather soggy salted crackers by the Vice-Chancellor. Murray Pearl, working overtime, printed 'Only Worne Once' on an adhesive label and stuck it to the surface of a very fake ocelot swagger-length coat. Even the residents of Primrose Close, their gossiping gaggles now dispersed, presumably continued to eat beans on toast and watch *Crossroads*.

It was the feeling of cosmic indifference that was so hard to take, that generated such a terrible sensation that could only be described as anticlimax, after the arrival of the doctor and the police, after Colette and Don had been led from the house and Jinx had driven Hilary Roberts back home and delivered her to Gavin's tender loving care and then confessed to Christina that, actually, she had no valid driving licence.

Christina didn't care. 'Come back with me,' she pleaded. 'I don't want to be on my own. Come back with me, please. You've no pressing reason to go home?'

No babies crying might have been the phrase that would have tripped off her tongue in normal circumstances.

'Do we get pissed, or what?' Jinx said, when they were back at Gwen's.

Christina stole a bottle of claret – a Léoville Barton – from the case in the cellar that was kept for special occasions, and they each had a couple of glasses, but for all the appreciation it aroused in them, they might have been drinking the cheapest untitled supermarket red ink. Nor – it soon became apparent – was it going to render them inebriated, not if they broached the entire case. Each of them kept opening her mouth as if to begin a sentence and then closing it again. And then Jinx said, all in a rush, as if to catch herself unawares and confound the natural reticence that prevented utterance, 'You know what was the worst thing, worse even than . . .? All those baby clothes that were packed away in tissue paper, all those fancy little frocks and jackets and so on, and yet the kid was dressed in that plain white thing, like . . .'

Like a shroud. Colette had explained: Sharon Mary Theresa had sicked on or soiled every single one of those exquisite garments that had been prepared for her during all the years her mother had been obliged to await her arrival; it made much more sense to pack them away and clothe her in something cheap and dispensable until she was of an age to appreciate and care for nice clothes.

She had spoken as if unaware of the terrible flaw in this argument. She had looked at them in a puzzled way. In fact, puzzlement had been her reaction to everything that had happened: she didn't understand why it was necessary to call the doctor, was nonplussed at the arrival of the police, utterly at a loss to know why they wished her to accompany them to the station. 'What's the matter? What *is* it?' she kept asking, more and more plaintively. 'Everything's all right now. Everything's in order.'

Everything certainly was. As neat and tidy as you could wish for: the baby clothes folded away, the christening gifts arranged upon the white-painted shelves, the child's cot-sheets tucked in with precise hospital corners. And, neatest and tidiest of all was the child that lay within the cot, not disturbing the symmetry of its surroundings by the slightest of movements: not the curling of a tiny fist, nor the kicking of a dimpled leg, nor the inspiration of the merest breath.

Jinx laid aside her glass. 'I can't drink this,' she said. 'Let's have a cup of tea instead.'

She made toast too. There were times when nursery food was appropriate.

They crouched in front of the fire, trying to warm themselves, trying to thaw that internal chill. Jinx discarded her crusts around the edge of her plate more in the manner of Jennifer Weatherby, spoiled only daughter of Dr Weatherby, general practitioner and Freemason, and Mrs Weatherby, Tory councillor and magistrate, than Jinx No-Surname who ate whatever was on the go out of the communal pot. 'How come nobody *knew*,' she asked, savagely shredding the last of the crusts, scattering charcoal crumbs all over Gwen's shag pile. 'How come nobody *checked*?'

'Who, for instance?'

'*I* dunno. Health visitors. Social workers. Aren't they supposed to *monitor?*'

'Only, I think, if there's reason to believe that a baby might be at risk. I don't suppose there are the resources available for that sort of blanket surveillance. Besides, most people would consider it to be an unwarranted intrusion into their privacy. Personal freedom, all that . . .'

To run their lives according to their own lights, to buy their council houses and shun their neighbours, to shave their skulls or spike their hair or cock their snooks . . .

'Freedom to kill their kids,' Jinx said.

There was a little silence during which each knew the other was remembering the child, tucked neatly into its cot, and how it might have been possible to imagine that it was simply asleep, but for the fact that the state of death differed in some dreadful, indefinable way from the state of sleep.

'*Had* she gone potty, do you think?' Jinx said.

Such a middle-class, girls' dormitory word, that was, such a tennis-club, church-social, privet-hedged word; how much more was involved in breaking free of your origins than dyeing your hair pink and festooning your jacket with ironmongery.

'Or was she just being sly?'

Until that afternoon Christina would have disbelieved in the possibility: a wanted child, wanted for years, welcomed into the world with gifts and rejoicing; only derangement of some sort could explain what had happened. But anything seemed possible, with anybody.

'You think of them as being monsters,' Jinx said, overtaken suddenly with an attack of the shivers. 'You practically expect horns and tails and then they publish their photos in the papers and they look such pathetic – *prats*, that's all.'

She pulled her jacket round her shoulders, moved nearer the fire. 'It *couldn't* have been one of those cot deaths, could it?'

'You heard what she said.'

Explaining, patiently, to the doctor, apparently unable to understand why the expression on his face was growing grimmer by the minute, why he demanded to know where the nearest functioning telephone was situated and cared not a jot that his conversation would be overheard – by the time the police escorted the Donaldsons to the car, there was quite a crowd gathered to watch them go. 'Bastards,' someone had shouted. No doubt if and when the Black Maria delivered them to court someone would shout 'Murdering bastards.'

'I was giving her too much to eat,' Colette had said, her doll face pink and earnest. 'That's what was making her cry so much. When I reduced it she was better. She started to sleep right through. She's a real good sleeper now. It was the food, you see. Too much. It was giving her wind. That's why she was crying. It's awful painful, wind.' Then she had yawned widely. 'Oh I *am* tired,' she had said. 'Can I go back to bed now?'

'More tea?' Jinx said.

It was stewed but Christina nodded. They huddled together in front of the fire, sipping and shivering. Jinx said, 'How long d'you think it actually takes for a baby to – die – of – of starvation?'

'I've no idea.'

She didn't want to think about it. But the terrible facts and dwelling upon them were inescapable: dehydration, stupor, coma? Movements becoming feebler, crying diminishing in volume. The skin harsh and dry, the eyes gumming up, crusts of mucus blocking the nasal passages. Tissues starved of nutrient, the saltatory conduction of the nervous system ceasing, the pump of the heart stuttering and failing, the atrophy of the brain cells, until that final, imperceptible ceasing to be when Sharon Mary Theresa would never again be capable of causing mess and noise and confusion, but might remain as inert and unbother-some as any of the ornaments that Colette dusted so diligently and replaced precisely in position.

'And *him*,' Jinx said. 'What the hell was *he* doing while all this was taking place?'

'Head-the-ball,' they'd called Don, those jeering teenagers

who baited him from the garden gate. It was the most contemp-
tuous phrase in their vocabulary.

'Working. Earning money. She didn't want him to take that
job and he didn't want to go, but it was the only thing available
and they'd adopted a standard of living that demanded a lot more
money than the state is willing to provide.'

'But he must have suspected that there was something up, that
she wasn't coping . . .'

'Oh yes, I think he did. He just wasn't bright enough to make
sure that his suspicions were put into words and breathed into
the right ear.'

He should have gone to the relevant authorities, Christina
thought; instead – I realise now, with hindsight – he came to
me.

'You got a spare bed at all?' Jinx asked, staring with studied
concentration at the backs of her hands. 'It's pissing down
outside.'

'Lots of them. You can take your pick.'

She borrowed a nightdress and bathed sybaritically using
Gwen's bath-oil and body-gel and peach-kernel moisturiser.

'Your cousin got any kids?' she asked, uninhibitedly rummaging through the contents of the bathroom cabinet: Anusol
suppositories, anti-fungal cream, Feminax and Aquaban on the
one side; on the other: wintergreen for when Corky strained a
ligament, Blisteze, and Rinstead Pastilles to heal the ulcers that
tended to form between gum and plate if she kept her teeth in
and ground them while she slept.

'No.'

'Thought not. Place is too un-battered. I expect that's how
Colette wanted hers to stay.'

'I've no doubt she did. I suppose she just never realised what
having children entails.'

An unhappy combination of lack of example, lack of close
friends and lack of supervision, coupled with what Christina
called privately the Max Conway Syndrome: a desire for order
so obsessive, a horror of the untidiness and ambiguity that any
kind of healthy vitality tends to breed so profound, it seemed
that the ultimate aim of all the energy expended in maintaining
such frozen symmetry, such immutable certainty, could only be
stasis. Or, otherwise, death.

'I shall never, ever, have any kids,' Jinx said later on. She sat in the armchair in Christina's room with a blanket across her knees. Though she had started off in the other spare bedroom, the prospect of staying there, alone and sleepless, re-running the events of the day, was too bleak to be endured. Trailing her blanket, she had knocked at Christina's door and Christina, thoughts trapped within the same profitless process of rumina-tion, had welcomed her in.

'I mean – quite apart from the question of whether you'll be able to love them enough – '

'It happens. They make you love them.'

'It *made* me,' Adam used to say whenever, as a small child, he'd broken something or been caught red-handed in some misdemeanour. 'It *made* me,' he'd say, pointing accusingly towards the shattered fragments of a cup or a dismembered toy or a pool of water on the floor.

'Not always. Apparently.'

No, not always. Something goes wrong, gets in the way, poisons the affection within its natural course.

'Maybe some people shouldn't be *allowed* to have kids,' Jinx was saying. 'Maybe those eugenics goons were quite right. You know, you read all the stuff about doctors performing sterilisa-tion operations on mental-defectives without their informed consent, and it makes you wild that their rights are ignored, but maybe they have a point . . .'

Her voice faded out and her head fell forward upon her chest. Christina led her, half-asleep, back into her own room and her own bed. She was tough, Jinx, unsentimental, nobody's fool; it seemed strange that despite all that, despite the coxcomb and the tattoo and the ball-bearing earrings, she could seem so child-like, vulnerable, too soft not to be horrified if her sensible theory were ever to be translated into brutal fact, too young to understand that the best will in the world is all that anybody can feasibly hope for.

∽ 2 ∽

Hilary Roberts needed to take a week off work. Gav rang to tell them. 'It's really knocked her for six,' he said. 'Poor girl. She can't stop thinking about it.'

Jinx said the same: 'I keep seeing it: the baby. I can't get it out of my head.'

Neither could Christina. Its image appeared behind her closed eyelids, swam up from her subconscious to haunt her dreams. Alone in Gwen's house, she was no longer afraid of the darkness falling because of creakings and rattlings and persons with felonious intent; she was afraid because the night meant sleep and sleep meant dreams and then that little white waxen face would appear, with its accusing, sightless, eyes.

Colette was in hospital being treated for puerperal psychosis. They reckoned that she hadn't been responsible for her actions, so she could hardly be punished for them. One night Christina watched a television programme about infertility: a woman who'd been trying desperately for years to conceive finally held a tiny baby in her arms and wept tears of joy on to its downy skull. Christina wept too, and then felt bitterly ashamed. It was fitting that the passing of Sharon Mary Theresa should be marked by tears, but they ought not to be provoked by the mere judicious editing-together of emotive images. Easy tears, Max used to say, when he'd noticed her eyes brimming during a choirboy's solo, at the sight of blinded soldiers scrambling out of the Flanders mud, when the pot-bellied victims of African famine appealed mutely to the conscience and the pockets of the overfed West.

'Easy tears,' Max had sneered. 'Catharsis. It absolves you from doing anything about it.'

That wasn't true. She could lay a poppy on the cenotaph, put a contribution in the collecting plate or the charity envelope.

The easy tears prompted action; the other sort, it seemed to her, simply flowed and dried and emphasised her inability to change anything.

Nevertheless, the death of someone else's child at least alerted you to the necessity to protect and cherish your own. Back at Gwen's house, she pushed aside her work and she wrote two letters, one to each of her sons. 'By Easter,' she wrote, 'I hope to have moved out of here. Mr Rogers (the property-renovator I told you about whom I met through my job) has rung to say that the house he's converting should be ready for occupation by then and I can have first refusal on one of the flats. Gwen has been very good, but I suspect that I've outstayed my welcome and I never feel altogether easy about asking anyone back . . .'

She crossed out this last sentence. It sounded as though she was referring to the entertaining of men, and that was not what she meant.

She sat at the bureau in the bow window at the front of the house. It was growing dark but instead of getting up to turn on the light she sat where she was, determined to rack her brains until the exact phrase that would convey her love and concern for them, without making them cringe at her over-sentimentality, suggested itself.

The figure of a youth was visible at the corner of the square. Adam's come, she thought, and for a second joy bloomed within her, but the figure was too tall and heavily built for Adam. It moved differently too. It moved, in fact, in fits and starts, peering at the numbers on the gate-posts, pausing to glance over its shoulder, craning its neck to look up at the windows that overlooked the road.

Gwen's gate-post was consulted. There was a moment of hesitation and then the youth ran up the steps, pushed something through the letter-box, and ran down them at breakneck speed and carried on running until he disappeared around the corner.

She had caught only an indistinct glimpse of him but sensed a familiarity. By the time that she collected his message from the door mat – not, as she had supposed, some sort of circular or free newspaper, but an envelope bearing her name – she had assembled these sparse visual clues and realised that the messenger was Parkinson.

The envelope was crumpled and grimy. She unfolded the piece of exercise-book paper that it contained and read the terse, imperative, unsigned message: 'Make Adam tell you about the stuff.'

The stuff? The *stuff*.

Smack, they called it, and skag. And, before that, horse and H and shit. It was also known, then and now, as the stuff.

The letter: it couldn't – could it – be referring to *that* sort of stuff?

She put on the light and opened the cupboard in the telephone table and took out the directory and flicked through it until she reached 'P'. Even a Caliban like Parkinson must have parents, a home and – in all probability – a telephone number.

There were dozens of them, even when she'd eliminated those whose addresses suggested that they'd be unlikely to have sons at Adam's school. After one: 'I wonder if you can help me, I'm trying to locate a Mr and Mrs Parkinson who have a son called . . .' and then realising she didn't actually know Parkinson's Christian name and putting the receiver down, she recognised the futility of such an enterprise, so she rang her old home number and the phone was answered by Max with his mouth full.

'Whose name?' he said indistinctly. 'Parkinson? Which one's he? Oh, him! I've no idea. Do you want me to ask Adam when he comes in?'

'No,' she said. 'It doesn't matter.'

'Why on earth do you want to know Parkinson's name?'

'Or his address, do you know that?' she asked, ignoring his query.

'No, not offhand. What's it all about?'

'It's not important,' she said and put down the phone. Let him have a taste of his own medicine.

It was Tuesday tomorrow. On Tuesday afternoon the Fifth Year had Games. Adam, who was not particularly athletic, stayed in school and 'dossed around', as he put it, but Parkinson was in the rugger team – that much she knew. She would make her way to the playing fields and she would intercept him. If spite had motivated him to alert her to Adam's activities (and the degree of spite must be extraordinarily acute to lead him to break that unwritten law of adolescence: thou shalt at all times, no matter what, keep parents totally in the dark), then, presumably, he might be prevailed upon to spell them out more precisely.

*

287

The playing fields seemed to stretch for ever. She scanned the featureless horizon for evidence of rugby matches. Perhaps she was too late. And then a small boy, blue with the cold, came running out of the mist, running knock-kneed and oblivious to obstacle in the manner of certain sorts of spindle-shanked little boys. She put out an arm and arrested him in mid-hurtle. 'Are you the Fifth Form?' she asked.

He looked at her and then shook his head violently as though horrified at the thought that anyone might have taken him for such.

'But the Fifth Form *are* here today?'

He jerked his head over his shoulder. 'In the pav,' he said. And a beefy gentleman in a tracksuit with a whistle round his neck poked his head out of the pavilion door and shouted, 'Pilgrim! Get in here and get yourself changed.' And then looked enquiringly at Christina as if she might be in the process of attempting to molest one of the younger and more defenceless of his charges.

'I was looking for Parkinson,' she said. 'Lower Five X . . .'

He continued to survey her suspiciously for a moment, but then probably came to the conclusion that Parkinson was far too well-grown to be in danger of molestation and said, 'Righto, Mrs Parkinson. I'll get him for you.'

He came down the pavilion steps wearing his normal fugitive-from-a-chain-gang expression. She took a breath and plunged in at the deep end.

'That message. What was it all about?'

'What message?'

'The message you pushed through my door last night.'

'Not me.'

He didn't quite have the courage to walk away from her but he half turned, so that she was talking to the side of his head rather than his face.

'There is absolutely no point in lying. I saw you. So what's the meaning of it?'

She held it out towards him, the exercise-book page upon which were inelegantly scrawled those seven words that hadn't gone away as she had fervently hoped when she fell asleep, but been waiting to greet her when she woke up.

He wouldn't look at it. He hung his head until his chin

288

touched his chest and banged his sports bag against his thigh and drew circles in the dirt with his toe and he kept repeating, tonelessly, 'Not me.'

She recognised that only threat could force him to admit to it; she said, 'If you don't tell me I shall first of all inform your parents and then the headmaster, and I'm sure all three of them will take a pretty dim view.'

'Ask Adam,' he said, and kept on repeating the phrase, like a spastic parrot: 'Ask Adam.'

'I'm asking *you*. I suppose you've had a quarrel and this is your way of getting back at him.'

All the dislike felt by every mother in the world towards those members of her child's peer group who are, she believes, responsible for leading him astray, gathered itself within her, all those unspoken fears about Parkinson's detrimental influence, found a voice: 'I knew from the first moment he started to go about with you that there'd be trouble.'

It was unfair as well as being untrue and a look of outrage was appearing on Parkinson's face as though he recognised it as such.

'At least,' she said, 'have the courage to admit *your* part in this whole sordid business, whatever it is. Don't hide behind anonymous letters and try to get other people into trouble while saving your own skin . . .'

'Adam's my mate,' said Parkinson. It was the most articulate statement she'd ever heard him make. His spots blazed crimson against the winter pallor of his complexion. He said, 'I told you so you could do something before he ends up in the sh . . . before he gets into real trouble. I told you so you could warn him before anybody else finds out. And if you tell my old fella or my old woman or old Accrington Stanley Phipps there won't be *anything* down for him. I told you so's you could *help* . . .'

The members of Form Lower Five X began to emerge from the pavilion, barging each other out of the way, swinging their sports bags at one another's heads, yelling and whistling and shouting and jeering. 'What did you *mean*?' Christina enquired desperately of Parkinson, but he had disappeared into the heart of the throng. Perhaps Parkinson was something of a classical scholar and knew the fate that traditionally awaited the bearers of bad tidings.

'The old man's hired some ancient crone to pick up his socks from the carpet. A widow-woman,' David had said at Christmas.

But David's care for accuracy had always been in some doubt: Max wasn't the sock-dropping sort; and the ancient widowed crone was possibly a well-preserved fifty, with highlighted hair, wearing a slightly more restrained version of a Hilary Roberts flying suit.

In fact, so un-housekeeper-ish did she look, that Christina wondered at first if Max was in and she might be interrupting some late-afternoon idyll.

'Mr Conway isn't back yet. He doesn't normally get back until after six,' the woman said. And then she said, awkwardly, 'Well of course you'd know that . . .'

'Is my son in?'

His school bag was set down beside the stairs, his jacket hung from a hook.

'He's *been* in and gone out again. Said something about catching the library. Look,' the woman said, 'you don't mind if I get off, do you? I've to pick up my granddaughter from her dancing lesson. My son's wife doesn't finish work till late on a Tuesday.'

'I hope I did right,' she would say to Max when next she saw him; the ethics of the situation: whether it was the done thing to allow an almost ex-wife the run of the household, being unclear.

'If you could tell Mr Conway when he comes in that the beef will be ready to take out of the oven at seven o'clock?'

After she'd gone, Christina went upstairs to Adam's room and then paused outside the door, experiencing a few sudden and unexpected qualms. He had as much right to his privacy as anybody. Yet how else could she find out anything about him?

While a soul was searched, a life could be lost. With a firm hand she turned the doorknob.

Once, she'd visited David on campus. He'd deposited her in the bar while he went back to his room, 'to tidy up', he'd said. When she was finally invited in it was neat enough, but a furtive opening of *his* wardrobe door when he went to make coffee had revealed a mass of crumpled garments: clean, dirty and halfway between, all crammed together.

The contrast between that wardrobe and this could not have been greater. Clothes were hung on hangers, as neatly as if they had been displayed for sale. She was amazed at the amount of them and their quality: a suede jacket as soft as silk, shirts and trousers bearing every fashionable and expensive label to which the richest and most discerning Young Turk might aspire: Missoni, Armani, Pierre Cardin, Nike. The drawers at the side of the wardrobe contained sweaters, two of which were cashmere. Shoes were ranged in ranks: rows of those sort of hideously expensive trainers that are worn both for running and posing by anybody who is anybody.

Max had never been mean with money. He had provided his sons with a well-appointed home and good holidays. He had been prepared to purchase the finest of educations for them. He had acknowledged the validity of their need, at the appropriate times, for all that went with growing up in the dying days of the twentieth-century: cameras and telescopes, fishing rods and football boots, motor-bikes and cars and guitars.

But he had not been in favour of indulgence. Never would she have believed him capable of largesse on this scale. Further along the wardrobe rail she saw pairs of jeans hanging. 501s. Five pairs.

There was a crocodile belt and a matching wallet and a watch even more complicated in terms of its functions than the one that he normally wore. This one could probably not only measure your heartbeat and give you a reading of your brain waves but also tell you the traffic situation on the main roads of Ulan-Bator.

Through the drawers she went, sifting through piles of underwear, socks, handkerchiefs, shifting paints and pencils and sticks of charcoal, pulling books and records from shelves. She didn't stop even when she heard the front door opening and closing and footsteps on the stairs. If it was Adam all hell would break loose anyway – she was prepared for that. And if it was Max then let him suspect burglars and get the wind up.

But she relented and called, 'It's me. I'm up here.'

'Does Adam know that you're doing this?'

He had on his bad-drains face.

'Where is he?'

'Adam? He said something last night about going to the Leisure Centre to sign up for one of those Martial Arts classes. I imagine that's where he's gone. Origami, would it be?'

'That's paper-folding.'

'Akai, then?'

'That's a company that makes hi-fi equipment.'

'Oh God *I* don't know. Some name like that.'

'Doesn't matter, anyway, does it, whatever it's called?'

He said, 'You should be pleased he's actually getting off his backside and doing something.'

'I would have thought that, at this particular time, the best place for him to be would be on his backside – in view of the imminence of his exams.'

'The lad has to have some recreation,' Max said, and then, before she could open her mouth to tell him that that was what was worrying her, he said, 'Who let you in anyway?'

'Your – housekeeper-woman let me in. She was more or less on her way out. She said she had to pick up her granddaughter from a dancing lesson and to tell you that the beef would be ready at seven.'

'Oh yes,' he said. 'Tuesday. Little Stacy.'

'Little who?'

'Stacy. Her granddaughter.'

'My word,' she said, 'you *have* become pally.'

'Spare us the cheap sarcasm. What did you think: that we'd never exchange a civil word? Mrs Monks has been a tower of strength – hanging on here late at a minute's notice, baking for us when she could just as easily have bought cakes and so forth. She even made the cover for the sofa downstairs and wouldn't take a penny more than the cost of the material. We're damn lucky to have such a lovely person who puts herself out for us.'

'A lovely person'? Such fulsome phrases had never been part of Max's vocabulary. Weighed words, grudging praise, a critical eye that noticed the cracks in the ceiling while you were admiring the design of the wallpaper, a disinclination to believe in the best of anybody unless presented with incontrovertible proof, these were the qualities that had characterised Max Conway the husband; was it the resurgence of sexual arousal that was responsible for the change in Max Conway the employer of housekeepers? Did the well-preserved fifty-year-old form of Mrs Monks fill him with desire?

The smell of beef cooking drifted up the stairs. The street lamp going on outside the window displayed the sparklingly-clean glass of the panes. It was not a lover that Max had found, but a mother, one who would make a comfortable nest for him, see to it that his beef was cooked to the exact degree of tenderness that suited his palate, maintain him in terms of buttons sewn on and shirts ironed to perfection and socks sorted into whole and matching pairs, one who, because her livelihood depended upon it, would accord him the same sort of deference and uncritical admiration as that which had been provided by his real mother.

'She's been really good with Adam too,' he was saying. 'Making sure that he eats properly and gets down to his homework as soon as he gets in. Anyway,' he said, conscious of having demonstrated extreme forbearance thus far, 'what *is* this? How dare you come bursting in here and start ransacking the place?'

'Your precious Mrs Thing may be good with Adam but she's not good enough,' she said, and she held out Parkinson's note to him and explained its origin.

He read it. And read it again. 'Stuff?' he said.

'You know.'

'You mean – like David?'

'I mean perhaps worse than David.'

'And have you found any of this – stuff?'

'No. But I hadn't finished looking . . . Anyway, those two drawers are locked and I can't find the key.'

'Look here,' he said, 'are you sure that there's actually any basis to this – allegation? If Parkinson's the one I'm thinking of, then he always looked a very shifty customer to me . . .'

'I don't know. I thought maybe it was spite or something. But boys generally aren't spiteful, are they, not in that way?'

Max, unable to countenance untidiness even at moments of extreme stress, began to stack together the shoes that she'd pulled from the cupboard. 'I think you're making too much of a song and dance about it,' he said. 'As usual.'

'What! It was the first word out of your own mouth when the headmaster was telling us about his truancy. "Is he on drugs?" you said.'

'All right, all right,' he said peevishly and waved a hand at her to indicate that, having made her point, she should now shut her mouth.

'Max,' she said, 'it must have dawned on you that his truancy and the neglect of his schoolwork might be symptomatic of something more than dislike of school?'

He stopped fiddling with the shoes and sat down on the edge of the bed and he said, 'I thought it was just a phase – like David.'

'David's different from Adam.'

'Yes.'

She said, 'Have you looked in this wardrobe recently? Or those drawers?'

She watched him examining the shirts and the sweaters, the crocodile belt and the soft suede jacket and the five pairs of jeans. He wasn't a 'young' father. There had never been any question of exchange of clothes such as occurred in, say, the Harrington household where male garments provided a sort of communal pool, where you were just as likely to see Mr Harrington Senior attired in a school team rugby jersey as his seventeen-year-old son. Max was measured regularly for classic suits in discreet colours. He wore plain well-tailored shirts and Barkers shoes and a Burberry macintosh and rarely did his ties aspire to anything more eye-catching than the stripe of his regiment. David would have gone naked before raiding his wardrobe; Adam considered his tastes to be hopelessly antiquated.

But although he despised those sort of young men's clothes shops that looked as though they catered exclusively for what he called 'arse-bandits', he was sufficiently *au fait* with the prevailing trends to know the prices they charged.

'Have *you* bought him all these clothes?'

Max shook his head. 'I bought him that black leather jacket and some of those ridiculous sports shoes that cost a fortune. Oh, and he asked me for money to get a couple of shirts . . .'

'And he certainly couldn't have afforded these from his allowance. Those jeans cost nearly thirty pounds.'

Max fingered the finery. A little nerve jumped in his cheek. He said, 'What, exactly, are you suggesting?'

Little Adam, his tongue between his teeth, smearing a Christmas card with glue and scattering glitter on it and writing beneath the picture, with much effort, 'From your loving son'. Little Adam pointing at the spilled milk, the broken saucer, eyes wide with guilt and a fear surely out of all proportion to the mildness of any rebuke that might be expected: 'It *made* me.' Could she believe him capable of drug-taking, drug-*pushing*?

The mother in her found it inconceivable. The researcher, detached, knew that, statistically, there was little to suggest that drug-pushers, wife-beaters or foul murderers differed in any salient characteristic from anybody else.

'*Why* are these two drawers locked? I think we should open them. Can't you force them or something?'

He looked up at her. 'I think we should wait,' he said. 'And give Adam the opportunity to open them himself.'

So they waited. They went downstairs and he poured them both a drink and when the oven bell rang he made a gesture in the direction of the kitchen and said, 'Do you . . .?'

She didn't and neither did he. So she took it upon herself to turn it off, just as if she'd still been mistress of the house, and then they had another drink: a lot of gin, a little tonic – and another, and he said that perhaps they should slow down and she realised that rather than advocating restraint for no better reason than a soured prudence, he had a valid point: the drunk berating the drugged would be hypocrisy of the highest order.

'Have you noticed anything out of the ordinary?' she said, forcing herself to speak, if only to lessen the unbearable tension of waiting.

'Such as?'

She tried to remember every article she'd read on the subject. 'Needle marks,' she said eventually, 'up his arms.' But injecting was no longer the favoured method. Now they chased dragons or sniffed until their septums were destroyed. 'Silver paper in the ashtrays,' she said, remembering. 'Lots of spent matches.'

Max shook his head.

'I don't understand him, Chrissie. I don't understand either of them.'

He hadn't used that fond diminutive for years. And, judging by the startled look on his face, she was certain that he hadn't intended to use it now.

'I expect our parents thought the same about us.'

'No,' he said. 'They thought they knew us. They thought so because we let them think so. We weren't going to let them in on our real private lives, so we pretended to be what they expected of us to put them off the scent. Our kids can't be bothered to do that.'

He closed his eyes. From where she stood she could see the grey in his hair. 'I never feel entirely at ease with them,' he said. 'Either of them. I'm always conscious of having to make a tremendous effort.'

'I feel that way sometimes. As though if I try terribly hard and remain frightfully polite everything will be all right, but the minute that I forget and try to seek some acknowledgement that we are, actually, related, they look at me as though I'm guilty of the most appalling intrusion.'

He nodded. Oh Max, she thought, why couldn't we continue to love each other or, at least, continue to feel whatever it was we felt? Or, even if that was impossible, why couldn't whatever it was have changed into whatever it is that allows people to grow and change together and make allowances and become fonder?

~ 3 ~

Could I come back? She had asked herself this at intervals throughout the three hours during which they sat on the edge of their chairs and watched the clock and desisted from the gin that might have made the waiting more bearable. Could I come back? If he would have me?

Yes. It was possible. If a change of definition were to be agreed upon. If he were to be all the time as he was tonight: too saddened and shocked to care about dust and crumbs and curtains. If she were to submerge her desire for that which he couldn't supply.

They might rub along, managing to avoid the worst kind of abrasions. Things might even improve.

But if she came back, if he had her back, she knew it would be a failure of her nerve, a decision made against all her survival instincts, and that, having returned, she would never again, however desperate she became, pluck up the courage to leave.

The silence was broken by the sound of feet on the gravel. They froze and then looked at each other. How much easier it would be to say nothing, to hope that their suspicions were unfounded or – if they weren't – that the situation would resolve itself without the need for them to intervene.

You? Or me? Such was the gist of Max's glance. We're scared of our children, she realised suddenly; *that's* the difference between our parents and us and us and them. And then she saw him square his shoulders and accept the responsibility.

'Oh hello,' Adam said, entering the room and acknowledging her unexpected presence. 'Why are you sitting in the dark?'

This wasn't quite accurate. They had switched on a couple of wall lights, but the illumination provided wasn't bright enough to allow anybody to see anybody else at all distinctly. He put on the overhead light and, before the first comment was made that would start the ball rolling, or cause the balloon to go up, or trigger off the next world war, she took the opportunity for a long and comprehensive scrutiny of him. And anything further from the traditional media-dispatched image of the dilapidated junkie would have been hard to imagine. He looked well-fed, well-groomed, robust. His hair was glossy and his eyes were bright. He could have stepped out of the pages of some posh magazine as a teenage fashion model – except that, these days, posh magazines seemed to choose teenage fashion models for their close resemblance to heroin addicts.

'What's up?'

Max rose to his feet. It seemed necessary to emphasise that he was taller and broader and stronger than Adam, that they were still, indubitably, father and son, in that order of precedence.

'What's going on?' Adam said.

'That's what I want to ask you. What *is* going on? What are you involved in that you shouldn't be?'

Oh Max, she thought, the evil fairy excluded from your christening obviously withheld the gift of guile. If Max had been involved in torturing people, he'd have been the one who stood by with the cosh while the other man delicately inserted lighted matches beneath the victim's fingernails.

'You what?' Adam said, with a pointed glance towards their glasses. 'Are you drunk or something?'

'Where've you been?'

'Told you where I was going. Told Mrs Whatsit anyhow.'

'Oh yes. The library and/or this Akai business.'

'Akai? What d'you mean Akai? Kendo. Yeah, that's right.'

'Where are your books then? And whatever paraphernalia you need for – Kendo?'

'I went to the library to take books *back*. And you don't *have* paraphernalia, as you call it, for Kendo. You have swords and they supply them and I've only just signed *up*, I'm not a flaming Grand *Master* yet. Anyway, what *is* all this?'

'I'll show you. Or rather, you can show me. Come upstairs,' Max said. 'Come on!' And he said it so peremptorily that Adam obeyed, almost reflexively.

A long way up the stairs. Long enough for her to wish fervently that the clock could be turned back to the time of not-knowing, the time before the figure of Parkinson: head down and shoulders hunched, had moved through Lansdowne Gardens like a character from a *Carry on Spying* film.

Max opened Adam's wardrobe doors. He opened the drawers. He gestured to the wallet and the watch and the belt and the clothes. He said, 'How on earth have you managed to acquire all these, all of a sudden?'

Injured innocence had been evaporating all the way up the stairs. No longer the bright challenging stare that derives from the confident certainty that you know more than those who are accusing you; now there was only hostility left. And fear.

'Out of my allowance, of course. How else?'

'No. You'd need a salary, not an allowance like you get from me to afford all this.'

To convince, he should have stuck to his guns, but he didn't cotton on to that and kept changing his story. The variations became feebler and feebler: he had had those clothes for yonks, hadn't he? (Max, displaying a surprising amount of knowledge, said no, he hadn't, for the simple reason that, for instance, 501s hadn't been on sale in England long enough for him to have gradually acquired five pairs of them.) He had borrowed them from friends: they all operated a kind of clothes' exchange, didn't they? (Which friends, Max had asked. Well: John Pickering and Jeremy Willis and Mark Jones. Then these friends could confirm it? A move towards the telephone producing a change of tack.) He'd sold records, picked up the gear cheap on the markets, got a mate who worked in the shop and was given discount. (No, and no, and no again.) Loss of control seemed the best diversionary tactic. He began to shout, picked up a paperweight from his desk and hurled it to the floor. How *dared* they? What *right* did they have, to snoop, to rummage through his possessions and make their offensive insinuations?

Max said, with commendable coolness, 'I'm not picking on you or snooping for the sake of it. Your mother had an anonymous letter suggesting that you may be involved – in wrongdoing. That's why I'm asking you, quite reasonably, for an explanation.'

'What letter? Where is it?'

She would have pretended to have left it at Gwen's, but Max produced it. She prayed, as she watched Adam unfolding it and reading it, that he wouldn't recognise the clumsy printing as emanating from Parkinson's pen.

'And you believe this crap?'

'I would infinitely prefer *not* to believe it.'

'Thanks. Thanks a lot. Thanks very much.'

Hands trembling. Voice rising higher and higher and becoming louder and louder. Eyes darting from one corner of the room to the other.

'What's "stuff", Adam?' Max said.

'How the hell do I know?'

'Is it what I think it is?'

He stopped shouting and muttered scornfully, 'And what *do* you think it is?'

'It's a word they use for drugs, isn't it?'

'What!'

He looked at them both as if they'd suddenly switched to speaking a different language.

'Why,' Max continued, 'should anyone even suggest it? Why should they go to the trouble of writing a note like this?' Suddenly his expression altered. He held out his arms. 'Oh, Adam, what *is* it all about? Is there anybody who dislikes you enough to want to get you into trouble? Are you covering up for somebody?'

Adam spoke through clenched teeth. He said, 'You're disgusting. You're vile. Even *thinking* it . . .'

Max hung his head, wanting to feel sufficiently ashamed to be justified in ceasing his attack. But there were still the clothes. 'Why are those two drawers locked, Adam?' she said.

'Because I happen to want them that way, that's why.'

'Is there something in them that you don't want us to see?'

Let it be dirty mags, she prayed, French letters, *love* letters. Please God, let it be anything but folded squares of paper.

'No,' he said, 'of course there isn't.'

'Then you won't object to opening them?'

'I don't know where the key is.'

'I think you do.'

He started to dance up and down on the spot. 'I hate you,' he shouted, dancing faster, shouting louder, shaking off Max's restraining hand.

'Adam, you've been playing truant, you haven't done any school work for ages, you've a wardrobe full of expensive clothes that you can't account for, and we receive a note implying that you're up to no good – What are we *supposed* to do?'

'Get off my back. That would do for starters.'

'We want to *help* you.'

'You want to kill me. You want me to be what *you* want me to be, not what I am.'

Max was soft. Beneath the brittle shell of irritability there was a centre like fondant. 'Leave him,' Max said.

But softness could breed evil as often as it encouraged good. Softness inclined one to the easy option. 'Leave him': to get away with it, to continue to do it – whatever 'it' was. 'The key, Adam?' she said.

It would never be forthcoming. So Max went downstairs. Adam had barricaded himself in the corner behind the desk, had stopped shouting, crying, twitching or dancing, stood frozen into immobility, gave no indication whatsoever that he heard what she was saying to him: 'I love you. I can't let you go headlong into situations from which you may never be able to extricate yourself. I can't do it.'

Max winced even before the screwdriver had split the wood, but persevered until the first drawer was broken from its restraining lock mechanism and could be pulled out to reveal its secrets.

There were three cigarette lighters and two digital watches and a silver identity bracelet. There were four pewter napkin rings and a St Christopher medal. There was a leather-cased travelling alarm clock and another wallet and a couple of examples of what they called executive toys. There were scarves and cufflinks and a crystal paperweight and a man's dress ring. And there were two pairs of brightly-coloured, patterned mittens, mittens that matched the pair in Christina's pocket, the pair that Adam had, supposedly, brought her back as a souvenir from his skiing holiday.

'Why?' they said, inspecting the items, rearranging them, hoping that a pattern would emerge that might form some link between them other than that provided by a marketing strategy that placed them in close proximity upon the counters and within the display cabinets of department stores.

'Why?'

But he was not capable of inventing an answer that could allay their qualms by establishing some sort of logical – and licit – reason for this magpie hoard. They knew it and he knew it. It was the desperation born of this knowledge that furnished him with a hitherto undemonstrated athletic ability and allowed him to vault the vandalised desk and run for freedom.

Max lifted the telephone from her grasp and put it out of her reach and held her firmly, her arms pressed to her sides. For a moment or two she struggled within the straitjacket of this un-tender embrace and then she said, 'All right. We'll leave it for a while. But only for a while. I don't care what you say.'

What he had said was that a rash – and premature – appeal for the help of the law in tracking down and apprehending the fugitive might not be too smart a move in view of the all-too-obvious evidence of the fugitive's undoubtedly unlawful activities.

'Anyway,' he said, 'there's very little that the police could do – or would do – at this stage.'

It was cold still. The night temperatures plummeted, causing severe ground frosts. A child, in the news last week, lost and wandering, had died of hypothermia.

'Where would he go? Where *could* he go?'

Max could not deny the logic of ringing the homes of his friends, despite the lateness of the hour. She rang the parents of John Pickering and Jeremy Willis and Mark Jones. None of them had seen Adam and *their* sons were safely accounted for.

'What about Parkinson?' Max said. 'Isn't he the obvious one?'

'Haven't got his number.'

'*We* have.'

And there it was, inscribed as large as life on the pad. She need not have contemplated with dismay those endless columns of Parkinsons in the phone book; she could simply have asked Max for the number, rather than the name and address. Why had it not occurred to her? Once, she had won a prize for an essay on Kierkegaard, but Gwen was right: that kind of intelligence was of absolutely no use when it came to coping with life.

She took a deep breath and made the call and was much taken aback when a gentle female voice answered her and told her pleasantly that Justin had gone to bed, but she'd get him down if necessary.

Justin!

'If *I* can help in any way?' Mrs Parkinson said, and Christina covered the receiver with her hand and mouthed the words at Max and he shook his head vehemently, so she said, 'Oh, I expect he's just forgotten what time it is. You know what they're like.' And Mrs Parkinson, true to her cue, replied that she did indeed, and a few more pleasantries were exchanged and then she said goodbye.

'You don't think it might have been an idea to enlighten her about her son's part in all this?' Christina asked, thinking of Parkinson, snug in his bed, and Adam wandering the city streets beneath a cold moon.

'No. Not yet. Not until we get the facts. This Parkinson may be as guilty as Adam, or he may simply have been trying to bring the problem to somebody's attention before Adam ended up in a police cell.'

Once again they contemplated the cache: the mittens, the napkin rings, the cufflinks set with large and vulgar tiger's eyes – items he could not possibly need or want or even find attractive.

'It's stealing for the sake of it,' Max said. He couldn't stop wringing his hands. And, except for when she'd been making the phone calls, neither could she. 'Oh – not the clothes. I can see that those would be carefully chosen, but all this – stuff.' And he looked at her and she looked at him and both of them expelled great relief-laden sighs, and even after they'd finished being glad that Parkinson's stuff might only refer to stolen property and not to dangerous drugs, such was the climate of the times and their adaptation to it that it still seemed preferable to discover that your son was a thief (and she amended this definition to 'had been thieving', which had altogether different implications) than having to accept that he was an addict.

They went downstairs and they took it in turns to make cups of tea, and at midnight, when the heating went off, Max turned it back on again, but all the same she shivered as uncontrollably as she had done after finding the dead Donaldson baby, so he poured her a very stiff gin and that seemed to help so he poured her another, and one for himself and they sat drinking, so quietly that they could hear distant train whistles and ships' hooters and car brakes squealing at the traffic lights.

At two o'clock, and a lot of gin later, she asked him *when* they ought to ring the police.

'Not until tomorrow, I think. Well – later today.'

Max was alternating his gin with Neutradonna.

'He might have done something – foolish.'

'More foolish than what he's already done? Stop reacting,

Christina, and think. If I call the police, they're going to want to know why he left. Even if we keep our mouths shut about that little haul upstairs, there's no guarantee that, if they pick him up, *he* will. He might well panic and land himself in serious trouble. Very serious trouble. I don't think we should involve the police until we have to.'

'And when is that: when we have to involve them?' she persisted, and he lost his temper then and snarled at her, saying that he didn't *know* when, only not just yet and she cried back at him, asking how she was supposed to endure the interim period without going totally off her head, and he said well, *that* wouldn't be very far for *her* to go, would it? And then they both recognised the old familiar road down which they were travelling and they made an effort and she said, 'At least, you'll understand that I can't go home until something has been resolved,' and he said, 'No, of course not,' because, in such circumstances, if you couldn't summon your best friend to give you support, then you must be glad of your worst enemy.

They couldn't eat and they couldn't sleep. They could only drink and talk: had Adam gone off the rails as a consequence of the domestic upheavals, or was there some constitutional weakness? Had there been signs in his childhood that they should have picked up? Wasn't kleptomania supposed to be associated with the desire to be loved? Hadn't they loved him enough, in their respective ways, regardless of whether they were together or apart?

By half-past three they had talked themselves hoarse. By half-past three she was certain that he would never return, that he'd be discovered, as dawn broke, on the railway line, or fished from the river. She could no longer hold back her tears. It was a tidal wave of grief that seemed to encompass not only Adam's wrongdoing and her fears for his safety, but the end of her marriage too and Livingstone's defection and poor silly Albert's crisped corpse and Kenneth Little's pathetic attempts at wooing and the Donaldson baby clad in that plain white garment that couldn't be spoiled.

Max left the room and walked in the garden while she cried. She could hear his feet on the paving stones of the terrace as he completed each aimless circuit. Once he opened the french windows and poked his head into the room but she was still crying so he closed them again. She was still crying and consequently he was in the garden when the phone rang, but he'd heard it and had sprinted to answer it before she'd had time to cross the room.

She heard him say only, 'Hello,' and 'But let me ring you back,' and 'Be sure that you do,' and 'Goodbye,' but the expression on his face told her what she needed to know well before he repeated the other half of the conversation.

The caller was David. 'Dad?' he had said. 'Now listen because I've only got this one ten pee. No, shut up and listen. Adam's here. He's OK, so don't start sending for the Seventh Cavalry or anything dumb like that. I'll ring you tomorrow – well, later today. All right? Yeah, right. Bye.'

Her tears didn't cease, but they soothed now rather than scalded. From amidst them she managed to say, 'How on earth did he get there? There wouldn't have been any trains after he left here.'

'He must have hitched. I'll ask David tomorrow – today, when he rings.'

'He *will* ring? You know David.'

'Yes, I think, this time, he will ring. He knows that I'll go straight over there if he doesn't.'

He sat down and yawned enormously. 'God,' he said, 'is it *worth* going to bed? What time is it?'

'Ten to four.'

'Then I suppose we'd better or we'll feel even more like bloody hell tomorrow – today – than we do now.'

She went upstairs while he attended to the locks and the lights. She could have slept in Adam's bed, or equipped herself with sheets and a quilt and gone into what they still called David's room, or the spare bedroom where she had spent every night of the last six months of her sojourn beneath this roof. But none of these alternatives occurred to her; she made, instinctively, for the matrimonial bedroom.

'Can I borrow some pyjamas?'

Max stood looking at her for a moment and then he opened a drawer and took out a pyjama jacket.

She sat down to take off her shoes and then she must have fallen asleep and woke briefly to find that he was lifting her legs into bed. She noticed that she was wearing the pyjama top and nothing else, and wasn't sure whether she'd undressed herself or he'd done it. She didn't care either way. She wanted only to go back to sleep, secure in the knowledge that her son was safe and that tomorrow – or today – was, in terms of sleep-time at any rate, light years away.

'Got a pen?' David said. 'Take this number and ring me back. And then just listen, will you, for a bit?'

From the hall where she was listening in on the extension, Christina could see Max's agitated gestures: the fingers of his free hand beating time on the wall, occasionally indulging in wild bouts of doodling on the telephone pad, scratching his chin, pulling at his ear. But he listened, as requested. For her own part, the main problem was not stifling her comments but stifling her yawns.

They had woken at eight forty-five. Max had rung first the admirable Mrs Monks to tell her that her presence today would not be required, and then his secretary, informing *her* of the revised *ordres du jour*, given that he would not be going into the office.

But that had been the second awakening. Her first had been at seven-forty, his, presumably, some time earlier, since the reason for her awakening was his parting of her thighs.

She had gone to their bed as she used to do in times past, and times past had incorporated conjugal relations. Normal procedure. Consequently she had allowed the pyjama jacket to be unbuttoned so that he could put his mouth to her breast, allowed her hand to be guided downwards for the purpose of caressing his erect penis; it was only when she felt his weight on top of her that she remembered that intercourse between them was not, any longer, normal procedure, that had the Queen's Proctor been alerted to their conduct (was there still a Queen's Proctor?) Max could have whistled for his divorce.

But she was too tired to point this out to him, and once he was inside her it seemed pointless to object.

He came quickly and immediately fell asleep. For a few moments she was crushed beneath his weight. But Max was ever the gentleman and the necessity to behave like one woke him for long enough to roll off her; he even mumbled an apology for having scratched her with his stubble.

He was up and making his telephone calls before she got out of bed. A glance at his face, and vice-versa, was enough to lead each of them to the understanding that what had happened during the night was best forgotten, that it had not been prompted by any desire to reanimate their relationship but rather was due to propinquity: a man deprived of normal sexual relations for some considerable time, who finds himself in bed with a woman, particularly one naked from the waist down, may be pardoned for becoming aroused. When Christina pulled back the coverlet they both pretended not to notice the incriminating stain.

She thought: I hope I'm not pregnant, but beyond that she didn't dwell upon it. Had she been less tired, it might have been enjoyable – their sexual relations had often been enjoyable – but, enjoyable or not, it made absolutely no difference.

She prepared breakfast and they sat down opposite each other to eat it, each being excessively polite in terms of passing the butter and wielding the coffee pot. Then she washed their few dishes while Max made a pretence of reading the paper. They knew it would be hours yet before David surfaced, let alone sought out a telephone and put them out of their misery.

She gazed through the french windows. Rain fell remorse-lessly. Frost-blackened evergreen shrubs bowed what little of their foliage they had left beneath this onslaught; flower beds were churned into mud baths. A single bird, venturing recklessly out of its nest in the chestnut tree, changed its mind and flew back again.

'Don't you need to let anyone know that you won't be going in to work today?' Max asked, obviously irritated by her aimless wandering to and from the window, her switching on of the radio and switching it off again, her picking up and replacing (always just that annoying fraction to the right or to the left of their original positions) of the ornaments on the shelf.

She shook her head.

'Well for Christ's sake, sit down, can't you!'

She offered to heat up Mrs Monks' beef casserole for lunch, but he didn't trust her. He put on the oven gloves and did it himself. He cut some cheese and buttered some crackers and opened a bottle of Perrier water (it was alcohol as well as propinquity that had aroused him, and he wasn't going to allow it to happen again).

At quarter-past one the phone rang. It was Max's secretary seeking guidance on how to deal with a certain difficult customer. Max explained, slowly and carefully. Christina fretted with impatience; undoubtedly David was at this very moment putting down the receiver, having got the engaged signal. Leave it till later, he'd think; and for David later usually meant never.

It was three o'clock when he rang. Despite Max's protests, she had worn a path across the carpet, pacing to and fro, and Max had read the same few paragraphs of *Jude the Obscure* perhaps two dozen times.

'Got a pen?' David said. 'Take this number and ring me back. And then just listen, will you, for a bit?'

Max motioned her to the hall where she picked up the extension and prepared to bite her tongue.

'He's told me all about it,' David said, 'the stupid little jerk. Apparently it's been going on ever since he moved into the Lower Fifth. He and that ugly one – Justin Parkinson, is that his name? – got caught up with a crowd from Westbourne.' (Westbourne was the school with the appallingly bad record with which the boys' grammar had been amalgamated.) 'Real smart-arses, apparently. The craze was to see who could accumulate the most knock-off. Parkinson got cold feet early on and backed out and the rest of them stopped nicking when they formed a group – well, they only nick instruments now, but Adam just sort of carried on. Incidentally, he reckons it must have been Parkinson who ratted on him. Is that right?'

'Where *is* Adam?' Max asked, loath to reply to this question if he happened to be at David's shoulder.

'Gone with Jools to the take-away.'

'Yes, between you and me and the gate-post, it *was* Parkinson. We thought it showed a certain degree of maturity. We felt that we'd been misjudging the lad.'

'Adam reckons that he was shit-scared of being implicated. And with his dad being a vicar – '

'A vicar!'

Christina, at this point, stopped yawning, disobeyed orders and interjected, so amazed was she at this announcement.

'– yeah. St Mary's. Anyway, Parkinson doesn't want anything mucking up his chances. Very bright, apparently. White hope of the Lower Fifth. He tried to persuade Adam to knock it on the head. Adam carried on, so Parkinson probably thought the best thing was to try to get you to do something.'

'And how *is* Adam?'

'He seems more relieved than anything. As though he was

waiting for something like this to make him stop. Anyway, he won't be seeing Parkinson again for a bit. He wants to stay here.'

'What?'

'He wants to stay here for a bit. Lie low till the heat's off.'

'What do you mean: the heat's off? Do you mean he's been found out? Is *that* what you mean?'

Interjections were coming now, thick and fast. When he could make himself heard, David said, 'I don't think he's scared that the Bill are going to grip him. Apparently he's always got away scot-free. And the rest of those nerks aren't going to open their gobs, are they? Least of all Parkinson. Wouldn't look too good, would it, on the Cambridge Entrance? No, it's you two. He knows he'd have a dog's life if he came back now.'

Their interjections were silenced as each of them contemplated with bewilderment the mental processes that produced an attitude refuting the idea that a dog's life might be all that he could reasonably expect. Then Max said, 'But he can't just not go to school.'

'Why not? It's nearly Easter. He's not done any work. He's obviously not going to do any now. So I can't see that it matters.'

'And what am I supposed to tell them?'

'You'll think of something.'

Max ceased to be calm. Flippancy, Max said, was hardly the right approach. Adam was guilty of stealing; Adam had misappropriated, over a long period of time, a large amount of other people's property. And not only was Adam a thief, but there had been some suspicion that drugs might be involved.

'They're not,' David said. 'Forget drugs, Dad, scrub round them. Adam's just a tea-leaf, right?'

'David,' said Max, acknowledging that the son whose advent into the world had been welcomed with purple gladioli, whom he'd rocked to sleep and taught to drive and carried upstairs to bed when drunk, now held the whip-hand. 'David, do you honestly think that he should be allowed to run away from the consequences of his actions?'

David considered. Eventually he said, 'No, I suppose I don't, *theoretically*, but you haven't got many options, have you? Even if he goes back to school tomorrow, you can't make him work. And he might start nicking again. Or else take off. At least here he's safe. He can try and get his head together without you two giving him a hard time.'

'He's done wrong, David,' Max said with a weary persistence, as though, should the whole world depart from an acknowledgement that moral absolutes existed, he would continue to uphold them.

'He got caught up with a crowd of dingbats and he made a daft mistake. He's young. Were *you* never young?'

They had no choice but to capitulate: Adam would attempt to get his head together; David would watch him with a careful eye; Christina would kindly desist from boarding an Intercity train for the sake of holding his little hand and checking that he had on clean underwear and laying a big guilt-trip on everyone within earshot; and Max – perhaps it would be as well if Max got rid of any incriminating evidence.

They had to wait for the rain to stop and then Max lit a bonfire at the far end of the back garden and, furtively, under cover of darkness, they carried down the jeans and the shoes and the shirts and the sweaters and threw them on to the petrol-assisted blaze. The other stuff – that which wouldn't burn – they packed into a dustbin liner and left for the refuse men.

The flames leapt as Max stoked the fire. 'Do you remember,' she said, 'that Guy Fawkes night – it was when we were still at the other house – when you used too much petrol and the fence caught fire and horrible Mrs Whatsit next door called out the fire brigade?'

He poked the last of the jumpers into the heart of the blaze, kicked back an ember that had rolled out of it. 'Good God, yes,' he said. 'We'd put it out in about two minutes flat with half a bucket of water and then two damn great fire engines came clanging down the street. She was an old cow, wasn't she? Tried to claim compensation off me. It wasn't even her fence!'

'She was always accusing the boys of stealing her apples or her pears or her raspberries – whatever happened to be ripening at the time . . .'

'Well she was right, wasn't she, at least on one occasion . . .?'

She remembered: the pockets of the five-year-old David's grey school shorts bulging with juicy William pears. 'But she's got *loads* and we haven't got *any*,' he'd said in mitigation, couldn't understand why they were so horrified. 'I think we've bred a little Marxist,' Max had said at the time. Now he raked the ashes and said, 'Perhaps it runs in the family.'

It was very dark by then but there was still a glow from the fire's embers and she could have sworn that he'd smiled.

And it became possible, briefly, to believe that she'd imagined all the bad years that had intervened between that bonfire and this, that they could go back to being as they were, wanting now only what they'd wanted then.

But his smile, like the joys of life, was fleeting. He was frowning when he flicked his fingers at her impatiently, indicating that he wanted her to pass him the spade so that he could damp down the ashes with soil.

He said, 'My father must be turning in his grave.'

'Why's that?'

'Do you think he'd have done this for me?'

'I hope he would.'

'You don't know what I'm talking about, do you?' he said. 'For all his faults, my father knew that covering up for somebody was an abdication of responsibility. He wouldn't have let me crawl away to get my head together – whatever the bloody hell that *means*; he'd have punished me and made damn sure that it fitted the crime. He'd have acknowledged that it was his fault not society's if I behaved badly, for failing to instil proper values into me.'

There was a hiss as damp soil fell on to live coals. He leaned on the spade. He said, 'There's a tribe of South American Indians whose language, apparently, doesn't cater for the concept of personal accountability: they say "The cup fell from my hand" and so forth.'

Adam, at three, beside the spilled milk: 'It *made* me.'

'And are all *their* heads done in because of it?'

Adam, at fifteen, obliged to do anything he didn't want to do: 'It's doin' me 'ead in.'

'I don't know,' Max said. 'I only know mine's going that way.'

⌐ 4 ⌐

'What *did* God make mothers for?' said Murray Pearl, reading the labels on the 78 records as, together, they stacked them on a trestle table next to the secondhand paperbacks and the pile of *People's Friends*.

'Suffering, I should imagine. What else? Who's going to buy these anyway?' she said. 'You can't play them. Unless you've a record-player of the same vintage, and I shouldn't think that there are many of those around any more.'

'Mind your backs!' shouted Joyce Perrot as she and one of the twins manhandled a trestle across the room. Then she yelped and dropped her end of it and started sucking furiously at her forefinger. The twin – Maureen – had prudently put on gloves, and Joyce had mocked her, saying, 'Oh surely you're not fussing about the odd little splinter?'

Now she sucked and yelped and attempted vainly to dislodge the sliver of wood with blunt, nail-bitten fingers until Christina, using a flame-sterilised darning needle, manoeuvred the foreign body from the spot where it was embedded.

'There!'

She drew out the splinter whole. Joyce bound her finger with a dirty handkerchief and decided to appoint the other twin, Linda, to take over at her end of the trestle. 'I'll help you with these cardis,' she said, dislodging a heap of them that Christina had just finished arranging.

'I say! This is quite nice, isn't it?'

She held up a sweater, hand-knitted in a particularly revolting shade of green. One sleeve looked to be slightly longer than its fellow.

'I might have this myself. How much?'

Christina indicated Murray Pearl's laboriously-printed price tag which said fifty pence.

'Twenty-five then?' Joyce Perrot said, laying it aside, beyond the reach of customers. 'That's usually the way we work it – half price.'

Christina felt like saying: 'What is the point of trying to raise funds when the fund-raisers cream off the profits?' but thought better of it.

Joyce's assistance proved to be not a help but a hindrance. Christina refolded cardigans, rearranged *Girls' Crystal* annuals, removed a stack of not-quite-set and not-quite-sealed home-made jams from where they were leaking on a pile of raffia table mats to a safer place. She endured the realignment of the shoe collection according to a different (and incomprehensible) criterion and an alternative scheme being worked out as regards the manning of the stalls. She had no option: the hall in which The System's bring and buy sale was being held was that attached to Robin Perrot's church.

That the event was taking place at all was no small achievement. And due almost entirely to Murray Pearl. The badly-washed cardigans, the yellowed underwear with its perished elastic, the leaking jars of jam and the collectors' item discs, every aspect of the organisation and advertisement that had brought people who might be willing to purchase these goods to the door was solely attributable to his industry.

Joyce said that you could always tell a good worker. She did not mean 'you' generally; she meant 'I' specifically. She said that if only The System had been able to call upon the services of Murray Pearl from the beginning it might not now be fighting for survival. She said that if only everybody would make a similar effort even now it might not be too late. Joyce never stopped saying. When she wasn't praising Murray Pearl, exhorting the other members to pull their weight, or entreating her children to stop quarrelling over ownership of a *Blue Peter* annual, she was touring the stalls and passing on her experience as to which sort of arrangement would attract purchasers and which would not. 'Oh no, no,' she said to Christina, 'you don't put your books at the *front*. Anybody'll buy a *book*. You put them at the *back*, then they've to reach over and look at the other things. You'll learn,' she said kindly, 'when you've done as many of these as I have.'

313

'Ever thought of offering Terence Conran the benefit of your advice?' Christina asked, but Joyce had already moved on to interfere with Norman and John and their potted plant arrangements.

As bring and buy sales go, it differed in no way from any that Christina had ever been obliged to attend or preside over before. People brought and people bought. People rummaged and wrinkled their noses and haggled over pennies. People elbowed their way to the front of the queue as though the Crown Jewels were on display rather than an assortment of plastic hairslides and gilt bangles and glass beads. The chief attraction was the tea urn.

As bring and buy sales went, it was as tedious as any other. She yawned till her eyes watered and had to be nudged, *en passant*, by Murray Pearl, who'd noticed that a gentleman actually wished to buy 'Come Back to Erin' and 'That's What God Made Mothers For'.

A few of the records went and most of the books and some of the shoes. Even the pot dog with the smashed nose was sold. Joyce Perrot, periodically acting as assistant to every stall alternately, had a line in sales patter and a capacity for haggling that wouldn't have seemed out of place on a Berwick Street barrow. Christina, whenever her turn came round to be assisted, suffered agonies of embarrassment as the virtues of a pair of lace-trimmed camiknickers with a rotted gusset were extolled with the kind of lewd frankness that is the prerogative of the invincibly naïve.

She spied Corky in the doorway and waved, thankful for the diversion, surprised that she had actually turned up after her assertion that bun-fights, bring and buys, Mothers' Unions and suchlike get-togethers were not at all her sort of thing. 'Oh do drop in and buy a tea cosy, at least,' Christina had begged.

'Don't need a tea cosy.'

It was no use asking Gwen. She'd say, very slowly, 'A bring and buy sale? At the Witnesses' Hall?' as though you'd invited her to the abattoir to watch pigs being slaughtered.

'Will it do *you* some good if I come and buy a tea cosy?' Corky had asked.

'Well, not directly. But if the thing goes well then my boss will be pleased because her project might be kept going, and the better pleased she is, the better it is for me.'

'I know the feeling,' Corky had said, with a meaningful nod in Gwen's direction.

'Not the same, is it? You two are equal partners.'

'No such animal, darlin',' Corky had replied.

'You *will* drop in though?'

'Well I was going to try and get a bit of practice in . . .'

'Oh come on! You've had a fortnight's solid practice. You can't need much more.'

Burned black, she was, by that relentless East Coast wind against which, daily, she had pitted herself. She'd arrived back a couple of days ago, at lunchtime. Gwen was due around dinner. She'd announced her immediate plan as a bit of a run and then an evening at the cinema (not that you could call it an evening these days: lucky if you got a couple of hours and that including the hot dog adverts and the Pearl & Dean). 'I'll leave you to hear all about the tropical sunsets and Him in his white dinner jacket, kissing her hand,' she said to Christina. 'I don't think my stomach would stand it.'

And of course, come dinnertime and Gwen's luggage-laden arrival, there had been a fair amount of 'My Holiday' to be absorbed by way of Polaroids and anecdotes involving the blueness of the sea and the whiteness of the sand and the obliging nature of black servants.

But Gwen had seemed preoccupied, a state of affairs that could not wholly be attributed to jet-lag, because it lasted long after jet-lag had evaporated, after she'd assured herself that her house and possessions were as she'd left them, after she'd checked that the rebuilding of Klosters was proceeding according to plan.

Gwen was pondering something very deeply indeed and it didn't take clairvoyant powers to deduce the nature of that something. An unused packet of Anusol suppositories had been returned to the bathroom cabinet, an unsqueezed tube of anti-fungal cream. Presumably one bedroom only had been occupied in the Hotel Splendide, or whatever it was called, Nassau, rather than two.

'I say! Over here.'

Corky came loping across the room. She'd been running in the rain and her cropped grey hair was plastered to her skull and her dark-brown, deeply-lined face shone with moisture so that it looked like a highly-polished woodcarving.

'I'm so glad you've come. I was starting to wilt. What can I sell you? A nice propelling-pencil: "Unwanted Gift"? A butter dish with a picture of Charles and Di? A frightfully tasteful vase for a single rose?'

She remembered, too late, that these were the kind of ornaments that Corky displayed on her shelves.

But she appeared not to make the connection. 'Wouldn't give them house-room,' she said, picking up and putting down a Spanish-flamenco-dancer-with-a-flounced-skirt toilet-roll cover as though it carried contagion. 'Haven't you got any buns or anything like that? I wouldn't mind a bun.'

'There was some jam, but it got sold.'

To the woman who'd donated it, a woman of strong charitable inclination, which was as well because, so runny was it and prone to mould, so much did it leave to be desired as jam, no one else would have bought it.

'And there were the cakes the twins baked . . .'

But as with Joyce Perrot's cardigan, these had been snapped up long before the general public got a look in.

'Oh don't go away empty-handed. Something for everybody. Support a good cause. What about a tea towel?'

Joyce Perrot had come bounding across. She picked up the tea towel, unfolded it and held it aloft to display its design: 'Birds of East Anglia'.

'Everybody needs a tea towel. You can't have too many. Only seventy-five pee.'

But Corky had stopped listening. Corky's whole attention appeared to be fixed on the tea-urn stall where, now that the rush seemed to be over, Robin was dispensing tea to the helpers. So intent was her focus, so tense was she in every muscle, that she seemed to quiver.

'Is something the matter?'

Christina craned her neck to see whether there had been some ghastly accident or supernatural apparition, but there was only Robin pouring tea and Klaus and Linda and Murray Pearl and Norman drinking it.

Corky's wood-sculpture face was no longer mahogany, it was ash.

'Are you all right?'

She didn't reply. She didn't even say, 'I don't want a tea towel,' or 'Goodbye, see you later.' She simply turned on her heel and strode out of the hall. But she moved blindly, oblivious to whatever obstacles might beset her path, and barged into the pot-plant stall and sent two African violets and a tradescantia hurtling to the floor and everyone turned to look, but she just carried on walking, totally ignoring Norman's infuriated request to know what, exactly, she thought she was doing.

'Who *is* that woman?'

Christina helped him to scoop up spilled compost. 'No real damage done,' she said, concealing a broken blossom beneath her foot.

'Flaming vandal! Was she drunk?'

'Drunk? No, she wasn't drunk.'

Just another of her turns, by the look of it, a rapid mood-swing of the sort that had heralded the start of that period of gloom and irritability coinciding with Boysie's death and Stephen Millward's courting of Gwen. One hoped that *this* bout would not last as long.

Whatever the duration of the mood was likely to be, she'd carried it back home with her. Christina entered the house to the sound of battle well into its full strident stride, the spectacle of suitcases, packed, and stacked in the hall. She followed the noise up the stairs and into Gwen's bedroom where she caught the tail-end of what seemed to be the latest in a long list of swapped insults: 'I wonder if your little lap-dog knows just what he's letting himself in for if he takes you on?' (from Corky); from Gwen: 'You can go where you like as soon as you please, and the further away and the sooner, the better, as far as I'm concerned.'

'My accountant will be in touch. And my solicitor. You'll have to get some other mug to put up the money. Perhaps you can get lover-boy to cough up. Or does he only do the honours when there's a chance of a bit of leg-over?'

'You haven't got an accountant, or a solicitor. And I wonder if your boarding-house friend quite realises the instability of your temperament? I mean, the odd visit is all very well, but day in, day out . . .'

'Poncin' around like the Lady of the friggin' Manor: "Yes, it *is* quite a success, isn't it?"' (Here: a mock genteel accent adopted to emphasise such pretension.) '"Just a little recipe I've been experimenting with." Can't boil water without burning it!'

'Does she know your charming habit of leaving your teeth all over the place? *Not* a big plus, I'd have thought, when it comes to attracting customers.'

'Is he prepared to push your piles back? Lovely end to a romantic evening that'll be, won't it?'

It was all to do with whose control snapped first. Usually Gwen held out longest, disdain being a more powerful weapon than mere vituperation.

'Were you aware that there's a drop on the end of your nose?'

'Bit old for you, isn't he? Thought you didn't much care for them when they got past twenty-two.'

'Whatever is the matter now?'

It was unwise to interfere, she knew that. But very difficult to resist.

Gwen turned round very slowly on her dressing-table stool. Corky threw her a glance brief enough to acknowledge her total irrelevance to these proceedings. She'd got some of her colour back, Christina noticed, but not all of it.

'You can practically be heard on the street.'

Gwen took up a mascara brush and, with a deceptively steady hand, began to colour her lashes. 'I'm not surprised,' she said. 'The shouting that's been going on would put a fish-wife to shame. Not to mention the language.'

'Language!' Corky said. 'I never heard anything like some of the things you come out with, not in all my years in the Forces . . .'

'But what's it *about*? *Why* are you quarrelling?'

'Ask her,' Corky said. 'She needs an excuse to get me out so that she can get her fancy man in.'

And at the same time Gwen said, 'Ask her. She wants an excuse to pack her bags and leave. I suppose that Scarborough woman has come up with a better offer.'

'If you could only be *straight*. You've wanted me out for a long time now. Ever since you decided to start husband-hunting.'

'God, you're eaten up with jealousy, aren't you? There's nothing unnatural in my having a man-friend. You're the unnatural one – letting it eat into you all these years . . . We've all had problems. We don't all embroider them on banners and go through life waving them . . .'

'Problems! What problems have you ever had? You've been carried through life on a silken cushion. You've always had someone to spoil you to death: your father, your husband, me . . .'

'You! Your manner towards me alternates between brusque and unpleasant and downright obnoxious. That's why it's such a relief to escape for an evening into the company of someone who possesses a few of the social graces . . .'

The doorbell rang. Nobody moved. Eventually Christina said, 'Are you expecting Stephen?' And Corky replied, 'No, he's been called away on business. That's why *she's* on the turn. Funny business, I call it: over the weekend?'

'I am *not* on the turn – whatever that may mean . . .'

The doorbell rang again and Christina went downstairs to answer it. Murray Pearl was standing on the step and he said, 'Will you tell my mother I'd like to see her?'

'Your mother?' she said. And, presuming that this was some sort of joke, started to smile.

His face didn't alter. 'There's nothing to smile about,' he said.

There wasn't. Not unless you had a really strange sense of humour.

He pushed past her and was into the hall before she had a chance either to invite him in or to ask him to explain his business. He stood dripping rain on to Gwen's Persian rug. There was rain on his face too, or beads of sweat; she couldn't tell which.

'Your mother?' she said. 'What do you mean: your mother?'

If it was meant to be a joke, then it was a very unfunny one.

They heard Corky come thundering down the stairs. 'Social graces?' they heard her say, 'he'll need more than social graces. Can you see him fannying around you like I've done? I can't.' And then she came round the bend of the staircase and stopped dead.

'My mother,' Murray Pearl said.

When Max was puzzled and scratched beneath his chin he looked exactly like David; she and Adam had an identical way of sighing histrionically if obliged to repeat an explanation – or so people said; where have I seen that gesture before, Christina had wondered, apropos Murray Pearl, who does he remind me of? As soon as she saw them together, he and Corky, she wondered how she could have failed – all these months – to make the connection?

Corky looked down from the landing. She was motionless except for the spasms of quivering – clearly detectable even from that distance – which shook her from top to toe. 'Get out,' she said. 'Get the hell out.'

He didn't move. None of them moved. Gwen emerged from her bedroom and walked into a tableau. 'Still here?' she said to Corky and then noticed their visitor and said, 'Who's this?'

A moment passed. 'Who's this?' Gwen asked again, passing Corky, descending the staircase, changing the query – when, still, nobody answered her – to 'What's this?', walking up to where Murray Pearl stood, dripping still, confronting him.

'I just wanted to see my mother,' he said. And it was said in a tone so agreeable that you'd have thought that this was nothing more than a normal social visit.

Then Corky moved, came running down that last flight of stairs as though she had wings on her heels. 'Get out,' she shouted. 'Get out of here, whoever you are!'

You'd have thought her momentum would have propelled her to crash into him, but she checked herself at the last minute, braked sharply, snatched back the hand that seemed to be moving, of its own volition, to shove him towards the door and out into the street.

'You know who I am,' Murray Pearl said. 'You know all right.'

'What's this all about?' Gwen said impatiently. 'This *is* my house, you know.'

And one could have been forgiven for assuming that, whatever it was all about, it had nothing whatsoever to do with Gwen.

'Well?'

'I waited,' Murray Pearl said. 'I had to make sure . . .'

But he wasn't answering Gwen, he was addressing Corky.

Waited. Watched. Prowled? Dogged one's footsteps? Enlightenment was bestowed, at last, upon Christina. 'It *was* you, wasn't it?' she said. 'I wasn't imagining things, was I?'

She shot Gwen a triumphant glance, but Gwen wasn't paying her any attention. Gwen was looking from Murray Pearl to Corky and saying, in a tone that suggested her patience was at an end, 'Will someone tell me what's going on?'

Reluctantly, he changed the direction of his gaze. 'I told you,' he said equably. 'I just want to see my mother.'

'Your mother? Are you mad?'

But it seemed as though it was Corky who might be mad. She

plunged towards him, flailing her arms as though attempting to disperse a cloud of troublesome flying insects. 'Out, out, out!' she shouted, like Lady Macbeth with her needle stuck.

'No,' he said. 'No,' and ducked to avoid her indiscriminate blows. 'No,' he said, 'don't make me.'

Gwen tried to catch hold of Corky's tracksuit top in order to impose some measure of restraint upon her. Christina reached out a hand towards Murray Pearl's arm with the idea of leading him gently out of harm's way; but he almost jumped away from her and then, in the dimness of the hall, there was a flash as the light suddenly caught some hard, bright, reflective surface, and he shouted, 'Get off me, get away.' And she saw, and Corky too and Gwen, that the thing that was throwing back the reflection was a knife, a thin-bladed, sharp-edged, elegantly-turned, steel knife.

He moved so very quickly then. He'd grabbed Gwen and twisted her arm behind her back and brought the knife to her neck while Christina's mouth was still in the process of dropping open, while Corky's arm – final directionless lunge completed – was still falling to her side.

'Get in there,' he said, motioning towards the sitting-room. 'Get in there and sit down and shut up.'

It's Murray Pearl, Christina thought. It's only Murray Pearl. I know him. I've helped him to count the petty cash, drunk cups of coffee that he's made for me, exchanged glances of complicity with him across the Perrots' crowded room. Once I rolled a matchstick in the corner of a handkerchief and removed a foreign body from under his eyelid, once I sewed him a button on. I *know* him, and people you know don't suddenly produce knives and threaten you, not people you *know*.

He pushed Gwen down on one sofa and then sat by her side, keeping the knife as close to her skin as was possible without actually touching it – her eyes were opened so wide that you could see white right round the iris – and motioned Christina and Corky to sit down opposite on the other. Corky sank down on to it like a ton of bricks. With the appearance of the knife all her aggression seemed to have evaporated.

It *was* sweat on his face. Great beads of it broke forth from his hairline, rolled across the surface of his skin and dripped from his brow, his chin. He dashed them away with his free hand; the other one, the one that held the knife, never wavered.

And Gwen moved not a muscle. She was rigid with fear. This was it, Christina realised, the real thing; the threat that had been implicit in all those creakings and rustlings in Swinburne Court, in the obscene phone calls and dark alleyways and footsteps that kept pace with her own, had finally become manifest in the unlikely surroundings of Cousin Gwen's brightly-lit, comfortably-appointed sitting-room at six-thirty of an ordinary Saturday evening.

The knife glittered. She could see a cross-hatching of little marks on the cutting edge that showed where it had been sharpened. But although merely looking at it made her toes curl in her shoes as she thought of the damage that it could inflict, apart from that, she kept waiting to feel as terrified as she'd felt when alone in the flat, when walking along the dark and deserted alley, trying to invest the shape of the shadows with a non-sinister identity. This was only Murray Pearl, with whom she'd shared a chocolate bar for elevenses, who'd prevented her from being assaulted, who'd offered her his protection on the home-ward journey through the darkened streets.

'Murray,' she said placatingly. But she might not have been there for all the impression she made. All his attention was focused on Corky, who, Christina saw, had pressed her hands to her mouth and was making the sort of noise that old sick animals sometimes make before they are taken to the vet to be put out of their misery.

'They don't know, do they?' he said. 'Why don't you tell them? Go on,' he said. He said it almost cajolingly as though trying to wheedle out of a relative one more repetition of a favourite family anecdote. But the sweat continued to drip from him and his eyes were as wide as Gwen's.

'About the kid,' he prompted. 'Tell them about the kid you dumped twenty-six years ago without once bothering to check up on it. Shall I tell them instead? Would you like me to do it? About the Home where the principal's favourite pastime was interfering with little boys, or the foster home where they sent him back for wetting the bed, or the one where they thought they might adopt him but then they saw a nicer kid and adopted him instead?'

Corky moved her hands from her mouth and covered her eyes with them. She was trembling violently. Christina, at the other end of the sofa, could feel the vibration.

'You'd think, wouldn't you,' he said, 'that that kid wouldn't want anything to do with a mother like that? But kids are soft. They always think that their mothers *must* love them. It's what makes them try to find them when they get old enough. It's what makes them go up to London and search through the records until they find their birth certificate, and even though there's just a blank space on one side of it, well, that's to be expected, isn't it? Important thing is: it's your mother's name there. Can't get away from that. Can't pretend it never happened, can you?'

Gwen, despite herself, drew in breath sharply. He turned to her. She cringed. He said, 'Oh by the way, I want to apologise about the cat. I thought it belonged to her. Didn't think someone like you would have a cat like that. Also the wine bar,' he added, as if as an afterthought. 'Wasn't aimed at you personally.'

'Thank you,' Gwen said, faintly, ridiculously.

For a moment he looked blank and then he seemed to struggle to recapture his train of thought. 'I was telling you, wasn't I,' he said, 'about this kid going to Somerset House? Well it's not that now, but it was then . . . Sixteen, he was, Junior Leaders Regiment. Wanted to fly like Dad, but there'd been measles when he was small and perforated eardrums, so that put paid to that. Anyway Dad's was the Canadian Airforce. He was getting round to giving that kid his name, you know.'

This time it was Christina's turn to be focused upon. She returned his glance but there seemed to be nothing in his eyes that might respond to appeal.

'Couldn't adopt, wouldn't let him adopt – too old. But he was going to give the kid his name, by deed poll. All official, above board. Wouldn't have to be called Tommy McCorquodale any more. That was her dad's name: Thomas. Saw it in the records. Came from Cumberland. "Grace McCorquodale, born April 21st, 1926. Father: Thomas, farmer; Mother, Edith." Very remote, it was, the farm. Sheep.'

Grace!

'Dad died before he could make it official. Took his name anyway. Dad wanted him to have it. Murray Pearl. Murray Pearl the Second.'

His expression suddenly changed. He reminded her of the way that Max had looked the day she told him she was leaving him; as though a great struggle was taking place to fight back the tears. His mouth worked for a moment and then he said, 'That

323

cow of a wife of his: Ruby – she sent the kid back. Never liked him. Jealous. He and Dad got too close. Squeezed her out. Big fat cow, she was. Worked him until he had a heart attack. Then went looking for another mug. Kid was in the way. Sent him back pronto.'

Gwen licked her lips, opened her mouth and managed to croak out some words. 'Excuse me,' she said. 'Excuse me but I need to use the bathroom.'

He regarded her steadily. Then he said, 'I'm afraid you'll have to wait.'

'I can't wait,' she said, blushing dully.

'You'll have to.'

Tears ran down her cheeks. Perhaps they would relieve the pressure on her bladder.

'So this kid, he joins up and he looks a real star in his uniform and he thinks his mother would be as proud as punch if she could see him and he sets out to look for her. He's a bright kid and he finds out all the places to go: Somerset House and the farm in Cumberland – they're all dead, but there's always someone that can tell you. Local paper still had a photograph, from when she won the Sports. She was good at sports. Like me.'

The hand that wasn't holding the knife disappeared into an inside pocket of his anorak. He took out a photograph, made them pass it from one to the other. It showed Corky, in the voluminous singlet and shorts of the day, clutching a silver cup upon which was probably inscribed (although the photograph was too small and blurred for this to be deciphered): 'Awarded to the best fat goose in the show'. It was a grainy picture, but what was clearly apparent was the young girl's resemblance to the man who took back the photograph and replaced it in his pocket and said, 'When the old man died, she joined the army. Funny, isn't it, these coincidences – her and him doing all the same things?'

Corky's hands jerked away from her eyes for a second and then she re-covered them as though it might be possible to blot out what was happening.

'It took ages, tracing her. She was discharged from the army not long before the kid was born. Got herself into trouble. No pill in those days, was there? Moved round then, kept moving round: hotels, restaurants. Couldn't keep still. Always had to be on the move.'

Running, faster and faster. But she couldn't run fast enough.

'Found her eventually. Ten years ago. He was sixteen. She was staying with her friend Phyllis in Bournemouth. Worked together then at the Royal Albion. Not a bad woman, Phyllis. But in the dark, of course. "Corky hasn't got a son," she said. "Corky's never been married." *She* came back late – big do on at the hotel. It was dark and it was bitter cold and pouring with rain. "It's Tommy," he said, "Tommy McCorquodale" – he hadn't changed it officially then. He thought she'd be pleased when she saw what he'd made of himself. "A natural leader" the CO had put. Know what she did?'

The knife touched Gwen's skin. She yelped.

'Denied all knowledge, that's what she did. Right in front of Phyllis. She said, "Go away. Get the hell out of it, whoever you are." Said she'd call the police. Said she had no knowledge or cognisance of him. Even though he showed her the papers. She said, "Piss off out of it." So, in the end, he asked her if she'd just tell him who his father was – not Dad, his real father. Everybody has a right to know that, haven't they? She pretended she didn't know what he was talking about.'

'Please,' Gwen said faintly. 'Please.'

'Shut up,' he said. 'When I'm talking. She moved then. Found her in Whitley Bay. And then she went to Hunstanton. And Abergele. Lost her after that.'

Corky, running and running but not so fast that she could hope to escape.

'It was only a matter of time though, wasn't it? He told her he'd never leave it until she told him, and he never will. Right, you!' he said, turning towards Gwen. 'You want the bog? Come on then. Look sharp.'

Gwen rose, like a cobra from the depths of its basket towards the sound of the flute. Her eyes never left his face. But it was too late. The Sanderson 'Gold Lily' cushion cover was soaked; urine dripped down her leg.

Christina's bladder was almost as full as Gwen's had obviously been. She prayed for control. She also prayed, 'Somebody come, please, please, somebody come,' knowing full well that there was nobody to come until Mrs Crowther arrived to clean the house on Monday morning.

Her prayers were rarely answered, at least not with such unnerving alacrity; she jumped a foot when the phone rang.

It rang twelve times before it stopped. There was a pause of a few moments and then it rang again.

It is difficult to resist answering a ringing telephone. All three of them had automatically made to get up before he motioned to them to remain where they were. 'Leave it,' he said. 'It'll stop.'

It did of course. This time after ten rings. When it started again, five minutes later, he got up and lifted it off the hook. A voice issued from the receiver for a little while afterwards – too indistinct to be identified – and then ceased.

Corky was making a strange whistling noise through her nose, like an engine being required to supply more power than it was capable of converting. 'Stop that!' he said. 'Stop it. Just tell me what I want to know. It isn't *you* I want any more. I have no mother. I've wiped her out. She doesn't exist. She's been rubbed out. Look!'

From the same anorak pocket that contained the photograph, he produced a piece of paper. 'Look!' he said again and thrust it at Christina. It was a shortened birth certificate, the sort you're provided with if you lose the original and apply for a replacement.

'She's been rubbed out all right, hasn't she?'

But there was no provision to do this as his was the only name mentioned on the document.

Christina handed it back to him and looked up, past the knife and into the authentic face of madness.

'Tell me.'

Corky licked her lips. She said, hoarsely, 'I can't tell you.'

'Oh yes you can.'

'I don't know.'

'How can you not know? Tell me, tell me. Or she gets ripped.'

He stood up, lifting Gwen with him, pulling her head back, placing the knife at her throat. Gwen screamed: 'She doesn't know. She doesn't know.'

Slowly the knife was moved from that lethal position. Gwen's scream died on the air. She raised a hand to her neck as though to check that her head was still attached.

'What do you mean,' he said, 'she doesn't know?'

'She was raped,' Gwen said, babbling the words as though she had only a limited amount of time to impart the information. 'She was raped in a train on her way back from leave. She was raped by a man who got into the carriage. Somewhere between Northallerton and Richmond. She never told me she got pregnant though,' Gwen said. 'She never told me that.'

He looked from her to Corky and back again. 'Is that right?' he said.

'Is it right?'

They said that raped women rarely conceive. These days, Christina thought, with the tiny portion of her brain that was still working normally, these days you'd be offered an abortion.

'Yes, it's right.'

Corky's eyes were closed. She said, 'Go away, will you? Go away and leave us alone.'

He released Gwen and stepped forward, towards Corky. She cringed. So did Christina, at a loss to predict how this information would affect him, which way the pendulum was likely to swing.

From the look on his face it seemed that he too was unsure as to how he should react. The look on his face reminded Christina of the look on Adam's face when he'd cowered in the corner of his bedroom, realising that all was discovered: infinitely pathetic, rather than totally deranged. For a moment, her heart went out to him and she ceased to be afraid. She said, 'Murray, let's talk. Let's discuss it. Let's put that thing down and have a cigarette and discuss it . . .'

She made a gesture towards him, saw that, mingled with the sweat beads, there were tears on his face. She kept her hand extended. Slowly, he came towards her.

Then they heard a car in the square. They heard it slowing to a halt. They heard a door open and close, feet on the pavement, running up the steps, and then the ringing of the doorbell: once, twice, a third time.

Not *now*, Christina thought, not *now*. And then, as the footsteps retreated, wondered why she'd thought that.

But the sound that they had expected: that of a car starting, did not occur. There was an inexplicable hiatus and then it must have dawned on all four of them simultaneously: you wouldn't hear footsteps if someone was walking round to the back door because the path led around the other side of the house.

Murray Pearl seemed incapable of movement. Only when they heard the door opening (Corky had been out to the bin earlier and, as usual, had failed to drop the latch. 'You're just asking for burglars,' Gwen always said) and the footsteps distinct on the tiled kitchen floor, did he turn from them and move towards the door. It opened and Max walked in.

At first he didn't seem to notice the knife. He glared at Corky, he glared at Gwen, he glared most of all at Christina. 'What the hell's going on?' he said. 'I've tried to ring you about a dozen times and then somebody takes the phone off the hook and I can hear somebody else screeching in the background and now you won't open the door even though I can see your shadows through the curtains. Just what the hell is going on?'

When they didn't answer him he looked for explanation to the other occupant of the room. Then he noticed the knife and instead of fainting or running or holding up his hands, he said, as testily as if he'd just caught David or Adam out in some piece of mischief, 'Oh, for God's sake, what are you playing at?'

The colour had gone from Murray Pearl's face. 'Go away,' he said, quietly, feebly. 'Go away.'

He brandished the knife. Gwen screamed. And then, at last, it must have dawned on Max that some sort of drastic action was required. He stepped forward. And as he did so, Murray Pearl seemed to shrink in size, dwindle. 'Get away,' he said, and Max said, 'Oh stop being so bloody silly,' and took hold of him and for a second or two grappled with him and then they both fell to their knees and the knife was on the floor and Murray Pearl scrambled to his feet and ran out of the door and out of the house.

Max remained where he was, staring fascinatedly at the carpet upon which a dark red stain of blood was beginning to spread.

They kept Max in hospital not because of his wounds, which were fairly superficial, but because of his ulcer. The shock to his system had caused slight internal bleeding and they wanted to keep him under observation.

A policeman came to take a statement from him, but it appeared to be a formality. He was just leaving Max's bedside when Adam and David came in. Adam went white and turned on his heel. David gripped his elbow, anchoring him to the spot. 'No need to look down in the mouth, son,' the policeman had said. 'Your dad's going to be all right.'

When Christina went in to visit him they'd pushed those occupants of Men's Medical who weren't only just beginning to recover from operations or just about to die as a result of them, through to the Day Room, where, together with various nursing staff and some dressing-gown-clad Fibroids and Hysterectomies from Gynae, which was just along the corridor, they were obliged to watch the television on which a royal personage and his fiancée were answering a selection of deferential or impertinent questions put to them by members of the press.

Max looked very cross. Although he approved of the monarchy, he deplored conspicuous consumption and the drain on the public purse every time one of them decided that his kite-flying days were over.

'For God's sake, push me back to bed,' he demanded of her.

Apart from the odd groan issuing from behind the screens that enclosed the bed in the corner, it was quiet in the ward. Sun streamed through the windows – it was the first proper spring day they'd had.

'How's your shoulder?' she asked.

'Fine. It's my knee that's sore.'

He'd been stabbed in the shoulder: the knife had bounced off the bone, and at the back of his knee (more or less in the same place that Murray Pearl had shot himself some four years earlier in order to escape what might have been a lethal wound from an Argentine weapon. The natural leader, coping with mock hostilities in Catterick Camp or on Salisbury Plain, had turned into a gibbering wreck when obliged to participate in the real thing).

'Everyone's very impressed,' she said. 'It seems you're quite the hero.'

'I was annoyed,' he said, as if that explained everything. 'I thought it was one of Gwen's cronies acting the fool.'

'What did you want?'

She had asked him this when they were waiting for the ambulance to arrive. And the police.

Blood had saturated Max's trouser leg and Gwen's shag pile. Clutching his shoulder and groaning, he'd said, 'Do we have to have the police?' He was obviously incapable of distinguishing the police who would come to his assistance and apprehend his assailant from the police who might identify a dustbin bag full of stolen property and charge him with conspiracy.

'Don't be ridiculous,' Gwen had said. It was the second thing she'd done. The first thing she'd done was to go upstairs and change her knickers.

'What did you want?' Christina had asked while they waited. She didn't know what else to do or say; she felt shy of him. He'd allowed her to cut open his trouser leg and bind him up and brush the hair away from his forehead, but when she'd picked up one of his hands and started to chafe it between her own (an action she'd seen performed by heroines for their wounded-hero lovers in films) he'd snatched it away.

'Why did you come?' she'd asked.

'Well it wasn't for the pleasure of seeing you, I can tell you that for nothing,' he'd replied.

Afterwards, of course, she'd found out the reason: his sales manager, due to travel to the annual trade fair in London, had been struck down with flu, which meant that Max would be obliged to go in his place. He would be away for three or four days and though, in normal circumstances, he wouldn't have felt any need whatsoever to inform her of his movements, now there was the small matter of a letter containing a spurious reason for

Adam's absence from school which had been dispatched to the headmaster and which might elicit a reply. It would be up to her to allay any suspicions, to supply any embellishments, while Max was away.

A renewed burst of groaning was to be heard from behind the screens that surrounded the end bed. 'A goner,' Max whispered, but she didn't need to be told; the end bed was where they put you when your next destination was likely to be the morgue. She remembered her mother travelling from bed to bed, moving nearer and nearer to the door. She remembered Max walking beside her down the corridors.

Max wouldn't be doing any travelling. They would discharge him in a day or two. 'I'll be glad to get out,' he said, pouring himself a glass of Lucozade. 'I'm bored stiff.'

He'd re-read *The Trumpet-Major* and *Far from the Madding Crowd* and filled in all the crosswords and listened to the radio until he couldn't tolerate it any longer. She put him a last clean pair of pyjamas in his locker. When he'd first noticed her collecting clothes for washing he'd asked anxiously whether she'd moved back to Winchester Road.

'No. I'm popping in, but Mrs Monks seems to be looking after everything – including the boys – perfectly well.'

His brow had cleared, and she knew that, more than anything, he wanted to return to the house and find it as he'd left it: neat and orderly, with his spectacles keeping his place in *The Mayor of Casterbridge* and the smell of one of Mrs Monks' safely-bland casseroles wafting in from the kitchen.

'I thought we might go away,' he said. 'For Easter. I'd originally intended to take Adam. Walking. Obviously I can't do that now. But we could have a few days sightseeing instead. Scotland, I thought. David can share the driving.'

It sounded an inviting prospect. But she was not invited. If she were to be present, then the atmosphere would alter: small irritations would assume the dimensions of major crises; he would criticise one or other of the boys, she would leap to their defence; she would look at the map and make a suggestion and he would pooh-pooh it; at night, he'd want sex and she wouldn't, or vice-versa.

Without her, harmony would be far more likely to prevail. They would have a pleasant holiday, and then he'd return to his well-appointed, efficiently-run home. He'd come back from work and eat the meals that Mrs Monks prepared for him, before settling in his armchair to read his book or listen to his music, a glass of wine at his side. Every so often he'd look around him and smile with satisfaction at everything just so: no spills, no crumbs, no clutter.

No Christina.

At heart he was a solitary; she understood that now. His sex-drive had led him towards women and – eventually – one woman, whose constant proximity could guarantee him regular release; his instinct to reproduce himself had brought forth two sons, and that he had made even a reasonably successful stab at being a husband and father was no small achievement, considering that he had never been taught to share, to be tolerant, to regard others as having equal rights and deserving of equal respect.

'And how's life in Lansdowne Gardens? Returned to normal, has it? Though I don't see how it can.'

Neither did Christina. Knives, woundings, revelations – surely it would take years for these events to fade from the memory, surely relationships would be obliged to undergo radical redefinition?

Or cease to be?

They'd called the police and the ambulance and Christina had gone with Max to hospital and when she came back they told her that Murray Pearl's body had been found on the railway line, on that stretch of it that was intersected by unmanned crossings. He had been killed by the last train, the 11.47 to Crewe. No one could say whether this had been a deliberate act or an accident. The state of his mind at the time of his death was not ascertainable – and, anyway, by all accounts he was well and truly out of it.

The policeman told them that there'd be an inquest. Mrs Swallow would once again wear black and give her evidence in a high, clear, carrying voice; Miss McCorquodale would never once raise her eyes from the floor and have to be requested, time without number by the coroner, to raise her voice to a level that was audible to the court.

Meanwhile there was a doctor, and some pills to be swallowed which rendered them insensible until the middle of the following day. So it wasn't until then that Corky had zipped her anorak and picked up her suitcases from where they had stood in the hall since she'd packed them subsequent to the previous evening's row.

'Where do you think you're going?' Gwen had asked.

She wore no make-up except what remained from yesterday, and her hair was scraped back from her face behind an Alice band. She looked plain and pasty; Stephen Millward wouldn't have recognised her.

'Got to go,' Corky said, walking to the door. She hadn't even combed *her* hair; it stood up on end.

'Where? *Where* are you going?'

'I don't know,' Corky said. She reached the hallstand and put down her cases and took her key-ring from her pocket and began to detach the house keys from it. All her movements were very deliberate and very slow, as though the effect of the sleeping pill hadn't yet worn off.

'Why? *Why* are you going?' asked Gwen.

'Got to go,' Corky repeated.

She put down the keys and picked up the cases and carted them to the door.

'You can't just go,' Gwen said. 'You can't just walk out. What about the party we've got booked for tomorrow night?'

'You'll manage.'

She put down a case and reached out a hand towards the latch.

'*How* will we manage? You were going to do that soufflé . . . You can't just walk out and leave everything. We've got a partnership . . .'

'It's yours,' Corky said. 'All of it.'

She turned the latch and began to open the door. Gwen came running along the hall, tripping in her high-heeled mules. Christina, watching from the sitting-room, noticed for the first time the little signs of ageing that were normally so cleverly concealed: double chin, sagging breasts, a cluster of blue veins tending towards varicosity just below the knee.

'You *can't* go,' Gwen said.

'I can't stay.'

'But what about me? What am I going to do?'

'Ring your boyfriend, get him to come round. He'll be only too pleased. You'll be all right.'

She held the door open with one foot while she manoeuvred her cases into the porch.

Gwen started to cry. She said, 'I can't be on my own. I can't.'

'I told you: ring Millward. He'll look after you.'

'I don't want him to look after me. I want you.'

Tears and dilute mascara poured down her face. Gwen never cried – except for a dead cat; it had never been known. 'Don't leave me, Corky,' she said. 'Please don't leave me.'

And then the doorbell rang and all three of them froze, but it was only the taxi come to take Christina to the hospital. When she got back, the suitcases were still in the porch but their owner was in the sitting-room. Gwen was curled up in one corner of the sofa; Corky was stroking her hair. 'Never mind, lass,' Christina heard her say, as she passed the door. 'You'll be all right now.'

And then, astonishingly, things did return to normal. Or very nearly. Gwen's first priority appeared to be the redecoration of the sitting-room: from bled-into shag pile carpet to urine-drenched sofa cushion. When Christina came back from her next hospital visit, Jason-the-interior-designer was already installed. He and Gwen had their heads bent over paint cards and fabric samples and Gwen was saying, 'I've always felt that that very subtle shade of sea-green – oh no, not *that* one, that's the colour of fuller figure frocks in catalogues – was very much me . . .'

In the kitchen, Corky, wearing Gwen's spectacles, was knitting some sort of garment that involved the casting-on of a great many stitches. Her lips moved as she recited the pattern to herself.

'Mr Stewart phoned,' Christina said, cautious as to how the message might best be worded. 'He said that now the body has been released for burial, he'll go ahead with the funeral arrangements.'

It was that same Mr Stewart, the social worker, under whose wing Kenneth Little had so uneasily resided. He'd called at the house the day after the body had been found on the railway line.

'You, as the next of kin, will be entitled to whatever the residue of the estate may be after the deduction of funeral expenses,' he'd told Corky. Corky, without raising her eyes, had said, 'Give it to the Widows and Orphans.' Later that day she'd started knitting.

'It's a dreadful thing,' Mr Stewart had said when Christina was showing him out. He looked very down in the mouth.

Probably losing two clients in the space of three months wouldn't look too good on his record.

And normality continued to prevail: Jason discussing paint colours and curtain fabric, Corky taking her car in for its MOT and playing hell when they failed it, she and Gwen overseeing the final touches to the rebuilt Klosters.

In the mornings strong tea was brewed as before, the disc-jockeys of Radio Whatever were subjected to vilification, as were Leon Brittan and Derek Hatton and any other prominent political figures who happened to feature in that day's *Sun*. 'Shut your row,' Corky would say, drinking from her George VI Coronation mug, when the voice on the radio introduced a particularly cacophonous record; or, upon reading an account of the Council's continued refusal to fall into line with government policy: 'Why don't they rechristen this city "Moscow" and have done with it?' or, gazing speculatively at a picture of Princess Diana: 'D'you think she ever gets a square meal?'

The only difference was that knitting had, apparently, taken the place of running.

Christina consulted Gwen, saying, 'Don't you think it's a bit odd, the way she's carrying on as if nothing untoward had happened? Shouldn't she – well – be externalising it a bit more?' Gwen had frowned fiercely, not really understanding the principles of abreaction, but suspecting it belonged to the school of psychological clap-trap.

'Why? What difference would it make? She's got to go on living her life, hasn't she?'

'But she must be feeling terrible. After all, he was her son. She *was* responsible . . .'

'Why?' Gwen said again. 'She didn't ask to be raped, did she? And I expect, when she put the boy into the orphanage, she thought that'd be the end of it. And it wasn't her fault that he turned out to be wrong in the head. I should think, uppermost in her mind, is relief that it's all over.'

Christina told Max all this as she sat at his bedside in the hospital. It was uncanny, *eerie*, she said, the way they were carrying on as though nothing had happened. Max said that perhaps that theory about unburdening yourself in order to come to terms with an unpleasant experience was unsound; perhaps if you kept your mouth shut about it and made a determined effort to put it out of your mind you'd forget it a damn sight quicker.

'Perhaps you're right,' she said. 'Anyway, it's really none of my concern. I'm moving out on Saturday.'

'Oh? Where to?'

'Radclyffe Street.'

He raised his eyebrows. 'Bit rough round there, isn't it?'

'I suppose you might say that.'

She wasn't terribly concerned about it. A respectable neighbourhood was no guarantee of one's safety. She'd been menaced by terrors in Swinburne Court and held at knife-point in Lansdowne Gardens: dead babies could be found inside owner-occupied houses with Philippine mahogany front doors, fried dwarfs among the debris of up-market wine bars.

'It's only temporary anyway. Until the divorce comes through.'

She had, at last, seen a solicitor who had informed her of her entitlements. 'We don't talk in terms of "fault" any more,' he had said. 'You are entitled to half of everything that has been accumulated during the time of the marriage. We're not talking about gold-digging here, Mrs Conway. We're talking about your due.'

She had to learn to stop feeling guilty, or grateful. She had to learn to stop devaluing herself. After all, for twenty years, she had kept his house and brought up his sons – however unsatisfactorily. With Max's money, she would look for another place, a better place. Perhaps a flat in the nice new development at Badger's Green . . .

Max looked down, plucked at a loose thread on his pyjama trousers, and then looked up at her and for a long moment they exchanged a glance, seeking to recognise in each other's face the young man and the girl who had said, 'always' and 'forever'. But they had vanished, beyond recall.

'There won't be any fuss about custody or access . . . They'll consult Adam anyway. And I shan't make any objection . . .'

He appeared to be engrossed in the pattern of his dressing gown. She said, 'There wouldn't be any point, would there? It's what's for the best now – for him, not us.'

Best of a bad job. All you could do.

*

336

Her project was now nearing completion. All the questions had been asked, all the replies categorised, translated into symbolic form and subjected to analysis. Now she knew, officially, that people's attitudes towards each other vary just as widely when they are involved in non-profit-making transactions as they do in any other circumstance.

It was confirmation of what she'd suspected all along, although she also suspected that there might not actually be any such thing as a non-profit-making transaction; that no one did anything unless there was the hope of some sort of personal bonus to be derived. Even mother-love, supposedly purely altruistic, was never totally free from self-interest. Even mother-love untainted by a child's not being wanted, or being wanted too much, or being nothing but a reminder of a violation that, for your sanity's sake, you needed to forget.

She looked at her sons and she wanted them to be happy, but on her terms. She had borne them and weaned them and clothed them in Cherub vests. She had spooned Virol down their throats and read stories to them and made shapes with Plasticine and sewn shepherds' robes for nativity plays and fed neglected pets and swallowed back all the questions that could have been construed as inquisitorial.

And, in return, she had expected them to demonstrate their gratitude by advertising themselves as products of her supremely successful nurturing.

Nothing aberrant about that though, was there? Dr and Mrs Weatherby must surely have yearned for Jennifer in a frilled skirt rather than Jinx with spider's web tattoos on the backs of her hands.

Though, at least, Jinx was now growing out her Mohican. There was a fine blonde fuzz to be seen on her skull when she stood with her back to the light. She was debating whether to kick the whole academic thing into touch and join the Peace Convoy or the Greenham Women, or to take up the offer of a place at Chicago University. America sucked, of course, but sociologically . . .

'Where's the problem?'

'Principles, innit?' Jinx said. The hair would probably regrow as curly as it had done originally when Dr and Mrs Weatherby had entered their daughter for the Miss Pears competition.

Somehow you never connected Nihilism with principles. 'I know what I'd do,' Christina said.

'Go?'

'Like a shot.'

But then her circumstances were somewhat different. By the end of the academic year she'd be out of a job, the Standish Trust, unimpressed even by Murray Pearl's efficiency, having decided to withdraw its funding.

So the organisation was to be dismantled. Robin and Joyce, Norman and John, Jim and Klaus and the twins would have to find a different cause to espouse, another club to join; Hilary Roberts would need to bring her research to its conclusion.

And Christina – unless her application to join a research team at Manchester University, and at the same time to register for a higher degree, was successful – would be signing on.

She discussed it with David after they'd finished their flat-warming meal. She said, 'I've got an interview, but the competition is bound to be stiff – and I've no one to put a word in for me this time.'

'You can only give it your best shot.'

He wrung out the dishcloth with a flourish and hung it over the taps and then started to sneeze. He was allergic to house plants (they'd never been able to have any in Winchester Road) and she'd placed a Bleeding Heart that she'd brought from the dismantled System office on the windowsill above the sink. It was her first independently-acquired possession, a fact – despite the plant's unfortunate colloquial appellation – of some significance.

'Oi,' David said, looking around the edge of the kitchen door and into the living-room, where Adam appeared to be utterly transfixed by some sort of costume drama on the television, which featured Mario Lanza surrounded by a lot of powdered cleavage, all filmed in the fiercest sort of technicolour. 'Oi,' David said, 'get off your bum and come and put these pots away.'

'It's all right,' she said, starting to stack the dishes herself.

'It's not all right,' David said sternly, as Adam came ambling reluctantly towards his task. The duties entailed *in loco parentis* had been taken very seriously indeed and he wasn't having all his good work spoiled by her lack of moral fibre.

They were her first guests, the first people to sit upon her

Habitat unbleached-cotton-covered sofa and eat off her MFI pine dining table with an assortment of supermarket-bought cutlery.

And it was a scratch meal that she had cobbled together: smoked meats and pickles, spiced sausages, ripe cheeses and hot pitta bread – all the sorts of food that Max detested, that had been banished from his table in favour of steamed cod and semolina pudding.

'I'll go out and get us a few cans,' David announced, and then came back, poked his head round the door and said, 'Mum, can you lend me some money?'

Equipped with her purse, he'd gone to the off-licence, leaving her to the moment she'd looked forward to with apprehension ever since he'd returned to his wounded-hero-father's hospital bedside: being alone with Adam.

'How was Scotland?' she asked.

He managed to nod his head and shrug his shoulders simultaneously. It had been – OK, he intimated, it had been – all right.

'We never talked,' she said, 'what with the drama, about – you know . . .'

'I've talked,' David had said, with the confidence born of *naïveté*. 'Told him to behave himself. He'll be all right. But he's dead set on leaving school. Might be a good idea, of course, get him away from that bunch of idiots . . .'

She had closed her eyes, obliterating the glowing future that she had always envisaged for him, towards which end all the Virol and Cherub vests and visits to the orthodontist had been directed.

She had closed her ears, too, to the rest of the arguments that David had put forward to support his case: Adam was only young, education could be re-entered, exams re-sat; she knew how irrevocable certain steps taken at certain times could be.

This she tried to convey to Adam while David was out. He was fixing a plug on to the end of the table lamp cord for her. He appeared to be absolutely engrossed in the activity. 'I had to give up my education,' she said. 'I always regretted it and it took me years and enormous effort to get back to where I was.'

He coaxed the live wire through the copper terminal.

'So you see . . .' she continued.

'But you're not me,' he said. 'Are you?'

It was probably the hardest of all the parental lessons to learn:

the acceptance that your child is an individual rather than simply an extension of yourself.

'And the other business?' she said hesitantly. If Adam was to be recognised as an individual and his right to autonomy respected, must that recognition and respect embrace his criminal habits?

Max believed in moral absolutes, but she saw the world now as offering no certainties. Right, wrong, courage, integrity: for Adam's generation, brought up to judge themselves and others in a climate of ever-changing standards, these were probably just words on paper. She hoped, she prayed, that he was still young enough for example to prevail. She remembered the look on his face when he came to his father's hospital bedside. Max was no hero, but Adam wasn't to know that.

He put down the screwdriver, plugged the lamp into the socket and switched it on. His face was haloed by the sudden illumination. For an instant, he looked exactly like the young Adam who had once allowed his hand to rest so trustingly in hers and she stopped wondering about what had happened and why it had happened and the degree of her culpability. He was her son and she loved him. She put her arms round him and she said, 'I'm sorry.'

'So'm I.'

For a moment he allowed himself to be embraced. For a moment she felt faint traces of a reciprocal affection. Then they heard David clanking beer cans at the door and he sprang away from her as if he had been an illicit lover caught *in flagrante*.

'So'm I.' And a hug. It wasn't much, but it was more than she had expected, and perhaps more than she deserved.

✑ 6 ✑

Late in April she saw Livingstone through the window of an Indian restaurant. It was a basement restaurant. She'd been walking along, thinking about nothing very much in particular and she'd happened to glance idly downwards.

He was drinking lager and eating what looked like Chicken Biriani. He appeared to be engaged in earnest conversation with his companion: a pretty, blonde-haired woman who might have been Louise but, on the other hand, might not. At the critical moment: that instant before she looked away and walked on, he looked up and their glances met and she saw him say something to the woman and then he got to his feet and came outside and up the steps to where she was standing.

'I've been trying to get in touch with you,' he said. He said it accusingly, as though she'd deliberately been avoiding contact. 'I rang Swinburne Court. Some woman said you'd left a forwarding address but she'd lost it. Then I rang the Poly. I spoke to Whatshername – Hilary Roberts. She gave me an address in Lansdowne Gardens and a number, but when I rang there I got no reply at all. I rang several times.'

'When did you get back?'

'A month ago.'

A month ago Corky and Gwen had left for a recuperative week in Torquay.

He kept glancing back over his shoulder into the restaurant where the woman: Louise, or not Louise, having finished her meal, was now showing signs of impatience.

'Look, I've got to go back. Can I see you? What *is* your address?'

He looked completely, absolutely, as he had looked when last she saw him. He always would. Nothing would ever touch him enough to change him.

'We could meet for a coffee perhaps,' she said. She was in a hurry too, to get to the library before it closed; she had some references to check before she submitted her final report to Dr H E Roberts – or Dr H E Robber, as she had been christened in Scrabble tiles upon her desk, when Christina last went into the Department: Jinx's ultimate act of mischief before she took wing for Chicago.

'What about Wednesday?' Livingstone said, from halfway down the steps.

'No, I can't manage Wednesday. Adam comes round on Wednesdays. Tuesday afternoon? Four o'clock in the Adelphi?'

He nodded rapidly, not wishing to prolong the conversation. Time was of the essence. Besides, he'd probably realised the take it or leave it nature of the offer.

'So what's been happening?'

He waved the waiter away and began to pour her coffee. Prior to that he had helped her off with her coat and spread it carefully over the back of her chair. An ex-lover must be treated gently, like an invalid. There would always be a sympathetic hand at her elbow, an arm about her shoulders, a shared glance, brimming with fond recollection, across the room.

He awaited her reply.

What's been happening? I stepped out from under Max's wing and found that you hadn't a wing to offer and then met life head on.

'What's been happening? Well, the job at the Poly's come to an end. I'm getting a divorce. And I've moved into another flat.'

He waited for her to tell him where the flat was. When she didn't oblige, he said, 'You're not frightened any more then – of being on your own?'

She shook her head. Somehow, real life had cured her of her imaginary terrors.

'You *are* on your own?'

He said it in an unconvincingly casual manner, not looking at her.

'I thought you might have gone back to Max.'

'No,' she said. 'I couldn't go back.'

'This job collapsing must have come as a blow. What happened, did the funding dry up?'

She nodded and he said, 'What will you do?'

'Something will turn up.'

She wasn't unduly concerned. One consequence of being touched by tragedy was that you no longer tended to worry so much about problems that weren't life and death.

'It's nice here, isn't it?' she said. She remembered drinking coffee here in the same spot, in virtually the same seat, with Stephen Millward. Poor Stephen Millward, twice-unlucky in his wife-hunt through Lansdowne Gardens.

'It's all right.'

But he was not at ease, never could be when engaged in illicit rendezvous in so public a place. Obviously his companion in the Indian restaurant had been Louise; she should have remembered his pusillanimity – caution, she'd called it, six months ago.

He smiled at her, that same dream-haunting smile that used to cause her to wake up crying. He said, 'You look lovely.'

She could see her reflection in a distant mirror and saw that, distantly, she did look rather nice. Close up, as well. She'd used some of her maintenance to buy new clothes. She'd bought a vividly-patterned dress and a red jacket. 'Bright colours suit you,' the shop assistant had said encouragingly. No doubt, if she wore them long enough, she'd get used to them.

She knew, by the mistiness of his eye and the slightly goofy expression on his face, that he was going to say: 'I've missed you terribly.' It was what he had said so often before: whether they'd been separated for the weekend or by two months' holiday in Switzerland. So, to forestall him, she said quickly, 'So what about you? How did you get on in America? Did you get much work done? Did Louise clinch the deal?'

Yes, and yes again. But he didn't particularly want to talk about those things. He wanted to say, 'You realise why I didn't get in touch?' and reach for her hand.

'No. Why?' she said. She allowed her hand to be held, discreetly, under cover of the tablecloth, was aware of their sexual chemistry beginning to reassert itself.

Sexual chemistry seemed to be like allergic reactions: beyond one's voluntary control: you didn't choose to sneeze your head off if you came into contact with a house plant any more than you 'chose' to be attracted to one man rather than another.

Well, you might have to adapt your lifestyle because of your allergy, but you'd be an idiot if you allowed it to dominate your every action. She was thinking this as he told her that the reason he hadn't contacted her all the time he'd been away was that a state of total incommunicado was essential if he was to sort out his feelings, come to a decision concerning the possibility of their life together.

'And did you reach a decision?' she said, freeing her hand from his in order to scratch her nose.

'I want to give it a try,' he said. His eyes sought hers but she was concentrating on rubbing her nose which itched furiously; they said it was a sign of an impending quarrel. She didn't want to quarrel with him.

'What do you say?'

'What exactly do you mean?'

'I mean we'll do what you wanted. Move in together, see how it goes. You *did* want that, didn't you? I wasn't just an excuse to leave Max, was I?'

Oh, she'd wanted it, she'd wanted it more than anything. Last October.

She stopped fiddling with her nose and looked at him. He was a lovely looking man. He hadn't changed at all. She had though.

She said, 'You mean, you'd leave Louise?'

'We'd have a sort of trial separation, yes.'

She wasn't lonely at present; she was too busy at present to be lonely: finishing her project, house-hunting – both here and further afield, depending on whether she got the Manchester job. In the event that she'd need to commute, she'd booked herself a course of driving lessons: Gwen could drive (Gwen who'd peed herself with fright and clung to Corky, crying that she couldn't be alone), Hilary Roberts could drive (she who'd fled from the sight of a dead baby: locking herself into her car and curling herself into a foetal position and bleating for the browbeaten Gavin); even Corky could drive.

She'd had the first lesson at the weekend; she wasn't nearly as bad as she thought she'd be.

Again he took her hand. 'You don't hate me?' he said.

She didn't hate him. She loved him. And she would continue to do so, as long as they remained in contact. And though she hadn't time to be lonely now, the time would come when she would be lonely. Lonely and loving him. Perhaps, if she had him to herself, she could make him love her as much, make him as dependent upon her as he obviously was upon Louise.

'I never thought I'd miss you as much as I did,' he was saying.

He was saying everything she'd wanted him to say. In October.

'What do you say?'

Loving and lonely. But accepting his proposition, as it stood, would mean losing something that had been so painfully achieved since he'd left her. Something. She couldn't even put a name to it.

'I think it's got to be something you do off your own bat,' she said. She said, 'If you want to leave, leave, and we can take it from there. Do you understand what I mean?'

She had not got things clear in her own mind yet: not worked out either what she wanted or what she didn't want. But one thing she was certain of: for the first time in her life she felt that she had freedom of choice and she knew what a privilege that was, and how it must not be abused by reason of fear or timidity or the need to have her identity confirmed by seeing her reflection in somebody else's eyes.

She looked at her watch and got to her feet. 'Alan,' she said (for how could she address him any longer by that entirely inappropriate surname? Once, she'd thought of him as an explorer, intrepid; now she realised that he would never be without a ball of string, having first made sure that Louise was holding it firmly at the other end – or perhaps, more appropriately in Louise's case, it was a ball of wool), 'Alan,' she said, 'I've got to go now. A colleague of mine is going to the States and she's having a farewell party in the Department. I promised I'd look in.'

He said, 'But how do I get in touch with you?'

'I have no phone at present,' she said. 'Let me ring you.'

She watched the London Marathon with Corky on the television set in Gwen's sitting-room. Corky watched it with the avidity of a penniless child gazing through a sweetshop window. Even when the commentator announced that they were now leaving the event for the News or *Farming Today* or whatever, her eyes never left the screen. She wouldn't even break for lunch; she ate a symbolic Mars Bar instead.

Down they came, from the Red Start and the Blue, from

Greenwich and Blackheath: the athletes, tightly-muscled and trim, their training carefully timed so that they were due to peak, the professionals, stern-faced, knowing exactly how the race must be run, knowing how to pace themselves, to make the tactical move at the critical moment – and the others: the cripples and the clowns, the sad and the slow, the game-spirited hopeless cases who knew they must rely upon the goodwill of others and had come to accept this necessity without resentment.

Down they came: the wheelchairs and the hundred-pound training shoes, the waiters tossing pancakes as they ran, the runners dressed as bears, ringmasters, gorillas, those draped in Union Jacks, puffing cigars, juggling, rattling their collecting boxes on behalf of others whose disabilities prevented them from even reaching the starting-post.

Down they came, from Rotherhithe, along Jamaica Road, past the Tooley Street doss-house, and over Tower Bridge: the young, the fit, the old, the dependent and the determined.

Gwen, passing through, enquired frostily how long the wretched thing actually went on for. But she was going out anyway, driving to the coast with Stephen Millward. There, in some four-star lounge, they would take tea and she would inform him that, having considered all the relevant factors, she had decided not to marry him. She would tell him very nicely, because although, on balance, the enhanced social status of parading a husband was not sufficient to outweigh the disadvantage of having her freedom curtailed, he was a pleasant companion, a satisfactory sexual partner and, most important of all, a jolly good accountant.

'Now you won't forget to take Boris outside as soon as he wakes up?' she said. 'We must get him into a routine.'

At the moment he was curled up on Corky's lap. Her veined hand moved rhythmically, stroking the tabby fur, scratching between the tiny pointed ears. 'I don't care for cats,' Corky had said. Though it was at her suggestion, apparently, that Boysie's successor had been acquired. *Not* a replacement – Gwen had been firm on that point – Boysie was irreplaceable.

They had visited Klaus's pet shop, intending to buy something highly-bred, with a pedigree and an official title as long as your arm. A Shaded-Cameo Persian, he had suggested, a Chocolate-point Siamese. He had spent ages, showing them pictures,

recommending top-class breeders, attempting to match requirements to environment. And then Gwen had spotted a hand-
written notice in his window that said: 'To good home: tabby
kitten (spaded) – owner forced to part.' And they had left Klaus
describing the relative merits of American Wirehairs and Russian
Blues in his ponderous Teutonic way, and driven to the council
estate where neighbours had spray-painted 'Murderers' across
the Donaldsons' Philippine mahogany front door.

In a nearby avenue the owner of the 'spaded' kitten: an old
lady who was moving into a council home, explained tearfully
that only those who would love and cherish little Fluffy could be
considered for ownership; she would rather have him put down,
as his mother – who would never have taken to a new home –
had been put down, than have him go just anywhere.

Fluffy was asleep on a cushion. He had opened one eye,
exposed his cat tonsils and little white needle-teeth in a great
pink yawn and winked, very deliberately, at Gwen.

So, rechristened Boris (he had a square face and, in repose, a
rather grim expression reminiscent of members of the Politburo
watching a May Day parade), he had come to Lansdowne
Gardens and repaid charity by piddling not only on the kitchen
floor but also in the middle of the sea-green carpet and Gwen's
Mary Quant duvet cover. Gwen hadn't complained. Love had
made her tolerant.

At half-past two they switched from the Marathon yet again
to show a local arts programme. Somebody had written a book
about urban decay and the contribution made to it by modern
architecture. They had the book's author, a modern architect,
and Alan Livingstone, senior lecturer in Urban Studies at the
University, gathered together for a studio discussion. When
Corky got up to turn the sound down, Christina said, 'No, leave
it. I'd like to listen.'

But for all she actually heard (or took in) of the discussion, the
sound might as well have been turned down. She watched him:
his smile, his gestures, the way he had of uncrossing and re-
crossing his legs when he wanted to emphasise a point, the
involuntary flicking back of the hair from his forehead. She
thought, again, how strange it was that you could be so close to
somebody and yet so incalculably distant.

She thought of the flat she'd viewed at Badger's Green,
thought of him there with her: lying in bed with her, looking

across a dinner table at her, helping her to plant roses. And then she thought: we've been here before: fantasy-land, and it's not where I want to be. Reality can be terrible, but at least it's *real*.

'How did you get on with that interview?' Corky asked, discarding the *Sunday People* and picking up her knitting – it appeared to be the same garment still: a parachute case? A gorilla suit?

'I'm still waiting to hear. It seemed to go all right, but you never know how good the opposition is, do you?'

She didn't know how she'd come across to the interviewing panel; she wasn't experienced enough to tell. But she knew that her project had impressed them. As well it might. It was perhaps a trivial proposition that she had been employed to investigate and its result a foregone conclusion, but she had worked hard on it: her methodology was sound, her presentation immaculate. Nor had she allowed Hilary Roberts' impatience to force her towards corner-cutting or too-hasty assumptions. She'd lost her husband and her lover and, briefly, her son. She'd been on the verge of nervous collapse. She'd been besieged by a madman. A baby had died that she might have saved. She'd been frightened and lonely and alienated. But somehow, despite everything, she'd managed to produce a decent piece of work. And she was proud of it, such as it was, whether it got her a job or it didn't. Something to do with self-respect, with finding a reason for your existence that didn't depend wholly upon your reflection in somebody else's eyes.

The race was reaching its end when Gwen returned. She was humming. Stephen Millward had accepted her decision with a fairly good grace.

'Good God!' she said. 'It's not *still* on, is it?'

Corky was on the edge of her seat. As the winner breasted the tape, she slumped back against the cushions and, with a surreptitious forefinger, wiped a tear from the corner of her eye. There was none of the bombast, the rough confidence that had characterised the time of her training. 'I probably would never have finished the course,' she said, 'let alone come in with the winners.'

'Why's that?'

'Too old. Can't run fast enough. Probably never could. Still, we can all dream.'

She rose to her feet, not like an athlete, but an elderly lady whose hobby was knitting. 'Better start on the dinner,' she was saying. 'Before Madam gets a cob on.'

Christina said, 'That reminds me, I had the most vivid dream last night.'

'What was it about?' Corky asked, but without much interest, being a committed member of the toasted-cheese-for-supper school of interpretation.

'The usual. Trains. Missed them as usual too.'

But she was getting closer.